A NEW YORK TIMES EDITORS' CHOICE

"Phenomenal...powerful...brilliant."
Publishers Weekly (starred review)

"A moving reflection on loss, memory, and the past...
Heartwarming and heartrending. Highly recommended."
Library Journal (starred review)

"Electrifying...A commanding family memoir."
Foreword Reviews (starred review)

"Exceptional." *Shelf Awareness* (starred review)

"Unique...moving." *BookPage* (starred review)

"Moving...engrossing...Let's hope that a book like this,
which encompasses both the monstrosities of the past
and the dangers of the present, will guard us from
complacency." Heller McAlpin, *The Wall Street Journal*

"Intimate, profound, essential." *ELLE*

"Combines the excitement of a thriller with the emotional
power of a requiem." *Le Point*

"A gift...It is as though Berest has taken us by the hand to
lead us through the family home."
Virginia Reeves, *New York Journal of Books*

"Wonderfully constructed, sweeping...As addictive as it is
transformative." *La Croix*

"Both personal and universal, timely and eternal...
Magnificent." *Madame Figaro*

Photo © DR

Anne Berest is the bestselling co-author of *How to Be Parisian Wherever You Are* (Doubleday, 2014) and the author of a novel based on the life of French writer Françoise Sagan. With her sister Claire, she is also the author of *Gabriële*, a critically acclaimed biography of her great-grandmother, Gabriële Buffet-Picabia, Marcel Duchamp's lover and muse. She is the great-granddaughter of the painter Francis Picabia. For her work as a writer and prize-winning showrunner, she has been profiled in publications such as French *Vogue* and *Haaretz* newspaper. The recipient of numerous literary awards, *The Postcard* was a finalist for the Goncourt Prize and has been a long-selling bestseller in France.

Tina Kover's translations for Europa Editions include Antoine Compagnon's *A Summer with Montaigne* and Négar Djavadi's *Disoriental*, winner of the Albertine Prize and the Lambda Literary Award, and a finalist for both the 2020 National Book Award for Translated Literature and the PEN Translation Prize.

THE POSTCARD

Anne Berest

THE POSTCARD

*Translated from the French
by Tina Kover*

Europa
editions

Europa Editions
27 Union Square West, Suite 302
New York NY 10003
www.europaeditions.com
info@europaeditions.com

Copyright © Editions Grasset & Fasquelle, 2021
First publication 2023 by Europa Editions
This edition, 2024 by Europa Editions

Translation by Tina Kover
Original title: *La carte postale*
Translation copyright © 2023 by Europa Editions

Library of Congress Cataloging in Publication Data is available
ISBN 979-8-88966-035-4

Berest, Anne
The Postcard

Cover design by Ginevra Rapisardi

Cover photo: Noémie Rabinovitch, 1941

Prepress by Grafica Punto Print – Rome

Printed in Italy

CONTENTS

THE POSTCARD

M y mother lit her first lung-charring cigarette of the morning, the one she enjoyed most, and stepped outside to admire the whiteness blanketing the entire neighborhood. At least ten centimeters of snow had fallen overnight.

She stayed outside smoking for a long time despite the cold, enjoying the otherworldly atmosphere of the garden. It was beautiful, she thought, all that blankness, that erasing of colors and blurring of edges.

Suddenly she heard a noise, muffled by the snow. The postman had just dumped the mail on the ground at the foot of the mailbox. My mother went to collect it, putting her slippered feet down carefully so as not to slip.

Cigarette still clamped between her lips, its smoke dissipating in the freezing air, she made her way quickly back to the house to thaw fingers numbed by the cold.

She flipped through the stack of envelopes. There were the usual holiday cards, most of them from her university students, a gas bill, a few pieces of junk mail. There were also letters for my father, from his colleagues at the National Centre for Scientific Research and the PhD candidates he supervised, all wishing him a happy new year.

All very typical for early January. Except for the postcard. Slipped in among the other envelopes, unassuming, as though it had hidden itself deliberately.

What caught my mother's attention right away was the handwriting, strange and awkward, like no handwriting she had ever seen before. Then she read the four names, written in the form of a list.

Ephraïm
Emma
Noémie
Jacques

They were the names of her maternal grandparents, her aunt, and her uncle. All four had been deported two years before she was born. They died in Auschwitz in 1942. And now, sixty-one years later, they had reappeared in our mailbox. It was Monday, January 6, 2003.

Who could have sent me this terrible thing? Lélia wondered.

My mother felt a jolt of fear, as if someone were threatening her, someone lurking in the darkness of the past. Her hands began to tremble.

"Look, Pierre! Look what I found in the mail!"

My father took the postcard and examined it closely, but there was no signature, no explanation.

Nothing. Just those four names.

At my parents' home in those days, one picked the mail up off the ground, like ripe fruit fallen from a tree; our mailbox had gotten so old that it was like a sieve—nothing stayed inside—but we liked it that way. It never occurred to any of us to get a new one; that wasn't how our family solved problems. You simply lived with things, as if they deserved the same respect as human beings.

When the weather was bad, the letters would get soaked, their ink running and the words becoming permanently indecipherable. Postcards were the worst, bare like those teenage girls who run around with exposed arms and no coat in wintertime.

If the author of the postcard had used a fountain pen to write to us, their message would have been obliterated. Had they known that? The names were written with a ballpoint pen.

The following Sunday, Lélia summoned the whole family: my

father, my sisters, and me. Sitting around the dining-room table, we passed the card from hand to hand. None of us spoke for a long time—which was unusual for us, especially during Sunday lunch. Normally, in our family, there's always someone with something to say, and they always want to say it *right now*. But on that day, no one knew what to think about this message that had shown up out of the blue.

The postcard itself was nothing special, just a touristy postcard with a photo of the Opéra Garnier on the front, the kind sold by the hundreds in tobacco shops and kiosks all over Paris.

"Why the Opéra Garnier?" my mother asked.

No one knew the answer.

"The postmark is from the Louvre post office."

"You think they could give us more information there?"

"It's the biggest post office in Paris. It's *huge*. What do you think they'll be able to tell you?"

"Was it mailed from there for a reason, do you think?"

"Yeah. Most anonymous letters are sent from the Louvre post office."

"It's not recent. The card itself must be ten years old at least," I observed.

My father held it up to the light and looked at it carefully for a few moments before declaring that the photograph dated from the 1990s. The print's chroma, with its saturated magentas, as well as the absence of advertising panels around the Opéra Garnier, confirmed my hunch.

"I'd even say it's from the *early* '90s," my father clarified.

"How can you be so sure?" my mother asked.

"Because in 1996 the green and white SC10 buses, like the one in the middle ground of this picture, were replaced by RP312s. With a platform. And their engines in the rear."

No one was surprised by my father's knowledge of Parisian bus history. He'd never driven a car, much less a bus, but his career as a researcher had led him to learn countless details on a myriad of subjects as varied as they were specialized. My father invented a device that calculates the moon's influence on Earth's tides, and my mother has translated treatises on generative grammar for Chomsky. Both of them know an unimaginable number of things, almost all of which are completely useless in everyday life—most of the time. But not that day.

"Why write a postcard and then wait ten years to send it?"

My parents continued their musings. But I couldn't have cared less about the postcard itself. No—it was the *names* that were calling to me. These people were my ancestors, and I knew nothing about them. I didn't know which countries they'd traveled to, what they'd done for a living, how old they'd been when they were murdered. I couldn't have picked them out of a photo lineup.

I felt a wave of shame.

After lunch, my parents put the postcard away in a drawer, and we never talked about it again. I was twenty-four years old, my mind full of my own life, of other stories to be written. I erased the recollection of the postcard from my memory, though I kept hold of the vague intention to ask my mother, one day, about our family's history. But the years slipped by, and I never took the time to do it.

Until ten years later, when I was about to give birth.

My cervix had dilated too early, so I was on bedrest to keep the baby from arriving prematurely. My parents had suggested that I spend a few days at their house, where I wouldn't have to lift a finger. Suspended in a state of anticipation, my thoughts turned to my mother, my grandmother, and the whole line of women who had given birth before me. It was then that I felt a pressing need to hear the story of my ancestors.

Lélia led me into her study, where she spends most of her time. The little room always reminded me of a womb, its air thick with cigarette smoke, its walls lined with books and filing cabinets and bathed in the pale winter sunlight that streamed through windows overlooking the Parisian *banlieue*. I settled myself beneath the bookshelf and the ageless objects on it, all those memories blanketed with a film of dust and cigarette ash, as my mother retrieved a black-speckled green archive box from among twenty identical ones. As a teenager, I'd known that these neat rows of boxes contained the relics of our family's dark past. They'd made me think of little coffins.

My mother reached for a pen and a sheet of paper—like all re-tired professors, she views everything as a teaching opportunity, even parenting. Lélia's students at Paris 8 University Vincennes-Saint-Denis adored her. Back in the good old days, when she could smoke in the classroom, she used to do something that fascinated her linguistics students: with rare dexterity, she could finish an entire cigarette without the ash dropping to the floor, keeping the thin gray cylinder between her fingertips. No need for an ashtray, she'd set the worm of ash down on her desk, deli-cately, and light up another one. It was a skill that demanded respect.

"I should warn you," she began now, "that what I'm about to tell you is a blended story. Some of it is obviously fact, but I'll leave it up to you to decide how much of the rest comes from my own personal theories. And of course, any new documentation could flesh out those conclusions, or change them completely."

"Maman," I said. "I don't think cigarette smoke is very good for the baby's brain development."

"Oh, it's all right. I smoked a pack a day during all of my preg-nancies, and in the end, I don't think you three turned out so bad."

Her answer made me chuckle. Lélia took advantage of the pause to light another cigarette. Then she began to tell me about the lives of Ephraïm, Emma, Noémie, and Jacques. The four names on the postcard.

BOOK I
PROMISED LANDS

CHAPTER 1

J ust like in all the Russian novels," my mother began, "it started
with a pair of star-crossed lovers. Ephraïm Rabinovitch
was in love with Anna Gavronsky, whose mother, Liba
Gavronsky, born Yankelevich, was a cousin of the family. But the
Gavronskys didn't approve of Ephraïm and Anna's love."

Seeing that I was already completely lost, Lélia paused.
Cigarette wedged in the corner of her mouth, squinting against
the smoke, she began rummaging in the archive box.

"Hold on, let me read you this letter; it'll make things clearer.
It was written in Moscow in 1918, by Ephraïm's older sister."

Dear Vera,

My parents' troubles continue to pile up. Have you heard
about the mess between Ephraïm and our cousin Aniouta? If
not, I can only tell you in complete confidence—even though
it seems that some in the family are aware of it already. Simply
put, An and our Fedya (he turned twenty-four two days ago)
have fallen in love—they've gone utterly mad with it—and it's
upset us all terribly. Auntie doesn't know about it, and it would
be utterly catastrophic if she found out. They see her all the
time, and they're in agony. Our Ephraïm adores Aniouta, but
I'll admit, I'm not sure I believe her feelings are sincere. Well,
that's the news from us. Sometimes I'm completely fed up with
the whole thing. Must stop writing now, my dear. I'm going to
post this letter myself, to make sure it doesn't go astray.

With love,

Sara

"So if I understand what's going on here, Ephraïm was forced to give up his first love."

"And another fiancée was quickly found for him: Emma Wolf."

"The second name on the postcard."

"Exactly."

"Was she also a distant relative?"

"No. Emma came from Lodz. She was the daughter of a wealthy industrialist, Maurice Wolf, who owned several textile factories, and her mother was called Rebecca Trotsky—no relation to the revolutionary."

"How did Ephraïm and Emma meet? Lodz must be a thousand kilometers from Moscow."

"Far more than a thousand! Either the families used the services of the synagogue *chadkhanit*—the matchmaker—or Ephraïm's family was Emma's *kest-eltern*."

"Her what?"

"*Kest-eltern*. It's Yiddish. How can I explain it . . . Do you remember what I told you about the Inuktitut language?"

Lélia had taught me, when I was little, that the Inuits have fifty-two words for snow. *Qanik* is falling snow, *aputi* is fallen snow, *aniou* is snow they melt for water, and so on and so on.

"Well, in Yiddish, there are various terms that mean 'family,'" my mother continued. "There's one word for the nuclear family, and another for in-laws, and a third term that means 'those who are considered to be like family' even when there's no blood tie. And then there's a basically untranslatable term, something like 'foster family'—*di kest-eltern*. 'Host family,' you might say, because traditionally, when parents sent a child away to university, they looked for a family who would provide lodging and meals for that child."

"And the Rabinovitches were Emma's *kest-eltern*."

"Yes. Now relax. Just listen. It'll all make sense in the end, don't worry."

Very early in his life, Ephraïm Rabinovitch broke away from his parents' religion. As a teenager, he became a member of the Socialist Revolutionary Party and declared to his mother and father that he didn't believe in God. Deliberately provocative, he made a point of doing everything forbidden to Jews on the holiday of Yom Kippur: smoking cigarettes, shaving, eating, and drinking.

In 1919, Ephraïm was twenty-five. He was a modern young man, slim and fine-featured. If his skin had been fairer and his mustache not so black, he could have passed for an ethnic Russian. A brilliant engineer, he'd just earned his degree despite the *numerus clausus* in effect, which limited the number of Jews admitted to university to 3% of total enrollment. He wanted to be part of the great wave of progress sweeping the nation and had great ambitions for his country—and for the Russian people, *his* people, whom he hoped to join in the Revolution.

Being Jewish meant nothing to Ephraïm. He considered himself a socialist, first and foremost. He lived in Moscow, led a Moscow lifestyle. He agreed to marry in the synagogue only because it was important to his future wife. But, he warned Emma, theirs would not be an observant household.

Tradition dictates that, on his wedding day, the groom must smash a glass with his right foot after the ceremony, a gesture representing the destruction of the temple in Jerusalem. After this, he makes a vow. Ephraïm's vow was to erase the memory of his cousin Aniouta from his mind forever. But, looking at the shards of glass littering the floor, he felt as if it were his heart lying there, broken into a thousand pieces.

CHAPTER 2

On Friday, April 18, 1919, the young newlyweds left Moscow and traveled to the dacha owned by Nachman and Esther Rabinovitch, Ephraïm's parents, fifty kilometers from the capital. Ephraïm had agreed to celebrate Pesach, the Jewish Easter, only because his father had insisted with uncharacteristic vehemence and because his wife was pregnant. This was the perfect opportunity to announce the news to his brothers and sisters.

"Was Emma pregnant with Myriam?"
"Your grandmother. Yes."

On the way, Ephraïm confided to his wife that Pesach had always been his favorite holiday. As a child he had loved its mystery, the strangeness of the bitter herbs and salt water and honeyed apples on a platter in the middle of the table. He'd loved it when his father explained to him that the sweetness of the apples was meant to remind Jews to be wary of ease and comfort.

"In Egypt," Nachman insisted, "the Jews were slaves—meaning, they were fed and housed. They had a roof over their heads and food on the table. Do you understand? It's *freedom* that is unreliable, that is gained through pain. The salt water we put on the table on the evening of Pesach represents the tears of those who broke loose from their chains. And the bitter herbs remind us that the life of a free man is inherently painful. Listen carefully, son—the instant you feel the touch of honey on your lips, ask yourself: of what, of whom, am I a slave?"

Ephraïm knew that his revolutionary soul had been born at that very moment, listening to his father's words.

That evening, arriving at his parents' dacha, he hurried to the kitchen to breathe in the bland but unique scent of the matzos, unleavened flatbreads baked by Katerina, the elderly cook. Suddenly emotional, he took her wrinkled hand and pressed it against his young wife's belly.

"Look at our son," Nachman said to Esther, watching the scene. "Proud as a chestnut-seller showing off his wares to everyone who passes."

The parents had invited all the Rabinovitch cousins on Nachman's side and all the Frant cousins on Esther's. *Why so many people?* wondered Ephraïm, toying with a silver spoon that shone brightly from being scoured for hours with ashes from the fireplace.

"Have they invited the Gavronskys, too?" he asked his younger sister Bella, worriedly.

"No," she assured him, carefully concealing the fact that both families had agreed to avoid a face-to-face meeting between Emma and Cousin Aniouta.

"But why are they having so many cousins over this year? Are they planning some sort of announcement?" pressed Ephraïm, lighting a cigarette to hide his anxiety.

"Yes, but don't ask me. I can't say anything about it until dinner."

On the evening of Pesach, it's traditional for the patriarch to read aloud from the Haggadah, the story of Moses leading the Hebrew people out of Egypt. When the prayers had concluded, Nachman rose and tapped his knife against his glass.

"I've chosen to read these final words from the Book," he said, addressing the whole table: *Rebuild Jerusalem, the holy city, speedily in our days, and bring us up into it.* This is because, in my role as head of the family, I must warn you."

"Warn us about what, Papa?"

"That it's time to go. We must all leave the country. As quickly as possible."

"Leave?" his sons repeated incredulously.

Nachman closed his eyes. How to convince his children? How to find the right words? It was as if there were an acrid tinge to the air, like a cold wind blowing to signal a coming freeze: invisible, almost nothing, and yet it was there. It had come to him in nightmares first, nightmares shot through with memories of his boyhood, when, on some Christmases, he'd been hidden behind the house with the other children from drunken men who'd come to punish the people who killed Christ. They'd gone into the houses and raped the women and killed the men.

The violence had calmed down somewhat when Tsar Alexander III, intensifying the state's anti-Semitism, had enacted the May Laws, stripping Jews of most of their liberties. Nachman had been a young man when everything was suddenly forbidden to Jews—attending university, traveling from one region to another, giving Christian first names to their children, putting on theater productions. These humiliating measures had mollified the Russian people, and for some thirty years now, the bloodshed had lessened. Nachman's children had never known the terror of Christmas Eve, of a mob rising from its dinner tables filled with the urge to kill.

But for the past few years now, Nachman had noticed a smell of sulfur and decay returning to the air. The Black Hundreds, an extreme-right monarchist group led by Vladimir Purishkevich, were gaining strength in the shadows, the Tsar's former courtier spreading rumors of a Jewish conspiracy. He was only waiting for the right moment to come back. And Nachman didn't believe for a moment that the new Revolution fomented by his children would banish old hatreds.

"Yes. Leave. Listen to me well, my children," Nachman said calmly. "*Es'shtinkt shlekht drek*. It stinks of shit."

His words caused the clinking of forks against plates to cease abruptly. The children stopped chattering. Silence fell. Finally, Nachman could speak.

"Most of you are young married people. Ephraïm, you will soon be a papa for the first time. You have spirit, bravery—your whole life ahead of you. Now is the time to pack your bags."

Nachman turned to his wife and squeezed her hand. "Esther and I have decided to go to Palestine," he continued. "We've bought a piece of land near Haifa, where we will grow oranges. Come with us. I'll buy land for all of you there."

"Nachman—you aren't *really* going to settle in the land of Israel?"

The Rabinovitch children had never imagined that anything like this could be possible. Before the Revolution, their father had belonged to the first guild of merchants, which meant that he was among those rare Jews who had the right to travel freely around the country. It was an unheard-of privilege for Nachman to be able to live as a Russian in Russia. He had risen to an enviable position in society—and now he wanted to abandon it for exile on the other side of the world, in a desert country with a hostile climate, and grow oranges? What a bizarre idea! He couldn't even peel a pear without the cook's help.

Nachman picked up a small pencil and moistened its tip between his lips. His eyes still fixed on his children and grandchildren, he added, "Now, I'm going to go around the table. And I want each of you—*every one* of you, do you hear me?—to give me a destination. I will go and buy steamer tickets for everyone. You must leave the country within the next three months; is that understood? Bella, I'll begin with you—it's simple; you're coming with us. I'll write it down: *Bella, Haifa, Palestine*. Ephraïm?"

"I'll wait to see what my brothers say."

"I could picture myself in Paris," piped up Emmanuel, the youngest brother, leaning back in his chair nonchalantly.

"Avoid Paris, Berlin, Prague," Ephraïm advised seriously. "All

the respectable places in society have been occupied for generations in cities like that. You'll never establish yourself. You'll be
seen as either too clever or not clever enough."

"I'm not worried; I've already got a fiancée waiting for me
there," retorted Emmanuel, to make the rest of the table laugh.

"My poor boy," sighed Nachman, irritated. "You'll lead the
life of a pig. Stupid and brief."

"I'd rather die in Paris than in the damned middle of nowhere, Papa!"

"Ach!" Nachman snapped, shaking a fist at his son. "*Yeder
nar iz klug un komish far zikh*: Every idiot believes himself to be
intelligent. I'm not joking here. Go. If you don't want to follow
me, try America," he added, sighing. "That would be very good,
too."

Cowboys and Indians. America. No, thank you, thought the
Rabinovitch children. Its landscapes were too remote, impossible to picture. At least they knew what Palestine looked like,
because it was described in the Bible. A bunch of rocks.

"Look at them," said Nachman to his wife, gesturing to their
children. "Just a bunch of veal chops with eyes! *Think* for a moment! There is nothing for you in Europe. *Nothing.* Nothing
good, at any rate. But in America, in Palestine, you'll find work
easily!"

"Papa, you always worry for nothing. The worst thing that
can happen to you here is your tailor turning socialist!"

It was true that, looking at Nachman and Esther, sitting side
by side like two plump little cakes in a pastry-shop window, it
was hard to imagine them as farmers in a foreign land. Esther was
still girlishly pretty despite her snow-white hair, which she wore
in a low knot. Still stylish, with her dainty cameo brooches and
pearl necklaces. Nachman still wore his trademark three-piece
suits, custom-made by the best French couturiers in Moscow.
His beard was white as cotton, his only whimsical touch the
polka-dotted ties he matched to his pocket handkerchiefs.

Exasperated by his children, Nachman got up from the table now, the vein in the side of his neck throbbing so furiously that it seemed on the point of bursting all over Esther's beautiful table-cloth. He would have to go and lie down to calm his racing heart. Before closing the dining-room door, Nachman asked them all to think carefully, concluding, "You must understand something. One day, they'll want us all to disappear."

After this dramatic exit, the conversation around the table resumed cheerfully, lasting until late into the night. Emma sat down at the piano, the stool pushed back slightly to accommodate her bulging belly. The young woman had been educated at the prestigious National Conservatory of Music. She had wanted to be a physicist, but the *numerus clausus* had put an end to that dream. It was her fervent hope that the baby she was carrying would live in a world where he, or she, would be able to study whatever they chose.

Lulled by the snippets of his wife's music drifting in from the lounge, Ephraïm talked politics with his brothers and sisters at the fireside. The evening had been so pleasant, the siblings uniting in gentle mockery of their father. The Rabinovitches had no way of knowing that these were the last hours they would all spend together as a family.

CHAPTER 3

E mma and Ephraïm left the family dacha the next day, everyone parting in a good mood, promising to see one another again before the summer.

Gazing out the window of their carriage at the scenery sliding past, Emma wondered if her father-in-law was right, if perhaps it wouldn't be better for them to move to Palestine. Her husband's name was on a list. The police might come to their home to arrest him at any time.

"What list? Why was Ephraïm wanted by the police? Because he was Jewish?"

"No, not at that time. I told you; my grandfather was a member of the Socialist Revolutionary Party. After the October Revolution, the Bolsheviks began to eliminate their former comrades-in-arms, including the Mensheviks and the revolutionary socialists."

So, back in Moscow, Ephraïm was forced to hide. He found a place to hole up near his apartment so he could at least visit his wife from time to time.

On one evening when he had done just that, he wanted to bathe before leaving. To drown out the sound of water splashing in the kitchen washbasin, Emma had sat down at the piano, plunking hard on the ivory keys. She trusted neither their neighbors nor the informers that seemed to be lurking everywhere.

Suddenly, there was a knock on the door. A succession of quick hard raps. Commanding. Authoritative. Emma went to the door, one hand on her swollen belly.

"Who is it?"

"Emma Rabinovitch? We're looking for your husband."

Emma made the officers wait in the corridor just long enough for Ephraïm to stow his things and crawl into a hiding place they'd made, the false bottom of a wardrobe, behind stacks of blankets and household linens.

"He's not here."

"Let us in."

"I was having a bath. Let me dress."

"Send your husband out," ordered the police, whose patience was wearing thin.

"I haven't heard from him for over a month."

"Do you know where he's hiding?"

"No. I have no idea."

"We'll break down the door and turn this house inside-out."

"Well, if you find him, tell him I said hello!"

Emma opened the door and thrust her protruding belly at the officers.

"Look—you see the state he's left me in!"

The police trooped into the apartment. Spotting Ephraïm's hat lying on an armchair in the living room, Emma pretended to be overcome by faintness, dropping into the chair, feeling the hat crumple beneath her weight. Her heart thumped in her chest.

"Your grandmother Myriam hadn't even been born yet, but she had just experienced, physically, what it means to have terror fill the pit of one's stomach. Emma's organs clenched around the fetus."

As the officers completed their search, the young woman remained imperturbable.

"I don't believe I'll come with you," she said, her face pale, "as I'm afraid my waters might break. You'd have to help me give birth."

The police left, cursing pregnant wives. After several end-less minutes of silence, Ephraïm emerged from his hiding place and found his wife curled in agony on the carpet in front of the fireplace, gripped by cramps so painful that she couldn't stand. Fearing the worst, Ephraïm promised Emma that, if the baby survived, they would leave Moscow and go to Riga, in Latvia.

"Why Latvia?"

"Because it had just become an independent country—one where Jews could settle without being subject to laws restricting their commercial activity."

Your grandmother, Myriam—Mirotchka, as the family called her—was born in Moscow on August 7, 1919, according to the papers issued by the Refugee Office in Paris. The actual date was uncertain, however, because of the difference between the Gregorian and Julian calendars, so Myriam would never know the exact day of her birth.

She came into the world in the bright and gentle warmth of *Leto*, the Russian summer. She was practically born in a suitcase as her parents prepared to depart for Riga. Ephraïm had investigated the profitability of trading in caviar and was confident that he'd be able to establish a thriving business. To finance their new life in Latvia, Ephraïm and Emma had sold everything they possessed: the furniture, dishes, carpets. Everything but the samovar.

"The one in the living room?"

"Yes. That samovar has crossed more borders than you and I put together."

The Rabinovitches left Moscow in the middle of the night by horse and cart, traveling the empty country roads to the border under cover of darkness. The journey was long and difficult—nearly a thousand kilometers—but it would get them out of reach of the Bolshevik police. Emma entertained little Mirotchka by whispering stories to her when she grew fretful in the evenings, pushing aside her blankets to show her the world above the sides of the cart: "They say that night falls, but that's not true; look how the night rises up slowly from the earth . . ."

At twilight on the last day, a few hours before they reached the border, Ephraïm suddenly became aware of an odd sensation: his horse's burden seemed suddenly lighter. Turning, he saw that the cart was gone.

When the cart had come loose, Emma hadn't cried out for fear of drawing attention. Now she waited as her husband doubled back, hardly knowing what frightened her more—the Bolsheviks or the wolves—but Ephraïm came for them, of course, and their wagon reached the border before sunrise.

"Look," Lélia said. "After Myriam died, I found papers in her desk. Bits of old writings, letters—that's how I found the story of the cart. She ends it like this: 'Everything is always all right in the pre-dawn, in that gray hour before sunrise. Once we reached Latvia we spent several days in prison due to administrative formalities. My mother was still nursing me, and I have nothing but sweet memories of her milk, with its taste of rye and buckwheat, from those days.'"

"The next few sentences are virtually unreadable," I observed.

"That was the onset of her Alzheimer's. I've spent hours trying to puzzle out what's hiding behind some grammatical error or other. Language is a maze, and the mind can get lost in it."

"I knew that story about the hat that absolutely had to be hidden from the police," I said. "Myriam wrote it down for me when I was little, in the form of a fairy tale. She called it 'The Tale of the Hat.' But I didn't know it was a real family story. I thought she'd made it up."

"Those slightly sad little stories your grandmother always wrote for you on your birthday—they were all episodes from her life. They've been real treasures for me, as I've tried to piece together certain events in her childhood."

"But the rest of it—how have you managed to tell the whole story in so much detail?"

"I started from almost nothing, just a few things I found after your grandmother's death: photos with indecipherable scribbling on the back and some bits and pieces she wrote down on scraps of paper. Gaining access to the French archives in the early 2000s and eyewitness accounts at Yad Vashem, as well as accounts from survivors of the camps, are what allowed me to recreate these lives. Not all the documentation is reliable, though; it can lead you down some strange paths. Sometimes the French government made administrative errors. Only cross-checking everything in painstaking detail, with the help of archivists, allowed me to substantiate facts and dates."

I looked up at the shelves and shelves of books overhead. My mother's archive boxes, which used to frighten me, suddenly appeared to hold the mysteries of a body of knowledge as vast as a continent. Lélia had traveled through history as if she were going from country to country, gathering records and recollections of journeys that had brought landscapes to life within her, landscapes it now fell to me to visit in my turn. Pressing a hand to my belly, I silently entreated my daughter to listen as carefully as I would to the rest of the story, to this tale that was both old and deeply relevant to her brand-new life.

I n Riga, the little family settled in a pretty wooden house at Alexandra isl., No. 60/66 dz 2156. Emma adapted quickly and was readily accepted by the local community. She was full of admiration for her husband, whose caviar business rapidly took off.

"My husband has a true entrepreneurial spirit and wonderfully good business sense," she wrote proudly to her parents in Lodz. "He's bought me a piano, so I can whip my lazy fingers into shape again. He gives me all the money I could need, and he's also encouraging me to give piano lessons to the little girls in the neighborhood."

Ephraïm's success in the caviar trade soon allowed the couple to buy a little dacha in Bilderlingshof, where many of Latvian society's best families holidayed, and a German nurse was hired to assist Emma in her household duties.

"This way you'll be able to work more," Ephraïm said. "Women should be independent."

Emma took advantage of her new leisure time to make regular visits to the great synagogue in Riga, famous for its cantors and even more so for its choirs. She only went there to recruit new students, she assured her husband, not to pray. Arriving one day just as services were concluding, she was surprised to hear Polish spoken. There were members of old Lodz families in the congregation, and, with them, she could feel the community atmosphere of her home city. It was like finding a few scattered crumbs of her childhood.

It was the gossiping housewives at the synagogue who

informed Emma that Cousin Aniouta had married a German Jew and was now living in Berlin.

"Don't mention it to your husband, though, whatever you do. You must never revive the memory of your former rival," warned the rebbetzin, the rabbi's wife, whose unofficial role was to counsel the wives of the congregation.

Ephraïm, for his part, had received highly encouraging news from his parents. Their orange grove was prospering, and Bella had gotten a job as wardrobe mistress for a theater in Haifa. The brothers, now scattered all over Europe, had found good situations for themselves—all except the youngest, Emmanuel, who was determined to become a film star in Paris. "He has yet to land a role," his older brother Boris had written. "He's already thirty years old, and I'm worried for him. But thirty is still young, and I'm hoping he'll get a break. I've watched him perform, and he's good. I think he'll do all right in the end."

Ephraïm acquired a camera, to immortalize the sight of Myriam's little face. He dressed his daughter up like a doll, buying her the most luxurious clothes, the finest ribbons for her hair. In her pure white gowns, the little girl was the Princess of the Kingdom of Riga, a proud and confident child, fully aware of her importance in the eyes of her parents—and thus of the whole world.

People passing the Rabinovitch home on Alexandra Street invariably heard the sound of a piano, and the neighbors, rather than complaining, enjoyed the music. And so the weeks passed happily, the family's life suddenly one of ease. One evening during Pesach, Emma asked her husband to set out the traditional Seder plate.

"Please," she said. "You don't have to read the prayers, but at least tell her about the exodus from Egypt."

Eventually, Ephraïm agreed and showed Myriam how to arrange the egg, the bitter herbs, the chopped apples with honey, the salted water, and a lamb shank bone in the center of the plate. Abandoning himself to the theme of the evening, he told his daughter the story of Moses, exactly the way his father used to do.

"How is this night different from all the other nights? Why do we eat bitter herbs? Sweetheart, Pesach reminds us that the Jewish people are a free people but that this freedom has a price. Sweat and tears."

For Pesach dinner, Emma had baked matzohs using the recipe given to her by Katerina, her mother- and father-in-law's old cook, so that her husband could experience again, just briefly, that delicious blandness from his childhood. Ephraïm was in a jolly mood that night, making his daughter laugh by imitating her grandfather:

"Chopped liver is the best remedy for life's problems," he said in Nachman's Russian accent, taking a big bite of chicken liver pâté.

But suddenly, amid the laughter, Ephraïm felt a pang in his heart. *Aniouta.* His cousin's face flashed through his mind; he imagined her, at that very moment, celebrating Pesach with her own family, a husband and perhaps a baby, bent over the prayer book at a candlelit table. *How beautiful maturity must have made her*, he thought. Even *more* beautiful. A shadow passed over his face. Emma noticed it immediately.

"Are you all right?" she asked.

"Do you think we should have another child?"

Ten months later, Noémie—the Noémie from the postcard—was born in Riga, on February 15, 1923. This little sister, come to unseat Myriam from the throne of only-childhood, looked just like her mother, with a face round as the moon.

Ephraïm used some of the profits from his caviar business to buy a space in which he set up an experimental laboratory, where he hoped to invent new machines. He spent entire evenings explaining the principles of his inventions to Emma, his eyes shining with enthusiasm.

"Machines will be a revolution. They'll free women from the burden of housework. Listen to this: 'Within the family, the husband belongs to the middle class, while the woman is a member of the working class.' Don't you agree with that?" asked Ephraïm, still a devoted reader of Karl Marx despite the fact that he was now the owner of a thriving business.

"My husband is like electricity," Emma wrote to her parents, "traveling all over, bringing the light of progress wherever he goes."

But Ephraïm the engineer, the progressivist, the cosmopolitan, had forgotten that an outsider will always be an outsider. He'd made the terrible mistake of believing that he could rely on happiness in any one place. The following year, in 1924, a tainted barrel of caviar plunged his small business into bankruptcy. Bad luck, or the work of a jealous rival? These immigrants arriving in their wagon had become too successful, too quickly. Overnight, the Rabinovitches became *persona non grata* in the Riga of the goys. Their neighbors in Binderling Court demanded that Emma stop disrupting the peace and quiet of the street with her students' comings and goings. The gossips at the synagogue wasted no time in telling her that the Latvians had now targeted her husband and would harass him until he had no choice but to leave. They would have to pack their bags—again. But where would they go?

Emma wrote to her parents, but the news from Poland wasn't good either. Her father, Maurice Wolf, seemed anxious about the strikes breaking out all over the country.

"You know I'd love to have you near me more than anything, my dear," he wrote. "But I mustn't be selfish, and, as a father, it's my duty to tell you that you and your husband and the children should probably think about going even farther away."

Ephraïm sent a telegram to his younger brother Emmanuel, but unfortunately the latter was staying in the Parisian apartment of some painter friends, Robert and Sonia Delaunay, who had a little boy of their own. Ephraïm then wrote to Boris, the older brother now living in Prague, like many other members of the Socialist Revolutionary Party—but the political situation was highly unstable, and Boris advised the Rabinovitches against settling there.

Ephraïm was out of money and out of options. Sick at heart, he sent a telegram to Palestine:

"We're on our way."

Getting to the Promised Land meant going south from Riga in a virtually straight line for two and a half thousand kilometers. Traveling across Latvia, Lithuania, Poland, and Hungary, then taking a ship from Constanza, in Romania. The journey would take forty days—as long as it had taken Moses to reach Mount Sinai.

"We'll stop in Lodz to see my parents. I want my family to meet our daughters," Emma told her husband.

Crossing the Lodka river, Emma found herself once again in the home city she had missed so much. The din of the traffic, a mixture of trolleys, cars, and droshkys rattling noisily along the streets, terrified the children—but warmed Emma's heart.

"Every city has its very own smell, you know," she said to Myriam. "Shut your eyes and inhale."

Myriam closed her eyes and breathed in the lilac-and-asphalt-scented air of the Baluty quarter, the odors of soap and oil in the streets of Polesie, the aromas of cholent wafting from kitchens, and everywhere the cloth dust generated by the city's famous textile factories, drifting out of open windows. As they made their way through the working-class Jewish neighborhoods, Myriam saw for the first time those men dressed all in black like flocks of forbidding birds, with their dark beards and sidelocks bouncing like springs next to each ear, their tzitzit draped over their long rep shirts, their large fur hats. Some of them wore mysterious black cubes—phylacteries—on their foreheads.

"What are those?" asked Myriam, who, at the age of five, had never been inside a synagogue.

"These are religious men," Emma replied, her voice respectful. "Scholars of the holy texts."

"Doesn't look like anyone's told them the twentieth century has arrived," Ephraïm joked.

Myriam was busily soaking in the fantastical sights of the Jewish quarter. The face of a child her own age selling poppy-seed cakes on the street would remain etched in her memory, as would the figures of old women sitting on the ground, brightly colored scarves covering their hair, hawking rotten fruit and toothless combs. *Who would buy such dirty things?*, Myriam wondered.

In the 1920s, the streets of Lodz seemed transported from the previous century, or perhaps from an old book of fairy tales, stories of a world teeming with characters as wondrous as they were fearsome, a dangerous world where cunning thieves and beautiful prostitutes skillfully plied their trade on every corner; where men lived alongside beasts in a labyrinthine maze of streets; where rabbis' daughters came to study medicine and their spurned lovers led ribald urban lives in revenge; where live carp kept in tubs suddenly began to speak as in Yiddish legend; where people whispered stories of black mirrors; where you ate freshly baked buns spread with soft white cheese bought from street vendors.

All her life, Myriam would remember the sickly sweet scent of the street carts selling chocolate doughnuts in the heat of that bustling city.

At last, the Rabinovitches reached the Polish quarter, the air filled here, too, with the clack-clack of the weaving machines. But the reception that greeted them was startling, to say the least.

"*Hep hep Jude,*" they heard, as they made their way through the streets.

A group of children, several dogs straggling behind them, threw little stones at them. Myriam was hit by a sharp-edged pebble just beneath her eye. A few drops of blood spotted the pretty dress she'd worn for the journey.

"It doesn't matter," Emma told her. "They're just stupid kids."

Emma tried to dab away the bloodstain with her handkerchief, but a red mark remained under Myriam's eye, which would soon turn black. Ephraïm and Emma tried to comfort her, but the little girl could tell that her parents felt threatened by *something*.

"Look at that group of buildings with the red walls," said Emma, in an attempt to distract her daughters. "That's your grandfather's factory. He went to Shanghai once, to study different weaving machine techniques. He'll make a blanket for you out of silk!"

Then Emma's expression darkened, as she read the graffiti scrawled on the factory walls.

WOLF = WILK = JEWISH OWNED

"Don't ask," Maurice Wolf sighed, embracing his daughter. "The Poles don't want to work in the same rooms as the Jews anymore because they hate each other, but they hate me most of all. I don't know if it's because I'm their boss, or because I'm Jewish."

The hostile atmosphere in Lodz didn't prevent Emma, Ephraïm, Myriam, and Noémie from spending several pleasant days in the Wolfs' dacha near Piotrkow, on the banks of the Pilica river. Everyone deliberately overplayed the happy mood, and their conversations revolved around food, the children, and the weather. Emma described their plans for the move to Palestine with exaggerated enthusiasm, explaining to her parents how good this new adventure would be for her husband, how it would give him the freedom to work on all his inventions.

On the evening of Shabbat the Wolfs put out a magnificent spread for dinner, their Polish maids working busily in the kitchen, as they alone were permitted to light the stove and do all the other tasks forbidden to Jews after sundown on that day. Emma was overjoyed to be reunited with her three sisters. Fania had become a dentist and was now Mrs. Rajcher; the pretty Olga, married to a man named Mendels, was a doctor; and Maria, engaged to a young man called Gutman, was preparing to start her medical studies, as well. Emma was struck speechless by the sight of her little brother Viktor, whom she hadn't seen in such a long time. The teenage boy had turned into a young man with a curly beard. He was married now, and a practicing attorney, with an office at 39 Zeromskiego Street, not far from the center of Lodz.

Ephraïm had brought along his impressive camera to immortalize this day on which the entire Wolf family gathered on the front steps of their holiday home.

"Look," Lélia said. "Here's the photo."

"It's . . . strange to look at. Kind of disturbing," I said, examining it.

"Ah. You feel that, too."

"Yeah. The faces are fading away. The smiles are almost gone. It's like they're hovering on the edge of oblivion."

In the photograph, my grandmother Myriam is the little girl with the bow in her hair, wearing a white dress and white shoes, her head tilted to one side.

"I found this picture completely by chance," my mother said. "The nephew of one of Myriam's friends had it. She'd told him that on the day it was taken, the adults and children had all played duck, duck, goose in the garden together. And then Myriam told the nephew that on that day, right in the middle of the game, a thought had suddenly occurred to her: *Whoever wins this game will be the one who lives the longest.*"

"That is one hell of a morbid premonition—and a very strange thought for a little girl of five to have. And she remembered it?"

"Yes. She remembered it clearly, even sixty years later, I can tell you that. The thought haunted her for the rest of her life."

"But why tell a stranger a secret like that? She never talked to *anyone*. It's weird."

"It isn't, really, when you think about it."

I held the photograph closer, scrutinizing each of the faces. Ephraïm, Emma, Noémie—but also Maurice, Olga, Viktor, Fania. These ghostly figures were no longer abstract entities, no longer just numbers in the history books. I felt a contraction in my belly, strong enough to make me close my eyes. Lélia looked at me anxiously.

"Do you want to stop?"

"No, no. It'll be okay."

"You aren't too tired? Do you feel up to hearing the rest?"

I nodded. "In a few decades, my daughter's children will be the ones seeing old family photographs for the first time," I said, gesturing to my abdomen. "And we'll look like we belong to some other world, too, some ancient world. Maybe even older than this one."

The next morning, Emma, Ephraïm, and their two daughters set off on another journey of nearly two thousand kilometers. It was the first time Myriam had been on a train. She pressed her face against the window for hours, nose and cheeks squashed flat, never tiring of the spectacle. It seemed to her as if the train was creating the landscape for her, and she made up stories in her head as they rumbled along. The big stations in the cities impressed her; in Budapest, she felt as if the train were pulling into a cathedral. The little country depots, on the other end of the spectrum, looked to her like dolls' houses, with their red bricks and their brightly painted wooden shutters. One morning when she woke up, the beech forests had been replaced by a railway line dug into the rock, the sides of the narrow canyon so close she felt like they might crash down on them. A bit later, on a fog-shrouded bridge, Myriam said to her mother, "Look, Mama, we're up above the clouds!"

A hundred times a day, Emma reminded her little girls to behave, so they wouldn't disturb their fellow passengers. But Myriam continually escaped to roam the corridors, where a million adventures lay in store, especially at mealtimes, when the juddering of the train overturned plates into ladies' laps and drenched men's shirt fronts with beer. Myriam delighted in it all, with that spiteful glee children always feel when something embarrassing happens to a grown-up.

On one such occasion, Emma set off in search of Myriam after about an hour, making her way through the cars one by one, past the compartments where families played cards and bickered in a thousand foreign languages. The walk along the length of the train reminded Emma of the strolls she used to take with her parents and her sisters in Lodz in the spring, when people's home lives could be glimpsed through windows left open.

When will I see them again? she wondered.

She found Myriam in the caboose, being scolded by the babushka in charge of the samovar. Apologizing to the old woman, she led Myriam to the dining car where, in a setting resembling the canteen of an army barracks, they ate the same meal of fish and cabbage every day. That day, a man was telling fantastic stories in Russian about the Orient Express.

"It's an entirely different animal than this old monstrosity! Like a jewel-box—all glittering! And the drinking glasses are made of Baccarat crystal. Journalists from all over the world are served fresh croissants for breakfast every morning. The staff wear dark-blue and gold uniforms that match the colors of the tapestries . . ."

That night Myriam was rocked to sleep by the swaying of the train and dreamed that she was inside a living creature, a giant skeleton with steel veins. And then, one morning, the journey was over.

Reaching the port of Constanza, Myriam was deeply disappointed to discover that the Black Sea wasn't actually black. The family now boarded the ocean liner *Dacia* of the Serviciul Maritim Român, the state-run luxury steamship company that ferried passengers between Constanza and Haifa. Emma admired the elegant, pure-white vessel, its two slender smokestacks reaching upward like the arms of a newly married young wife.

The crossing was very comfortable, and Emma savored these last moments of European sophistication before their arrival in the Promised Land. On the first evening, they had dinner in the grand dining room, an excellent meal that ended with a dessert of apples candied in honey.

CHAPTER 7

Emma's first glimpse of her parents-in-law upon disembarking from the steamship made her feel incredibly strange.

What had happened to the three-piece suits? The pearl necklaces? The lace collars and polka-dotted ties? Esther wore a shapeless cardigan, Nachman overlong trousers and battered old shoes.

Emma glanced at her husband. What had happened? Her mother- and father-in-law had changed so much! Farming life had transformed their bodies. Both of them had gained muscle and thickened around the middle. Their features seemed coarser, their tanned skin deeply wrinkled.

They look like Indians, she thought.

Nachman's booming laugh echoed around the kitchen as he searched fruitlessly for the bottle of liquor he had picked out to celebrate their arrival in Migdal.

"'From dust we came, and to dust we shall return,'" he said, clasping Emma by the arm, "but in the meantime, it's good to drink vodka! I hope you haven't forgotten my cornichons!"

The glass jar had made it across four borders without breaking. Emma rummaged in her suitcase and took out the *malosol'nye*, which means "slightly salty" in Russian. The tiny pickles in brine spiked with cloves and fennel were Nachman's favorite.

How my father has changed, thought Ephraïm, watching him. *He's gained weight, and his temper has mellowed, too. He's laughing more. I suppose milk has to age in order to become cheese . . .*

He looked around at his parents' house. Everything there was extremely basic.

"I must show you the orangery!" Nachman exclaimed proudly. "Come, let's go!"

The little girls dashed toward the canals that snaked like miniature rivers through seemingly endless rows of orange trees, tiptoeing carefully along the canals' low walls, arms held out like tightrope walkers, so as not to fall into the shallow irrigation channels.

The farm laborers stared in surprise as the boss's granddaughters gamboled past them, their little shoes getting dirtier and dirtier as they darted among the trees. When it was time for the afternoon nap, the men would go and rest in the shade of the carob trees with their wide, gnarled, rough-barked trunks and their carmine-red flowers that left rusty stains on clothing—Myriam would always remember that their seeds could be ground into a flour that tasted like chocolate.

Once harvested, Nachman explained, the oranges were transported in carts to large warehouses where women seated on the ground wrapped them up one by one. It was tedious, painstaking work. The women moistened their fingers to envelop the oranges quickly in "citrus paper," a Japanese paper as thin and delicate as cigarette paper.

Ephraïm and Emma were still feeling the odd sensation that hadn't left them since their arrival in Palestine. They'd been expecting new, gleaming buildings, but everything seemed cobbled together from bits and pieces. Clearly, business wasn't as good as Nachman and Esther had boasted in their letters. Palestine was no land of abundance for the Rabinovitches. The truth was that Ephraïm's parents were struggling to make a success of their orangery.

Ephraïm had arrived with his suitcase stuffed with papers. Designs for machinery, drafts of patents. He'd assumed that his father would be able to finance the development of his ideas here in Palestine—but unfortunately, as it turned out, his parents' straitened circumstances meant that he would have to find work. Thanks to the close-knit Jewish community in the region, he was quickly hired by an electricity company in Haifa, the Palestine Electric Corporation.

"Oh yes, I'm a Zionist now!" Nachman announced proudly to his son one evening.

Fetching a dog-eared book filled with scribbled notes, he held it out to Ephraïm. "*This* is the true revolution."

The book was called *The Jewish State*. In it, the author, Theodor Herzl, laid the groundwork for the foundation of an independent nation.

Ephraïm didn't read the book. He divided his time between his parents' orangery, where there was serious need of help, and his work as an engineer at the PEC. This left only a few evenings a week for him to pursue his own work. He often nodded off to sleep over his schematics.

It hurt Emma to see her husband's dreams so cruelly thwarted. She herself no longer played the piano, as they didn't have one. To keep from forgetting the skill, she asked Nachman to make her a keyboard out of wood. Her daughters learned to play in silence, on a phony piano.

But Ephraïm and Emma took great consolation in seeing how happy Myriam and Noémie were in this rough-and-tumble out-door life. They loved to stroll beneath the palm trees, tugging on their grandparents' sleeves. Myriam attended the kindergarten in Haifa, where she was taught Hebrew, as was Noémie—a prac-tice strongly encouraged by the Zionist movement.

"You mean Jews didn't normally speak Hebrew before then?"
"No. It was solely a written language."
"So it's like if, instead of translating the Bible into French, Pascal had encouraged people to speak Latin?"
"Exactly. And so Hebrew was the third alphabet Myriam learned to read and write. At six years old, she could already speak

Russian; German, thanks to her nanny in Riga; and Hebrew. She knew some basic Arabic, too, and she could understand Yiddish. But she didn't speak a word of French."

In December, for Hanukkah, the festival of lights, the two sisters learned to make candles from oranges, by fashioning a wick from the stem and placing it in the hollowed-out peel of the fruit, into which a little olive oil was then poured. The children's year was marked by liturgical rites: Hanukkah, Pesach, Sukkot, Yom Kippur. And then a new event: a little brother, who arrived on December 14, 1925. They named him Itzhak.

In the wake of her son's birth, Emma openly renewed ties with religion. Ephraïm didn't have the energy to argue with her, though he did stage a subtle protest of his own by shaving on Yom Kippur. His mother had tended to sigh deeply whenever her son did anything to provoke God's wrath as a youth; now she didn't reprimand him at all. The whole family could tell that Ephraïm was unhappy, exhausted by the heat, by the long round-trips between Migdal and Haifa. He was not himself.

Five years passed in this way. These were cycles: just over four years in Latvia, nearly five years in Palestine. Unlike in Riga, where their fall from grace was as rapid as it was sudden, their situation in Migdal deteriorated year by year, slowly but surely.

"On January 10, 1929," my mother said, "Ephraïm wrote a letter to his older brother Boris. Here, look—this very letter. In it, he admitted that the Palestinian venture had been disastrous, both for his parents and for himself. He was without a penny to his name, he said, and without any prospects whatsoever. 'I have no idea where to go or if I'll have anything to eat tomorrow, let alone be able to feed my children. Our parents' business is riddled with debt.'"

Pesach celebrations in Palestine were nothing like they had been in Russia. The silver cutlery had been replaced by old forks with bent tines. Ephraïm watched his father dust off the Haggadahs, which grew dirtier each year. Yet he couldn't help but smile as he watched his daughters read, with varying degrees of skill, the story of the exodus from Egypt, the prayer books too large for their little hands.

"The Hebrew word *Pesach* means 'to pass over,'" Nachman explained. "Because God passed over Jewish homes to spare them. But it also means passage: the passage across the Red Sea, the passage of the Hebrew people to become the Jewish people, the passage from winter to spring. It's a rebirth."

Ephraïm recited the words silently along with his father. He knew them by heart, having heard the same words, the same phrases, every Pesach for nearly forty years.

Almost forty, he thought to himself, marveling.

That evening he couldn't keep himself from remembering his cousin. *Aniouta*. It was a name he never spoke out loud.

"*Mah Nichtana?* How is it different? How does this night differ from all other nights? We were slaves of Pharaoh in Egypt . . ."

Half-listening to his children's questions, Ephraïm let his thoughts drift. Suddenly he was afraid, afraid of dying in this country without having fulfilled his destiny. That night, he couldn't sleep. Depression overtook him, becoming a landscape in his mind through which he wandered desolately, sometimes for whole days. He felt as though his life—his real life—had never begun.

The letters he received from his brother only made him feel worse.

Emmanuel was happier than ever. He had applied for naturalization as a French citizen thanks to the support of the filmmaker Jean Renoir, who had written him a letter of recommendation. He was still working in movies and finally beginning to make a name for himself. He was living with his fiancée, the painter

Lydia Mandel, at 3 rue Joseph-Bara in the sixth arrondissement between the rue d'Assas and the rue Notre-Dame-des-Champs, very near the Montparnasse quarter. Reading these letters, Ephraïm felt as if he could hear the distant sounds of a party where his brother was having fun without him.

The changes in Ephraïm had not escaped Emma's notice. She went to the synagogue's rebbetzin for advice.

"It's not your fault if your husband is *troyerik*. It's because of the air in this country. He's like an animal, living in a climate that doesn't agree with his temperament. There's nothing you can do for him as long as your family lives here."

"For once, the rabbi's wife has said something sensible," Ephraïm agreed when Emma told him about it. "She's right. I don't like this country. I miss Europe."

"Fine," replied Emma. "Let's move to France."

Ephraïm took Emma's face in his hands and kissed her soundly on the lips. Surprised, she laughed—something she hadn't done in quite a long time. That same evening saw Ephraïm studying his schematics at the kitchen table again. He would conquer Paris, not by arriving empty-handed, but with an invention: a baking machine that made bread dough rise faster. After all, wasn't Paris the baguette capital of the world? Mind buzzing anew with plans, Ephraïm became once again the brilliant engineer able to spend whole nights working on a patent without getting tired.

On that June day in 1929, Emma waited for her daughters to come home from school to tell them the news. She spotted them in the distance, tripping single-file like two little gymnasts along the low white wall of the ditch that diverted the miraculous water of the Sea of Galilee. Emma drew Myriam and Noémie aside, into the orange warehouse, where the sharp, gasoline-like smell of orange peels was so strong that it still lingered in the girls' hair in the evening, scenting the air of their bedroom.

Emma unfolded one of the citrus papers, with its picture of a red and blue boat.

"You see this boat, that takes our oranges to Europe?" she asked. "Well, now *we're* going to sail on it! Think how exciting it will be to see the world!"

Then Emma picked up an orange and held it in her hand.

"Imagine that this is the Earth."

As her daughters watched, she pulled away small pieces of the peel, to show oceans and continents.

"See, this is where we are. And we're going to go . . . here! To France! Paris!"

Emma took a nail and stuck it into the flesh of the orange.

"Look—it's the Eiffel Tower!"

Myriam listened closely as her mother spoke, absorbing the new words: *Paris. France. Eiffel Tower.* She understood the message beneath the lighthearted speech.

They were going to have to leave. Again. That was just how things were. Myriam was used to it. The only way to keep from suffering, she knew, was just to move forward, to keep going, and never, *never* look back.

But little Noémie began to cry. She hated the idea of leaving her grandparents, those mythical gods reigning over this paradise of olive and date orchards, in whose laps she loved to doze in the shade of the pomegranate trees.

"Everything is ready, Papa," said Ephraïm to his father. "Emma will spend the summer in Poland, before joining me in Paris. She hasn't seen her family in a long time, and she wants them to meet Itzhak. Meanwhile, I'll go on ahead to France, to find us a place to live and prepare for the girls to come."

Nachman's cottony beard wagged as he shook his head. This departure was a very bad idea.

"What do you expect to gain from going to Paris?" he asked.

"Money! I'll make a fortune from my bread machine."

"No one will want anything to do with you."

"Papa . . . 'Happy as a Jew in France'—isn't that the expression?

The place has always been good to us. Think of Dreyfus—the whole country rising up to defend a humble Jewish nobody!"

"Only *half* the country, son. Don't forget the other half."

"Stop it, now. As soon as I have enough money, I'll send for you and Mama."

"No, thank you. *Besser mit un klugn dans gehenem eyder mit un nar dans ganeydn* . . . Better to be a wise man in hell than a fool in heaven."

CHAPTER 8

Emma and Ephraïm found themselves once again at the port of Haifa, in the very place they had disembarked five years earlier. They had one more child than they'd had then, and a few more gray hairs. Emma was more ample in the hips and bosom, while Ephraïm had become reed-thin. They were both older, and their clothes were threadbare. But none of it mattered; the prospect of this journey made them feel twenty years old again.

Ephraïm boarded a ship for Marseille, from whence he would travel to Paris. His wife's ship was bound for Constanza, en route to Poland.

Emma's family marveled at the sight of Itzhak, the toddler they had never met. Maurice, his grandfather, would teach him to walk on the magnificent ivy-covered stone stoop. The little boy would be called "Jacques" from now on, Emma decided. It sounded chic. French.

"You should know that all the characters in this story have multiple first names and multiple ways of spelling them. It took a while before I realized, reading so many letters, that Ephraïm, Fedya, Fedenka, Fyodor, and Théodore were all the same person! And listen to this—it was *ten years* before I realized that Borya wasn't some female Rabinovitch cousin; Borya was *Boris!* Don't worry; I'll make you a list of all the names so you can keep track. You see, over the centuries, Russian Jews picked up some characteristics of the Slavic soul, including a taste for changing their first names— and, of course, the refusal to give up on love. The Slavic soul."

*

In the summer of that same year, 1929, the Wolfs received a visit from Ephraïm's brother, Uncle Boris, who arrived from Czechoslovakia to spend a few days in Poland with his nieces and sister-in-law. He, too, had been forced to flee the Bolsheviks.

In his youth, Uncle Boris had been a true *boevik*, a militant. At age fourteen he had set up a *kruzhok*, a political circle, in his high school. Rising to become head of the military arm of the SRP, then the 12th Army, and then vice-president of the Executive Committee of the Soviets of the Northern Front, he was made a delegate to the Soviets of Peasants' Deputies and named to the Constituent Assembly by the PSR.

"But then suddenly, after having dedicated twenty-five years of his life to the Revolution—after experiencing the exhilaration of the grand political assemblies—he gave it all up. Overnight. To become a provincial rustic."

For Myriam and Noémie, he was the same old Uncle Boris, with his funny straw hats and his head now bald as an egg. He had become a farmer, a naturalist, an agronomist, and a collector of butterflies. His travels had deepened his knowledge of plants. Everyone loved this Czechoslovakian uncle. The little girls went on long walks with him in the forest, learning the Latin names of flowers and the properties of mushrooms. He taught them how to whistle on a grass stem held between their fingers. You had to choose one that was both wide and strong, so the sound would be loud.

"Look at these pictures," Lélia said. "They were taken that summer. Those short-sleeved dresses Myriam, Noémie, and their cousins are wearing were all sewn from the same pattern, the same flowered fabric, same white pinafore."

"They remind me of the dresses Myriam used to make for us when we were little."

"Yes. She liked you to pose in those traditional dresses to take pictures just like this one, in height order—tallest to shortest."

"Maybe seeing us that way reminded her of Poland. I remember she used to get this distant look in her eyes."

On the steamship from Haifa to Marseille, Ephraïm had the strangest feeling. It had been ten years since he'd been alone. Alone in bed, alone with the time to read a book, alone to eat when he felt hungry. For the first few days, he thought constantly of his children, missing their laughter and even their squabbles. And then, suddenly, the delicate, evanescent image of his cousin filled the space where they had been. She remained on his mind for the rest of the crossing. On deck, gazing out at the ship's frothy wake, he imagined the letters he might write to her. *An . . . Aniouta, dearest . . . Anouchkaia, my little ladybug . . . I'm writing to you from an ocean liner, on my way to France . . .*

In Paris, Ephraïm was reunited with his younger brother Emmanuel, now a French citizen with a new stage name: Manuel Raaby. No more Emmanuel Rabinovitch.

"You're an idiot! You should have chosen a French name!" Ephraïm exclaimed.

"Pah! I needed an *artistic* name. And it's pronounced 'Rrrah-bee,' American-style."

Ephraïm snorted with amusement. His little brother looked anything but American.

Emmanuel was working with Jean Renoir. He had had a small part in *The Little Match Girl* and then a leading role in *The Sad Sack*, an anti-war comedy filmed in Algeria. He would also appear in *Night at the Crossroads*, an adaptation of one of Simenon's *Maigret* novels.

The advent of talkies had obliged him to take voice lessons

to smooth out his Russian accent. He was studying English, too, and had an obsession with Hollywood.

Through his connections, Emmanuel had found a house for Ephraïm near the film studios in the Parisian suburb of Boulogne-Billancourt, and so in the late summer of 1929, the five Rabinovitches—Ephraïm, Emma, Myriam, Noémie, and the toddler now known as Jacques—settled at number 11, rue Fessart.

School began in September, but the little girls weren't yet ready to go. Instead, a tutor came to the house to teach them French, which they mastered much more quickly than their parents did.

Emma began giving piano lessons to the daughters of well-heeled Parisian families; it had been five years since she'd played on a real instrument. Ephraïm managed to secure a place on the board of directors of an automotive engineering firm, the Fuel, Lubricant, and Supply Company. It was a promising start for a man wanting to establish himself in France's business world.

Much like the early days in Latvia, everything went very well, very quickly. Two years passed. Ephraïm wrote a letter to his father, in which he congratulated himself on his decision to settle in France.

On April 1, 1931, the family left Boulogne and moved much closer to the city, to a house at 131 boulevard Brune, near the Porte d'Orléans. The newly built residence had all the modern conveniences a family could desire and was supplied with municipal gas, water, and electricity. Ephraïm was proud to provide his family with such luxury. At the time, he was passionately interested in the Yellow Expedition, a trek from Beirut to China by automobile, organized by the Citroën family.

"A Jewish family from Holland that sold lemons before making their fortune in diamonds, then cars," he explained to Emma. "*Citrons*—Citroën!"

Destinies like the wealthy Dutch family's always fascinated Ephraïm, who was determined to become a naturalized French citizen like his brother. The process would be long and arduous, he knew, but he was resolved to see it through to the end.

He had decided that his daughters would attend the best school in Paris. That spring, the director of the Lycée Fénelon escorted the Rabinovitch family on a private visit to the school. Founded in the late nineteenth century, the Lycée Fénelon was the first secular academic institution "*d'excellence*" for girls.

"Our teachers have extremely high expectations of their students," the director warned.

For a pair of little foreigners who hadn't spoken a word of French two years previously, it would be very difficult to do well.

"But you mustn't let that discourage you," she continued.

Passing the window of the gymnasium, the Rabinovitches saw the young pupils' arms and legs whirling silently, moth-like, in the air.

Myriam and Noémie were impressed by the art room, which was decorated with Greek busts in plaster.

"It's like the Louvre," they marveled to the director.

The little girls were sorry they wouldn't be eating their lunch in the cafeteria. The tables were so lovely, with their white cloths, their wicker breadbaskets, their bouquets of flowers in small vases. It was like a restaurant.

The rules were strict at the Lycée Fénelon, and the proper uniform imperative: a cream-colored blouse with the pupil's name and class embroidered on it in red thread. No makeup allowed.

"And it is not permitted to have a young man wait for you outside the school," said the director dryly, "even a brother."

The girls were fascinated by the bronze statue of a blind Oedipus, guided by his daughter Antigone, that stood beneath the grand staircase.

Out in the street again, Ephraïm knelt and took both of his daughters by the hand.

"You must be first in your class," he said solemnly. "Understood?"

*

In September 1931, the Rabinovitch daughters were enrolled in the primary school at the Lycée Fénelon. Myriam was almost twelve; Noémie was eight. Their registration form read "Palestinians born in Lithuania. No nationality."

To get to school, Myriam and Noémie took the metro each morning, traveling the ten stations from Porte d'Orléans to Place de l'Odéon and then walking through the narrow cour de Rohan, which opened onto the rue de l'Éperon. The journey took thirty minutes from start to finish if they didn't hurry, and they did it four times a day; as day students rather than boarders, they were obliged to go home at noon and gulp down a hurried lunch. The cafeteria cost more than metro tickets.

These daily trips were trying for the girls. But they stuck together like brave little soldiers, Myriam always looking out for Noémie to make sure she didn't get into trouble on the metro and Noémie making enough friends for both of them in the schoolyard. The sisters had come to operate like the government of their own tiny country, over which they reigned as a pair of queens.

"Maman, when I was putting together my application for the Lycée Fénelon in 1999, did you know that Myriam and her sister had been students there seventy years earlier?"

"I had no idea, if you can believe it. I hadn't gotten to that point in my research. Otherwise, I would have told you, obviously."

"Don't you find it surprising?"

"What?"

"Going to the Lycée Fénelon was my dream back then, remember? I was *so* determined to get in. Almost as if . . ."

The family moved once again in February 1932. Ephraïm had found a larger apartment at 78 rue de l'Amiral-Mouchez, on the sixth floor of a brick building that's still there. It was a three-bedroom apartment with a kitchen, bathroom, WC, and foyer. Municipal gas, water, and electricity. The phone number was GOB(elins) 22-62, and there was a post office on the ground floor. The building overlooked the Parc Montsouris and was very close to the Cité Universitaire train station. Now Myriam and Noémie were a mere two stops from school, which made their lives much easier; from there it was a simple matter of cutting through the Luxembourg Gardens, past the merry-go-round with its wooden horses and brass rings that didn't earn you a prize even if you managed to grab one.

For Emma, this was her fifth move since becoming a mother, and it was always an ordeal, with everything needing to be sorted and washed and folded and put away again. She disliked the feeling, on arriving in a new house or a new neighborhood, of having to find her routines and habits again as if they were an object she'd mislaid.

And so the months passed, and the Rabinovitch daughters grew older, their characters asserting themselves. Jacques, the youngest member of the family, remained the chubby-cheeked toddler still clinging to his mother's skirts.

The future seemed full of promise. Myriam, at thirteen, was already picturing herself studying at the Sorbonne once she passed her final exams. In the evenings, she wove tales for Noémie of the life awaiting them: the smoky bistros of the Latin Quarter, the Sainte-Geneviève library. Both sisters had wholly absorbed the idea that it was up to them to fulfil the destiny their mother had been denied.

"I'll rent an attic room on the rue Soufflot."

"Can I come and live with you?"

"Of course. You'll have your own room, right next to mine."

The daydreams made them both shiver with happiness.

A pupil at Fénelon was having a tea party for her birthday, and all the little girls in her class had been invited. All but Noémie. She came home from school flushed with anger. Ephraïm was even more indignant than his daughter; the celebration was being thrown by a venerable French family at their grand home in the 16th arrondissement.

"Knowledge is the true essence of nobility," Ephraïm told his daughters. "We'll go and visit the Louvre while those little madams are stuffing themselves with cakes."

Still fuming, he set off toward the Place du Carrousel with the girls. On the Pont des Arts, a man abruptly grabbed his arm, and he tensed, ready to fight—but the man, he quickly realized, was an old friend from the Socialist Revolutionary Party whom he hadn't seen in almost fifteen years.

"I thought you moved to Germany during the trials!" Ephraïm exclaimed.

"I did, but I left and came here a month ago with my wife and children. Times are difficult for us in Germany, you know."

The man mentioned a fire that had ravaged the Reichstag building, home of the German parliament, a few days prior; Communists and Jews had been blamed for setting it, of course. The party now controlling the Reichstag—the National Socialist Workers' Party—was, he said, deeply anti-Semitic.

"They want to ban Jews from working in any civil service profession! *All* Jews! I can't believe you didn't know!"

That night, Ephraïm discussed the encounter with Emma.

". . . but, as I recall, that fellow had a habit of panicking about every little thing," he said, so as not to frighten her.

But Emma was worried. This wasn't the first she'd heard of Jews being mistreated in Germany, and more seriously than it might seem. She asked her husband to find out more.

The next day, Ephraïm went to the news kiosk at the Gare de l'Est and bought a few German papers. In them, he read articles accusing the Jews of every crime under the sun. And, for the first time, he saw the face of Germany's new chancellor, Adolf Hitler. Then he went home and shaved off his mustache.

July 13, 1933, was the day prizes were handed out at the Lycée Fénelon. The director and the teaching staff gathered on a rostrum decorated with tricolor rosettes, and the student choir sang "La Marseillaise."

Myriam and Noémie stood together near the front. Noémie had her mother's round face with her father's fine features; she was a beautiful little girl, impish and sunny-tempered. Myriam's features were rather stern, and, serious and earnest, she was less popular in the schoolyard—but every year, without fail, she was elected class president.

Madame la directrice now began to hand out the awards for achievement—the first prizes, the honorable mentions, the honor roll. In her speech, she cited the Rabinovitch sisters as an example; their performance since the day of their arrival at the school, she said, had been truly remarkable.

Myriam, who was about to turn fourteen, was named top of her class and took first and second prizes in every subject except gymnastics, sewing, and drawing. Noémie, aged ten, came in for her share of commendation, as well.

Emma wondered, almost fearfully, if all this wasn't too good to be true. Ephraïm, though, was beside himself with pride. His daughters were now part of the Parisian elite. "Proud as a chestnut-seller showing off his wares to everyone who passes," Nachman would have said.

After the ceremony, Ephraïm decided that the whole family would walk home together. The charm of the Luxembourg Gardens on that midsummer day was irresistible. Butterflies fluttered among the famous sculpted *Queens of France and Famous Women*; babies took their first unsteady steps near the pond filled with wooden toy boats. Families strolled leisurely homeward, enjoying the beauty of the flowerbeds and the murmur of the fountains; they nodded to one another in greeting, gentlemen doffing their hats and wives smiling graciously, when their paths crossed near the rows of olive-green chairs where students from the Sorbonne loved to lounge.

Ephraïm pressed Emma's arm to his side. It was hard to believe they were really part of this scene that was so wholly, perfectly French.

"We'll need to think of a new last name for our family soon," he mused, a faraway look on his face.

Her husband's confidence that they would obtain French citizenship frightened Emma, who squeezed her youngest child's hand tightly, as if to conjure up the destiny Ephraïm was projecting. She thought of the murmurs she had overheard behind them during the school director's speech, a few of the mothers' whispers.

"How vulgar these people are—positively *gloating* over their children."

"They're so *pleased* with themselves."

"They nearly trampled us just to make sure those daughters of theirs could stand at the front of the room . . ."

That evening, Ephraïm offered to take Emma and the girls to the neighborhood dance being held for Bastille Day, as any good Frenchman would.

"The girls have done so well; surely that's reason to celebrate!"

Seeing her husband in such a jolly mood, Emma pushed the dark thoughts from her mind.

Myriam, Noémie, and Jacques had never seen their parents dance. They gazed in wonder at the two of them, twirling together to the strains of a brass band.

"Remember that date, Anne. July 13, 1933. It was a wonderful day for the Rabinovitches. Such happiness. Complete joy."

The next day, July 14, 1933, Ephraïm read in the paper that the Nazi Party had officially become the only political party in Germany. Further, the article stated that sterilization would be forcibly imposed on those suffering from physical and mental disabilities to preserve the purity of the Germanic race. Ephraïm closed the newspaper. Nothing, he decided, would ruin his good mood today.

Emma and the children spent the rest of July in Lodz with the Wolfs. There, Maurice, Emma's father, gave Jacques his tallit, the large prayer shawl worn by Jewish men.

"Now he will wear his grandfather on his back the day he is called to the Torah," said Maurice to his daughter, evoking his grandson's future bar mitzvah.

The gift designated Jacques as his grandfather's spiritual heir. Emma was touched as she accepted the ancient shawl, its fabric worn threadbare by time. And yet she felt, as she tucked it into her suitcase, that it might spell trouble for her marriage.

In August, Emma and the children spent two weeks at Uncle Boris's experimental farm in Czechoslovakia while Ephraïm remained in Paris, taking advantage of the quiet apartment to perfect his baking machine.

These visits were a time of deep happiness for the Rabinovitch children. "I miss Poland," Noémie wrote a few days after their return to Paris. "We were so happy there! I feel like I can still smell Uncle Boris's roses. And I miss Czechoslovakia—the house, the garden, the chickens, the fields, the blue sky, the walks, the countryside."

The next year, Myriam competed in the prestigious Concours Général in Spanish—her sixth language. She was passionately interested in philosophy, as well, while Noémie was a devotee of the humanities, writing poems and short stories in her diary and winning first prize in French and geography. Her teacher, Mademoiselle Lenoir, noted that she had "great literary promise" and encouraged her to keep writing.

At night, Noémie fantasized about being a published author as she drifted off to sleep.

A teenager now, she wore her long dark hair in braids wound coronet-fashion around her head, like the young female intellectuals at the Sorbonne, and was a great admirer of Irène Némirovsky, whose work she'd discovered by reading the novel *David Golder.*

"I've heard she depicts Jews in a bad light," Ephraïm objected, worriedly.

"Not at all, Papa. You haven't even read her books."

"You'd do better to read the Goncourt Prize winners, and French novelists."

On October 1, 1935, Ephraïm registered his company: SIRE, the Société industrielle de radio-électricité, or Radioelectricity Manufacturing Company, headquartered at 10–12 rue Brillat-Savarin in the 13th arrondissement. In the records of the Parisian commercial court where the registration papers were filed, Ephraïm was listed as "Palestinian." SIRE was a limited liability company with a capital of 25,000 francs composed of 250 shares at 100 francs each. Ephraïm owned half these shares, and the other half was split between two other associates, Marc Bologouski and Osjasz Komorn, both Polish. Like Ephraïm, Osjasz was a member of the board of directors at the Fuel, Lubricant, and Supply Company located at 56 rue du Faubourg Saint-Honoré. The new company was immediately added to the files of the government's counterespionage service.

"Maman, wait. Wait a minute," I said, getting up and opening a window to air out the smoky room. "You don't have to go into every tiny detail. I don't need all the street addresses."

"It's *all* important. These details are what made it possible for me to piece together the fate of the Rabinovitches—and don't forget I started with absolutely nothing," Lélia reminded me, lighting a new cigarette from the stub of the previous one.

One day, Jacques, who was almost ten, came home from school in tears. He locked himself in his room and refused to speak to anyone. All because of something one of his classmates had said in the schoolyard: "Pull the ear of one Jew, and they'll all have trouble hearing."

At the time, Jacques hadn't understood what it meant. But then a boy from his class had chased him, trying to yank on his ears. And then several other students had joined in.

The incident was deeply disturbing to Ephraïm, who grew angry.

"All of this," he told his daughters, "is because of all the German Jews flooding into Paris. The French feel invaded. Oh yes," he insisted, when they disagreed with him, "I'm telling you."

Myriam and Noémie had become friendly with Colette Grés, a Fénelon pupil whose father had just died suddenly. Ephraïm was pleased that his daughters were friends with a goy, and he urged Emma to follow their example.

"We have to do everything we can to make sure our citizenship application goes through," he told her. "Stop spending so much time with Jews."

"Then I'll just stop sleeping in your bed, shall I?" she retorted.

The girls laughed. Ephraïm did not.

Their friend Colette lived with her mother on the corner of the rue Hautefeuille and the rue des Écoles, on the third floor of a building with a cobbled courtyard and a medieval turret.

Noémie and Myriam spent leisurely afternoons in that strange circular room filled with books, and it was there that they continued to dream of their future. Noémie would be a writer and Myriam a professor of philosophy.

CHAPTER 13

Ephraïm had followed with great interest the ascent of Léon Blum, whose political enemies now grew more vicious by the day, as did the scathing attacks of the right-wing press. Blum was called "the vile lackey of London bankers"; "a friend of Rothschild and other bankers who are obviously Jews"; and "a man who should be shot," as journalist Charles Maurras wrote, "but in the back." As it turned out, this last article was not without consequences.

On February 13, 1936, Léon Blum was attacked on the boulevard Saint-Germain by members of the Camelots du Roi, an anti-Semitic group belonging to the far-right Action Française. Recognizing Blum, the men injured his neck and leg and threatened to kill him.

In Dijon, shop windows were vandalized, and in the same week, a number of merchants received an anonymous letter that read: "You belong to a RACE that wishes to destroy France and start a REVOLUTION in our country that isn't your own, because you're a Jew, and Jews have no homeland."

A few months later, Ephraïm bought a copy of Louis-Ferdinand Céline's long pamphlet *Trifles for a Massacre*. More than 75,000 copies had been sold in only a few weeks, and he wanted to read what the French were reading.

Book in hand, he sat down at a café and, despite the fact that he never drank alcohol, ordered a glass of Bordeaux like any good Frenchman would. And then he began to read.

"A Jew is 85% bravado and 15% hot air . . . As for the Jews, they have no shame of their own Jewish race, quite on the contrary, *nom de Dieu*!... Their religion, their glib tongue, their reason for being, their tyranny, their entire arsenal of fantastic Jewish privileges . . ."

A sudden tightness in his throat, Ephraïm put the book down, finished his glass of wine, and ordered another.

"I no longer recall which cack-handed little twit of a Hymie (I forget his name, but it was a Hymie name) who took the trouble, over the course of five or six issues of a supposedly medical journal (Jewish lapdogs in reality), to take a shit all over my works and my 'grotesqueries' in the name of psychiatry . . ."

Thinking of how many people had already bought this outpouring of madness, Ephraïm felt as if he couldn't breathe. He rose and left the café, a bit unsteady on his feet, nausea rising in his gut. Walking up the boulevard Saint-Michel, past the gates of the Luxembourg Gardens, he remembered the passage in the Bible that had so terrified him as a child:

"Then the Lord said to Abram, 'Know of a surety that your descendants will be sojourners in a land that is not theirs, and will be slaves there, and they will be oppressed for four hundred years.'"

Myriam left school with an honors diploma and the annual prize given by the Association of Former Fénelon Pupils "to the ideal student, for impeccable moral, intellectual, and artistic conduct."

Noémie moved on to the upper class with the warm approval of her teachers. Jacques, a student at the Collège Henri IV, performed less well than his sisters academically, but was a promising athlete in gymnastics. In December, he would enter his fourteenth year, the one traditionally marked by a bar mitzvah. This was the most important ceremony in the life of a male Jew, marking his passage to adulthood and his entrance into the community of men. Ephraïm, however, refused to consider it.

"I'm trying to file our application for French citizenship—and you want to dive headfirst into all that old-fashioned nonsense? Did you fall and hit your head or something?" he chastised Emma.

The issue of Jacques's bar mitzvah drove a wedge between the couple. It was the most serious disagreement they'd had since getting married. Emma was forced to accept that she would never see her son form part of a minyan, the ten-man quorum required for public prayer, his shoulders draped in his grandfather's tallit. It was a profound disappointment.

Jacques himself didn't really understand what was going on—he knew nothing of Jewish liturgy—but he sensed deep down that his father was denying him something, though he couldn't have said precisely what.

Jacques turned thirteen on December 14, 1938, without

setting foot in the synagogue. In the second trimester of his school year, his grades dropped. He fell to the bottom of his class, and at home he clung to his mother's skirts like a toddler. By the spring, Emma had begun to worry.

"Jacques has stopped growing," she remarked. "He's not getting any taller."

"Just a phase," Ephraïm reassured her. "It will pass."

CHAPTER 15

Ephraïm had devoted the bulk of his attention to the citizenship application for himself and his family, and at last he submitted the necessary papers to the relevant authorities, including a letter of reference from the writer Joseph Kessel. The police commissioner's opinion was favorable: "Well assimilated, speaks French fluently. All information in good order . . ."

"We'll be French soon," Ephraïm promised Emma.

For now, the family was listed on their application as "Palestinians of Russian origin" by the government.

Ephraïm was confident, but he knew it would be several weeks before they could expect an official response. In the meantime, he had already chosen a new name, one that he thought rolled off the tongue like that of a hero in some nineteenth-century novel: Eugène Rivoche. Sometimes he repeated it aloud to himself as he stood in front of the bathroom mirror.

"Eugène Rivoche. It's elegant, don't you think?" he asked Myriam.

"How did you choose it, Papa?"

"Well, I'll tell you. Have you ever read anywhere, maybe in a genealogy book, that we're cousins of the Rothschilds?"

"No," Myriam answered, laughing.

"Ah. Well, then, I had to find a name with the same initials I have now, so I wouldn't need all my shirts and handkerchiefs re-monogrammed!"

Ephraïm felt sure that the doors of Paris were about to be thrown wide open for him. He stepped up his efforts to spread the word about the baking machine he had invented, filing patents with the French and German ministries of commerce under both names, Ephraïm Rabinovitch and Eugène Rivoche.

"In life you will find, son," he explained to Jacques, "that you have to know how to anticipate things. Hold on to that. Being one step ahead of the game is more useful than being a genius."

"At first I didn't understand why I'd found two identical patents in the archives," Lélia said. "They had the same date but different names. It was such a puzzle! It took me quite a while to realize that both names referred to the same person."

Ephraïm Rabinovitch, alias Eugène Rivoche, had invented a machine that reduced the time necessary to produce bread by speeding up the dough fermentation—thus saving two hours per oven-load, a remarkable gain of time in a baker's day.

The machine rapidly attracted interest. The *Daily Mail* ran a lengthy article on Ephraïm/Eugène's invention, entitled "A Major Discovery" ("I'll let you read it later," Lélia told me). According to that article, experiments and performance tests were being conducted near Noisiel, backed by the industrialist and senator from Seine-et-Marne, Gaston Menier—yes, of the Chocolat Menier family. Ephraïm had dreams of becoming a major overnight success like Jean Mantelet, who had struck it rich just a few years prior with his first invention, the hand-cranked food mill, and gone on to found the home-appliance company Moulinex.

While he waited for his dough-fermenting-machine patent to receive the adulation that was its due, Ephraïm/Eugène turned his attention to new intellectual endeavors—specifically, researching the mechanical breakdown of sound; he planned to start manufacturing coils for crystal radio sets. He bought a lot of thirty radios, which filled the apartment. The girls learned to assemble and disassemble them along with their father, which they thought was great fun.

A few weeks later, the Rabinovitch family's application for naturalization was denied. Ephraïm was stunned, and quickly assailed by pains in his chest and esophagus. He tried desperately to understand the reasons for the refusal. He was advised to wait six months and resubmit a more complete application.

Now Ephraïm began to see government agents hiding behind every lamppost, waiting to pounce on any doubts about the completeness of his "assimilation." He turned his back on anything that might evoke his foreign roots. He'd been embarrassed to say his name before; now he tried to avoid uttering it altogether. If he heard Russian, or Yiddish, or even German spoken in public, he crossed to the other side of the street. Emma was no longer allowed to do her shopping on the rue des Rosiers, and Ephraïm devoted himself to banishing his Russian accent and speaking with more "sophistication," like his children.

The only Jew Ephraïm spent any time at all with now was his brother.

"I'm having more and more trouble getting roles," Emmanuel lamented to him. "There are too many Jews in the movie industry, they say. I don't know what I'm going to do."

Ephraïm thought back to his father's words twenty years earlier: "My children, it stinks of shit."

So he decided to act. He bought a country house to get the family away from Paris—a farm called Le Petit Chemin in Eure, near Évreux, in the tiny hamlet of Les Forges. It was a lovely building with a slate roof and a cellar, an old well and a barn and a pond, standing on just over twenty-five acres of land.

"Let's try to be discreet, please," he said to his wife and children when they arrived in the village.

"Be discreet, Papa? What does that mean?"

"It means no shouting from the rooftops that we're Jewish!" Ephraïm replied, in the Russian accent that, more than anyone else in the family, immediately betrayed his origins.

But a Yiddishkeit wind would blow through their home in

that summer of 1938. Nachman was traveling from Palestine to spend some time with his grandchildren.

"He doesn't look like a Jew," sighed Ephraïm, watching his father disembark at the port in Normandy. "He looks like a *hundred* Jews."

CHAPTER 16

N achman shook his head at the sight of the Rabinovitches' neglected garden, his long white beard wagging. The whole thing would need to be tidied up, a vegetable garden planted, the well restored to working order, and the little barn transformed into a henhouse. They must plant some flowers, too, for his daughter-in-law, who loved pretty bouquets. But Emma urged him to rest and relax, instead of getting so worked up about everything.

"'*Kolzman es rirt zikh an aiver, klert men nit fun kaiver.*' As long as one limb stirs, one does not think of the grave," was Nachman's answer.

Rolling up his sleeves, he began to dig in the soil of Normandy. "It's like butter compared to the ground in Migdal!" he exclaimed, laughing.

Nachman's hands seemed to breathe new life into anything green and growing. At the age of eighty-four, he was the hardiest member of the family, fresh as a daisy, everyone happily obeying the orders he gave—especially Jacques, who was meeting this grandfather properly for the first time. The boy pushed wheelbarrows full of pebbles, turned soil, planted seeds, and nailed down loose boards from sunrise to sunset without a single word of complaint. At lunchtime, the old man and the teenage boy stayed out in the garden, eating a simple meal on their worksite like two farm laborers.

"We've got things to do," they explained to Emma, when she suggested they dine more comfortably in the kitchen.

Jacques loved his grandfather's accent, the way he spoke using his entire throat, from the base of the palate to the larynx. And he was exposed for the first time to Yiddish, that language with its honey-sweet words that rolled in Nachman's throat like bonbons. Jacques loved his grandfather's blue-gray eyes, bright as glass and washed pale by the Migdal sun, with something wistful and faraway in their depths. The grandson fell completely under the spell of this grandfather from Palestine. As for Esther, her rheumatism made it too difficult for her to make long journeys these days.

Emma watched, delighted, as the slight, wiry figure of her son flitted excitedly around the slower, bulkier one of the old man. Occasionally Nachman stopped in his tracks, his heart racing, and pressed a hand to his chest. Jacques would rush to his side at these times, terrified that his grandfather was about to collapse amid the gardening tools—but Nachman always recovered himself and rolled his eyes, shaking his head.

"Don't worry, my lad. I plan on sticking around for a good while yet!" he would boom, adding, with a wink, "If only out of curiosity!"

Myriam, soon to begin her studies in philosophy, spent these months absorbed in reading the books on her syllabus, while Noémie had begun to write both a novel and a play. They would work side by side, seated on chaises longues, straw hats on their heads, awaiting the arrival of their friend Colette, who was spending her summer holidays just a few kilometers away in a cottage her father had bought shortly before his death.

When they felt they had worked enough, the three of them would set out on their bicycles to explore the nearby forests, then come home for a big family dinner. The atmosphere was merry. Uncle Emmanuel came to visit; he had separated from the painter Lydia Mandel and was now living with Natalia, who was originally from Riga and worked as a salesgirl at Toutmain, a couture boutique at 26 avenue des Champs-Elysées. The couple had moved into a flat at 35 rue de l'Espérance in the 13th arrondissement.

"You see how nice life is, when you stop worrying so much about every little thing?" Emma said to her husband, lighting a candle.

To please Nachman, Ephraïm had agreed that on Fridays Emma would make challah, the braided loaves of bread traditionally eaten on the Sabbath.

"Does it make you sad that your son doesn't believe in God?" Jacques asked his grandfather.

"It used to, yes. But now I tell myself, the important thing is that God believes in your father."

Jacques, Emma realized, had begun growing again. He seemed visibly taller every day. They nicknamed him Jack and the Beanstalk, and, until they could get him fitted for new clothes, he started borrowing his father's trousers. His voice changed, and downy fuzz began to appear on his jaw. The boy who had never taken an interest in anything except football and marbles suddenly realized that his parents had been young once, that they had lived in several countries—Russia, Poland, Latvia, Palestine. He asked questions about the family and wanted to know the first names of the many cousins scattered across Europe. He began to drink wine—not because he liked the taste, but because he wanted to do as the adults did.

"How did you make our little boy grow up so fast?" Emma asked her father-in-law.

"That's a very good question, and I'm going to give you a very good answer. Wise men say that you must take a child's character into account when educating them. And Jacques has a very different character than his sisters. He doesn't like the strictness of school rules; he doesn't care to learn just for the sake of learning. He's a young man who needs to understand the immediate interest of what he's doing. He's what the English call a 'late bloomer.' You'll see. Your son will be a builder of things. He will make you proud of him, in the fullness of time."

That evening, the adults sat around the table telling old family stories and sipping glasses of slivovitz from a bottle brought from Palestine. Emma was thoughtful; Nachman, she could tell, still didn't dare mention the Gavronsky relatives. For twenty years—*twenty years*—her father-in-law had avoided that subject in her presence. Spurred on by a combination of pride, tipsiness, and defiance, she adopted her most detached expression and asked, "Do you ever hear anything about Anna Gavronsky?"

Nachman cleared his throat, casting a furtive glance at his son. "Er . . . yes, yes," he said after a moment, slightly flustered. "Aniouta lives in Berlin now, with her husband and their only son. She nearly died giving birth to him; the baby was too big. I believe she was unable to have more children after that, unfortunately. The three of them had a plan to move to America at one point, but I don't know if anything came of it."

Listening to his father's words, Ephraïm began to tremble all over; hearing the news of Aniouta's death could hardly have been worse. So overcome was he that even later, as he and Emma prepared for bed, he couldn't hide his disquiet.

"Why did you ask my father that question?" he asked his wife.

"I felt humiliated. Your father avoids talking about her, as if she were still a rival."

"It was a mistake," Ephraïm said.

Yes, it was a mistake, Emma repeated silently.

For the whole of August, Ephraïm allowed memories of his cousin to sweep over him. Aniouta appeared to him as he napped in the afternoon heat; he saw again her slim waist, so tiny he could encircle it with his two hands. He imagined her naked, yielding, offering herself to him.

As summer drew to a close, the family prepared to shut up the house and return to Paris after an absence of two months. Thanks to Jacques and Nachman, the place had become a proper little farm—and now Jacques confided to his grandfather that he wanted to become an agricultural engineer.

"*'Shein vi di zibben velten!'* Sublime as the seven worlds!"
Nachman exclaimed. "You'll come to work with me in Migdal!"

"Nachman," Emma said, "stay with us a few more weeks. You
can see the sights of Paris; the city is so lovely in September."

But the old man shook his head.

"*'Un gast iz vi regen az er doi'ert tsu lang, vert er a last.'* A guest
is like rain; he becomes a nuisance when he lingers too long. I
love you, my children, but I must return to Palestine to die alone,
like an old animal."

"Papa, stop," Ephraïm protested. "You're not going to die."

"You see, Emma; your husband is like all men! He knows he
will die one day, and yet he doesn't want to believe it. You know
what? Next year, you will come visit my grave. And then you will
settle in Migdal, because France . . ."

Nachman didn't finish his sentence, just swept a hand through
the air as if batting away an invisible swarm of flies.

The young Rabinovitches went back to school in September 1938. Myriam was in her first year of a philosophy degree at the Sorbonne. Noémie passed the first part of her baccalaureate at Fénelon and enrolled to continue her studies with the Red Cross. And Jacques was in his fourth year at the Collège Henri IV.

Ephraïm kept up his efforts to push the family's citizenship application through—but it seemed to him now that, at every meeting with the authorities, he took a step backward. There was always a new problem, a missing document, a detail that required further explanation. He always came home from these sessions grim-faced, shaking his head as he hung up his hat in the foyer of their apartment, remembering an expression his father was fond of repeating: "A whole crowd of people, and not one true human among them."

In early November, he began to become seriously worried by the masses of refugees streaming in from Germany. Terrible events had driven them out overnight; some had fled carrying only what they could fit in a suitcase, leaving everything else behind. Sighing, Ephraïm refused to talk about the situation, or even to hear it discussed in his presence.

"Because I already know the most important part," he sighed. "All these Jews arriving in France aren't exactly going to help my case . . ."

A few days later, Emma came home with a bombshell. "I met your cousin Anna Gavronsky today," she announced. "She's in Paris with her son. They had to flee Berlin; her husband was arrested by the German police."

Ephraïm was so shocked that he couldn't speak. He stared unseeingly at the jug of water on the table.

"Where did you see her?" he managed eventually.

"She was looking for you, but she'd lost your address, so she went into some different synagogues and came across . . . me."

Ephraïm didn't even seem to register the fact that his wife was still frequenting houses of worship despite his instructions.

"You spoke to her?" he asked hoarsely.

"Yes. I invited her to come to the house with her son for dinner, but she refused."

Ephraïm felt a contraction in his chest, as if someone were pressing on it very hard.

"Why?" he murmured.

"She said she couldn't accept the invitation, because she can't return it."

That sounds like Aniouta, Ephraïm thought. He laughed nervously. "Even in the midst of chaos, she considers etiquette. She's a Gavronsky through and through."

"But I told her we were family, and that we wouldn't think of it that way."

"You did well," said Ephraïm, standing up so abruptly that he knocked his chair over backward.

Emma had something else important to tell her husband. She rummaged nervously in her pocket for the scrap of paper Aniouta had given her containing the address of the hotel where she was staying with her little boy. In truth, Emma was reluctant to give Ephraïm this message. His cousin was still beautiful, her body still slim despite having given birth. Certainly her face had a few new lines, and her bosom was less generous than it had once been, but she remained a very desirable woman.

"She'd like you to visit her," Emma said finally, holding out the piece of paper.

Ephraïm recognized his cousin's delicate, rounded handwriting immediately. The sight was overwhelming.

"What should I do?" he asked Emma, shoving his hands into his pockets so she wouldn't see them shaking.

Emma looked her husband straight in the eye. "I think you should go and see her."

"Now?" Ephraïm stammered.

"Yes. She said she wanted to leave Paris as soon as possible."

Ephraïm went to fetch his coat and put on his hat. His body felt as taut as a bowstring, his blood pulsing wildly in his veins the way it had when he was young. He walked rapidly northward through Paris, across the Seine, as if his feet were floating above the ground, his thoughts whirling, his legs remembering their boyish muscularity. He'd been waiting for this moment for so long, he realized, hoping for it and dreading it at the same time. The last time he'd seen Aniouta was to inform her of his engagement to Emma in 1918—twenty years ago, almost to the day. Aniouta had pretended to be surprised, but in fact she'd already known of her cousin's plans. She had been teary-eyed at first. Aniouta had always cried easily, but even so, it had cut Ephraïm to the quick.

"One word from you, and I'll call off the wedding," he'd said.

"Oh, *you!*" she had exclaimed, shifting from tears to laughter in an instant. "How dramatic you are! It's ridiculous, but you make me laugh. Go. Go on. We'll still be cousins."

It was an unhappy memory for Ephraïm. Deeply unhappy.

Aniouta's hotel, tucked away behind the Gare de l'Est, was startlingly shabby.

Of all the places for a Gavronsky to be staying, thought Ephraïm, noting the state of the carpet, as threadbare and careworn as the woman behind the reception desk.

Behind her glass partition, the clerk consulted the hotel register but did not find Ephraïm's cousin among the guests.

"Are you sure that's the right name?"

"Sorry—it's her maiden name . . ." Ephraïm realized that

he couldn't remember her husband's last name, though he had known it once. "Try 'Goldberg.' No—'Glasberg.' Wait, maybe it was 'Grinberg' . . ."

He was still racking his mind when he heard the door open behind him. Wheeling around, he saw Aniouta make her entrance in a leopard coat and white fur hat. The cold air outside had brought a rosy flush to her cheeks and made her skin glow, making her look like one of those Russian princesses with whom men fall madly in love. She was carrying a few prettily wrapped packages.

"Oh—you're already here," she remarked, as if they'd just seen one other the day before. "Wait for me in the tearoom. I'm just going to put these things in my room."

Ephraïm stood frozen, breathless, silent, gazing at this almost supernatural vision—it was as if Aniouta hadn't changed a bit in twenty years.

"Be an angel and order me a hot chocolate. *Do* forgive me, but I wasn't expecting you to be here so soon," she said, in an adorable French accent.

Ephraïm wondered if her words contained a subtle reproach. It was true that he had responded to her summons with the haste of a dog called by its master.

"My husband and I woke up one morning," Aniouta recounted a short time later, taking a dainty sip of hot chocolate, "and *every* shop window on our street belonging to a Jewish merchant had been smashed. There was glass all over the pavement; the whole street was sparkling like a crystal chandelier. You can't *imagine*. I'd never seen anything like it in my life. Then someone called and told us that a friend of my husband's had been killed in his *own home* in the middle of the night, right in front of his wife and children! We'd only just hung up when the police were pounding on the door to arrest my husband. Before they took him away, he made me promise to leave Berlin with our son immediately."

"He was right to do that," said Ephraïm, his knee jiggling nervously under the table.

"But just *think* of it—I didn't even have time to put the house in order, I simply took David and left with the bed unmade and a single suitcase, in the most terrifying hurry."

The blood was pounding so wildly in Ephraïm's temples that he could hardly concentrate on her words. Aniouta was exactly the same age as Emma—forty-six—but she looked like a young girl. Ephraïm wondered how such a thing was even possible.

"I'm traveling south to Marseille as soon as possible, and from there we'll sail to New York."

"How can I help?" Ephraïm asked. "Do you need money?"

"No, but you're a *darling* to offer. I've got the money my husband put aside so David and I could get to America quickly. I don't know how long we'll be there . . ."

"Then tell me, how can I be of use to you?"

Aniouta laid a hand on Ephraïm's forearm. Once again, he struggled to focus on what she was saying.

"Dearest Fedya, you must leave, too."

Ephraïm was silent for a moment, unable to tear his eyes from Aniouta's delicate hand resting on his coat-sleeve, the sight of her shell-pink fingernails almost unbearably titillating. He pictured himself on a luxury liner with Aniouta, along with David, whom he would treat as another son. He could almost smell the salty air, feel the blare of the foghorn restoring his vigor. The image was so vivid, so visceral, that a vein began to throb in his neck.

"You want me to come with you?" he asked.

Aniouta stared at her cousin, frowning. Then she burst into laughter. Her little white teeth gleamed.

"*Lord*, no!" she said. "Oh, how you make me laugh! I don't know how you'd even manage it, with the way things are! Be serious, now. Listen to me. You must leave as quickly as possible with your wife. Your children. Settle your affairs; sell your possessions. Everything you have—change it all into gold. And buy steamship tickets to America."

Aniouta's laugh, high and piping like the chirping of a little bird, rang unpleasantly in Ephraïm's ears.

"Listen to me," she said again, shaking her cousin's arm. "What I'm telling you is important. I got in touch with you so I could warn you—so you would know. They don't just want us to leave Germany. This isn't about expelling us; it's about destroying us! If Adolf Hitler succeeds in conquering Europe, we won't be safe anywhere anymore. *Any*where, Ephraïm! Do you hear what I'm saying?"

But Ephraïm could hear nothing except that sharp, cruelly fond little laugh, the same now as it had been twenty years ago when he'd offered to call off his wedding for her. He only wanted one thing at that moment: to get away from this woman. She was nothing but a snob, like all the Gavronskys.

"You've got a spot of chocolate by your mouth," he said, getting up from the table. "But I've listened to what you have to say. Thank you. And now I've got to go."

"Already? I wanted to introduce you to my little boy, David!"

"I'm sorry, I don't have time. My wife is waiting for me at home."

Ephraïm could tell how vexed Aniouta was that he was leaving her so quickly. He took it as a victory.

What did she think, that I was going to spend the evening at her hotel? In her room, perhaps?

Ephraïm took a taxi home, relieved to see Aniouta's hotel receding in the rearview mirror. He laughed to himself, a strange laugh. The cab driver thought he must be drunk—and he was, in a way: drunk with newfound freedom.

"I don't love Aniouta anymore," he said aloud, like a crazy man, there in the back seat of the car. How ridiculous she was, repeating her husband's words like a parrot; surely the husband was one of those fat, rich men who were horrible bosses and made people hate Jews. And really she wasn't so beautiful anymore, after all. Her eyelids were sagging with age—her whole face was. And there'd been a few liver spots on her hand . . .

Ephraïm had begun to sweat, as if his body were ridding itself of all his love for his cousin, expelling it from every pore.

"You're back already?" Emma exclaimed, surprised. She concentrated on the vegetables she was peeling, glad to have something to occupy her shaking hands.

"Yes, already," Ephraïm said, bending to kiss Emma on the forehead, happy to be back in the warmth of the apartment, to smell dinner cooking and hear the sounds of the children in the hall.

Never had home felt so welcoming.

"Aniouta just wanted to tell me that she's sailing for America. It isn't as if we were going to spend the whole evening together. She says we should get our affairs in order and leave Europe as soon as possible. What do you think?"

"What do *you* think?" Emma returned.

"I don't know. I wanted to hear your opinion."

Emma was silent for a long while, considering. She got up from the table and dumped the vegetables into a pot of boiling water on the stove, the steam hot on her face. Then she turned back to her husband.

"I have always followed you. If we have to leave and start all over again, I'll follow you this time, too."

Ephraïm gazed at his wife with love. What had he done to deserve such a loyal and devoted wife? How could he ever have loved any woman but her? He got up and took her in his arms.

"Here's what I think," he said. "If my cousin Aniouta had any real political insight, we'd have known about it long ago. I think she's too emotional. What's happening in Germany is terrible, of course . . . but Germany isn't France. She's getting everything confused. And you know what? Her eyes looked a bit crazed.

Her pupils were dilated. And what would we do in America? At our age? You'd end up ironing trousers in New York for a pittance. And what about me? No, no, no, there are already far too many Jews there. All the good jobs will already be taken. Emma, I don't want to put you through that."

"You're sure?"

Ephraïm took a moment to reflect seriously on his wife's question, and said, "It would be utterly foolish to leave now, just when we're about to get our French citizenship. Let's not even talk about it anymore. Call the children and tell them it's almost time for dinner."

CHAPTER 18

After eleven years of research, Uncle Boris had perfected a method for determining the sex of chicks before they hatched. By watching the development of the weblike blood vessels in the egg, the red threads that make up the veins of the future chicken, he could predict whether the embryo would become a hen or a rooster. It was a revolutionary idea, commented upon in several Czech newspapers including the *Prager Press* and the *Prager Tagblatt*, a French-language Prague newspaper, and the Czech-language *Narodni Osvobozeni*.

In early December 1938, Boris traveled from Czechoslovakia to file the patents for his invention in France. He had enlisted Ephraïm's company, SIRE, to act as official representative of his scientific research. The two brothers spent whole days closeted in the office drawing up the documents, and their excitement spread to include the whole household. Emma felt as if she could finally breathe a bit; for the time being, her husband had forgotten his angry brooding against the government.

For the Christmas holidays, the whole family decamped to the country house at Les Forges in Normandy.

"A true kolkhoz!" Boris exclaimed when they arrived, using the Russian term for a collective farm. "Nachman's been here, I see! Could use a *few* improvements, though . . ."

Uncle Boris, who had given up a high-ranking position in the Socialist Revolutionary Party to become a farmer, knew everything about raising livestock. Under his tutelage, the Rabinovitches' little farm expanded to include chickens and a few pigs. Myriam and Noémie loved their dreamer of an uncle;

childless adults always fascinate children as much as they reassure them.

Emma would have loved to celebrate Hanukkah together as a family, but both brothers objected. Faced with their united opposition and not wanting to spoil her husband's good mood, she didn't insist.

"But I promise you, my dears," Ephraïm announced to the children, "as soon as we have our French nationality, we'll celebrate Christmas—and we'll buy a Christmas tree!"

"And a mini nativity scene with baby Jesus, too?" asked Myriam playfully, teasing her father.

"Er, no," he replied, glancing at Emma. "No need to go overboard . . ."

Back in Paris, on January 5, 1939, Boris received an invitation from the University of Maryland to attend the next global conference on poultry raising, entitled *Speeding Up Production, Seventh World's Poultry Congress*. It was a significant honor, and Ephraïm bought a bottle of champagne to mark the occasion. Emmanuel came to dinner at the house on the rue de l'Amiral-Mouchez to celebrate, and that evening he announced to his brothers that he intended to go to America, to try his luck in Hollywood.

"Now I wish I'd listened to Papa when he told us to move to America. I'd have struck it big, like Fritz Lang and Ernst Lubitsch and Otto Preminger and Billy Wilder—they went at just the right time. I was young and stupid; I thought I knew better than my father . . ."

But Boris and Ephraïm advised him to wait, to think it through a bit more.

After Uncle Boris's return to Czechoslovakia, worried postcards began arriving in Paris from Prague. The situation in Europe was deteriorating further and further.

"We didn't realize," Boris wrote.

Germany invaded Czechoslovakia in March. Boris found himself trapped, unable to travel to Maryland for the world poultry congress. It was a huge disappointment. Thinking back to the conversation with Emmanuel, he wondered if perhaps he'd been wrong not to encourage his brother to leave for America while he still could.

Nachman asked the whole family to come to Palestine for the 1939 summer holidays. But Emma and Ephraïm, remembering uncomfortable weeks in the sweltering heat, preferred to stay in the coolness of their farmhouse in Normandy. Besides, Ephraïm was always thinking of their pending citizenship, and a trip to Haifa wouldn't look very good in the file.

In May, France committed to providing military aid to Poland in the event of a German attack. Emma wrote to her parents in Lodz every day. She was careful not to let anyone see her fear, especially the children.

Myriam spent the school holidays that summer painting still lifes—baskets of fruit, glasses of wine, and other meaningless objects. She preferred the English term for the style to the French *nature morte,* or "dead nature." Still life. Still alive. Noémie made a point of writing in her private journal every day, while Jacques doggedly studied Lasnier-Lachaise's *Sommaire d'agronomie.* In early September, just before their return to Paris, Myriam and Noémie went to Évreux to stock up on paint and canvases.

As they walked their bicycles past the imposing façade of the savings bank, the girls heard the clock-tower bell begin to chime, a lengthy, insistent knelling that went on and on and on. Then all the church bells began clanging, as well. When they reached the art dealer's, the man was hastily pulling down the shutter of his shop with a loud metallic clatter.

"Go home!" he told the sisters sharply.

A cry rang out from an open window.

Myriam would remember declarations of war, later, as being very noisy.

The girls rode home on their bicycles as fast as they could. On either side of the path, the verdant countryside remained the same as always. Indifferent.

The Rabinovitches, who had been on the point of shutting up their country retreat, now unpacked their bags. Paris was under threat of bombardment; they would not go back.

Ephraïm and Emma went to the town hall and registered the Les Forges house as their principal residence, so that Noémie and Jacques could attend high school in Évreux.

They felt safer in the country, and the neighbors were friendly. Food wasn't a problem, thanks to the vegetable garden Nachman had planted, and Boris's chickens provided large fresh eggs. In the midst of such chaos, Ephraïm congratulated himself on having purchased the farm when he did.

Noémie and Jacques went back to school the next week; the former was in her final year, and Jacques in his third. Myriam traveled into Paris and back for her philosophy classes at the Sorbonne, and Emma had a piano brought in to keep her skills honed. Ephraïm played chess on Sundays with the husband of the village schoolteacher.

We're at war, the whole family kept reminding themselves, as if that would give the words some tangible meaning in this strangely normal life.

For now, those words were just something bandied about on the radio, read in the newspapers, and repeated in conversation with the neighbors or at the bistro.

"Still, I don't want to die," Noémie wrote in a letter to Uncle Boris. "It's so nice to be alive when the sky is blue."

And so the weeks passed in that surreal, resolutely carefree atmosphere common to troubled times, the rumors of war impossibly distant, the large numbers of dead merely an abstraction.

"I found a few pages from one of Noémie's notebooks among

Myriam's papers. She wrote, 'And the rest of the world goes about its business; we eat, we drink, we sleep, we attend to our needs, and that's it. Oh yes, we know people are fighting somewhere. How do you expect me to feel about it—I, who have everything I need. No, but really, people are dying of hunger out there, we say, while stuffing ourselves with every kind of dish imaginable. I want music, and I turn the wireless dial, tuning out the news and replacing it with Tino Rossi's beautiful voice, cooing about Barcelona again. There, that's better. Indifferent. We are completely indifferent. Eyes closed, naïve and innocent, we do nothing but talk—we shout—we fight and make up—and all that time, men are dying.'"

The Germans had invaded Poland. France and England launched half-hearted offensives, not really seeming to believe in them. The English even nicknamed it "the phony war"—and then a French journalist confused that with the word "funny," and it became forever immortalized as the "funny war."

Emma's father, Maurice Wolf, wrote letters to his daughter describing the September campaign and the entry of tanks into the city of Lodz. The Wolfs would be forced to vacate their home in favor of the invaders and were faced with the threat of having to do the same with the factory and even the pretty dacha on whose ivy-clad stone stoop Jacques had taken his first steps. It was painful to imagine German soldiers climbing those stairs. The city was reorganized and the quarters divided into territories, with Miasto, Baluty, and Marysin reserved for Jews. The Wolfs had to move into a small apartment in Baluty. A curfew was imposed, with residents forbidden to leave their homes between 7 P.M. and 7 A.M.

Ephraïm, like most Jews in France, failed to understand fully what was happening.

"Poland isn't France," he kept repeating to his wife.

As the school year ended, so did the funny war. Exams were postponed or cancelled. The girls weren't sure how they would get their diplomas. Ephraïm read in the paper that the Germans were in Paris: a strange threat, near and distant at the same time. Then, the first bombardments. On June 23, 1940, Hitler paid a visit to the capital with his personal architect, Speer, so that the latter could draw inspiration from Paris for the project called *Welthauptstadt Germania*—"Germania, capital of the world." Adolf Hitler wanted to turn Berlin into a model city, reproducing Europe's greatest monuments but on a scale ten times greater than the originals, including the Champs-Élysées and the Arc de Triomphe. His favorite building was the Opéra Garnier, with its neo-Baroque architecture.

"The stairwell is the most beautiful in the world," he said. "When the ladies stroll down in their costly gowns and uniformed men form a gauntlet . . . Herr Speer, we must build something like that, too!"

Not all Germans shared Hitler's enthusiasm for coming to France. The occupying soldiers were forced to leave their homes, their country of birth, and their wives and children. Accordingly, the Nazi propaganda office launched a major publicity campaign promoting the quality of French life, and a Yiddish expression was cynically misquoted to become a Nazi slogan: *Glücklich wie Gott in Frankreich*—"Happy as God in France."

The Rabinovitches did not return to Paris after the armistice was announced on June 22, 1940. Instead, they became one of the many families who went west, staying for several weeks in Brittany, in the town of Le Faouët, near Saint-Brieuc. The girls were surprised at first by the scents of kelp and salt on the seaside air but soon became used to it. One morning they found that the tide had gone out very far, so far that the ocean was no longer in view. They had never seen anything like it in their lives, and for a moment they didn't speak.

"It's like the sea is afraid, too," Noémie said at last.

For a few days, there were no newspapers, and so the occupation of Paris became something abstract, unreal, especially as they soaked in the last rays of the sun on the beach, eyes closed, face turned toward the ocean, hearing the sound of waves and of children making sandcastles. More than ever, those final days of August gave the vague impression that these happy times would never come again. The carefree interludes, the moments with no real purpose. That melancholy feeling that these were the last days, that life as it was had been irretrievably lost.

CHAPTER 19

Back to school, 1940. On orders from Berlin, France aligned itself with German time. Local governments were obliged to set all clocks forward one hour, creating mass confusion, particularly when it came to train schedules. Letters were now stamped with the *Deutsches Reich* surcharge, and the swastika fluttered atop the National Assembly building. Schools were requisitioned and a curfew imposed between 9 P.M. and 6 A.M. The streetlights no longer burned at night, and ration coupons were needed to go shopping. Civilians were required to black out their windows by covering them with cloth or paint to prevent Allied planes from detecting towns and cities. All of these things were checked and enforced by German soldiers. The days grew shorter. Pétain had been named head of the French government. He announced a policy of "national renewal" and signed the first of the Jewish Status Laws. This was where it all began, with the first German ordinance of September 27, 1940, and the law enacted October 3. Myriam, summing up the situation, wrote later, "One day, everything was turned upside down."

The uniqueness of this catastrophe lay in the paradox of its insidious slowness and its viciousness. Looking back, everyone wondered why they hadn't reacted sooner, when there had been so much time to do so. How they had been so blithely optimistic? But it was too late now. The law of October 3, 1940, stated that "any person with three grandparents of the Jewish race, or with two grandparents of that race if his/her spouse is Jewish" would be considered a Jew themselves. It also prohibited Jews from holding any sort of public office. Teachers, military personnel, government employees, and those who worked for public authorities—all were obliged to resign from their positions. Jews were also forbidden to publish articles in newspapers or participate in any of the performing arts: theatre, film, radio.

"Wasn't there also a list of authors whose books were banned?"
"Quite. The *Liste Otto*, named after the German ambassador to Paris, Otto Abetz. It listed all the books withdrawn from sale in bookstores. All the Jewish authors were there, of course, but also communist ones and French writers who were considered 'disruptive' by the regime, including Colette, Aristide Bruant, André Malraux, Louis Aragon, and even some dead authors, like Jean de la Fontaine."

On October 14, 1940, Ephraïm became the first person to register himself as a Jew at the prefecture in Évreux. He, Emma, and Jacques were assigned numbers 1, 2, and 3, respectively, in a register composed of large-format copy sheets on grid-lined paper. As Ephraïm had never been granted French citizenship, the family was listed as "foreign Jews." They had lived in France for more than a decade. It was Ephraïm's hope that, one day, the French government would remember his willingness to obey. He was required to disclose his identity and specify his profession, which posed a problem. The new German ordinances made it illegal for a Jew to be a "business owner, director, or administrator," so Ephraïm could not tell the truth: that he ran a small engineering company. And yet he didn't want to say that he was unemployed. And so he was obliged to lie, to invent a job for himself from the list of authorized professions. He chose "farmer"—he, who had loathed the farming life in Palestine so much. When he signed the register, Ephraïm wrote in the margin that he was proud of those who had fought against Germany in 1939–1940 and signed his name a second time. Later, Myriam and Noémie, made uncomfortable by their father's attitude, would find the ridiculous gesture embarrassing.

"You think Pétain's going to read the register?"

They refused to go and register themselves. Ephraïm was angry; his daughters had no idea of the danger they were putting themselves in. Emma, distraught, begged the girls to comply, and so four days later, on October 18, 1940, with great reluctance, Myriam and Noémie went to the prefecture together to sign the register. They declared themselves to be without religious affiliation and were listed as numbers 51 and 52, then given new identity cards bearing the word "Jew." The cards were issued by the prefecture of Évreux on November 15, 1940, number 40 AK 87577.

. Emmanuel was still hoping to leave for America, but he lacked funds for the ocean crossing; he'd had no work since the proclamation forbidding Jews from acting in films. He hadn't yet found a way to obtain the money to travel, and he hadn't registered himself, either. Ephraïm grew more and more frustrated with his younger brother, who was always so determined to set himself apart from the crowd.

"It's compulsory to register yourself at the prefecture," he remarked.

"I don't give a shit about the government," retorted Emmanuel, lighting a cigarette nonchalantly. "They can go fuck themselves."

"Emmanuel didn't register himself?"

"No, he chose the illegal route. Nachman and Esther had worried about their youngest son all his life; he'd been rebellious even as a child, didn't want to apply himself in school or do anything that everyone else did. And it was that rebelliousness that would save his life. Look at them, Ephraïm and Emmanuel, two brothers who were polar opposites. Two mythological brothers. Ephraïm had always been hard-working, faithful to his wife, and mindful of the common good, while Emmanuel had never kept a promise to a woman, tended to make himself scarce at the first sign of difficulty, and now wanted to leave France behind the way you'd cast off a dirty shirt. In times of peace, it is the Ephraïms who are the backbone of a people—because they have children and raise them with love, patience, and intelligence, day by day. They are the guarantors of a functioning country. But in times of chaos, it's the Emmanuels who save their people—because they refuse to submit to any rule and because they sow their oats in other countries, creating children they will never acknowledge . . . but who will survive them."

"It's horrible to think of Ephraïm being so obedient to the very government planning his destruction."

"But he didn't know that. He couldn't even conceive of the possibility."

One day, an official order was given for foreign nationals "of the Jewish race" to be "interned in camps," "in assigned residence." The wording was brief, terse. And vague. Why should they be interned in camps? And for what purpose? There were rumors of departures for Germany "to work there," but with no further clarification. In the orders, foreign and unemployed Jews were said to be "surplus to the national economy." And so they would serve as labor in the land of the conquerors.

"It's also very important to note that the first deportments involved only 'foreign Jews.'"

"I'm sure that was deliberate."

"Of course. Naturalized citizens who were well assimilated into French society had too much support. If the orders had begun by targeting 'French' Jews, people would have had more of a reaction; these would have been their friends, work colleagues, customers, spouses. Look what happened during the Dreyfus affair."

"Foreigners were less established in the country, so they were 'invisible.'"

"They existed in the gray area of indifference. Who would take offense if someone attacked the Rabinovitch family? They didn't even know anyone outside their family circle! The important thing, at first, when these orders were implemented, was to put Jews into a 'separate' category. With other categories present within that category. Foreigners, French, young, old. The whole thing was very carefully planned and organized."

"Maman . . . there comes a point when you can't just keep saying 'but people didn't know' . . ."

"Indifference is universal. Who are you indifferent toward today, right now? Ask yourself that. Which victims living in tents, or under overpasses, or in camps way outside the cities are *your* 'invisible ones'? The Vichy regime set out to remove the Jews from French society. And they succeeded."

Ephraïm was summoned to the prefecture. Other than that trip, he was no longer allowed to travel anywhere.

The purpose of the summons? To update the information on file pertaining to him and his family.

"When you were last here, you declared yourself a farmer," noted the government clerk who was interviewing him.

Ephraïm, remembering his lie, felt a wave of unease.

"How many hectares do you own? Do you employ any workers? Farmhands? Which agricultural machines do you use?"

Ephraïm had no choice but to tell the truth. He had a small orchard, three chickens and four pigs, and a modest vegetable plot he shared with a neighbor . . . but it couldn't really be said that he was the owner of a large farm.

The clerk updating Ephraïm's file briskly crossed out the word "farmer" on his form and wrote in pencil, in the margin: "Monsieur Rabinovitch possesses a 25-acre property on which he has a few apple trees. He raises chickens and rabbits for his personal use."

"You see what they were doing here, right? There was no way anyone could outsmart the system."

"Yes. They forced you to lie, and then they treated you like a liar. They prevented you from working, and then they told you that you were a drain on society."

"On Ephraïm's file, the word 'farmer' was replaced with 'sp,' for *sans profession*.' And there you have it—he'd been transformed into an unemployed, stateless parasite, reaping the fruits of a piece of French land he never should have been able to buy in the first place. And that's not all. He wasn't even actually listed as 'stateless' anymore, but as being of 'unknown origin.'"

"I get it. Being stateless is one thing. Being unknown—that's suspicious."

At the same time as this was going on, businesses and assets belonging to Jews were being sequestrated. Merchants and business owners now had to register themselves at their local police headquarters. This was what was called the "Aryanization of commerce." Ephraïm was forced to turn SIRE over to French administrators—and with it his inventions and patents, and his brother's. Twenty years of work, handed to the Compagnie Générale des Eaux, just like that.

As the French government and the occupying Germans wove their net bit by bit, the Rabinovitch sisters went about their lives with the same vital energy as ever. Noémie wrote a novella and showed it to her former teacher at the Lycée Fénelon, Mademoiselle Lenoir, who had some connections in publishing. It would be necessary for Noémie to use a pen name, of course, but she believed in her own talent.

As for Myriam, she met a young man near the Sorbonne one day, named Vicente. He was twenty-one years old. His father was the painter Francis Picabia, his mother Gabriële Buffet, a prominent member of the Paris intelligentsia. They weren't parents—they were geniuses.

Vicente Picabia was a young man who had grown up alone, like quack grass, the bane of a gardener's existence, like dandelions, impossible to eradicate. He'd spent his twenty-one years of life being shuffled from place to place, wanted nowhere, preceded everywhere by a bad reputation, disliked by his teachers, bouncing from boarding school to boarding school. As a child, he had often been the only one left behind in the grand foyer on the first day of school holidays, after all his classmates had gone home. His parents, too busy acting like children themselves, would simply fail to come and pick him up.

Gabriële spent as little time as possible with her youngest son, whom she viewed as quite a dull, wishy-washy sort of child. She had nothing to say to him and was waiting for him to become more interesting before she took the trouble to get to know him. Vicente had been born well after his brothers and sisters—an accident, undoubtedly, as his parents were long separated by the time of his birth. As soon as he was old enough, Gabriële had enrolled him at the École des Roches in Verneuil, in the Eure department in northern France—a modern establishment whose educational methods drew inspiration from the English system, placing great importance on outdoor sports and practical work. Like everyone else, Vicente's mother had read Edmond Demolins's 1899 bestseller, translated into more than eight languages, *Anglo-Saxon Superiority: To What It Is Due*, a question answered immediately on the back cover of the book, putting paid to any suspense: "It is due to education."

Despite these initiatives, Vicente didn't learn a thing at the École des Roches. He often had to search for the right words, repeating the beginning of a sentence over and over. He had extreme difficulty concentrating, and when he was called to read in front of the class, the letters and numbers inverted themselves.

"But school doesn't mean anything, son," said his mother. "The important thing is to *live*, to *feel*."

"Don't concern yourself with spelling," advised his father. "You know what's brilliant? *Inventing* words."

When he met Myriam in October 1940, Vicente was a young man without a high-school diploma or even a middle-school certificate. Before the war he had worked as a dishwasher in a restaurant. Now, he aspired to become a mountain guide and poet. The problem was his grammar. He had posted a notice at the Sorbonne seeking a student to tutor him. That was how he met Myriam. They'd been born three weeks apart; Myriam in Russia sometime in August, and Vicente in Paris on September 15.

"That's not by chance," I said to Lélia.

"What?"

"It's not by chance that I was born on September 15, the same day as my grandfather."

"Well, they say there are three ways to define chance. It brings about miraculous events, random events, or accidental events. Which category are you putting yourself in?"

"I don't know. I feel like some sense of memory makes us attracted to places our ancestors knew, celebrate dates that were important in the past, and become drawn to people whose family once crossed paths with ours without our even knowing it. Call it psychogenealogy, or cellular memory . . . all I know is, this isn't just chance. I was born on September 15; I studied at the Lycée Fénelon and then the Sorbonne; I live on the rue Joseph-Bara just like Uncle Emmanuel did. The similarities are pretty shocking, Maman."

"Maybe. Who knows?"

Myriam and Vicente had arranged to meet twice a week at the L'Écritoire bistro in the Place de la Sorbonne. Myriam arrived equipped with Claude Vaugelas's grammar textbook, notebooks, and a selection of pens for writing. Vicente arrived with his hands in his pockets and his hair uncombed, smelling vaguely of a stable. He dressed oddly, wearing an old cloak to one session and his Mountain Infantry uniform to the next, but never showing up in the same clothes twice. Myriam had never met anyone like him.

Very quickly, she realized that Vicente was having trouble with his diction, getting hung up on difficult words. He didn't have much of an attention span, either—but he was funny and charming and loved to make her lose her professorial gravity by cracking jokes. Soon it became common for Myriam to burst out laughing in the middle of a discourse on irregular verbs and past-participle agreements.

Vicente would order hot toddies and then, slightly tipsy, make up absurd sentences for the dictation exercises, deliberately showcasing the illogical nature of French grammar rules. He poked fun at the pontificating seriousness of the Sorbonne students and imitated the professors sipping primly at their tea.

"We'd be having more fun at the Lutetia swimming pool," he concluded loudly.

When the lesson was over, Vicente bombarded Myriam with questions, asking about her parents, her life in Palestine, the countries she had visited. He asked her to repeat the same sentence in all the languages she knew and then watched raptly while she did it. No one had ever been so intensely interested in her.

He revealed little about himself, however. All Myriam could find out was that he had left his job selling barometers.

"They fired me after a month. I'd have been better at selling books—I love the American authors. Do you know *The Savoy Cocktail Book*?"

From the very first, Myriam found herself flustered by the dark Spanish beauty of his face, his black hair and the shadows beneath his eyes, as if he were haunted by some old pain. He'd inherited his looks from his grandfather, a phlegmatic man who'd never done a lick of work in his life. Slim as a young bullfighter, the elder Picabia had married for a second time to an Opéra ballerina young enough to be his daughter. He'd had dark circles beneath his eyes, too.

After a few weeks, the sessions with Vicente became the only thing Myriam cared about. All around her, space and time were growing ever narrower because of the curfew and the last metro and the closed shops and banned books and forbidden travel; there were barriers everywhere now. But it didn't matter. Vicente was her new horizon.

She, who had never flirted, now turned coquettish. At a time when resources were so scarce that they had to do their laundry in cold water without soap, she managed to get her hands on a half-empty bottle of Edjé shampoo and an almost-empty vial of perfume that cost her entire savings, Bourjois's *Soir de Paris*, a heady bouquet of damask roses and violets that had had a reputation for being a "love potion" since it first hit the market.

At the sight of that bottle of perfume, Noémie realized that her big sister had met someone. Hurt at not having been taken into Myriam's confidence, she let her imagination run free. The lover must be a married man, she decided, or maybe one of her sister's professors at the Sorbonne . . .

One day, Vicente failed to show up for their tutoring session. Myriam waited, made up and perfumed, eager to begin the lesson. Then she began to worry; perhaps her pupil was stuck in the metro due to some emergency? But after four more hours of waiting, she was humiliated and angry with herself for having missed Gaston Bachelard's class on the philosophy of science.

The next time, when Myriam arrived at the bistro, the waiter informed her that "the usual young man" had left an envelope for her. Inside was a sheet of paper with something scribbled on it in pencil. A poem.

You know, women,
You can't try to hold them back
They are like hair
You can delay their leaving a bit
But in the end they always go.
You don't react like the others
What era are you from?
The friends around me make me feel as if
No one is there.
You are the dark-eyed moon
I had so much to tell you,
But I've forgotten it all.
I feel exhausted
My skull being gently crushed,
There are cigarettes left but my lighter has stopped working
And all the matches in the world are damp with tears
Life is not the opposite of death,
Any more than day is the opposite of night
They are twins, perhaps, but who don't have
The same mother.
Beginning of the world
You or I
End of the world
I'm out of ink.
Lucky for you?

On the back of the paper, Vicente had made a point of spelling everything wrong: "Id like to in vite you too a par tee at my mothers hous tommorow eevning. Pleaze come." Myriam laughed, but her heart was suddenly thumping in her chest.

"He wrote the address but didn't say what time," Myriam said to Noémie later, showing her the sheet of paper. "What do you think I should do? I don't want to get there too early, or too late."

All at once, Noémie understood. Her sister was in love with a poet, and he was handsome, and he threw parties at his mother's house.

"Can I come with you?"

"No, not this time," replied Myriam, whispering the words as if to soften their impact.

How could she explain to Noémie that this night belonged to her, that she wanted to have an experience all to herself, for once? The sisters had always been a pair, but in this case, that was impossible.

Noémie, wounded, felt a deep sense of rejection. She hated this man who was drawing her sister away from her. She hated it that he wrote beautiful, strange poems. Myriam was supposed to marry some young student who'd been a classmate in her philosophy course; the poets, the painters' sons, the boys who lived on the edge—they were for *her*, Noémie! *She* was the one they were supposed to be writing poetry and organizing soirées for; *she* was the beautiful dark-eyed moon! She locked herself in her bedroom and wrote furiously in the notebooks she kept stashed under her bed.

The next evening, Myriam had her friend Colette draw a line up the backs of her legs with a black pencil, to make it look like she was wearing stockings.

"There," said Colette, wielding the pencil with a steady hand and laughing. "You can let him touch you, but don't get too carried away or the jig will be up!"

Myriam arrived at Vicente's mother's building feverish with excitement. Climbing the stairs, she realized that she could hear neither voices nor music. Just silence. Had she gotten the day wrong? Embarrassed, she rang the doorbell of the apartment. She would count to thirty and then leave, she told herself—but suddenly the door opened and Vicente was standing there, his handsome face in shadow. The apartment was empty. He looked as if he'd been asleep.

"I'm sorry . . . I've come on the wrong night . . ." Myriam stammered.

"I called it off. Wait a minute; I'll get a candle."

Vicente came back in a few moments, barefoot and wearing an oriental-style robe that gave off a scent of incense and dust, the light from the candle in his hand sparkling on the hundreds of tiny mirrors sewn to the fabric. He gestured for Myriam to enter, looking for all the world like a young maharajah.

She followed Vicente through the apartment, lit only by the flame of his candle, the rooms crammed with old furniture and knick-knacks like an antique shop, with stacks of paintings leaning against the walls, the bookshelves filled with photographs and African statuettes.

"Don't make any noise," whispered Vicente. "Someone's sleeping."

Silently, he led Myriam to the kitchen where, in the bright electric light, she saw that he had lined his eyes with kohl. He opened a bottle of wine and took a gulp directly from it before offering Myriam a glass. He was nude beneath the woman's robe, she realized.

"I loved the poem," she said.

He didn't thank her. The truth was that the poem wasn't his; he'd stolen it from a letter Francis Picabia had written to Gabriële Buffet. Despite the fact that they'd been divorced for fifteen years, they still corresponded like lovers.

"You want some?" he asked, gesturing to a basket of fruit.

He selected a pear and peeled it, then sliced the flesh off in small morsels which he held out to Myriam one by one, dripping with juice. She ate them obediently.

"I didn't want to have the party after all because this morning I found out that my father got remarried," he said. "Six months ago. No one bothered to tell me. No one gives a damn about me in this family."

"Who did he marry?"

"A Swiss German woman. An idiot. She used to be our au pair. I always thought it was spelled '*au père*,'" he said, bitterly. "You know, '*for Father.*' It would have made perfect sense."

Myriam had never met anyone with divorced parents before.

"Didn't it ever bother you?" she asked.

"Oh, you know. 'My ass contemplates those who talk behind my back.' My father and the Swiss woman got married on June 22. The day of the armistice. Says a lot about their marriage, don't you think? And I wasn't even invited. I'm sure the twin was, though."

"You have a twin brother?"

"No. That's just what I call him, 'the twin.' I can't bring myself to say the word 'brother.'"

And then Vicente told Myriam the strange story of his birth.

"My parents were separated. My father had moved in with his mistress, Germaine, and my mother was living here with Marcel Duchamp, who was my father's best friend. Get it?"

Myriam didn't get any of it, but she listened avidly. She'd never heard anything like these stories.

"Germaine got pregnant by Francis on purpose. But when she found out that Gabriële was pregnant, too, she threw a fit— accused my father of still being secretly in love with his wife. But Francis convinced her that Gabriële's baby was Marcel's, not his. You following me?"

Myriam didn't dare say no.

"Both women got pregnant at the same time. My mother and my father's mistress. Simple, really, isn't it?"

Vicente got up to look for an ashtray.

"Germaine was still really upset, though. She wanted my father to marry her so the baby wouldn't be illegitimate. But Francis wrote 'God invented cohabitation; Satan invented marriage' on the walls of his building. The neighbors complained. It was a whole saga . . ."

Of the two babies, Vicente was born first. Marcel delivered him. Perhaps he'd hoped he was the father of this ready-made new life? But Vicente came out as dark as a little Spanish bull, and there could be no doubt that he was Francis Picabia's son. Everyone was very disappointed—most of all Francis, who, as the father, was now obliged to choose a name. He decided to call the baby Lorenzo. A few weeks later, Marcel Duchamp, relieved of any responsibility, left for America. And the other woman gave birth in her turn, to a little boy with black hair. Francis had to think of a second name and, running short of ideas, he called this baby Lorenzo, too.

"One must be practical, you know," he said.

Vicente loathed both his first name and his half-brother. He was forced to spend vacations with him in the south of France when he went to visit his father.

"I'd like you to meet my sons, Lorenzo and Lorenzo," Francis liked to joke.

Vicente hated it.

Francis hired a young au pair, Olga Molher, whom the boys referred to as "Olga Malheur"—"misfortune"—or "Olga Molar." She was less intelligent than Gabriële, less beautiful than Germaine, but she knew how to wrap Francis around her little finger. He gave her anything she wanted, and it was then that her true nature emerged: she had no real interest in children.

"I truly belonged nowhere, and no one wanted anything to do with me. At six years old, I tried to kill myself. It was at boarding school—I jumped out a second-floor window. Unfortunately, all I ended up with were two cracked ribs and a broken arm. No one bothered to tell my parents about it. One morning when I was eleven, I decided that I didn't want to be called Lorenzo anymore; I'd go by Vicente. And in 1939, I joined the 70th Mountain

Infantry Regiment as a private second class. My mother had taught me to ski, and I thought she'd be proud of me for once in her life. Then I requested to be deployed with a mountain infantry battalion on a campaign in Norway. I fought in the Battle of Narvik and was evacuated in June with the Polish, disembarked at Brest. Even Death isn't interested in me, I guess. That's just how it is."

Vicente kept slicing pieces of pear for Myriam as he spoke. She ate them all, afraid to refuse a single one in case it made him stop talking.

"Fuck, can you tell I'm crying?" He wiped at one kohl-rimmed eye, his fingers sticky with pear juice.

He got up to fetch a dishtowel. Myriam caught his hands in hers and brought them to her lips, then licked his fingers. He pressed his mouth to hers, awkwardly, without moving. Myriam could feel his naked torso beneath the robe. He took her by the hand and led her toward a small room at the end of a corridor.

"This is my sister Jeanine's bedroom. You can stay over, because of the curfew," he murmured. "I'll be right back."

Myriam lay down fully dressed on the bed, not daring to turn down the covers. Waiting, she thought back to the scent of his fingers, to his dark and smoldering beauty, to that strange kiss. An unfamiliar heat burning in the pit of her belly, she watched the dawn light filtering through the closed shutters. Suddenly there was a noise from the kitchen. *Vicente must be making coffee*, she thought.

"Would you like anything?" enquired a petite woman wrapped in the same spangled Indian dressing gown her son had worn the night before.

Before Myriam had a chance to respond, Gabriële handed her a cup, adding, "The two of you left quite a mess in the kitchen."

Myriam blushed, taking in the empty wine bottle, the fruit peels and cigarette butts.

Gabriële observed her. She wasn't as pretty as the last one, little Rosie. Her son broke hearts with a dedication he didn't seem to apply to anything else.

"Things always end badly with him," she remarked to Myriam now.

Gabriële would have preferred for her son to be homosexual; she found it chic, provocative. "Boys are simpler, believe me," she often said to Vicente.

"What would you know about it?" he always retorted brusquely, unable to bear his mother's frank talk.

Vicente had the kind of beauty that aroused instant desire in everyone from young girls to old men. At boarding school he'd engaged in the usual experimentation—and endured the groping of lecherous teachers, too. And his trips home had brought him into contact with a group of adults whose sexual mores were far too dissolute for a little boy to handle. Even then, he'd been able to recognize the smell of sex on their sheets. All of it had warped him somehow. His relationships were always strange. But his mother had never known what to do about it.

Vicente came into the kitchen now, eyes still puffy with sleep. At the sight of his mother's annoyed face, he did the first thing that came into his mind. Taking Myriam's hand, he said in a solemn tone, "Maman, I'd like you to meet Myriam. We're getting married."

Myriam and Gabriële both froze at the same instant. The young woman felt as if the floor were falling away beneath her feet, but the mother's face remained impassive; she didn't believe a word of it.

"We've been seeing each other for two months," Vicente continued. "I never told you about her because I knew it was serious."

". . . I don't know what to say," said Gabriële at last, frowning now.

"Myriam's studying philosophy at the Sorbonne. She speaks

six languages—yes, six! Her father was a revolutionary, and she's crossed Russia in a wagon, spent time in a Latvian prison, seen the Carpathian Mountains from a train, sailed the Black Sea, learned Hebrew in Jerusalem, harvested oranges with Arabs in Palestine . . ."

"Your life's like a book!" Gabriële said to Myriam, gently mocking her son's enthusiasm.

"Jealous?" asked Vicente flippantly.

Myriam stepped back out into the streets of Paris feeling as if she'd lived her whole life in a single night. She was hurrying home in the wee hours, just like in a fairy tale, and the moon had given her a fiancé. Nothing would ever be the same again, because of this complicated, handsome boy, so beautiful she could die of it.

I n the following weeks, Myriam introduced her fiancé to Noémie and Colette over hot chocolate at the Pâtisserie Viennoise on the rue de l'Ecole-de-Médecine. Colette thought he was simply *dreamy*, while Noémie, viewing her sister's romance as an abandonment, was more reserved.

"Be careful. Don't throw yourself at the first boy that comes along," she warned Myriam. "Pétain wants to make divorce illegal, or have you forgotten?"

It was clear to Myriam that jealousy lurked beneath her sister's supposedly well-meaning advice. She chose not to take the bait.

Vicente, too, introduced his fiancée to his friends. They were an odd, ill-bred bunch fond of indulging in hashish jam; they hated the middle class, were frequently drunk, wore gusseted jackets and long, slicked-back hair, and refused to venture outside the triangle created by Montmartre, Montparnasse, and the Villa Montmorency where, on some nights, Vicente slept at André Gide's house on the avenue des Sycomores.

They thought Myriam was too serious.

"She's dull. Plodding. Rosie may have been middle-class, but at least she was pretty."

Vicente always responded with something his father had said to him one day while they were watching the sun set: "Beware of what is pretty. Seek out the beautiful."

"But what do you find beautiful about her?" his friends persisted.

And then Vicente said, looking them in the eye and emphasizing each word, "She's Jewish."

Myriam was his battle-cry. His fragment of dark beauty. His ticket to pissing off the whole world. The Germans, the middle class, and Olga Molar.

Noémie, who had always been a brilliant student, now began to falter academically. Her German teacher wrote on her report card at the end of the first term: "Confusing student. Does either very well or very poorly."

She left *hypokhâgne*[1] and audited literature classes at the Sorbonne instead, which had the added benefit, to her mind, of putting her near her sister. She would happily wait for hours outside the Amphithéâtre Richelieu just to be able to go home on the metro with Myriam, the way they used to when they were in school together.

"She's smothering me," Myriam complained to her mother.

"But she's your sister, and you're lucky to have her," Emma replied, her throat tight.

Myriam could have kicked herself. She knew her mother hadn't heard anything from her parents or sisters in several weeks. The letters Emma sent to Poland remained unanswered.

One morning in Lodz, Emma's parents had woken up as prisoners. Their neighborhood had been sealed off during the night with wooden barriers topped by barbed wire. Regular police patrols kept anyone from leaving. It was impossible to get in, and impossible to get out. The shops weren't stocked. Germs and bacteria ran rampant. Week by week, the ghetto became an open-air morgue, with dozens dying of starvation or disease every day. Bodies no one knew what to do with were left piled in carts. Putrid miasmas drifted through the air. The Germans did not enter, for fear of infection. They simply waited. This was the

---

[1] The first-year intensive foundation course in the two-year academic cycle taken by humanities students in France to prepare for the entrance competition of the *École normale supérieure* in Paris.

beginning of the extermination of the Jews, through death by "natural causes."

It was why Emma had had no word from her parents, or her sisters Olga, Fania, and Maria, or her little brother Viktor.

Noémie enrolled in an accelerated teacher-training course, which would allow her to earn a certificate in July if the exams weren't delayed—and to earn a living, while still continuing to write.

"Look at this letter," my mother said. "You can see that, despite the fact that the Germans had forbidden Jews from publishing books, Noémie wasn't giving up on her plans."

> Sorbonne, 9:00 A.M., waiting for the teacher
> Dear Mama, Papa, and Jacquot,
> Three weeks ago I had a kind of "emotional shock." And ever since then I've written a lot of little prose poems; they've just flowed out of me so easily!
> Out of everything I've written, they're definitely the most publishable, in the sense that they're mature, and there's a completeness about them. I sent them to Mademoiselle Lenoir, and yesterday she asked me to come see her and talk about them. She liked them. She even told me the exact things she liked most about them—I felt so self-conscious! But anyway, she's very excited.
> Sorbonne Library, 3:20 P.M.
> She typed them up on her typewriter and sent them to someone who can give a much more objective opinion, because she's afraid of being too harsh, or not harsh enough. Yesterday really was a big day for me!
> I don't know exactly how to put it into words, but yesterday I felt so strongly that later on—not later on in the way people say "one day . . . ," but in two or three years, maybe sooner, maybe later—I'll be a published writer.

I wish I could be more specific, but I can't. It's too complicated, and sometimes too painful. But this—a lot of this—is
because of someone. Someone I love very much.

With that, I send you all a big hug, and I'll see Jacquot on
Friday. I'll be waiting at the station.

Love,

No

This undated letter was written before June 1941. That was
when Myriam and Noémie learned that a *numerus clausus* had
been enacted, limiting the number of Jewish students enrolled
at the university. They would both have to give up the Sorbonne.

Numerus clausus. The words were like a bucket of freezing
water. They'd heard them before, from Emma, who hadn't been
allowed to pursue her dream of studying physics. The Latin term
evoked a period far distant in place and time, nineteeth-century
Russia. They had never imagined that it would concern them one
day.

In Paris, German soldiers were being attacked—and in retaliation, some prisoners had been shot. The theatres, restaurants,
and cinemas were temporarily shut. The girls felt as if they no
longer had the right to do anything at all.

A few days later, Ephraïm learned that the Germans had entered Riga. The great synagogue where his wife had loved to go
and sing had been set on fire by nationalists. They had locked
people into the synagogue and burned them alive.

Ephraïm didn't tell Emma about any of this, just as she hadn't
told Ephraïm that the letters from Poland had stopped arriving.
Each was protecting the other.

They were summoned to the prefecture to sign the registers.
Ephraïm, who had heard talk of departures for Germany, asked
the administrative agent about it. "What exactly are people doing there, in Germany?"

The man handed him a leaflet, on the front of which was a

drawing of a worker gazing eastward. In capital letters, the leaf-
let read, "IF YOU WANT TO EARN MORE MONEY, COME
WORK IN GERMANY. FOR MORE INFORMATION,
CONTACT THE GERMAN PLACEMENT OFFICE,
FELDKOMMANDANTUR, OR KREISKOMMANDANTUR."

"Why not?" Ephraïm said to Emma. "Maybe working there
for a few months, representing France, could help us get our
citizenship. It would show that we're hardworking, and, most of
all, it would be a sign of good faith."

In the hallway, the Rabinovitches ran into Joseph Debord, the
husband of the schoolteacher in Les Forges, who worked at the
prefecture.

"What do you think?" Ephraïm asked, showing him the
leaflet.

Joseph Debord glanced in both directions and then, without
speaking, took the leaflet from Ephraïm's hands and tore it in
half. The Rabinovitches watched him walk silently away.

A cross from the Opéra Garnier rose an Art Deco building that looked like an enormous pink biscuit tin, with its shopping arcade; its movie theater, the Berlitz; and its nightclub with murals painted by Zino. A dozen workers, suspended from ropes like trapeze artists, were busily hoisting a gigantic advertisement. It showed a drawing of an old man several meters high with gnarled fingers and thick lips, clutching a terrestrial globe as if he wanted to possess it. Red capital lettering read, "THE JEW AND FRANCE." The exhibition had been organized by the Institute for the Study of Jewish Questions, whose principal mission was to orchestrate large-scale anti-Semitic propaganda on behalf of the German occupiers.

The exhibition opened on September 5, 1941, with the purpose of explaining to the citizens of Paris why the Jews as a race were dangerous for France. It sought to provide "scientific" proof that Jews were greedy, lying, corrupt, and sexually obsessed. It was a manipulation of public opinion that would demonstrate to the French that the Germans weren't their enemy. The Jews were.

The exhibition was both informative and entertaining. Upon first entering, visitors could have themselves photographed in front of a huge reproduction of a Jewish nose. Mock-ups displayed various features: hooked noses, thick lips, dirty hair. A wall at the exit was covered with photographs of numerous Jewish celebrities: Léon Blum, Pierre Lazareff, Henri Bernstein, and Bernard Natan, all of whom were said to represent "the Jewish threat in every area of national activity."

France was symbolized by a beautiful woman, "the victim of her own generosity."

After this, visitors could buy a ticket to see a German-made documentary at the Berlitz, the production of which had been overseen by Goebbels, entitled *The Eternal Jew*. The writer Lucien Rebatet had declared it a masterpiece.

This manipulation of public opinion had consequences. In the month of October, six Paris synagogues were mined with explosives by collaborationist militants whose weapons had been supplied by the occupiers. On the rue Copernic, the bomb destroyed part of the building and blew out its windows. The next day, an intelligence report stated that "news of the attacks committed yesterday against the synagogues has caused neither surprise nor agitation in the public. 'It was bound to happen,' people are saying, with a certain indifference."

This propaganda was also used to justify anti-Semitic measures, which continued to intensify. Families that owned a radio were ordered to turn it over to the police when they reported to the prefecture to sign the registry. All bank accounts were subject to administration by government-appointed French trustees. Arrests began, mainly of Polish men of working age.

The prefectures organized an inventory of the assets of each family residing within their territory, so that the government could confiscate whatever interested them. Soon, Jews would be ordered to pay a million-franc fine.

"As you can see from this document I found, the Rabinovitches didn't have much in the way of possessions."

> Order concerning a fine imposed on Jews.
> Surname: Rabinovitch
> First names: Ephraïm Emma and their children
> Residence: Les Forges
> Itemization of objects of value seizable without damage to

the general economy or French creditors (silver, jewelry, art-works, movable assets, etc.):

One automobile and basic furniture

Every Sunday, Ephraïm played chess with Joseph Debord, the teacher's husband.

"I think the Jews should try to leave France," Debord said to Ephraïm during one of their meetings, moving a pawn on the chessboard.

"We don't have any identification, and we're under house arrest."

"Maybe . . . you could look into it anyway?"

"But how?"

"Well, someone could do it for you, for example."

Ephraïm was well aware of what Debord was trying to say. But he was used to managing his own affairs, particularly when it came to his family.

"Listen," Debord continued, whispering now. "If you ever have a problem . . . come and see me at home—but never at the prefecture."

Despite himself, Ephraïm thought about what Debord had said and began to consider the possibilities of moving abroad. Why not go back to live with Nachman for a while, if they could find a way to travel clandestinely? But the United Kingdom no longer allowed Jews to emigrate to Palestine under British mandate. So Ephraïm looked into the United States, but the immigration policies there had become stricter. Roosevelt had imposed restrictions. One ocean liner fleeing the Third Reich, the *Saint-Louis*, had been forced to turn around, and the thousand passengers aboard it were sent back to Europe.

Barriers were springing up everywhere. What had been possible just a few months before was no longer so.

Leaving would take money, but everything they possessed had been seized by the French government. And they would have to travel secretly, start over from scratch. Ephraïm felt too old for all of that. He wasn't brave enough anymore to load his family into a wagon and navigate snowbound forests.

His tired body was a limit, too. His own personal barrier.

Vicente and Myriam were married on November 15, 1941, in the town hall of Les Forges, without fuss or photographs. The Picabias, for whom the event held little interest, did not attend. Myriam wore a traditional Polish dress of her mother's, of heavy white linen embroidered in red. To reach the town hall, they'd had to pass through the village. The residents watched their little procession: those odd-looking Rabinovitches, Noémie wearing a little hat with a veil lent to her by the schoolteacher, Madame Debord, and Myriam a tablecloth draped like a scarf. They were like those circus performers you sometimes saw loitering on the edges of town, the mayor thought: half-artists, half-thieves.

"How strange these Jews are," he remarked to his secretary.

No one in Les Forges had ever seen anything like it: a wedding with no mass, no singing, no dancing to the strains of an accordion. It was a rather Spartan ceremony, to be sure, but it was Myriam's deliverance: she was removed from the list of Jews in Eure and transferred to the list for Paris.

And so Myriam became an official resident of the capital, settling in an apartment on the top floor of a building on the rue de Vaugirard. Three former servants' rooms linked by a long corridor.

As a young newlywed, Myriam tried to keep a tidy house. But Vicente didn't want to change any of their habits.

"Stop it," he would say. "We haven't turned into the petit bourgeois all of a sudden. Who gives a damn about housework?"

Still, they had to eat. When she wasn't in class at the Sorbonne, Myriam was standing in line at one shop or another. As a Jew, she wasn't permitted to run her errands at the same time as the French but was confined to the single hour between three and four o'clock. A "DN" ration coupon would get you some tapioca; "DR" was peas, "36" snap beans. Sometimes, by the time she got to the front of the line, there was nothing left. She always apologized to Vicente.

"No need to apologize! We'll drink; that's better than eating anyway."

Vicente preferred to imbibe on an empty stomach. He loved to take Myriam with him to prohibited drinking spots, like the Dupont-Latin on the corner of the rue des Écoles, and the Café Capoulade on the rue Soufflot. One of Myriam's diary entries read, "Spent the evening on the rue Gay-Lussac with Vicente. The people at the neighboring table thought we were making too much noise and called the police, so I escaped out a window. It was pitch-black outside. Made it to the rue des Feuillantines, and then I heard two French police officers coming. I crouched in a dark corner and hid."

Escaping, hiding, eluding the police: it was like a game where the only goal was to survive. Myriam, with all the fearlessness of youth, felt herself to be invincible.

"After the war, a lot of members of the Resistance developed a kind of depressive disorder, maybe because they'd never felt so alive as when every moment contained a brush with death. Do you think Myriam might have felt that way?"

"My father certainly did. The return to 'normal' life was extremely hard for Vicente. He needed that adrenaline rush that goes along with risk."

Little by little, as the government conducted its painstaking "delousing" operation, seeking to count every single Jew living on French soil one by one, new orders were issued continuously, restricting their liberty ever further. The work proceeded slowly, insidiously—and effectively. Between late 1941 and early 1942, Jews were forbidden from traveling more than five kilometers from their homes. An eight o'clock curfew went into effect, further hampering their movements. By May 1942, they were required to wear a prominent yellow star on the lapel of their coats to facilitate the job of the police, tasked with verifying that they were respecting the curfew and the travel restrictions.

In an act of protest, the students of the Sorbonne sewed yellow stars bearing the inscription 'Philo' onto their jackets and were promptly arrested in large numbers in the Latin Quarter, driving their parents mad with worry. "Don't you realize what a risk you're taking?" became a common refrain.

The Rabinovitches were trapped in their country cottage, no longer allowed to travel, go out in the evenings, or take the train.

Myriam and Vicente, however, *were* permitted to travel back and forth between Paris and Normandy. On the way out, their bags were stuffed with household essentials, on the way back, with food from the farm. These movements gave the Rabinovitch household a bit of room to breathe.

It was Noémie who suffered most from the situation, especially when she watched her big sister leave to catch the train for Paris with her young, handsome husband.

One evening Myriam sat on the terrace of La Rhumerie Martiniquaise at 166 boulevard Saint-Germain, drinking with Vicente and his pals. It was getting late, and the curfew prohibited Jews from being out in public after eight o'clock at night, but Myriam was in no hurry to leave the company of this group laughing uproariously amid the alcohol fumes. She was an adult, after all, and a married woman, and she wanted to feel the tingle of freedom on her skin. She leaned back and closed her eyes to better appreciate the burn of the rum on her lips and down the back of her throat.

When she opened her eyes again, the police were there. Identification check. It had happened as quickly as a tidal wave. Just a few seconds earlier, she could have gotten up and left. Escaped. But now, in the span of a breath, she was caught, collared. Finished. She felt as if icy fingers were brushing against her cheeks and neck and the undersides of her arms. She felt as if she were drowning. And yet, she could almost have burst out laughing; the alcohol made everything feel unreal, like a scene in a movie.

The tension among the drinkers on the terrace was growing; the presence of uniformed police was not pleasant. There was a certain sense of hostility emanating from the customers; the men groped in their pockets for their IDs just a bit longer than necessary to annoy the officers, and the ladies sighed loudly as they rummaged in their handbags.

Myriam knew she was done for. Useless thoughts flashed through her mind. Should she hide in the bathroom? The police would search there. Pay for her drink and leave as if nothing were the matter? No. They'd already seen her. Make a break for it? They'd catch her in no time. She was trapped. Suddenly everything seemed absurd. Her glass of rum. The ashtray. The cigarette butts. She was going to die for the sake of feeling free, drinking alcohol on the terrace of a Parisian café. What a senseless way for her life to end. She held her ID card out to the officer, the word "Jew" stamped on the front.

"You're in violation of the law."

Yes, Myriam knew that. It was punishable by internment. She could, even tonight, be sent to one of those strange "camps" where nobody knew quite what went on. Silently, she got up from her chair. She gathered her things, her coat, her bag, gave Vicente a little wave, and followed the officers. The other customers watched them handcuff her and lead her out. For a few minutes, the room rippled with indignation at the fate of the Jews.

"That young woman didn't do anything wrong."

"These laws are humiliating."

Then the laughter began again, and people went back to their rum cocktails.

Distraught, Vicente went to his mother's and told her what had happened.

"What were the two of you doing out in the first place?" Gabriële shouted. "Idiots—both of you! Do you think this is a game? I told you Myriam shouldn't keep going out at night."

"But Maman—she's my wife," Vicente protested. "She can't stay cooped up at home every night."

"Listen to me carefully, Vicente, because I'm not joking. You and I need to have a serious talk."

While mother and son had the first real conversation of their lives, Myriam was taken to the police station on the rue de l'Abbaye, where she spent the night. In the morning, she was transferred on foot—though without being handcuffed—to the police headquarters on Île Saint-Louis, where she spent her second night as a prisoner.

On Sunday morning, a police officer came to fetch her. His expression was hard, closed. He never looked Myriam in the eye but kept his gaze on the ground. Once they were out in the street, he indicated his car and said, "Get in. Don't argue."

As the man walked around to the driver's side of the car, Myriam sniffed her underarms and realized, embarrassed, that, after two days in jail, she smelled truly awful.

She asked if she was being transferred to another prison somewhere else in Paris, but the police officer didn't reply. The city streets were silent and empty. Parisians had been forbidden to drive their cars, and the capital was hideously quiet. Everywhere there were black-bordered white signs with directions printed on them in German, to help the occupiers orient themselves.

Eventually Myriam realized with a jolt that the officer was taking her to the train station, as the car systematically followed the signs toward *Der Bahnhof Saint-Lazare*. She wondered if she was about to be sent to one of those camps far from Paris. The thought was terrifying.

She gazed out the window at the office workers scurrying

along the pavement with their gold-framed glasses and leather briefcases, their dark suits and polished shoes, running to catch one of the rare buses that crisscrossed the city—slowly these days, due to faulty gas generators. She wondered if she would ever again be part of a scene like this, which now seemed like a pantomime being played out behind a glass screen.

The car abruptly pulled off into a narrow side street and stopped. The police officer took three ten-franc coins from the pocket of his uniform and handed them to Myriam. His fingers were long and slender, she saw, and his hand was trembling.

"For a train ticket," he said. "Go to your parents' house."

The instructions were simple. Yet Myriam sat frozen, staring at the coins in the man's hand, with their sheaves of wheat beneath the national motto of France: *Liberté, Egalité, Fraternité.*

"Hurry up," the officer urged, nervously.

"Is it my parents who—"

He cut her off. "No questions. Go into the station. I'll be watching."

"Just let me write a quick letter. I want to tell my husband."

"Wait, Maman—I find this whole police officer story really strange. Is this just the way you're imagining it happened?"

"No, darling. I haven't made up a thing. All I've done is research and reconstruct. Look—or read, rather."

Lélia handed me a page torn from a school notebook, covered with grid lines on both sides. I recognized Myriam's handwriting.

It's true that I've been lucky so many times in my life. The yellow star? I never wore it. At the Rhumerie Martiniquaise in Saint-Germain-des-Prés—did my identity card already have JEW stamped on it in red, or was it just my name? An evening ID check at eight o'clock at night? Jews were supposed to observe the curfew, so I was *arrested* and taken to the police station on the rue de l'Abbaye. I slept leaning against the shoulder of a very charming fellow. A pimp by profession. Riton, I think his name was. In the morning, very quietly and without handcuffing me, an officer in civilian clothes took me on foot to the police station on Île Saint-Louis. They'd give you a cup of coffee there, if you could pay for it. I was next to a very large Spanish woman who was cursing out the French at the top of her lungs. I had a little bit of money with me, so when the coffee boy came back for the empty cups, I slipped him a note along with a few coins as a tip. It said: "I'm giving you all the money I have. Please call telephone number xxxx and tell them I'm here." I spent the night there, and the next morning, which was a Sunday, an officer came to fetch me. "I've been told to take you to the train station," he said; "I have money for your ticket." I wasn't able to stop at home first. The officer let me write a quick letter to my husband. He gave me back my identification papers, and from there I went straight to Les Forges.

"Remember when I told you to remember the date July 13, 1933, as a day of complete happiness?"

"The day the Lycée Fénelon handed out the prizes."

"Yes. Well, this was exactly nine years later, to the day. July 13, 1942. In Les Forges."

J acques had completed the first part of his baccalaureate studies. He went to Évreux to get his results with the yellow star on his coat. On the way back, Jacques and Noémie rode their bicycles to Colette's house, to tell her the good news.

It was a hot day, and the three of them had a wonderful time. Since Myriam's marriage, Jacques had taken her place in the trio of friends, and Noémie was savoring their new, unexpected closeness, getting to know her younger brother's sunny personality. Colette thought of inviting the two of them to spend the night but ended up abandoning the idea.

Cycling back to their parents' home, Jacques and Noémie stopped in the village square in Les Forges, which was being readied for the Bastille Day celebrations, with a stage and strings of paper lanterns.

"You think we can come back here for a bit after dinner?" Jacques asked Noémie.

She ruffled his hair playfully, and he protested loudly. Jacques hated having his hair touched.

"Come on. You already know the answer to that," Noémie said.

They walked their bicycles the rest of the way home, taking off their jackets and draping them across their luggage racks so the yellow stars couldn't be seen. Luck was on their side; some Germans passed them on motorcycles, and it was already curfew.

Emma had somehow scraped together a tasty dinner and set the table prettily outside in the garden, beneath the trees, to celebrate Jacques's results. Since he'd made the decision to be an agricultural engineer, his academic performance had risen to equal his sisters'.

Emma had scattered the tablecloth with wildflowers. Myriam was there; she hadn't returned to Paris since her miraculous liberation from prison, and so the whole family would dine together in the garden behind the house. They were there, all five of them, in the same seats they'd occupied around the table in Palestine, and then in Poland, and then in Paris on the rue de l'Amiral-Mouchez. It was their little ship, this table. Their barque. The night seemed reluctant to fall, the air still heavy with the sweet-scented warmth of the day.

Suddenly the roar of a motor pierced the evening calm. A car was approaching the farmhouse—no, *two* cars. Conversation around the table broke off, ears pricking up like those of nervous animals. They waited for the noise to fade into the distance again, but it persisted, grew even louder. Their hearts clenched. All five of them held their breath. They heard the sound of car doors slamming, the crunch of boots on gravel.

They groped for one another's hands beneath the table, fingers intertwining, hearts already beginning to break. Fists pounded on the door. The children flinched.

"Everyone stay calm. I'm going to get the door," Ephraïm said.

He walked through the house and stepped outside. There were two cars parked there, one with three German soldiers in it and the other with two French policemen, one of whom would be tasked with translating any orders. But Ephraïm, who spoke German, already understood what they were saying to one another.

The police had come for his children.

"Take me instead," he said to the French officers at once.

"Not possible. Tell them to pack a suitcase for the journey, quickly."

"What journey? Where are they going?"

"You'll be informed in due course."

"They're my children! I need to know!"

"They're being sent away to work. No one's going to hurt them. You'll receive news of them."

"But where? When?"

"We aren't here for discussion. We're under orders to bring in two people, and we're taking those two people."

Two people?

Of course, Ephraïm thought. *Myriam's on the Paris lists. They're talking about Noémie and Jacques.*

"Everyone's asleep," he said. "My wife's in bed. It would be easier for you to come back tomorrow morning."

"Tomorrow is Bastille Day. The police won't be working."

"Then give me just a few minutes, so my wife and children can get dressed."

"One minute. No more," the officer replied.

Ephraïm turned and walked calmly back into the house, thinking. Should he tell Myriam to take the children and run? She was the oldest and most resourceful. She could leave with the two younger ones, help them get away—she'd gotten out of jail all by herself, hadn't she? Or should he tell Myriam to hide, to avoid running the risk of being arrested herself?

The rest of the family was waiting for him silently in the back garden.

"It's the police. They've come for Noémie and Jacques. Go and pack your suitcases. Not you, Myriam. You're not on the list."

"But where are they going to take us?" Noémie asked.

"To work in Germany. So pack some warm sweaters. Go on, hurry up."

"I'm going with them," Myriam said.

She rose from the table, ready to go and pack her own bag. A distant memory flashed through Ephraïm's mind, the vague recollection of that night the Bolshevik police had come to arrest him. Emma had become ill, and he'd pressed his hands to her belly, terrified that the baby she was carrying had died.

He gripped Myriam's arm firmly. "Go and hide in the orchard."

"But, Papa—" she protested.

Ephraïm could hear the police hammering on the door again. He seized his daughter by the collar, grasping it tightly enough to choke her. Looking her straight in the eye, he murmured, through lips twisted by fear, "Get the hell away from here, as far as you can. Understand?"

CHAPTER 24

W hy did the Rabinovitch children get arrested, but not their parents?"

"Yes, it does seem strange, because we've all got those images in our head of whole families being arrested together—parents, grandparents, children. But there were different kinds of arrests. The Third Reich's plan to exterminate millions of people was so vast that they had to proceed in stages over the span of several years. The first part of it, as you saw, was to enact ordinances aimed at neutralizing the Jews, to prevent them from acting. You see the sleight of hand there?"

"Yes. They separated the Jews from the French population; they distanced them physically, made them invisible."

"Even on the metro, where Jews could no longer travel in the same cars as the French."

"But not everyone turned a blind eye. I remember what Simone Veil said: 'In no other country was there a burst of solidarity comparable to what happened in France.'"

"And she was right. The proportion of Jews saved from deportation during the Second World War in France was higher than in other countries occupied by the Nazis. But to go back to your question, no, whole families of Jews weren't usually deported together. Not at first, anyway. The first deportees, in 1941, were all men of working age. Most of them Polish. They called it 'the green ticket roundup,' because the men who were deported all received their summons in the form of a green card or ticket.

"First they took strong, healthy men, to lend credibility to the idea that they were being sent away to do physical labor.

Young fathers of families, students, blue-collar workers; you get the idea. So Ephraïm, who was over fifty, wasn't affected. This allowed them to get rid of the strong, fit men first. The ones who could fight, the ones who knew how to use a weapon. You see—when you said you didn't understand how people could let this happen to them, as if they were dead men walking, when you said the idea was unbearable . . . well, those men, the 'green tickets'? They didn't just sit back and let themselves be sent away without objecting. First of all, almost half of them didn't respond to their summons. And then they fought. Many of them escaped, or tried to escape, from the French transit camps where they were held. I've read stories about some of those escapes, of terrible clashes with the camp overseers. Out of the 3,700 green tickets arrested, almost 800 managed to escape, although most were recaptured.

"All of this was done in a very calculated, deliberate way, to make people believe the whole thing was 'just' about imprisoning Jews and sending them to work somewhere in France. Not killing them. They were broadly associated in people's minds with prisoners of war. And then, gradually, younger Jews like Jacques and Noémie began to be arrested, too, and then other nationalities, and eventually, little by little, everyone was targeted: young, old, men, women, foreigners, non-foreigners . . . even children. It's an important point about the children. You might know that the Germans wanted to wait and deport the children *after* their parents had already been taken. But the Vichy government wanted to get rid of the Jewish children in France as quickly as possible. The French government expressed to the German government 'the desire for transports to the Reich to include children, as well.' It's all there in black and white.

"The Germans used a code name, *Vent de printemps*, or Spring Breeze, for the operation aimed at accelerating the deportation of Jews from western Europe. The original idea was to arrest every Jew in Amsterdam, Brussels, and Paris on a single day."

"In *one* day? How incredibly delusional the anti-Semitic dream was . . ."

"But things proved more difficult to organize than they'd expected. On July 7, 1942, representatives from both countries met in Paris. The Germans laid out their plan, but they left it up to the French to execute it. The directive specified, among other things, the deportation by train of four convoys per week, 1,000 Jews to a convoy. That was 16,000 Jews sent to the East per month, with the goal of deporting an initial contingent of 40,000 Jews from France in the first quarter. An *initial* contingent. And that was only the beginning. It was a clear, straightforward, concise plan.

"On the day after the July 7 meeting, the police commissioners of every French department received the following orders—I'll read them to you exactly as they were written: 'All Jews aged 18 to 45 years inclusive, of both sexes, of Polish, Czechoslovakian, Russian, German, and, as previously, Austrian, Greek, Yugoslavian, Norwegian, Dutch, Belgian, Luxemburgish, and stateless nationalities, must be immediately arrested and transported to the transit camp at Pithiviers. Jews who are visibly crippled, as well as Jews who are the issue of mixed marriages are not required to be arrested. Arrests must be wholly completed by July 13 at 8:00 P.M. The Jews arrested must be delivered to the transit camp no later than July 15 at 8:00 P.M.'"

"July 13 was when the Rabinovitch children were arrested. Noémie was nineteen, so she fit the criteria—but Jacques? He was only sixteen and a half. Eighteen years old is eighteen years old, and the government usually followed the rules."

"You're absolutely right. Jacques shouldn't have been arrested. But the French government had a problem. In some departments, the number of Jews available for deportation didn't meet the efficiency target set by the Germans. Remember what I told you? A thousand Jews per convoy, four convoys a week, and so on. And so the official order was given to reduce the age limit for arrests to sixteen years. I think that's why Jacques was on the list."

"What about Myriam? What would have happened to her if she'd turned herself over to the Germans that night?"

"She would have been sent away with her brother and sister, to meet the—"

"The efficiency target."

"But she wasn't on the list that night, because she'd just gotten married. All of our lives were spun from that impossibly slender thread of luck."

N oémie and Jacques huddled together in the back of the police car as they were driven toward an unknown destination. Jacques rested his head on his big sister's shoulder. Eyes closed, he thought back to the game they used to play, where they would try to think of words starting with the same letter in different categories: sports, famous battles, heroes. One of Noémie's hands clutched her brother's; with the other she gripped the handle of their suitcase. She made a mental list of everything she had forgotten in the rush to pack: her Rosat balm for chapped lips, a bar of soap, her favorite dark red cardigan. She regretted bringing Jacques's bottle of Pétrole Hahn hair tonic, which took up so much pointless room in the case.

Pressing her cheek to the window, she gazed out at the village streets, which she knew by heart. On this particular night, all the young people her own age were on their way to the dance, strolling in small groups. The car's headlights lit up their legs and torsos, but not their faces. Deep down, she thought it was better that way.

The ordeal to come would make a writer out of her, she mused. Yes—one day, she would write it all. She made sure to observe everything carefully so she wouldn't forget, each detail: the girls walking in bare feet, carrying their shiny shoes so as not to scratch them on the gravel-dotted sidewalks, their breasts straining against too-tight blouses. She would write about the boys walking their bicycles, their brillantined hair gleaming in the moonlight, hooting and howling like animals to make the girls laugh. And she would describe the erotic promise of the dance hovering in the air, the young people drunk without having imbibed anything, intoxicated by the strains of the brass band, already floating on the warm July breeze. The humid, sweet-smelling atmosphere of a summer night.

The police car exited the village now, heading toward Évreux. On the edge of the woods, a young couple emerged from the bushes, as if caught in *flagrante delicto* in the car's headlights. They were holding hands. The sight was like a knife in Noémie's heart, as if she knew, already, that this was a pleasure she would never experience.

The car plunged into the forest, silence enveloping the road and the house where Ephraïm and Emma sat alone, paralyzed with fear, and the garden where Myriam hid, waiting for something to happen without knowing exactly what.

Much later, in the mid-1970s, on a very hot afternoon in a dentist's office in Nice, Myriam would suddenly realize what it was that she had been waiting for, flat on her belly in the darkness. The memory of that waiting would flood through her. The feeling of the grass against her lips. The fear in the pit of her stomach. She had been waiting, she would realize, for her father to change his mind. It was as simple as that. She'd been waiting for him to come and find her, to ask her to go and catch up with her brother and sister.

But Ephraïm did not change his mind. He told Emma to close the shutters and go to bed, still maintaining his calm. Panic must not take over this house.

"Fear leads to bad decisions," he said, blowing out the candles.

Myriam, seeing that her parents had closed their bedroom shutters, waited for a little while longer. Deep into the night, when she felt sure that no one was coming for her out in the garden, she made her way to her father's bicycle, even though it was too large for her. Curling her fingers around the handlebars, she felt Ephraïm's hands inhabit her own, giving her courage, and then the whole bicycle became her father's body, fine-boned but solid, with strong, supple muscles that would carry his daughter through that long night, all the way to Paris.

She felt confident, trusting in the generosity of the darkness that would cloak her and in the mercy of the forest, which judges no one and offers shelter to every fugitive. Her parents had so often told her the story of their escape from Russia, the incident of the detached cart. To flee, to get out, to get away—these things, she knew how to do.

Suddenly, she glimpsed the shape of some animal lying at the side of the path. Pulling up short, she found herself looking down at the corpse of a dead bird, dark blood mingling with scattered feathers. The grisly sight was troubling, like a premonition of evil. Myriam covered the mangled, still-warm body with soil and recited, in a whisper, the Aramaic verses Nachman had taught her in Palestine, the *kaddish* for the bereaved, and only then, after uttering the ritual words, did she feel strong enough to go on. As if she were a bird herself, she flew, taking side roads and byways, hiding in the edges of the forest, slipping and creeping as adroitly as the animals that crossed her path—with them she was never alone; they were her companions in invisibility.

At the first quiver of morning, the first bright gleam of dawn, Myriam glimpsed the Zone of Paris in the distance at last. She was almost there.

"What they call the Zone," Lélia explained, "was originally a large belt of open land that encircled Paris. A firing zone reserved for French artillery cannons. *Non aedificandi*. But gradually the poorest denizens of the capital were pushed outward into the area. The *misérables* Hugo wrote about, the families with too many children to feed, and all those whom Baron Haussmann's grand rebuilding project had driven from the city center crowded into the Zone, in shanties, wooden huts, and caravans; hovels

142 · ANNE BEREST

sunk inches deep in fetid mud and stagnant water; shelters cobbled together from odds and ends. Every part of the area had its specialty; there were the rag-pickers in Clignancourt and the scavengers with their flea markets in Saint-Ouen, the gypsies in Levallois and chair-menders in Ivry. There were the ratcatchers, who resold the creatures to the laboratories along the Seine for experiments, and the collectors of animal droppings who resold shit by the kilo to the glovemakers, who used it to whiten leather. Every quarter had its own community, too; there were Italians, Armenians, Spanish, Portuguese—but all the people who lived in the zone were nicknamed *zonards* or *zoniers*, regardless of origin."

At the time of day when Myriam crossed the dark belt of the Zone, everything was quiet in this area, which was without electricity or running water but didn't lack humor, for the people who lived there amid the mud and mildew had given their streets punny little names, like "rue-Barbe," after the plant, "rue-Bens," after the painter, and "rue-Scie"—though whether this last was actually home to a Russian community, she didn't know.

It was six o'clock in the morning. The Zone's painted ladies had finished their night's work, and the laborers and tradesmen were beginning their day. The overnight curfew ended at that hour for the factory workers streaming toward the capital in the dawn light, dreaming of a *café crème*. Myriam waited with them for the city gates to open and then joined the crowd of cyclists passing through the *portes de Paris*, taking care to abide by the rules that everyone riding a bicycle in the capital was required to follow. *Do not let go of the handlebars. Do not put your hand in your pocket. Do not take your feet off the pedals. Yield to vehicles whose license plates bear the letters WH, WL, WM, SS, or POL.*

The Paris through which Myriam now rode was virtually deserted, the few pedestrians seeming to keep to the shadows. But the beauty of the city gave her renewed hope. The rising sun dispelled her forebodings, the freshness of the summer morning banishing the night's dark thoughts.

How could I have thought that my brother and sister were going to be sent to Germany? It's ridiculous. They're minors.

Myriam remembered a night in the house in the suburb of Boulogne, the first place the family had lived after arriving from Palestine. Noémie hadn't been able to sleep that night because of a spider near their bed. But when dawn came, she'd realized that the terrifying creature wasn't a spider at all, only a tangled wisp of thread. They were like that, Myriam thought, the dark imaginings—mere trifles given fur and fangs in the blackness of the night and banished by the light of day.

She crossed the Pont de la Concorde toward the boulevard Saint-Germain, ignoring the immense banner draped from the façade of the National Assembly building that read "*Deutschland siegt an allen Fronten,*" crowned with an enormous V for victory. Her parents would get Jacques and Noémie back before they were sent to Germany. She was sure of it.

When they realize that my brother and sister hardly know how to do any manual work at all, the Germans will send them home, she told herself resolutely, to give herself the strength to climb the stairs, two at a time, to her sixth-floor flat on the rue de Vaugirard.

Vicente opened the door in a cloud of smoke. He ushered Myriam into the apartment and went to finish his coffee in the living room, still immersed in the thoughts that had kept him awake all night, judging by the dark circles beneath his eyes and the full ashtray on the table. Myriam shakily told him the story of Jacques and Noémie's arrest and her long ride back to Paris by bicycle—but he wasn't listening, his mind elsewhere. He had passed a sleepless night, too. He lit a fresh cigarette with the stub of the previous one and went silently to the kitchen for a cup of Tonimalt, a hot malted drink that often stood in for coffee these days, and for which he paid a king's ransom at the pharmacy.

"Wait here; I'll be back," he said, handing Myriam the cup.

Smoke wreathed her husband's head as he vanished down the hall, and Myriam was reminded of a locomotive entering a long tunnel. She lay down on the carpet, utterly spent. Her whole body hurt after the night spent on a bicycle, her legs throbbing from the hours of pedaling. Lying there on the dusty living-room carpet, trembling with exhaustion, she closed her eyes—and suddenly, from the back bedroom, there came a sound. The sound of a woman's voice.

A woman? A woman spent the night in my bed? With my husband? No. It's impossible.

And Myriam sank into sleep, until she was awakened by a petite, delicate woman, shaking her vigorously.

I'd like to introduce my *big* sister," said Vicente, as if the young woman's small stature might leave room for doubt. Jeanine was three years older than Vicente, but she barely came up to his shoulder. Just like Gabriële. In fact, Myriam found the girl's resemblance to the mother so striking as to be almost disturbing; they had the same broad, intelligent forehead, the same thin-lipped, stubborn mouth.

"In some of the archival photographs I couldn't even tell them apart," said Lélia.

"How had Myriam never met her husband's sister before?" I asked incredulously.

"Remember, the Picabias never had much interest in the concept of 'family,' except as a bourgeois notion that should be done away with. No one in Vicente's family had come to the wedding when he married Myriam—and it's also true that Jeanine was a very busy woman. She'd been certified as a Red Cross nurse two years earlier, in March 1940, and joined the medical support unit of the 19th Train regiment in Metz. After the armistice, and until her demobilization in December 1940, she was assigned to the medical support unit at Châteauroux, in charge of provisioning in the prisoner-of-war camps in Brittany and Bordeaux. What I'm trying to say is that she was no lady of leisure. This was a woman who drove ambulances. Even if she did look like a twelve-year-old from behind."

"Are you pregnant?" Jeanine asked, point-blank.
"No," Myriam answered.

"Good. We can put her in Maman's Citroën."

"Citröen?" echoed Myriam, confused.

But Jeanine didn't reply; she was speaking only to Vicente now.

"She'll sit where Jean's bags were going to go; you can bring them down on the train. Well, what am I supposed to do about it? We don't have a choice now. We'll leave tomorrow morning the moment the curfew is lifted."

Myriam didn't have a clue what was going on, but Jeanine waved a hand impatiently: *Don't ask questions.*

"You remember the 'miracle' of that police officer coming to get you out of prison? Well, that miracle had a face, a name, and a wife and children, my dear. And a rank: chief warrant officer. And that miracle was arrested by the Gestapo last week, get it? So that's the situation. You can't stay in an occupied zone. It's too dangerous now that we know the police might come for you, the same way they came for your brother and sister. You're in danger, and that means your husband is, too. And so am I. We're going to the free zone. We can't leave today because it's a public holiday. No cars allowed. We'll leave tomorrow morning, as early as we can, from my mother's apartment. Get yourself ready, because we're going there in a few minutes."

"I have to tell my parents."

Jeanine sighed.

"No. You can't tell them. You and Vicente are such *children.*"

Vicente could tell that his sister was running out of patience, and for the first time in his life he spoke to Myriam like a husband, "No more discussion. You're leaving with Jeanine. Right away. That's just how it is."

"Put on several layers of underwear," Jeanine advised Myriam, "because you can't bring any luggage with you."

As they left the building, Jeanine seized Myriam's arm.

"Don't ask any questions. Just follow me. And if we run into any police, keep your mouth shut. I'll do the talking."

Sometimes, the mind lingers on pointless things. Certain tiny, absurd details hold your attention when reality has lost all of its usual meaning, when life becomes so insane that you can't call on any past experience to know what to do. And as the two young women walked down the street past the Théâtre de l'Odéon, Myriam's brain became fixated on an image that would be forever burned into her memory: a poster for a play by Georges Courteline. Long after the war was over, perhaps because of the phonetic similarity between "*culotte*"—underwear—and "Courteline," any mention of the playwright would cause her to think automatically, ridiculously, of the five pairs of underwear she had pulled on that day, the five pairs of underwear that had made her skirt pouf out as she walked past the theater with its arcades of ochre stone. The five pairs of underwear that she would wear for an entire year, until they were falling apart, until the crotches were completely worn through.

When they reached Gabriële's flat, Jeanine said to Myriam, "Don't eat anything salty, and tomorrow morning, don't drink any water at all. Not a drop. Got it?"

Jacques and Noémie woke up in prison, like criminals. They had been incarcerated in Évreux the previous night, at 11:20 P.M., according to the prison records. Reason for incarceration: Jews. Jacques was now called Isaac. He shared a cell with Nathan Lieberman, a Berlin-born German aged nineteen; Israël Gutman, a thirty-two-year-old Polish man; and Israël's brother Abraham Gutman, thirty-nine.

Jacques thought back to his parents' stories. They'd been imprisoned, too, after they'd fled Russia and just before entering Latvia. Everything had worked out all right for them in the end.

"They were freed after only a few days," he told Nathan, Israël, and Abraham, to reassure them.

On this Bastille Day, every police brigade had been mobilized. The Germans were worried about patriotic displays and had prohibited all parades and gatherings. Prison transfers were delayed, and Jacques and Noémie would spend one more night in Évreux.

That morning, a few kilometers from the prison where his children were being held, Ephraïm lay sleepless in his bed. A phrase haunted him, something his father had said on the last night of Pesach when the whole family was together. "One day, they'll want us all to disappear."

No . . . it isn't possible . . . Ephraïm insisted to himself.

And yet.

He wondered why there had been no word from his parents-in-law in Lodz. No word from Boris in Prague. No word from their old friends in Riga. Everywhere, a deathly silence.

He remembered Aniouta's laughter—that cruel laughter that had kept him from taking seriously her plans to flee Europe. She'd been in the United States for four years now already. It seemed like an eternity. And what had he done in those four years? He'd allowed himself to become inextricably entangled in a situation from which there was no escape, trapped by rising waters while he simply stood there and watched them rise. Slowly but surely.

At the same moment, in Paris, Myriam was woken by Jeanine in Gabriële's apartment. She'd slept fully dressed and felt as if she'd spent the night on a train.

The two young women left the apartment and walked to a side street some distance away, where a car was waiting for them. Gabriële was behind the wheel, smartly dressed and wearing a hat and driving gloves, looking stylish and resolute, as if she were about to compete in an automobile race in her faux-cabriolet Citröen Traction Avant with its four-cylinder, overhead valve engine. The car's back seat was completely taken up by a heap of bags and suitcases, surmounted by a pile of wrapped packages. Myriam spied some dark, newspaper-wrapped shapes atop the mass and, protruding from them, the heads of four dead crows.

The sight was bizarre. She wondered where on earth she was going to sit amid all that clutter—but then Jeanine glanced left and right to make sure the street was empty, free of pedestrians or any other cars, and with a quick movement she shoved some of the bags aside, revealing a hatch in the back of the seat.

"Slip through here. Hurry."

Myriam realized that the seat had a false back, and the hatch led to the car's trunk.

Jeanine had enlisted the help of an auto mechanic friend to equip her mother's car with a secret space, and now Myriam slid into it. Like Alice in Wonderland, she made herself smaller to slip into the trunk and curl up in the hiding place—but, as she tried to straighten her legs a bit, she felt something move in the back of the space, something alive. She thought at first that it was an animal, but it was a man lying there, silent and still.

Myriam couldn't see all of him, just parts: his bright, heavy-lidded eyes; the curve of his hairline, like a monk's tonsure; the cleft in his chin.

"It was Jean Hans Arp, then aged fifty-six."

"The painter?"

"Yes. He was a close friend of Gabriële's. I learned about this incident when I was going through Myriam's papers after she died; she mentioned 'being driven over the demarcation line in the trunk of a car with Jean Arp.' Then I found out that he was on his way to Nérac, in the southwest, where his wife, the artist Sophie Taeuber, was waiting for him. They fled Paris because Jean was born in Germany but also because their art had been deemed 'degenerate' by the Nazis, and they were in danger of being arrested."

Lying side by side in the trunk, the young woman and the painter didn't exchange a single word. The era of silence began that day; the era of words that, for the sake of self-protection, you didn't say; the era of questions you didn't ask, even in your own head, to keep from putting yourself in danger. Jean Arp didn't know the girl next to him was Jewish, and Myriam didn't know that Jean Arp was fleeing Nazism for ideological reasons.

The car drove smoothly toward the Porte d'Orléans, where Jeanine and Gabriële would have to show their *Ausweis*, an attestation that they had permission to travel. This was a forgery, of course, but they displayed it to the soldiers with supreme confidence. Between them, the two women had come up with a cover story: Jeanine was traveling to meet her fiancé so that they could be married. In front of the soldiers, Jeanine played the role of the flustered bride-to-be to perfection, Gabriële the fond but harried mother. Never had either of them been so charming, never had they smiled more sweetly.

"If you only knew how many suitcases my daughter *insisted* I cram into the trunk! It's as if we're moving house! She was determined to bring her *entire* trousseau, even though we'll have to turn around and bring the whole thing right back to Paris. Absurd, don't you think? Are you married? I don't recommend it!"

Gabriële even got the soldiers to laugh. She spoke to them in German, which she'd learned in her youth, studying music in Berlin. They were quickly won over by this effervescent little Frenchwoman with such a perfect command of their own language. They congratulated her on her daughter's marriage; she thanked them; they lingered and chatted. Gabriële even offered to give the soldiers one of the dead birds in the back seat, which they were taking down for the wedding feast. Crows were a sought-after delicacy in the years of the Occupation, selling for up to twenty francs apiece. They were especially prized for making soup.

"*Wollen Sie eins?*" Gabriële asked the soldiers, smiling.

"*Nein, danke, danke.*"

The document check went off without a hitch, and the soldiers waved the two women through. Gabriële started the car casually and drove on as if she hadn't a care in the world.

Ephraïm and Emma Rabinovitch had spent a sleepless night, waiting for the morning to arrive and the local authorities' offices to open. Calmly, they dressed. Emma wanted to say something to Ephraïm, but he let her know with a movement of his hand that, for the moment, silence was all he could bear. Emma went down to the kitchen and set out the children's bowls and spoons and napkins. Ephraïm watched her do this without speaking, without knowing what to think. Then they went together, straight-backed and dignified, to the Les Forges town hall. It was Monsieur Brians, the mayor, who dealt with them that morning. He was a small man with black hair slicked across a pale forehead that gleamed fishbelly white. His only desire, since the day the Rabinovitches moved to the area, had been to see them gone.

"We want to know where our children have been taken."

"The police don't tell us anything," the mayor replied, in his reedy, high-pitched voice.

"They're both minors, which means you're required to tell us where they are!"

"I'm not required to do anything at all. And don't speak to me in that tone. I won't tell you again."

"We just want to give them some money, especially if they have to travel."

The mayor grunted. "I'd keep your money for yourselves, if I were you."

"What do you mean?"

"No, no, nothing," the man answered, like the coward he was.

Ephraïm wanted to hit him, but instead he put his hat back on and left quietly, hoping that his politeness, his good behavior, would allow him to see his children more quickly.

"We could call on the Debords," Emma suggested as they emerged from the town hall.

"We should have thought of that sooner."

But when they rang the doorbell, no one answered. They waited for a little while, hoping to catch the teacher and her husband coming back from the market. But a passing neighbor explained that the Debords had left for their summer vacation two days earlier.

"Monsieur Debord was carrying the suitcases, and let me tell you, he was loaded down like a pack mule!"

"Do you know when they'll be back?"

"Not before the end of summer, I believe."

"Do you have an address where I could write to them?"

"No, Monsieur, I don't. You'll have to wait until September, I'm afraid."

Fuel had been requisitioned by the Germans, and so Jeanine and Gabriële, like all the French, had to use other liquids capable of powering their combustion engines. A car would run on Godet cognac, eau de Cologne, fabric stain remover, the rubber-based glue used to repair tires, even red wine. That day, Jeanine and Gabriële were driving on a mixture of gasoline, benzene, and beet alcohol.

The fumes from the Traction Avant's engine intoxicated Myriam and Jean to the point of semiconsciousness. They were thrown together whenever the car rounded a curve and tossed against the roof of the trunk when it went over a bump. The sculptor tried as hard as he could to apologize without words whenever his arm or thigh made contact with the young woman. *Forgive me for touching you*, he said with his eyes; *forgive me for pressing against you*. Occasionally the car stopped at the edge of a wooded area, and Jeanine let Myriam and Jean out to walk a bit and restore their circulation. Then it would be back into the trunk for several more hours. Every kilometer brought them closer to the free zone. But they would have to get past the checkpoint on the demarcation line first.

This line stretched for nearly two thousand kilometers and cut France in half, not without a few points of absurdity: at the Château de Chenonceau, built spanning a river, you entered the castle in the occupied zone but could roam the grounds behind it in complete freedom.

Gabriële and Jeanine had decided to travel via Tournus, in Saône-et-Loire, which wasn't the shortest route to Nérac, but it was one that Gabriële knew like the back of her hand, having taken it countless times with Francis, as well as with Marcel and Guillaume.

The checkpoint to cross the *déma*, as the French had nicknamed the demarcation line, was at Chalon-sur-Sâone. Gabriële and Jeanine had timed their journey so as to arrive at lunchtime, when workers streamed into the city to eat their midday meal at home.

"The soldiers won't be in the mood to be overly zealous," Jeanine had reasoned.

As they drove through town, Gabriële and Jeanine passed the city hall, from which the Nazi flag fluttered menacingly. They stopped to ask directions and then made their way past the Carnot Barracks, which had been requisitioned to house German troops and rechristened the Adolf Hitler Barracks. In the Place du Port-Villiers, an immense, empty pedestal languished, its bronze statue having been removed and melted down by the Germans. It was easy to imagine the ghost of its occupant, a full-length rendition of Joseph Nicéphore Niépce, the inventor of photography, hovering in the air nearby, searching for its pedestal.

Finally the two women caught sight of the Pont des Chavannes, where the checkpoint was located. A wooden booth stood at the entrance to the bridge, in the very spot where tolls had been collected in the Middle Ages. The German side was staffed by Nazi border guards, while members of the French Mobile Reserve Unit manned the French side. There were a lot of them, and they looked far less friendly than the soldiers in Paris had. The

sweeping roundups of Jews that had just taken place all over occupied France meant that all police services were on high alert,
on the lookout for attempts to flee.

The hearts of both mother and daughter thudded loudly in
their chests. Fortunately, as they had hoped, they were far from the
only ones arriving at the checkpoint this time of day. There were
numerous cyclists crossing the bridge in both directions, people
who lived near the river and crossed the *déma* every day to work
and who were required to show their *Ausweis*, which was stamped
with the word LOCAL and valid within a five-kilometer radius.

While they awaited their turn, Jeanine and Gabriële read the
notice posted the previous evening, which laid out the consequences for families caught in the act of aiding fugitives sought
by the police:

1. All immediate male relatives in the ascending line, as
well as brothers-in-law and cousins *aged 18* and over will be
shot.
2. All women in the same degree of kinship will be sentenced to forced labor.
3. All children up to *age 17* of any man or woman known
to have aided a fugitive will be sent for correctional education.

Both women knew what was in store for them if they failed
in their mission. This was no time to falter. The French border
guards approached their Citröen for the check. Jeanine and
Gabriële handed over the false *Ausweis* and turned on the charm
once again: their excitement about the wedding, the bride's
dress, the trousseau, the dowry, the guests. These guards were
less agreeably chatty than the ones in Paris had been, but in the
end they let them pass; a mother on the way to marry off her
daughter was, after all, eminently respectable. Then it was the
Germans' turn, a few meters farther on.

They had to be convinced not to go through the suitcases or

open the trunk. Gabriële's perfect command of German was a considerable advantage; the soldiers were appreciative of the effort made by the lady, who asked for news from Berlin—the city had surely changed a great deal since she studied music there; that was back in 1906, and ah! how quickly time flies! *How* she had adored the Berliners . . .

Suddenly, the Germans' dogs began sniffing at the trunk of the Citröen with great interest. They pulled at their leashes insistently, barking louder and louder. There was something in the trunk, they were telling their masters. Something *alive*.

Myriam and Jean Arp could hear the dogs' muzzles thudding against the trunk lid. Myriam closed her eyes and held her breath.

Outside, the Germans were trying to figure out why their dogs were going mad.

"Tut mir leid meine Damen, das ist etwas im Kofferraum." Forgive me, Madame, but it's something in your trunk that's exciting them . . .

"Ah! Of course; it's our crows!" Gabriële exclaimed in German. *Die Krähen! Die Krähen!*

She reached into the back seat and retrieved the birds. "They're for the wedding dinner!" And Gabriële thrust the crows beneath the dogs' muzzles. They fell on the bait, the trunk instantly forgotten. Black feathers flew in all directions. The soldiers watched as the wedding feast vanished into their dogs' bellies.

Abashed, they waved the Citröen through.

Gabriële and Jeanine watched as the soldiers' booth grew smaller and smaller in the rearview mirror and then vanished. At the Tournus exit, Jeanine asked her mother to stop the car so she could reassure their passengers. Myriam was trembling from head to toe.

"It's all right. We made it," Jeanine said, to calm her.

Jeanine took a few steps away from the car and filled her lungs with the air of the free zone. Her legs suddenly felt very weak, and she sank to her knees. She stayed for a few moments like that, head down. Gabriële came to her side and put a hand on her shoulder.

"Come on, my girl," she said. "We've still got six hundred kilometers to drive before nightfall."

It was the first time she had shown real tenderness toward any of her children.

They drove without stopping. Just before midnight, at curfew time, the car entered the grounds of a large estate. Myriam could feel the car slowing down and hear voices whispering. They asked her to get out of the trunk, which she did with difficulty, because her arms and legs had gone numb. She was escorted like a prisoner to a strange room, where she fell asleep immediately.

When Myriam woke up the next morning, her body was covered in bruises. It hurt even to put her feet on the floor, but she crept to the window. She was in an enormous château, she discovered, the grand avenue leading up to it lined with towering oak trees. It resembled a sumptuous Italian villa, with its ochre façade and operetta-worthy balustrades. She, who had never crossed the Loire, now found herself marveling at the beauty of the dewy light sparkling in the trees.

A woman entered the room, carrying a jug and a glass of water.

"Where are we?" Myriam asked her.

"The Château de Lamothe, in Villeneuve-sur-Lot," the stranger answered.

"Where are the others?"

"They left early this morning."

Myriam looked out the window again. The Citröen was no longer in the courtyard.

They've abandoned me here, she thought. Her legs gave way beneath her, and she sank to the floor.

In the early hours of July 15, Jacques and Noémie left the prison in Évreux along with fourteen other people. Jacques was the youngest in the group. They were taken to the headquarters of the 3rd Gendarmerie Legion in Rouen, where all the Jews arrested in Eure during the July 13 roundup were being held.

The next afternoon, on July 16, 1942, Ephraïm and Emma learned that mass arrests had taken place in Paris that morning. Families had been rousted from their beds as early as four o'clock in the morning and forced to come away then and there, with just a single suitcase and under threat of being beaten. The arrests did not go unnoticed; the General Intelligence office in Paris reported that "Though the French population is, broadly speaking, quite anti-Semitic overall, these measures have been met with strong disapproval and deemed inhumane."

"They even took young women and their babies! My sister's a concierge in Paris; she's the one who told me that," a village neighbor told Emma. "The police came with locksmiths, and when people refused to open their doors, they forced their way in."

"And then," the woman's husband put in, "they told the building landlords to shut off the gas in the apartments, because the people who lived there wouldn't be back anytime soon."

"They took the families to the Vélodrome d'Hiver, apparently," his wife continued. "Do you know it?"

The Vél d'Hiv. Yes, Emma knew the stadium well. It was on the rue Nélaton in the 15th arrondissement, a venue for bicycle races, ice hockey, and boxing matches. One year when Jacques was little, his father had taken him to the "Patin d'or," a roller-skating race.

"What on earth is happening?" Ephraïm fretted, overcome by fear at last.

He and Emma went back to the town hall to find out more. Monsieur Brians, the mayor, scowled with irritation at the sight of the foreign couple, so unassailably dignified, haunting the corridors of his building.

"We've heard that Jews are being held in Paris. We'd like to know if our children are there, too," Ephraïm told the mayor.

"We would need special permission to travel for that," Emma added.

"Gonna have to go see the police," the mayor replied. He closed and locked his office door. Then he drank a restorative glass of cognac and asked his young secretary to keep those people away from him from now on. She had a pretty name, that girl: Rose Madeleine.

On July 17, Jacques and Noémie were transferred again, this time to an internment camp in Loiret, near Orléans, two hundred kilometers from the prison in Rouen. The journey took the entire morning.

The first things they saw when they reached the Pithiviers camp were the guard towers equipped with searchlights and the barbed wire. Behind these sinister fences were all sorts of buildings. It looked like an open-air prison, or a military encampment under close surveillance.

The police officers ordered everyone out of the truck. At the entrance to the camp, brother and sister lined up with all the others and waited to be registered. The policeman registering the new arrivals was seated behind a small wooden table, with a soldier next to him acting as his assistant. Jacques couldn't help but notice their gleaming helmets. Their leather boots shone in the July sun.

Jacques was entered into the register under number 2582, Noémie under number 147. Both of them filled out the special accounts form; neither of them had a cent on their person. Then their group joined the other new arrivals in the courtyard. Loudspeakers ordered them to line up in rows, quietly, to hear the rules of the camp. The schedule was the same every day: coffee at 7:00 in the morning, cleaning and construction duties from 8:00 to 11:00, lunch at 11:30, more cleaning and construction from 2:00 to 5:30, dinner at 6:00, and lights out at 10:30. The prisoners were requested to be patient and cooperative; if they complied, they were promised better living conditions when they were sent to work abroad. This was only a transit camp, and it was the responsibility of each inmate to look after themselves and be obedient. Next, the loudspeakers instructed them to walk in an orderly manner to their barracks. Pithiviers, Jacques and Noémie saw, was composed of nineteen barracks able to accommodate up to two thousand detainees. All of these barracks were made of wood, all built according to the "Adrian" model, named after Louis Adrian, a military engineer who had designed barracks that could be rapidly dismantled during the Great War of 1914–18. A barracks was thirty meters long and six meters wide. Tiered wooden bunks covered with straw lined each of the two long walls, separated by a central aisle. This was where the prisoners would sleep.

The barracks were smotheringly hot in summer and perishingly cold in the winter. The sanitary conditions in them were deplorable, disease spreading almost as fast as the countless rats that shared the space; the skittering and scratching of their claws against the wooden floor could be heard day and night. The sinks and toilets, Jacques and Noémie discovered, were outside—if they could even be called toilets, these crude latrines where you squatted over cement-lined pits, always in front of other inmates.

The kitchens were brick-and-mortar structures, as were the administration buildings. As they passed the infirmary, Noémie sensed the eyes of a woman in a white smock resting on her, a French woman of about forty with curly hair, who seemed to be taking her break outside on the front steps. She looked at Noémie for a long time, her eyes bright and intense.

Now Jacques and Noémie were separated again: Jacques was assigned to barracks number 5, and Noémie to number 9. Every separation was painful and sent Jacques into a panic. He wasn't used to being around so many men.

"I'll come and find you as soon as I can," his sister promised.

Noémie went into her barracks, where a Polish woman showed her how to hang up her clothes so that her things wouldn't get stolen during the night. She spoke in broken French, and Noémie replied in Polish. In July 1942, most of the prisoners were foreign Jews—Polish, Russian, German, Austrian. Many of them spoke little French, particularly the women, who stayed mainly at home. Yiddish was the common language of the camp, understood by virtually everyone. A prisoner was usually assigned to translate the orders relayed by the loudspeakers throughout the day.

As Noémie was unpacking her things, she suddenly felt a hand close firmly on her arm. It felt like a man's grip. But when she turned around, she found herself face-to-face with the bright-eyed woman who had been looking at her so steadily in front of the infirmary.

"You," the woman said. "Do you speak French?"

"Yes," Noémie replied, astonished.

"Any other languages?"

"German. I can also speak Russian, Polish, and Hebrew."

"Yiddish?"

"A little."

"Good. When you've finished unpacking, come to the infirmary. If the soldiers question you at all, tell them Doctor Hautval is waiting for you. Quickly, now."

Obediently, Noémie finished putting away her things. At the very bottom of her suitcase she found her little pot of Rosat lip balm, which she'd thought she'd forgotten. Then she went directly to the infirmary.

When she arrived, the woman with the intense gaze tossed her a white smock.

"Put that on. And watch what I do," she said.

Noémie looked at the smock.

"Yes, it's dirty," said the woman. "But it's all we have."

"But—who is Dr. Hautval?" Noémie asked.

"I am. I'm going to teach you everything a medical assistant needs to know. You'll have to memorize all the terms and abide by the rules of cleanliness, all right? If you do well, you'll come and work with me every day."

All that afternoon and into the evening, without a moment's pause, Noémie watched the doctor work. She was given the task of disinfecting medical instruments and realized very quickly that the main part of her job would consist of reassuring, listening to, and supporting the women who came into the infirmary. The day went by quickly, as the flow of patients was nonstop, women of all nationalities in urgent need of care.

"Well done," said Dr. Hautval at the end of the day. "You're remembering everything I tell you. I want to see you back here tomorrow morning. But be careful—you must never get too close to the patients. Never touch their blood or breathe in what they breathe out. Who will help me if you get ill?"

"Wait, Maman—how did you find out about the infirmary and this doctor?"

"I told you; I haven't made up a single thing. Doctor Adélaïde Hautval really existed. She wrote a book after the war, *Médicine et crimes contre l'humanité*. I have a copy; it's over there—grab it for me, will you? I've highlighted several passages. Look, she describes the day of July 17, when new internees arrived in waves: 'Twenty-five women. All foreigners living in France. I was immediately struck by one young woman, No Rabinovitch. Lithuanian-type face, sturdy body, healthy, solid. Nineteen years old. I quickly set my sights on her. She would become my best assistant.'"

"How touching, that she remembered Noémie and wrote about her that way."

"Oh, she talks about her a lot in the book; you'll see. Adélaïde Hautval was named Righteous Among the Nations by the State of Israel in 1965. At the time Noémie met her she was thirty-six years old, a neuropsychiatrist and the daughter of a pastor, transferred to Pithiviers to run the camp's infirmary. Her book wasn't the only place I found mentions of Noémie—she made a lasting impression on people everywhere she went. I'll tell you all about it."

At the end of that first day, Dr. Hautval gave her new assistant two small lumps of white sugar. She carried them carefully across the camp in her pocket, eager to give them to her brother. But when she found him, Jacques was furious.

"You didn't come to see me once! I waited for you all day!"

But the sugar melting in his mouth sweetened his temper, as well.

"What did you do today?" Noémie asked.

"Chores. They sent all of the young ones to clean the toilets. You should see them—these fat white worms, big as your fingers, squirming around in the bottoms of the latrines. It was disgusting. We had to sprinkle Crésyl on them—it's a disinfectant powder—but the smell gave me a headache, so I went back to the barracks. It's horrible here. You don't know. There are rats. You can hear them when you lie down on the bed. I want to go home. *Do* something. *Myriam* would have found a solution," Jacques said.

The remark cut Noémie to the quick. She grasped her little brother's shoulders and shook him.

"And where *is* Myriam? Huh? Go and find her, then. Ask her for a solution. Go on!"

Jacques apologized, his eyes downcast. The next morning, Noémie learned that the camp permitted its occupants to send one letter per person, per month. She decided to write to her parents immediately, to reassure them. It had been five days since their separation. Five days with no contact. She made sure to sound cheerful in her letter: she was working in the infirmary, she told them, and Jacques was doing well.

Then she reported for another day of work. When she arrived at the infirmary, the doctor was in the midst of an argument with

the camp administrator. She was furious about the lack of resources provided for her team. The man responded with threats,
and it was then that Noémie learned that Dr. Hautval wasn't an
employee of the camp, but a prisoner. Like her.

"When my mother died last April," Dr. Hautval confided to
Noémie at the end of that day, "I wanted to travel to Paris for
her funeral. But I didn't have an *Ausweis*. So I tried to cross
the demarcation line illegally at Vierzon, and the police arrested
me and put me in prison in Bourges. While I was there, I saw a
German soldier abusing a Jewish family, and I intervened. 'Since
you're so determined to defend the Jews, you can share their
fate,' he said. The soldier was furious that a woman, a *French*
woman, had dared to stand up to him. They made me wear a yellow star and an armband with 'Friend of the Jews' inscribed on
it. Not long after that, the Pithiviers camp needed a doctor, so I
was sent here to run the infirmary. I'm still a prisoner, but at least
I can help other prisoners this way."

"Speaking of helping—do you think I could have some paper
and a pen?"

"What for?" Dr. Hautval asked.

"It's for my novel."

"I'll see what I can do."

That same evening, Dr. Hautval brought Noémie two pens
and several sheets of paper.

"I managed to get these from the central office. But you have
to do me a favor."

"What can I do?"

"You see that woman over there? Her name is Hode Frucht."

"Yes, I know her. She's in my barracks."

"Well, tonight you're going to write a letter to her husband
for her."

"Was all of this in Dr. Hautval's book?"

"I just happened to find out, in the course of my research, that

Noémie had acted as scribe for the women of Pithiviers. Hode Frucht's descendants told me. They showed me letters handwritten by Noémie; her penmanship was beautiful. She was like all teenage girls with her embellishments; she wrote her capital 'M's with curlicues on the legs. You can see them in all the letters she wrote for her fellow internees."

"What did the women say in their letters?"

"They all wanted to reassure their loved ones. They didn't want them to worry. So they said everything was fine. They never told the truth. That's why the revisionists used those letters to argue their case, later on."

Jacques came to see Noémie at the infirmary. He was upset; everything was going badly—a soldier had taken away his Pétrole Hahn hair tonic, his stomach hurt, and he was lonely. Noémie advised him to make some friends.

That evening, the men of Jacques's barracks observed Shabbat in a corner of the camp. The boy joined them, hanging back at the rear of the group. He liked it, this sense of belonging. After the prayers, the men stood around talking, just like at the synagogue. Jacques listened to their conversations; they were talking about the trains that were departing. No one knew exactly where they were headed. Some mentioned East Prussia, others the area around Königsberg.

"It'll be to work in the salt mines in Silesia."

"I've heard talk of farms."

"That's good, if it's true."

"Says you! You think you're gonna go and milk cows?"

"*We're* the ones being sent to the slaughter. Lined up in front of pits, then a bullet to the back of the head. One by one."

This talk frightened Jacques. He told Noémie about it, and she asked Dr. Hautval for her opinion about the horrible rumors. The doctor gripped Noémie's arm tightly and looked her straight in the eye.

"Listen to me, No," she said, with quiet vehemence. "Around here, they call that kind of talk 'radio crapper.' Keep well away from those disgusting stories, and tell your brother to do the same. It's a hard life here. You have to be able to bear it. Those awful rumors are to be avoided. Understand?"

"At the time, Dr. Hautval sincerely believed that the Pithivier camp's prisoners were being sent to Germany to work. In her memoirs, she wrote: 'I still had a long way to go before I understood.' It was a discreet way of referring to what she would soon have to face. If you want to get some idea, just look at the subtitle of her book: *Medicine and Crimes Against Humanity: The Refusal of a Doctor, Deported to Auschwitz, to Participate in Medical Experiments*. Take it, if you want"—Lélia offered me the book— "but, if I were you, I'd keep a wastebasket handy nearby because I promise you, it'll make you want to throw up . . . literally."

"I don't understand why Dr. Hautval was sent to Auschwitz. She wasn't Jewish, or a political prisoner."

"She was too outspoken. She stood up for the defenseless too often. She was deported in early 1943."

July 17 and 18 were hot days, and there was a nonstop flow of patients in the infirmary. Fainting, sickness, pregnant women having contractions. One Hungarian woman asked for an injection of coramine. She was a doctor herself, and she knew she was having a heart attack.

The next day, July 19, the first families arrived at the Vélodrome d'Hiver. The eight thousand people imprisoned over the course of several days were distributed between the transit camps at Pithiviers and Beaune-la-Rolande. For the first time, the majority of them were women, children, and the elderly.

"A few days before the major roundups, there had been rumors in Paris that they were coming, and so the heads of some families were able to flee. Alone. Because no one had anticipated that the women and children would be taken this time, too. Can you imagine the guilt those fathers felt? How do you go on living after that?"

The Pithiviers camp didn't have the capacity to accommodate so many people at once. There was no more room in the barracks; there were no more beds anywhere. There was no plan, and the place was in no way fit for such an influx of detainees.

Buses arrived one after the other without stopping. The coming of whole families to Pithiviers sparked panic in everyone—the prisoners who had been there before them, the camp's administrators, the medical staff, and the police themselves. And yet the General Secretariat for Health had sent a letter to the secretary-general of the police, René Bousquet, warning that the camps at Pithiviers and Beaune-la-Rolande "are not equipped to receive an overlarge number of internees (. . .). They cannot house them, even for a relatively short time, without violating the most basic rules of hygiene and increasing the risk of epidemics of contagious disease, particularly during the summer months." But no sanitation measures were put in place. Instead, on July 23, the governor of Loiret sent the camp fifty additional police officers.

The penal authorities had made no provisions for very young children. There was no appropriate food for them and nothing to bathe or change them with. No medications specifically for children. The mothers' situation became intolerable in the July heat; they had no diapers or clean water, and the authorities had not thought it necessary to provide milk, or the accoutrements necessary to boil water. An inspection report on the subject was sent to the governor, who did nothing. But a large shipment of barbed wire, to double up on the existing barrier, was quickly delivered to the camp. The police were afraid that small children might be able to slip through and escape.

A report written by a police officer at the Pithiviers camp stated that "the contingent of Jews arriving today is composed of at least 90% women and children. All detainees are quite tired and depressed by their time in the Vélodrome d'Hiver, where they were very poorly accommodated and lacking in nearly everything." When Adélaïde Hautval became aware of this report, she declared the terms "quite tired" and "depressed" to be laughable euphemisms. The families arriving from the Vél d'Hiv were in a state of absolute despair. They had spent several days packed together in a stadium, sleeping on the ground, with almost no bathroom facilities, the bleachers streaming with urine, the smell oppressive. The heat was stifling and the air choked with dust, nearly unbreathable. The men were dirty; they had been treated like livestock, humiliated, beaten by the police, and the women were likewise stinking from heat and sweat, the clothing of those who were menstruating soaked with blood. The children were filthy and unimaginably exhausted. One woman had committed suicide by leaping from the bleachers onto the crowd below. Of the ten toilets in the stadium, five had been blocked off because they had windows that opened onto the street and might allow people to escape. This left only five toilets for almost eight thousand people. These had all overflowed on the first morning, forcing people to sit in human excrement. As they had been given neither food nor drink, the fire brigade had eventually turned on their hoses to provide water to men, women, and children who were literally dying of thirst. Like a punishment for civil disobedience.

On July 21, Adélaïde and Noémie were present for the transfer of a group of mothers and young children to the camp. They were being housed in hangars that had previously been used as machine shops, now requisitioned and transformed into crude dormitories. Straw was spread on the ground for them to sleep on. There weren't enough bowls or spoons, so soup was given to them in empty food cans. The children were given old canisters of Red Cross cookies. The tins acted as bowls and, later, as toilets during the night. Many children cut themselves on the sharp metal edges.

Sanitary conditions in the camp grew worse by the day, and epidemics began to break out. Jacques developed dysentery and spent as much time as he could resting in the barracks, which were "like rabbit cages, full of straw, dust, vermin, sickness, arguments, shouting. Not a single minute of solitude," as Adélaïde Hautval wrote in her memoirs. Noémie was kept busy handling the overflow of patients in the infirmary. Dr. Hautval added, "There were two of us in the infirmary, No and me. We encountered every possible disease: acute dysentery, scarlet fever, diphtheria, whooping cough, measles." The police clamored for fuel coupons for the trucks they kept at the Pithiviers train station and demanded new barracks to house the incoming arrivals. Nothing in their training had prepared them for this.

"What did they tell their wives, when they went home at night?"

"History doesn't record it."

Noémie continued to impress the doctor, not only with her capacity for hard work, but also with her wisdom. The girl often said that it was necessary for her to experience terrible hardship, and to demonstrate great courage. She could feel it, she insisted. "Where did she get such depth of understanding?" Dr. Hautval wondered in her memoirs. In the evenings, Noémie worked on her novel in the barracks until it was too dark to see.

A Polish woman came up to Noémie one day and said, "The one who slept there, where you sleep now. The woman before you. She was a writer, too."

"Really?" Noémie asked. "There was another author here?"

"What was her name again?" The Polish woman asked another detainee.

"I only remember her first name," the other woman said. "Irène."

"Irène Némirovsky?" Noémie asked, frowning.

"Yes, that was it!" the young woman exclaimed.

Irène Némirovsky spent only two days at the Pithiviers camp, in barracks number 9. She was deported in convoy number 6 on July 17, a few hours before Noémie arrived.

On July 25, Dr. Hautval, passing through the central administration building, learned that a new convoy would be departing soon. A thousand people were being sent to Germany, to relieve the overcrowding in the camp. She feared being separated from Noémie. "No was a wonderful assistant," she wrote later. "She looked life square in the face, demanding something meaningful from it, something rich. She was always ready to throw herself into living, body and soul, seeing it as overflowing with possibilities, certain in the knowledge that she would be one, someday, to whom many eyes turned." The doctor turned her mind to finding a way to keep "No" with her. She spoke about it to one of the camp's administrators.

"Don't take away my medical assistant. I've put a lot of time into training her. She's highly competent."

"Okay. We'll find a solution. Let me think on it."

That same day, Saturday, July 25, the letter Noémie had sent to her parents arrived in Les Forges. It reassured them greatly. Ephraïm then picked up his pen to write a letter to the governor of Eure. What were the French authorities planning to do with his children? he asked. How long would they remain at the camp in Pithiviers? What would the situation be in the weeks to come? He enclosed a stamped return envelope with his letter, in order to be sure of a reply.

"One day when I was in the prefecture archives in Eure, I

stumbled across Ephraïm's letter. It was overwhelming. I held in my hands the very envelope he had enclosed, with its 1.5-franc stamp bearing the likeness of Marshal Pétain. No one had ever bothered to reply."

"I thought the local authority archives had been destroyed after the war."

"Not really. It's true that the French government had a major cleanout of its regional archives, particularly anything incriminating—but three departments refused to comply, and lucky for us, Eure was one of them. It's incredible how much is still there in the archives, like an underground world, a parallel world, still alive. Like the embers of a fire . . . all you have to do is blow on them to rekindle the flame."

The days passed, punctuated by Ephraïm and Emma's attempts to make contact with the local authorities and remind them of their presence. What else could they do, other than wait to hear from their children?

In the meantime, Dr. Hautval and the Pithiviers camp administrator had found a way to make sure Noémie's name was not on the list of passengers for the next convoy. In July 1942, certain categories of people were still being spared the journey to Auschwitz: French Jews, Jews married to French citizens, Romanians, Belgians, Turks, Hungarians, Luxemburgers, and Lithuanians.

"Does your medical assistant fall into any of these categories?"

Noémie, Adélaïde remembered, had been born in Riga. She knew that was in Latvia, not Lithuania, but she took a chance, and indeed, the camp administrator didn't differentiate between the two.

"Find me her registration form proving her Lithuanian nationality, and I'll make sure she's not sent away."

Dr. Hautval hurried to the office to find Noémie's registration form, but unfortunately the young woman's birthplace was not listed on it.

"See if you can locate a birth certificate," the camp administrator suggested. "For now I'll just put down that her case isn't clear, and that her departure is on hold."

On a list dated that Tuesday, July 28, the camp administrator compiled a list entitled "Pithiviers Camp: Individuals Seemingly Arrested in Error." On this list, he wrote the names of Jacques and Noémie Rabinovitch.

"Maman . . . that list . . . you found it?"

Lélia just nodded. I could tell she was too overcome by emotion to speak. I tried to imagine what she had felt, reading those words: *individuals seemingly arrested in error*. Sometimes, though, imagining is impossible. All you can do is listen to the echo of the silence.

Adélaïde Hautval made a special request to the authorities for Jacques and Noémie's entry documents into France. She wasn't expecting miracles, but it would buy some time.

Word was spreading through the camp that the departure of another convoy was imminent. Where were these trains going? What would become of the children? Panic began to overtake the internees. Some women screamed that they were being sent to death, that they would all be killed. These women were quickly deemed "crazy" and isolated so as not to contaminate the morale of the others. Dr. Hautval wrote in her memoirs: "One of them kept insisting: 'They'll put us in trains and then, once we've crossed the border, they'll blow up the train cars!' Her words disturbed us. Could it be that she was right, that she had the kind of clairvoyance the mentally ill sometimes possess?"

Convoy number 13 was being planned at Pithiviers. Dr. Hautval checked the list of names in the central office—a risky thing for her to do, as she was not authorized—and found that the entire group of prisoners from Rouen was scheduled to be aboard, including Jacques and Noémie. She tried one more time to convince the director of the camp to delay the Rabinovitches' departure.

"I'm waiting for verification of their possible Lithuanian nationality," she said.

"No time for that," the director replied.

Dr. Hautval grew angry.

"How am I supposed to manage without her? We're drowning in work at the infirmary! You want disease to spread even faster? It will be a catastrophe—the guards will get ill, too, and the police officers . . ."

She knew that this was the administrators' greatest fear. Hired workers from outside Pithiviers no longer wanted to come to the camp because of the epidemics, and it was getting harder and harder to find laborers. The director sighed.

"No guarantees."

All of the prisoners were called into the central courtyard. The list was read out over the loudspeakers. 690 men, 359 women, and 147 children.

Jacques and Noémie were not on it.

The mothers who had been called to be part of the convoy, leaving their children—sometimes infants—behind in the camp, refused to leave. Some of them flung themselves to the ground. One woman was stripped naked by the police, put in a cold shower, and shoved back into the line without her clothes. The commandant of the camp asked Dr. Hautval to do something to calm the women who were making the situation unmanageable. He knew the doctor's words carried weight with the detainees.

She agreed to speak to them, on the condition that she be given an explanation of how the French government planned to treat the children. The commandant showed her a letter from the office of the governor of Orléans: "Parents will be sent ahead to prepare the camp. The greatest care will be taken to give these children the best living conditions possible." Reassured by this letter, with its promises of good treatment, Adélaïde promised

174 · ANNE BEREST

the mothers that their children would join them soon, and in good health.

"You'll all be together again in the end."

Jacques and Noémie watched their companions from Rouen file out the main gate. Through the barbed wire, they watched them line up in a large field near the camp. There, they were stripped of any valuable items they were carrying before being transferred on foot to the Pithiviers train station.

In the camp, the hours following the departure of the convoy were strangely quiet. No one spoke. In the middle of the night, a cry shattered the silence. A man had slit his wrists with the glass from his watch.

N oémie and Dr. Hautval now found themselves looking after very young children whose mothers had departed in the last convoy. "No and I were on night duty. *Pipi* and *caca* on all sides." Their small charges spoke a kind of camp children's language among themselves that the adults didn't understand. Many of them were ill with fevers, ear infections, measles, scarlet fever—all the diseases of childhood. Some were so infested with lice that not even their eyelashes were spared. The older ones roamed the camp in little bands, peering down into the latrines at items thrown there at the last moment by the inmates who had been forced to leave, not wanting to leave their precious mementos to the gendarmes. The children stared into the pits, fascinated by these objects glittering in the shit, half-concealed beneath paper and leaves.

The next day, August 1, Dr. Hautval learned that another convoy would be departing soon. The commandant of the camp, who worked for the judicial police, ordered her to prepare the mothers to be separated from their children.

"Tell them that once they're there, the children will go to school."

But these women refused to leave their children. They went mad, launching themselves at the guards, braving their blows. Some were beaten to the point of losing consciousness before they would let go of their children.

Noémie was given the task of embroidering the full name and age of each child in thread on little strips of white cloth.

"It's to make the transfers easier," the departing mothers were told. "So you can locate your children when they come to join you."

But the children didn't understand any of it. Hardly had the strips been tied around their wrists when they ripped them off or traded them with one another.

"How will we find our children again?"

"But she's too little to know her last name!"

"How are you going to send them to us?"

The children wandered the camp, dirty and confused, runny-nosed and vacant-eyed. Some of the officers used them as entertainment, the way they might have done with rats or pigeons, giving them ridiculous hairstyles with clippers, adding humiliation to misery. They were a game for the guards, a diversion.

In the hangars, it was easy to tell which children had been separated from their mothers by the previous convoy because they had stopped crying. Some had stopped moving at all, half buried in straw. Surprisingly docile now, they were like rag dolls, bereft, indescribably filthy. Clouds of insects hummed and buzzed around them, as if waiting for the moment when the living flesh would become carrion. The sight was unbearable.

The very little ones wouldn't respond during roll call; they were simply too young. It began to irritate the guards. One little boy approached an officer and asked, very politely, if he could play with his police whistle. The man turned to his superior for guidance, at a loss as to how to respond.

The next morning, Dr. Hautval saw that Noémie and her brother were again slated to be shipped out with the upcoming convoy. They would have to be saved once more.

Adélaïde had no choice but to count on the German commandant. He was her last hope. He supervised the convoys in person on departure days, and he had authority over the camp's French personnel.

As soon as he arrived, Dr. Hautval explained to the commandant the regrettable loss that the departure of her medical assistant would represent for the camp.

"And why is that?" the man asked.

"Because she doesn't have children."

"I don't see what that has to do with anything."

"Have a look in the hangar and you'll see that no mother could bear to work there. I need someone able to keep her composure."

"*Einverstanden*," the German commandant replied. "I'll have her stricken from the list."

August 2, 1942, was a very hot day. The convoy was scheduled to include 52 men, 982 women, and 108 children. The mothers being deported without their children began to shriek so loudly that it could be heard in the village of Pithiviers some distance away. Children who were students at the time would testify decades later that they had heard women screaming as they played outside in the schoolyard. In the midst of this chaos, the names of Jacques and Noémie were read over the loudspeakers. Dr. Hautval, furious, sought out the German commandant, who reassured her: "I haven't forgotten my promise. She won't be leaving. She'll be searched along with the others, but then I'll have her brought back."

The women were being lined up, to be marched into the field adjoining the camp. The children clung to their mothers, allowing themselves to be dragged along the ground, until the police made them let go with swift, hard kicks. Yet a survivor would one day recall seeing an officer weep at the sight of tiny hands straining to force the strands of barbed wire apart, to create a gap large enough to crawl through.

"Parents and children will be reunited later on," the loudspeakers repeated.

But the mothers didn't believe it. Women swarmed frantically in all directions. The French police were completely overwhelmed. The mob grew larger, pressing toward the main gate, pushing and pushing until the gate was on the point of being forced. Suddenly it was flung wide open, and a German truck pulled up in front of the crowd. Each of the soldiers inside it held a machine gun that he pointed directly at the women. A camp administrator was requested to explain over the loudspeaker that everyone must return to their barracks if they wished to avert a bloodbath—except for the people named on the list, of course, who were ordered to line up quietly.

Noémie and Jacques filed into the field for the search along with the others. They were made to line up, and each person was instructed to put their jewelry, along with any money they had, on a table. When the women didn't move quickly enough, their earrings were torn from their ears. They were then subjected to vaginal and anal searches, to be sure they weren't concealing any money or valuables inside their bodies. The hours passed, "the sun beating down mercilessly on the field with no shade anywhere," as Dr. Hautval wrote. The doctor grew more and more anxious when Noémie failed to return. Eventually she went looking for the commandant again.

"You promised me," she said. "They've been gone for hours."

"I'll go and see what's happening," the commandant said.

In the field, Noémie, from her place in line, saw the German commandant arrive. He spoke with the French camp administrators, then pointed in her direction. The men were talking about her, Noémie realized. Adélaïde must have intervened successfully on her behalf. Now the commandant was striding between the rows of prisoners, heading toward her. Noémie's heart beat faster.

"Are you the medical assistant?"

"Yes," she answered.

"Come with me," he said.

Noémie began to follow the man, then stopped, scanning the field for Jacques.

"What about my brother?" she asked the commandant. "We have to get him, too."

"He doesn't work in the infirmary, as far as I know. Keep moving."

Noémie explained that it was impossible, that she couldn't be separated from her brother. Exasperated, the commandant signaled to the police officers that the young woman should be returned to her place in line. The convoy was ready to depart. There was a whistle. The prisoners were told to start walking. From somewhere in the field a man's voice rang out, breaking the silence:

"Frendz, mir zenen toyt!"

Friends, we are all dead.

CHAPTER 30

It was 7 P.M. Convoy number 14, which would be known as the Mothers' Convoy, was being marched to the train station. Adélaïde Hautval tried to spot Noémie amid the crowd filing past beyond the barbed wire, but in vain.

At the Pithiviers station, brother and sister saw the train waiting for them: it had originally been a cargo train, with each car designed to hold eight horses. The soldiers counted off the men and women as they shoved them inside, until there were eighty people in each car. One woman resisted, refusing to board the train, and was rewarded with a blow to the face that broke her jaw.

"If any one of you tries to escape during the journey," the prisoners were told, "everyone in your train car will be executed."

The train remained in the station that entire night, the thousand people aboard it forced to wait, packed together like sardines in the cars, with no idea of what awaited them. The luckiest prisoners found themselves near the small, barred window slits, where it was slightly easier to breathe. Jacques, weakened by dysentery, was nauseated by the smells in the car. Toward dawn, he heard the departure whistle blow. As the train slowly began to move, a man's voice rose from one of the wagons: *"Yit-gadal ve-yit-kadash shemay rabba, Be-al-ma dee vra chi-roo-tay ve-yam-lich mal-choo-tay . . ."*

They were the opening words of the *kaddish d'rabbanan*, the prayer of mourning for the dead. A mother clamped her hands over her young daughter's ears and screamed furiously, *"Shtil im!* Make him shut up!"

To give themselves courage, the young people speculated about the sort of work they would do in Germany.

"You're a doctor," a little girl said to Noémie, "so you'll be able to work in a hospital."

"I'm not a doctor," the teenager replied.

"Quiet!" the adults ordered. "Save your saliva!"

They were right. The August heat quickly grew stifling. The prisoners, crammed together, had no water. When they stretched pleading hands out of the train cars and begged for something to drink, the police beat them with the butts of their rifles, breaking their fingers.

Jacques lay down and pressed his face against the floor, breathing in what little air flowed between the wooden planks. Noémie stood over his body to keep him from being stepped on and crushed. During the hottest hours of the day, some people stripped off their clothing, men and women sweltering in their underwear, half-naked.

"They're like animals," Jacques said.

"You shouldn't say that," Noémie retorted.

The journey lasted three days, and the prisoners were forced to relieve themselves in a bucket, in full view of everyone. When the bucket was full, only a pile of straw in a corner of the car remained. The temptation to leap off the train was strong, but no one did it, in case their captors killed the others in retaliation. To keep her mind occupied, Noémie thought about her novel, which she had left in her bedroom in Les Forges. She had only written the beginning of it, and now she rewrote it in her head, and imagined the rest.

After three days, the train, which hadn't whistled even once in any of the fifty-three stations it had passed through, emitted a shrill blare and braked suddenly. The doors of the cars were hauled open with a clatter. Jacques and Noémie were dazzled by searchlight beams far more blindingly powerful than the ones in Pithiviers. They couldn't see anything, had no idea where they were, could hear nothing but the ferocious barking of dogs straining to attack them and the furious shouts of the guards—*Alle runter! Raus! Schnell!*—as the thousand prisoners were herded off the train. Without ceremony, the guards began clubbing any sick people lying on the floor of the train car, to rouse anyone who had fainted and clear out the dead. Noémie received a blow to the face that left her with a swollen lip. The sudden violence of it made her head swim; she couldn't tell which direction to go in anymore and let go of Jacques's hand. A moment later she saw him, up ahead of her on the unloading ramp, and she was running to catch up with him, obeying the Germans' shouted orders, when suddenly a foul stench filled her nose and her lungs, like nothing she had ever smelled in her life, a thick, sickening smell, like charred animal horns and burnt fat.

"Say you're eighteen years old." Jacques heard the words without knowing where they came from in the melee of milling bodies.

It was one of the living corpses, clad in striped pajamas, that had murmured this advice to him. Gangling and skeletal, these beings looked as if they'd been completely drained of blood. On their heads, they wore the strange round caps given to criminals in prison. Their gazes were fixed, as if they were looking with horror at something invisible, something only they could see. *Schnell, schnell, schnell!* Hurry, hurry, hurry! The guards were ordering these men to clear the filthy straw from the train cars.

When all the new arrivals had been assembled on the ramp, the pregnant women, children, and any sick prisoners were lined up to one side. Anyone who was tired was permitted to join them. Trucks arrived to take them directly to the infirmary.

Suddenly, everything stopped. There were shouts, and the barking of dogs, and blows from the officers' truncheons.

"A child is missing!"

Rifles were aimed at the crowd of prisoners. Hands went up in terror.

"If one child has escaped, all the others will be shot."

The guns shone in the beams of the searchlights. The missing child had to be found. Mothers trembled. The seconds ticked by.

"Found it!" a uniformed man shouted, emerging onto the ramp. Dangling from one hand was the tiny corpse of a baby, no larger than a crushed cat, that had been discovered beneath the straw in one of the train cars. The rifles were lowered. People started to move again. The sorting of men and women began.

"I'm tired," Jacques said to Noémie. "I want to go in one of the infirmary trucks."

"No. We stay together."

Jacques hesitated for a moment, but in the end he joined the infirmary line.

"I'll find you later," he said, walking away.

Noémie watched helplessly as Jacques disappeared into the back of one of the trucks. Abruptly she received another blow to the head. *Keep moving.* The prisoners remaining on the ramp were being lined up to be marched toward the main building. This was a rectangular brick cube, perhaps a kilometer long. From the middle rose a tower with a triangular roof. This was the entrance to the interior of the camp, resembling some gaping hellmouth, overlooked by watchtowers like two hateful eyes. A group of SS men were briefly questioning each of the new detainees. Two groups were being formed: those capable of working on one side, those judged incapable on the other. Noémie was one of those selected to work.

"In the summer of 1942," Lélia told me, "they hadn't yet begun tattooing prisoners' forearms. Only Soviet prisoners were marked, using a metal stamp. The stamp held needles that made up the shapes of individual numbers, and the whole number was then punched into the chest, with ink rubbed into the needle-wounds. *Schreibers*—prisoners assigned the task of tattooing numbers on newcomers to the camps, one digit at a time—weren't used until 1943, when that system was introduced to make it easier for the Nazis to identify and count the dead."

Next, a high-ranking officer addressed all of the new arrivals. His uniform was impeccable, leather boots gleaming, brass buttons shining. He gave the Nazi salute, then announced, "You have arrived in the model camp of the Third Reich. Here, the parasites who have always lived off others are made to work. Here, you will finally learn to be of some use. Be happy that you are contributing to the Reich's war efforts."

Noémie was then directed to the left, toward the women's camp, stopping first in the disinfection center, called the "sauna." Here, all of the women were undressed and made to sit close together on benches. Each of them had to wait, naked, for their turn to be completely shaved—head, body, and pubic hair—and then showered. Only a few young women were spared the razor—and this, because they were to be sent to the camp's brothel.

When Noémie's turn came, her long hair, the hair of which she had always been so proud, the hair she had loved to wear twisted and pinned on top of her head like a coronet, fell to the floor, mingling with the hair of the other women, forming a vast, shining carpet. This hair would be used, according to the bulletin dispatched by Concentration Camps Inspector Richard Glücks on August 6, 1942, to make slippers for submarine crews and felt socks for railroad employees.

The new arrivals' clothes, along with any other objects of value, were taken to a cluster of warehouses nicknamed "Canada," where they were sorted. Handkerchiefs, combs, shaving brushes, and suitcases were sent to the Main Welfare Office for Ethnic Germans. Watches went to the SS Main Economic and Administrative Office in Oranienburg, eyeglasses to the Medical Office. In the camps, everything that could be made profitable was recovered and recycled. Even the prisoners' dead bodies themselves were exploited. Phosphate-rich human ashes were used to fertilize reclaimed marshland. Melted-down gold from dental work furnished several kilos of pure bullion every day; a foundry was established near the camp, shipping gold bars to secret SS vaults in Berlin.

Noémie was issued a bowl and spoon before being directed to her barracks. This camp, she discovered, was twenty times the size of the one at Pithiviers. She had to walk for a long time to cross it, always watched by armed guards, always accompanied by the sounds of men shouting and dogs barking. But it seemed to her that she could also hear violins, the strains of an orchestra. *That's impossible*, she told herself—but then she saw them: Jewish musicians on a platform, accompanying the activities of the camp. To amuse themselves, the guards had made the men wear dresses. The conductor wore a white wedding gown.

In the barracks, all the women had shaved heads, some of them bleeding from razor cuts. There were wooden bunks built in vertical tiers up the walls, just like at Pithiviers, but now Noémie found that she would have to share a bed with five or six girls. There was no straw; they slept on the bare boards.

Noémie asked a woman where she was. Auschwitz. Noémie had never heard the name, had no idea where it might be on a map. She explained to the other girls that her brother had gone off in a truck with some prisoners who were ill and asked where she could find him. One of the women grasped her by the shoulder, steered her to the door of the barracks, and pointed toward the chimneys, which were belching thick, greasy black smoke choked with gray ash. *That must be the way to the infirmary*, Noémie thought, resolving to look for her brother there tomorrow.

Jacques's truck crossed the camp toward a small birch forest. There were barracks in these woods where he could bathe, someone told him. When they got there, a guard asked him about his schooling. The adults were asked to give their profession. The prisoners were still meant to think they would be working.

Jacques did not lie about his date of birth, didn't pretend to be eighteen, as the skeletal prisoner had advised him to do—didn't dare, for fear he would be punished. He was directed toward an underground staircase that led to a changing room. From there a very long line formed, like a long, long black snake, because the first trucks had been joined by others carrying prisoners judged "unfit" to work.

Jacques was informed that he needed to shower with a special product to be disinfected before settling in at the camp. He was handed a towel and a piece of soap. After they had showered, the SS officers explained, they would be given something to eat. They would even be allowed to rest and sleep before starting work the next day. These words gave Jacques a glimmer of hope. He hurried: the quicker he could get through the chore of disinfection, the quicker he'd finally be able to fill his empty belly. Physical weakness made all the prisoners more passive, more docile.

There were numbers all along the walls of the changing room. Jacques sat down on a small bench to take off his clothes. He didn't like undressing in front of other men. He didn't like anyone looking at his genitals, and seeing the other men's naked bodies made him uncomfortable. An SS guard, accompanied by a French prisoner acting as interpreter, told him to remember the wall number beneath which he'd left his clothes and shoes, so he could find them again easily after his shower. He also instructed Jacques to tie the laces of his shoes together.

Everything had to be neatly folded and organized, to facilitate the sorting work when the prisoners' belongings arrived at Canada.

Schnell, schnell, schnell. Jacques and the other prisoners were jostled and shoved to keep up, to move quickly—but also so they would have no time to think, no time to react.

The SS guards used their rifle-butts to herd the prisoners into the shower room, cramming it with as many people as possible. Jacques received a fierce blow that dislocated his shoulder. Once the room was full to bursting, the guards closed and locked the doors. Outside, two men opened a vent to release gas into the room: Zyklon B, a hydrogen cyanide-based gas that killed in a few minutes. The prisoners looked up at the shower heads in the ceiling. Very quickly, they understood.

I can see Jacques's face, his ruffled boyish brown hair, on the floor of the gas chamber.
On this page, I gently close his wide-open eyes.

Noémie died of typhus a few weeks after arriving at Auschwitz.
Just like Irène Némirovsky.
History does not record whether they ever met.

CHAPTER 31

I n late August, Ephraïm and Emma Rabinovitch received a
visit from Joseph Debord, who had learned on his return
from vacation that the Rabinovitch children had been arrested at the beginning of summer.

"I can help you get to Spain," he told them.

"We'd rather wait for our children to return," replied
Ephraïm, walking the teacher's husband to the door.

Turning back into the house, Ephraïm set the table for four,
with plates and silverware for Noémie and Jacques, as he had
done every day since their arrest.

On Thursday, October 8, 1942, at four o'clock in the afternoon, there came a loud knocking at the Rabinovitches' door.
They had been expecting this moment for a long time. They
opened the door calmly to the two French police officers who
had come for them. A new general operation against non-citizen
Jews had been launched.

"I have the names of the two policemen," Lélia told me. "Do
you want to know them?"

I thought about it, and then told my mother I'd rather not.

Emma and Ephraïm were prepared. They had packed their
suitcases, tidied the house, draped the furniture in sheets to
protect it from dust. Emma had carefully filed Noémie's papers,
tucking her notebooks safely away in a drawer, in an envelope
she'd labeled "NOTEBOOKS—NOÉMIE."

Both parents allowed themselves to feel, to *know*, that they were going to join their children. They handed themselves over to the police. Truly, they handed themselves over willingly.

Ephraïm wore an elegant gray fedora, Emma her comfortable navy-blue suit, a coat with a fur collar, and a pair of red shoes whose heels weren't too high, to make sure she could walk easily. Her handbag contained one yellow pencil, one mechanical pencil, a pocketknife, a nail file, a pair of black gloves, a wallet, and a ration card. And all the money she and Ephraïm had.

They'd packed only one suitcase for the two of them. There wasn't much in it, mainly a few things that would make the children happy when they saw them again. Emma had brought Jacques his game of jacks, and for Noémie a new notebook with lovely, fine paper. They would be pleased.

Ephraïm and Emma left their home in Les Forges under police escort.

They didn't look back.

The car took them to the police station in Conches, where they were jailed for two days before being transferred to Gaillon, a small town in Eure. The administrative detention facility was a Renaissance château built into a hillside overlooking the town. It had been transformed into a prison under Napoleon. Since September 1941, it had been reserved for communists, common criminals, and persons engaging in "the illicit trafficking of foodstuffs"—that is, the black market. A few Jews were held there briefly, as well, on their way to the internment camp at Drancy.

Ephraïm and Emma were formally booked into the prison in an office at the town's police station. Ephraïm's registration form number was 165, Emma's 166. They were in possession of 3,390 francs and 3,650 francs, respectively.

Ephraïm's form noted that he had "slate blue" eyes.

A few days later, husband and wife were taken from Gaillon to Drancy, arriving on October 16, 1942. All of their money was taken from them. On that day, a total of 141,880 francs was stripped from new arrivals entering the camp and transferred to the Deposit and Consignment Office.

The camp at Drancy was organized differently from the one at Pithiviers. Rather than barracks, internees were housed in a large, U-shaped four-story apartment building, grouped by staircase number. The rhythm of life was dictated by whistle-blows that everyone had to learn to recognize. Three long blasts followed by three short ones was a message to the overseers of each staircase that a small group of new prisoners had arrived. Three long plus three short, repeated three times, signified the arrival of a large group. Three long was an order to close all windows. Two long meant potato-peeling duty. Four long: bread and vegetable duty. One long blast marked the beginning of roll-call, and another marked the end. Two long blasts and two short ones: general duty.

Roll-call on the evening of November 2 included around a thousand prisoners. Two of those prisoners were Ephraïm and Emma. They were corralled inside a fenced space in the courtyard serving the east wing, or staircases 1 to 4. These were the staircases reserved for those detainees whose departure was imminent.

"Departure staircase" prisoners were kept separate from the rest of the camp and could not mingle with the others. Emma was assigned to staircase 2, room 7, 3rd floor, door 280. Before the prisoners were sent away, there was one final search of their bodies for personal belongings. The weather was cold, and the women had been instructed to present themselves without shoes or underwear—the latest orders, to reduce overstock at the destination point.

Next, Ephraïm and Emma were taken to the train station at Le Bourget. Like their children, they spent a night aboard the train, waiting, before the convoy finally departed on November 4 at 8:55 A.M.

Ephraïm closed his eyes. Images. His mother's hands when he was a little boy, smelling pleasantly of moisturizer. Sunlight through the trees around his parents' dacha. The white dress his cousin had worn to a family dinner, which pressed her breasts together like two doves in a lacy cage. Broken glass beneath his feet on the day of his wedding. The taste of the caviar with which he'd made his first fortune. His joy at watching his two little daughters playing among his parents' orange trees. Nachman laughing in the garden with Jacques. His brother Boris's mustache bristling as he bent over his butterfly collection with intense focus. The patent he had filed under the name Eugène Rivoche and the feeling he'd had on the way home that, finally, his life was about to begin.

Ephraïm looked at Emma. Her face was a landscape he had traveled so many times over. He took his wife's feet, ice-cold in the freezing air of the livestock car, and breathed on them, and rubbed them with his hands to warm them up.

Emma and Ephraïm were gassed immediately after arriving at Auschwitz, during the night of November 6–7, because of their ages: fifty and fifty-two.

"Proud as a chestnut-seller showing off his wares to everyone who passes."

E ach week, Monsieur Brians, the mayor of Les Forges, was required to send a list to the prefecture of Eure. A list entitled: "Jews Currently Living in the Municipality."

This time the mayor was able to write, in his elegantly rounded script, with the satisfaction of a job well done:

"None."

Now you know," said Lélia, "how the lives of Ephraïm, Emma, Jacques, and Noémie ended. Myriam never spoke about them. I never once heard her say her parents' names, or her brother's, or her sister's. Everything I know, I pieced together from archives and books, and also because I found a few snippets among my mother's things after she died. For example, she wrote this during Klaus Barbie's trial. Here, I'll let you read it."

The Barbie Affair

Whatever form this trial took, it was going to bring back memories, and everything I have tape-recorded in my memory is playing back now, little by little, sometimes in order and sometimes not, with a few blank spaces and a lot of [illegible]. It would be wrong to call them memories; they're moments of life, that *man hat es erlebt*—one has lived. They're inside me, part of me, branded into my skin, you might say—but they're not memories I want to live with, because there's no experience to be gained from them. There are no words I can use to describe them that don't trivialize them. Some of us managed to stay alive, without looking for explanations, often powerless, and yet active, given the scale of the cataclysm. Can a man who survives a plane crash ever know where his luck came from? If it had happened a few minutes earlier, or later, would he have been the one in the wrong place? He's not a hero. He was fortunate; that's all.

It was luck, enormous strokes of luck, that saved my life.

1) During an ID check on the train taking me back to Paris after the exodus

2) After curfew on the corner of the rue des Feuillantines and the rue Gay-Lussac

3) When I was arrested at the Rhumerie Martiniquaise

4) At the market on the rue Mouffetard

5) Crossing the demarcation line at Tournus in the trunk of a car with Jean Arp

6) The two policemen on the plateau in Bououx

7) During the meetings of the Filles du Calvaire at the end of the war, when I went into the Resistance

The most <u>commonplace</u> situations: 1, 4, 6
The most <u>comical</u>: 2
<u>Unbelievable</u> luck: 3
Risky: 5
Accepted, planned risk: 7
Whether these situations were commonplace, risky, comical, unbelievable, or accepted, luck was on my side. I always tried to keep some hope and to stay as cool-headed as possible. I can remember it all in a split-second, but writing it down . . . well, that's something else. I'll stop here for today.

"The characters in this story are only shadows now," Lélia said, opening the window to let in the twilight air and lighting the last cigarette from her pack. "There's no one left who can describe their lives in exact detail. Myriam took most of their secrets to the grave with her. But soon we'll have to pick up where she left off. And write. Come on, we'll nip out for more cigarettes. The fresh air will do us good."

Waiting for Lélia in the car I'd double-parked at the Vache noire intersection, where the tobacconist stays open later than 8 P.M., I heard a faint noise and then felt a trickle of liquid between my thighs, a thin stream of water emerging uncontrollably from my body.

BOOK II
MEMORIES OF A JEWISH CHILD WITHOUT A SYNAGOGUE

G randma, are you Jewish?"
"Yes, I'm Jewish."
"And Grandpa, too?"
"No, he isn't Jewish."
"Oh. Is Maman Jewish?"
"Yes."
"So I am, too?"
"Yes, you are, too."
"Okay, that's what I thought."
"Why are you making that face, sweetheart?"
"I really don't like what you just said."
"But why?"
"They don't like Jews very much at school."

E very Wednesday, my mother drives her little red car into Paris to pick my daughter up from school in the late morning. It's their day, their special time together. They have lunch, and then my mother drops Clara off at judo and goes back out to the suburbs.

I was very early to pick Clara up that day, as always; the class wasn't nearly over. This was my favorite part of the week. Time stopped, here in this gym with its weary fluorescent lights. A portrait of Jigoro Kano, the inventor of judo, gazed benignly down at the little lion cubs facing off on dingy tatami mats. One of those cubs was my six-year-old daughter, her tiny body swamped by the overlarge white *gi* she wore. I watched her, entranced.

My phone rang. I wouldn't have picked up for just anyone, but it was my mother calling. Her voice was shaking. I asked her several times to calm down, to tell me what was wrong.

"It's a conversation I had with your daughter today."

Lélia tried to light a cigarette to calm her nerves, but her lighter wouldn't work.

"Go get some matches from the kitchen, Maman."

She put down the receiver and went off in search of a light. Meanwhile, my daughter threw a boy bigger than her to the floor with a swift, confident movement. I was smiling—a mother's pride—when my own mother came back on the line, her breathing slowing as the smoke flowed in and out of her lungs. And then she told me what Clara had said.

They don't like Jews very much at school.

My ears filled with a sort of buzzing. I had to hang up. "Maman, Clara's class is finishing. I'll call you back later."

I felt hot bile rise in the back of my throat, and the gym began to spin. To keep from drowning, I clung to my daughter's *gi* like a white lifeboat. Somehow I managed to do all the things a mother does: tell my daughter to hurry up, help her get dressed in the changing room, fold the *gi* and put it in her sports bag, retrieve the socks caught in the bunched-up cuffs of her trousers and the sandals that had slipped through the planks of the changing room bench, all the miniature objects—shoes, lunchboxes, mittens connected by a strand of yarn—designed to vanish into every nook and cranny. I put my arms around my daughter and hugged her as hard as I could, trying to calm my own racing heart.

They don't like Jews very much at school.

On the way home I felt as if I could see the words hovering in the air above us. The very last thing I wanted to do was talk about it. I wanted to forget the conversation, forget that it had ever happened. I crept on cat-feet through the evening routine, built myself a suit of armor out of bathtime and buttered noodles and tooth-brushing and books about *The Little Brown Bear*—all those repetitive tasks that leave no room for reflection. That allowed me to detach. To turn back into a solid, dependable mother.

Going into Clara's room to give her a goodnight kiss, I knew I should ask the question. *What happened at school?*

But at the crucial moment, I stumbled over something inside me.

"Goodnight, sweetheart," I said, turning out the light.

I had trouble falling asleep. I tossed and turned in the twisted sheets. I was hot, my thighs burning. I opened the window. Finally I got up, muscles knotted. I turned on my bedside lamp, but I still felt deeply uneasy. I felt as if water were rising up around my bed, murky and brackish, oily and gleaming. The dirty water of war, stagnating in underground pits, rising up from the sewers, seeping between the boards of my wooden floor.

An image flashed suddenly into my mind. Crystal clear.

A photograph of the Opéra Garnier, taken at twilight.

From that moment onward, I was on the case. I wanted to find the author of the anonymous postcard my mother had received sixteen years earlier, whatever it took. The idea of finding the culprit became an obsession. I had to understand why that card had been sent.

Why did the postcard come back to haunt me at that exact moment in my life? The thing that started it all was the incident at my daughter's school. But looking back, I think there was something else, too. A more subtle reason. I was about to turn forty years old.

The idea that I had already lived half of my life also explains my utter determination to solve this mystery, which occupied my every thought, day and night, for months. I'd reached the age where something, some force, pushes you to look back, because the horizon of your past is now more vast, more mysterious, than the one that lies ahead.

CHAPTER 1

The next morning, after dropping Clara off at school, I phoned Lélia.

"Maman, do you remember that anonymous postcard?"

"Yes, I remember."

"Do you still have it?"

"It must be somewhere . . . my office, probably . . ."

"I'd really like to have a look at it."

Oddly, Lélia didn't seem too surprised. She didn't ask me any questions, didn't ask why I'd suddenly brought up such an old subject.

"It's here at the house, if you want it. Come on over."

"Right now?"

"Any time."

I hesitated. I had work to do, pages to write. There was no logic to it at all, yet I heard myself saying to my mother, "I'll be right over."

There were two RER tickets left in my wallet, but they were expired. Since my daughter's birth, I never took the train to my parents' house anymore; I always drove. And even *that* was only once or twice a year at most.

Stepping onto the platform at Bourg-la-Reine, I thought back to the hundreds, maybe thousands of times I'd made this journey between Paris and the suburbs. As a teenager, I'd waited for the RER B on this very platform. The minutes always seemed interminable; the train could never arrive fast enough to take me to the capital with all its promise. I always sat down in the same spot, in the very back of the car, next to the window, facing forward. The red and blue fake-leather seats stuck to your thighs in summer. The smell of metal and hard-boiled eggs, so typical of the RER B in the '90s, that ever-present smell—to me, that was the smell of freedom. From ages thirteen to twenty I was always so happy on that train that took me away from the suburbs, my cheeks flushed, exhilarated by the speed and the grinding of the machinery. Now, twenty years later, I was impatient again, but this time I was going in the opposite direction. I wanted the train to hurry, to take me back to my mother's house so I could see the postcard.

"How long has it been since you were here for a visit?" asked my mother, opening the door.

"Sorry, Maman. I was just thinking I should come more often. Did you find it?"

"I haven't had time to look yet. I was just going to make some tea."

I didn't want any tea. I wanted to see that postcard.

"You're always in such a hurry, darling," Lélia said, as if she could read my mind. "But at the end of the day, the sun sets at the same time for everyone, you know. Have you spoken with Clara about what happened at school?"

She put the kettle on to boil and opened the tin of Chinese smoked tea.

"No, Maman. Not yet."

"It's important, you know. You can't just ignore something like that," she said, tapping a cigarette from her already open pack.

"I'm *going* to talk to her, Maman. Can we go up to your office and look for the postcard now?"

Lélia ushered me into her office, which never changed over the years. Other than a photo of my daughter thumbtacked to the wall, everything was exactly the same as it had always been.

The same furniture cluttered with the same objects and the same ashtrays; the shelves full of the same books and the same archive boxes. While she began to look for the postcard, I picked up a small pot of black ink from her desk, beveled on the sides and gleaming like a chunk of obsidian. It dated from the time when she refilled her cartridges herself, from when I used to watch her type her articles on a typewriter. From when I was Clara's age.

"I think it's in here," Lélia said, opening a desk drawer.

Her fingers groped in the darkness, rummaging among check stubs and energy bills and outdated day-planners and old movie tickets—all the scraps of paper we accumulate over the years, the kind future generations will hesitate to throw away when they're emptying out our drawers after we're gone.

"There it is! Got it!" my mother exclaimed, just like she used to do when extracting a splinter from my foot.

She handed the postcard to me. "What exactly are you planning to do with this?"

"I want to find the person who sent it to us."

"Is this for a script?"

"No, nothing like that. I just want to know."

My mother looked surprised.

"How do you think you're going to find them?"

I looked pointedly at the bookshelves. "Well, you're going to help me."

Lélia's archive had gotten even larger since the last time I was here.

"I have a feeling their name is somewhere in those boxes," I said.

"Listen, you can keep the postcard . . . but I don't have time to think about all that."

My mother was warning me, in her own way, that she wouldn't help with my investigation. Which wasn't like her at all.

"Do you remember, when the postcard first came, how we all talked about it together?" I said.

"I remember."

"Did you have anyone specific in mind back then?"

"No. No one."

"You didn't think *oh, so-and-so might have sent this*?"

"No."

"Strange."

"What?"

"It's like you're not even curious to know who—"

My mother cut me off. "Take it if you want, but I don't want to hear about it."

She went to the window to light a cigarette. The atmosphere in the room was suddenly tense, charged, and I could tell my mother was trying to calm herself by putting some physical distance between herself and me. And, like a sheet of paper whose watermark becomes visible when you hold it up to the light, when my mother stood in front of the window I saw a kind of ice-cold iron box appear inside her, its lid rusted shut. She had put the postcard in that box, for reasons that were suddenly obvious to me, but that I'd never been able to articulate before. Whatever my mother had locked away in the black depths of her iron box was, to paraphrase the American writer Helen Epstein, "so potent that words crumbled before they could describe it."

"I'm sorry, Maman. I didn't mean to snap at you. I understand that you don't want to hear about that postcard. Come on, let's have some tea."

We went back down to the kitchen, where my mother had put together a bag for me with a jar of Malossol cornichons, my favorite pickles, which I used to eat as an after-school snack—I loved their combination of softness and crunchiness and their bittersweet taste. Lélia often fed us pickled herring and sliced black bread when we were growing up, and cheese danishes and potato pancakes and tarama, blinis and eggplant caviar and chopped liver. It was her way of preserving a vanished culture. Through the flavors of *Mitteleuropa*.

"Come on, I'll drive you back to the station," she said.

Going down the front steps, I noticed the brand-new mailbox.
"You got a new mailbox?"
"The other one finally gave out."
I stood still for a few seconds, disappointed that our dilapi-dated old soldier had gone. It was like finding out that a key wit-ness in my investigation had died.

In the car, I reproached my mother for not telling me about the new mailbox. Astonished, she rolled down the window, lit her umpteenth cigarette, and said, "I'll help you find out who wrote that postcard. On one condition."
"What?"
"That you deal with what happened to Clara at school ASAP."

G azing out the train window at the landscape of the southern suburb where I'd grown up, every shopping center and apartment building and office block as familiar to me as the back of my hand, I remembered that it was this area, between Bagneux and Gentilly, that used to be the "Zone," the neighborhood of chair-bottomers and basket-makers through which Myriam had ridden for her life in 1942.

Past the Cité U station, older buildings began to appear, orange-red brick structures six stories high. They were called HBMs—*habitations bon marché*, or low-cost residences, the ancestors of modern low-income housing projects, built during the era when tax exemptions were granted for such things. They were still there. The Rabinovitches had lived in one of them, at 78 rue de l'Amiral-Mouchez, back when they were among France's "foreigners." Seventy-five years later, I had achieved Ephraïm's dream, the dream of integration. I didn't live on the outskirts of the city anymore, but in the center. A true Parisienne.

I took the postcard out of my purse and studied it. The Opéra Garnier instantly called to mind the dark years of the Occupation. It was no accident that the sender had chosen this particular monument; I was sure of that. It was the first place Hitler visited when he came to Paris.

But as the train pulled into my station, I wondered if maybe I shouldn't be looking at things in a different way altogether. Maybe the author had chosen this card randomly, just because they had it to hand. Maybe it wasn't meant to convey any particular message at all. If I were going to get to the bottom of this mystery, I would have to steer clear of the obvious—and especially of anything that seemed too novel-perfect.

On the back of the postcard were those four names, written one above the other in a staggered, zig-zag list, forming a sort of puzzle. The handwriting was strange, especially that of the names. It looked as if it had been deliberately disguised. I'd never seen an "A" written like the one at the end of Emma's name; it was like two backwards "S"s, perhaps meant to be read in a mirror, like Leonardo da Vinci's famous notebooks.

The photograph of the Opéra had been taken in the autumn, undoubtedly on one of those gentle October evenings when the clocks have just been turned back, when the streetlamps seem to have been lit by accident because the sky is still summer-blue. That was how I pictured him or her, anyway, the anonymous author, as a kind of twilight being, hovering between two worlds. A bit like the man seen from behind in the foreground of the photo, with a rucksack slung over his right shoulder. The transparent quality of his figure made him seem ghostly. Not quite alive, not quite dead.

The postcard had already been old when it was sent in 2003. What had happened? Had the sender changed their mind in front of the post office? Had they felt the need to stop and think about it a little bit more?

He hesitates . . . he is just slipping it through the slot in the mailbox, but at the last minute, he stops. Relieved, or maybe troubled, he turns around and goes back home, and puts the postcard back on his desk.

Until the next century.

That evening, after having dinner with my daughter, after giving her a bath and putting on her pajamas, after kissing her and putting her to bed, I didn't ask her to tell me what had happened at school. I'd promised my mother. But once again, something held me back.

Instead I went into the kitchen, and I held the postcard up to the light in the hood of the stove, and I looked at it for a long, long time, as if eventually, suddenly, it would make sense.

I ran my fingertips gently over the thick card, and it felt like I was touching skin, the skin of something alive; I could almost feel its pulse beating, weakly at first, and then stronger and stronger the longer I stroked it. I called out to them silently, Ephraïm, Emma, Jacques, and Noémie. I asked them to guide me in my quest.

Then I took a few seconds to clear my mind, and I thought about how to tackle the problem. I stood there in the kitchen, in the silence of my apartment. And then I went to bed. As I was drifting into sleep, just for a moment, I thought I could see them. The author of the postcard. It was only the briefest flash. In the dimness of an old apartment, a figure at the end of a dark hallway, as if in the depths of a cave. Waiting, as they had been for decades, patiently, for me to come looking for them.

"This might sound bizarre, but sometimes I feel like there's some invisible force, pushing me."

"Your *dybbuk*s?" asked Georges. It was the next day, at lunchtime.

"Kind of. I do believe in some form of ghosts. But I need you to take me seriously now, okay?"

"I'm taking you *very* seriously, I promise. You know what? You should show your postcard to a private detective. They have ways of finding people, old phone books, sources you wouldn't think of . . ."

"I don't know any private detectives," I said, laughing.

"You should go to the Duluc Detective Agency!"

"Duluc? Like in the Truffaut films?"

"That's the one."

"That agency doesn't exist anymore; it was the 1970s."

"Yes, it does! The Duluc Detective Agency. I pass it every morning on my way to the hospital."

I'd known Georges for a few months. We'd formed the habit of eating lunch together near the hospital where he was a doctor. And sometimes we spent Saturday nights together, when I didn't have my daughter and he didn't have his kids. I loved those evenings with him. Both separated from our spouses, we wanted to take our time, to savor these early days of the relationship. We weren't in any hurry.

"You haven't forgotten about the Seder, have you? It's tomorrow," Georges reminded me when lunch was over.

I hadn't forgotten. It would be our first social appearance as an official couple. It would also be my first time celebrating Pesach. And that made me uneasy. I'd told Georges I was Jewish, but I'd left out the fact that I had never set foot in a synagogue in my life.

I'd told him the history of my family on our first dinner date. The Rabinovitches' escape from Russia in 1919. And he'd told me about his parents; his father, also born in Russia, had been a member of the French *Francs-tireurs et partisans* Resistance group and part of the immigrant labor workforce. We'd talked for hours about our families' crossed destinies. We'd read the same books, watched the same documentaries. We felt like we knew each other already.

After that dinner, Georges had done some research on a website mentioned by Daniel Mendelsohn in *The Lost*, a repository of genealogical documents on nineteenth century Ashkenazi Jewish families. He'd learned that in 1816, in Russia, a Chertovsky had married a Rabinovitch.

"Turns out our ancestors were in love a long time ago," he'd told me on the phone. "They must have planned for us to meet."

As strange as it may seem, I'd fallen in love with Georges as soon as he said those words.

I went home after lunch and sat down at my desk to work, but I found it impossible to concentrate. I couldn't stop thinking about the postcard. Was it supposed to be some sort of reparation for people who'd been denied any kind of proper burial?

Was this 15 by 17 cm rectangle of cardstock meant to serve as the marker for their nonexistent grave? Or, at the other end of the spectrum, had it been sent maliciously? To frighten? Was it a macabre poem, a *memento mori* written with a sneering laugh? My gut feeling kept switching between the two, between light and shadow, like the two statues perching atop the Opéra Garnier. On the postcard, Harmony is lit up, while Poetry fades into the night, like two winged spirits pitted against one another by the light.

Instead of working, I Googled "Duluc Agency."

Founded 1913. Investigations, inquiries, surveillance (Paris).

The official portrait of Monsieur Duluc appeared on my computer screen: a diminutive, brown-haired gentleman with angular features, eyebrows arched like ram's horns, and an impressively large handlebar mustache that curled back on itself until it touched his nostrils, so ink-black it might have been made of felt.

Based at the same location in Paris's 1st arrondissement since 1945, the Duluc Agency has expanded its activities over the years to include all types of inquiries and investigations, serving both businesses and individuals. Available 24 hours a day, 7 days a week. Free consultations. "In order to decide, you need to know."

The motto piqued my curiosity. I immediately sent an e-mail with my contact information.

Hello. I'm writing because I need your services to help me find the author of an anonymous postcard mailed to my family in 2003. It's extremely urgent and important to me. I would appreciate a reply as soon as possible.

A minute later, my phone buzzed. It was a text from the agency detective. They weren't lying when they said 24 hours a day, 7 days a week.

Hello, I'm surprised that you're reacting so strongly 16+ years later! I'm currently on the way back to Paris and will be at the office in an hour. Cordially, FF.

After crossing the Pont des Arts, I spotted a neon-green sign in the distance, all in capital letters. It looked familiar. I'd seen it glowing more than once, crossing the rue de Rivoli near the Louvre late in the evening. Some of the letters had burnt out, and the sign now read DUC DE CIVE. I'd always thought it was an old-fashioned nightclub.

Next to the wooden door, a brass plate above the keypad read:
INVESTIGATIONS
2nd FLOOR

The door opened automatically, and I made my way down the corridor to a waiting room. There was no one in sight, and the place was silent. The original business license filed by Jean Duluc, the agency's founder, hung framed on the wall, confirming that I was in the right place. The room was empty except for a few knick-knacks in a display case. I wondered if the objects had sentimental value for the private detective, or if he'd simply bought them to decorate the waiting room. They were so incongruous that they had a kind of hypnotic effect on me. The first one was a porcelain miniature of the Chinese vase that Tintin and Snowy jump out of in *The Blue Lotus*. Next to this was a faucet made of glass with kissing goldfish figurines beneath it, as well as several tiny aquariums. Tintin's presence among the knick-knacks made perfect sense in this place; the young Belgian might not have been a private detective, but his journalistic investigations often led him to solve mysteries. The aquariums, on the other hand, stumped me completely.

I picked up one of the agency's brochures from the coffee table.

In order to decide, you need to know. But obtaining complete, reliable, useful information doesn't happen by accident. It requires many years of experience and skill, thoroughness and intuition, material and human resources—and total, guaranteed confidentiality.

The brochure went on to explain that Jean Duluc had been born on June 16, 1881, in Mimizan, in the department of Les Landes, and received his detective's license from the Paris police headquarters at age twenty-nine. The numerous photos of him in the brochure informed us that he stood a hair over five feet tall—a short man even for that period—but sported a magnificent, extraordinarily long handlebar mustache, curled at the ends like in the old *Tiger Brigades* TV series.

The door of the waiting room opened before I could finish reading the brochure.

"Come in," the detective said. He was out of breath, as if he'd just returned from some daredevil high-speed chase. "My train was late; I do apologize."

Thickset and avuncular, aged around sixty, with salt-and-pepper hair, Franck Falque wore large horn-rimmed glasses, burgundy velvet trousers that more or less matched his jacket, suspenders, and a shirt that had clearly never known the touch of an iron. His face was round and cheerful, the face of a man who enjoyed the good things in life.

I followed him into his office, a room so narrow that you could stretch out your arms and almost touch the walls. Its single window overlooked the beehive of activity that was the rue du Louvre. Just below it sat an immense aquarium lit by neon blue bulbs, in which swam twenty or so guppies, a tropical freshwater fish native to Latin America. They were all brightly colored, blue or yellow, and their black-bordered scales reminded me of the detective's glasses. Franck Falque must love these fish, I realized. Suddenly the "aquatic" knick-knacks in the waiting room made sense.

Behind the desk were stacks and stacks of files like eviscerated sandwiches, their contents spilling out.

"Now, about this postcard," he said. His accent marked him out as a native of southwestern France. It was probably much like the accent Mimizan-born Jean Duluc had had more than a century prior.

"I brought it with me," I said, taking it from my purse and handing it to him.

"So it was your mother who originally received this, is that right?"

"Yes. In 2003."

Falque read the postcard over carefully.

"And who are these people?" he asked. "Ephraïm . . . Emma . . . Jacques and Noémie?"

"My mother's grandparents, and her uncle and aunt."

"Ah. And couldn't it have been one of these four who sent the card?" he asked, in the kind of patient voice mechanics use when they suggest right off the bat that maybe you just forgot to fill your oil tank.

"No. They all died in 1942."

"All of them?" the detective asked, nonplussed.

"Yes, all four. At Auschwitz."

Falque stared at me, frowning. I couldn't tell if it was sympathy in his expression, or if he hadn't fully grasped the meaning of my reply.

"The concentration camp," I clarified.

But he was still silent, still frowning.

"Murdered by the Nazis," I added, just to make absolutely sure we were on the same page.

"*Oh là là*," he murmured, in his southwestern accent. "How terrible. How very tragic."

He waved the postcard back and forth as he said this, as if fanning himself. He must not have been used to hearing the words "Auschwitz" and "concentration camp" in his office. He was silent for another moment, his face still shocked.

"Do you think you might be able to help me find the person who wrote it?" I pressed, trying to restart the conversation.

"*Oh là là,*" he repeated, still fanning himself with the card. "My wife and I usually deal with cases of adultery . . . corporate espionage . . . problems with neighbors. Commonplace problems, you know. But not . . . this!"

"You never look into anonymous letters?" I asked.

"Well, yes—yes, of course," Falque replied, nodding vigorously. "But this . . . this seems much too complicated."

Now we were both silent, neither of us knowing what to say. Falque read the disappointment in my face.

"It was in 2003!" he protested. "You could have decided to do something sooner! Quite frankly, Madame, it isn't even very likely that the author is still alive . . ."

I put my coat back on and thanked him.

Franck Falque eyed me over the rims of his large tortoiseshell glasses. He'd begun to sweat, and I could tell that all he wanted was to get rid of me as quickly as possible. Nevertheless, he agreed to give me a few extra minutes.

"Okay," he said, sighing. "I'll just tell you the first few things that occur to me. Why the Opéra Garnier?"

"That's just it, I don't know. Do you have any idea?"

"Is it possible that any of your family members were hidden there?"

"Honestly, I don't think so. That would have been incredibly risky."

"Why is that?"

"During the Occupation, the Opéra Garnier was *the* place for German high society to see and be seen. The front of the building was covered in swastikas."

Franck looked thoughtful.

"Did your family live in the area?"

"No. Nowhere near it. They were in the 14th, on the rue de l'Amiral-Mouchez."

"Perhaps it was a meeting place? Were they in the Resistance? You know . . . one of the nearby metro stations, or something like that."

"It's possible. A meeting place . . ."

I deliberately left the sentence unfinished to draw the detective out, to encourage his train of thought.

"Were any of your family members musicians?" he asked, after a few seconds of silence.

"Yes! Emma—her name is on the list there—she was a pianist."

"Could she have performed at the Opéra? Been part of the orchestra?"

"No, she was just a piano teacher. She didn't give concerts. And of course Jews were forbidden to perform at the Opéra during the war. Even Jewish composers were stricken from the repertoire."

He looked at the postcard again, turning it over in his hands. "Look," he said finally. "I'm not sure what else I can tell you . . ."

Falque, it was clear, felt that he had done his job. He had taken the time to look at my postcard, and now he wanted me to leave. But I stayed put.

He sighed. "Okay—yes, something does actually come to mind here." He wiped his forehead in silence. I could tell he was regretting the words already.

"My father-in-law was a policeman," he went on after a moment. "He always used to tell us police stories . . ."

He trailed off. He was thinking of some far-distant memory. Lost in thought.

"That must have been interesting," I prodded.

"No, actually. He had a tendency to ramble. Told the same stories over and over again. But sometimes it was useful. You'll see what I mean in a minute. Have you noticed it? The stamp?"

"The stamp? Yes. It was put on upside-down."

Falque nodded. "There might have been a reason for that."

"You mean the author did it deliberately?"

"Quite."

"Like a message?"

"Exactly."

Falque gazed into the middle distance. I sensed that he was about to tell me something important.

"Do you mind if I take notes?" I asked.

"No, go right ahead," he said, wiping the fogged-up lenses of his glasses. "The first thing you should know is that once—in the nineteenth century, I mean—people paid the postman twice. You paid to send your letter, and then the recipient paid to receive it. Do you see?"

"You had to pay to read your own mail? I didn't know."

"Oh, yes. This was in the very early days of the post office. But you had the right to refuse any letter that was sent to you. And then, of course, you didn't have to pay. So people came up with a code, so they wouldn't have to pay twice. The positioning of the stamp on the envelope had a particular meaning. For example, if you put the stamp on one side, leaning to the right, it meant 'illness.' You see?"

"Yes," I said. "So there was no need to open the letter or pay the fee. The message was in the stamp. Right?"

"Precisely. And people have assigned meaning to the position of stamps ever since. Even today, aristocrats affix stamps upside-down as a sign of protest or challenge. A way of saying 'Death to the Republic.'"

"So you think that the stamp on my postcard might have been put upside-down deliberately?"

Falque nodded again and then gestured that I should listen closely.

"Among members of the Resistance, sending a letter with the stamp upside-down meant, 'read the opposite meaning.' For example, if a letter said 'everything is fine,' the reader was to understand that really, things were going badly."

The detective sank into his chair with a sigh, relieved to have gleaned at least something from the postcard.

"Okay. There's something I don't understand," he said. "You said this postcard was sent to your mother. Then who is 'M. Bouveris'? That's not your mother, is it?"

"Oh—no. 'M. Bouveris' is Myriam Bouveris, my grandmother. Her maiden name was Rabinovitch, and her first husband's last name was Picabia—he was my mother's father. Her second husband was named Bouveris. So the postcard was sent to my grandmother, but at my mother's address. Her name is Lélia."

"You've lost me."

"29 rue Descartes is my mother Lélia's address. But 'M. Bouveris' is my grandmother, Myriam. Got it?"

"Right, right, okay. I get it now. Well, what does she say about it? Myriam?"

"Nothing. She died in 1995. Eight years before the postcard was mailed."

Franck Falque squinted, thinking.

"It's just that, when you first showed me the card, I read it as *Monsieur* Bouveris. You know? 'M' for 'monsieur.'"

It struck me as a logical, and maybe important, observation.

"You're right," I said. "It never occurred to me that it could be taken as Monsieur Bouveris."

I scribbled a few notes in my notebook. I would have to talk to Lélia about all of this.

Franck Falque leaned toward me across his desk. I sensed that I was about to benefit from another of the detective's flashes of insight.

"So, who is Monsieur Bouveris? Can you tell me more about him?"

"Not very much. He was my grandmother's second husband, and he died in the early '90s. I think he was quite a moody person. He worked for the tax office for a while, I believe, but I'm not even completely sure about that."

"How did he die?"

"It's pretty vague. I think it was suicide. Like my grandfather before him."

"Your grandmother had two husbands, and they both killed themselves?"

"That's right."

"Good lord. Your family members don't tend to die peacefully in their beds, do they?" he murmured, raising his thick eyebrows. "So your grandmother lived at this address?" He indicated the postcard.

"No. Myriam lived in the south of France."

"Ah. That complicates matters."

"Why?"

"Was your grandmother's name—Bouveris—on the mailbox at your parents' house?"

I shook my head.

"Then why did the postman deliver it there, if there was no 'M. Bouveris' on the mailbox?"

"I never thought about it. That is strange, actually."

The office doorbell buzzed shrilly. We both jumped. Falque's next appointment had arrived.

I stood and shook the detective's hand gratefully.

"I can't thank you enough. How much do I owe you?"

He waved the question away. "Nothing."

Just as I was about to walk out the door, he handed me a battered business card.

"Here. This is a friend; you can say I told you to call him. He's a handwriting analyst. Specializes in anonymous letters."

I slipped the card into my purse. It was time to pick Clara up from school, and I took the bus so I wouldn't be late. On the way, I thought back to Georges's remark about *dybbuk*s, the unhappy spirits that enter people's bodies to have certain vital experiences through them—and remember how it feels to be alive.

CHAPTER 3

ppropriate outfit for Pesach
I typed the four words into my Google search engine.
Michelle Obama promptly appeared on my computer
screen. She was sitting at a table, surrounded by men wearing
yarmulkes. She wore her usual warm smile and a simple navy-
blue dress, not too different from one I had somewhere in my
own closet. That made me feel better; maybe dinner at Georges's
wouldn't be a complete disaster after all.

The babysitter arrived. While she read a story to my daughter, I continued my research. The photos that came up on my
screen showed Hebrew books on tables and plates filled with
a strange assortment of items. Bones, lettuce leaves, hard-
boiled eggs. A labyrinth of symbolism. An unknown world
in which I feared I might lose myself. Georges thought, because of some conversations we'd had, that I was familiar with
the liturgy of Jewish holidays, and that I knew how to read
Hebrew.

I'd never corrected him.

This was the first time I'd ever gone out with a Jewish man.
Before him, the questions of whether I knew the order of a Seder
or if I'd had a bat mitzvah had never come up. My last name
wasn't Jewish, and so the other men I'd dated had always exclaimed after a while, surprised, "Oh, really? You're Jewish?"

Yes, despite appearances.

At school, I'd become friendly with a girl, Sarah Cohen. She
had black hair and olive skin, and she'd explained to me once
that men just assumed she was Jewish. But her mother wasn't

Jewish, and so she wasn't either, under traditional Jewish law. Sarah had ended up developing a real complex about it.

I *was* Jewish but didn't look it. Sarah *looked* Jewish but wasn't, according to the texts. We'd laughed about it. It was all so silly. Ridiculous. And yet it affected both our lives deeply.

As the years passed, the issue remained complex, intangible, incomparable to anything else. I might have one Spanish grandfather and one Breton one, a great-grandfather who was a painter and another who'd captained an ice-breaking ship, but nothing—absolutely nothing—mattered as much as that I was descended from a line of Jewish women. Nothing else had ever characterized me as strongly in the eyes of the men I'd loved. Rémi had had a grandfather who was a *collaborateur*. Théo had wondered about his own possible hidden Jewish roots. Olivier looked quite Jewish and was often mistaken as such. Even now, with Georges. My Jewishness always mattered in some way; it was never insignificant.

I wore the navy-blue dress in the end. It was a little too tight in the waist now—I'd thickened in the middle since my pregnancy—but there was no time to find anything else. I was late. All of Georges's guests had already arrived.

"Finally!" he said, taking my coat. "I thought you'd never get here! Anne, I'd like to introduce you to my cousin William and his wife Nicole. Their two boys are in the kitchen. And this is my best friend François and his wife Lola. My sons had to stay in London for their exams, unfortunately. It's too bad; this will be my first Seder without them. Oh—and this is Nathalie, who has written a book; I have a copy to give you. And this—" he said, as a woman came into the living room, "is Déborah!"

I'd never met Déborah, but I knew very well who she was. Georges spoke of her often.

One look at her face told me two things. One, Déborah was a

confident, take-charge kind of woman. And two, she wasn't at all pleased about my presence at this dinner.

Déborah and Georges had known each other since boarding school. Back then, Georges had been hopelessly in love with Déborah, but she hadn't returned his feelings and had rebuffed his advances. How could he have imagined for a moment that a girl like her could be interested in a boy like him?

"I'd rather just be friends," she'd told him.

More than thirty years had gone by since. Georges and Déborah had each gone about their own lives, but had remained in contact. They'd worked in the same hospitals. Georges had had two sons and a lengthy divorce, Déborah one daughter and a rapid separation. They'd continued to see one another from time to time, at birthday parties for doctors they both knew, that sort of thing, but hadn't ever really talked.

"We've known each other slightly for a long time," Déborah would say about Georges.

"We used to know each other quite well," Georges would say about Déborah.

Until, thirty years after their school days together, Déborah had looked at Georges with new eyes and become interested in him at last.

She'd thought that Georges would be thrilled to have another shot with his teenage crush. But that didn't turn out to be the case.

"I'd really like for us to be friends," Georges had said.

Déborah had taken the words as a challenge. Reconquering Georges's heart, she concluded, would just be a little more difficult than expected.

So much the better, she'd thought.

Georges had maintained what he called a friendship with Déborah ever since, but the truth was that deep down it was a sort of revenge. An ego-boost. The girl he'd suffered so much over was now wooing *him*.

When Déborah saw me arrive at Georges's house, she was surprised at first. Georges had told her about me, but since I wasn't a doctor, she hadn't considered me a serious rival. My presence at the Pesach dinner made her think again. It hurt that Georges hadn't bothered to tell her I was coming. She felt that he had humiliated her.

"Let's start dinner," Georges said.

Buckle up, murmured Déborah to herself.

While the men were putting on their yarmulkes, Déborah made a joke about the difference between a Sephardic Pesach and an Ashkenazi Pesach, which everyone thought was hilarious. Except me, of course. Déborah made a show of apologizing to me, but in a way that emphasized my ignorance.

"Sorry," she said. "Jewish joke."

"But Anne's Jewish, too," said Georges.

"Really? I thought your last name was Breton," she said warily.

"My mother's Jewish," I replied, blushing.

Georges began to say the prayer in Hebrew. My heart started pounding. Everyone was following along with his words, periodically interjecting an *Amen*, which they pronounced *O-meyn*. That confused me, because I'd thought only Christians said *Amen*. I could feel Déborah watching every move I made. The whole thing was like a nightmare.

Georges asked one of his nephews, who was about to have his bar mitzvah, to explain the Seder plate.

"These are the *maror*, the bitter herbs that represent the bitterness of slavery in Egypt, the bitter lives of our ancestors, in remembrance of the suffering endured by the captive Hebrews. This is the matzoh, symbolic of the haste with which the Hebrews fled to freedom . . ."

While the young man recited his lesson, everyone sat down. As I was lowering myself into my chair, a seam tore in the side of my dress. Déborah couldn't keep herself from smiling.

"Pick up your Haggadahs," George said. "I found my parents' old ones, so there are enough for everyone, for once."

I picked up the book that lay on my plate. It was entirely written in Hebrew. I tried to keep the dismay off my face.

Déborah leaned over to me and said, loud enough for everyone to hear, "You open a Haggadah from the *right*."

I began clumsily murmuring apologies. Georges had begun to read the story of the exodus from Egypt, his voice deep and solemn.

"'This year we are slaves . . .'"

This part of the Haggadah was meant to remind everyone in the table about the terrible trials endured by Moses.

I allowed myself to be soothed by the responses, by the bittersweet beauty of the tale of the Hebrew people's liberation. The Pesach wine made me feel joyful, giddy—and like I'd lived this scene before, like I already knew every part of the ritual we were enacting. Everything seemed familiar: passing the matzohs around, dipping the bitter herbs in salted water, letting a drop of wine fall from my fingertip onto my plate, resting my elbow on the table. The copper platters holding the symbolic Pesach dishes were familiar, too, as if I'd seen them a million times before. My ears already seemed to know the Hebrew chants. It was as if time had stopped. I felt a sense of wonder, a deep, warm happiness that came from somewhere far away. The ceremony transported me back in time. I could feel hands sliding into my own, inhabiting them. Nachman's fingers, gnarled as the roots of an ancient oak tree. His face leaning toward me, over the candles, whispering, "We are all pearls in the same necklace."

The Seder was over. It was time to eat dinner.

Déborah, talkative and at ease with everyone, slipped naturally into the role of hostess. She had a compliment for everyone, a question for everyone. Except me, of course. I was the distant relative you invite so they won't be alone for the holiday, but to whom no one's got anything to say.

Chatty, pretty, and witty, Déborah began to tell a funny story about a dinner she'd cooked for Georges—the peppers she'd let burn, the eggplant caviar that was her mother's recipe, the marinated peppers that were her father's. She talked, talked, talked, and everyone listened.

"And how does *your* mother make gefilte fish?" she asked me suddenly.

I pretended not to hear her. She turned to Georges.

"You know what I'm struck by every year in the Haggadah?" she asked. "It's that ancient command for us to go to Israel to escape persecution. 'Rebuild Jerusalem, the holy city, speedily in our days.' It's been right there in black and white for more than five thousand years."

"You're thinking of moving to Israel, aren't you?" Georges asked his cousin.

"Yes, as a matter of fact. When I read the papers, when I see everything that's going on in France nowadays, it seems to me that people just want us to disappear."

"You always exaggerate, Papa," William's son said. "No one's persecuting us."

William pushed back his chair, disbelieving. "You want me to rattle off a list of all the anti-Semitic incidents that have happened so far this year alone?" he asked his son.

"Papa, there are ten times more incidents than that against Blacks and Arabs every year in France."

"Have you heard that they might publish a new edition of *Mein Kampf*? With 'expert commentary.' It's pure cynicism, that's all. Just a guaranteed moneymaker."

William's wife gave her son a warning look: *Don't get into this with him.* And François, Georges's best friend, changed the subject.

"Will you leave if the National Front wins the elections?" he asked Georges.

"No. I'm not leaving."

"Why not? You're crazy!" William said.

"Because I'll resist. And resistance will be a grassroots, domestic movement."

"I don't understand your reasoning. If you want to fight, why not do it now, before it's too late? The whole point is to keep things from crashing down on top of us," put in Lola, François's wife.

"She's right. Here we sit in our comfortable chairs, just waiting for the disaster to happen."

"What's driving you, deep down, is a desire to experience the same kind of thing your father did during the war and the Resistance. But we can't let history repeat itself just so you can play vigilante!"

"It's true," Georges admitted; "It's always been kind of a family fantasy . . ."

"Well, there's the problem," said William's son, keen to distance himself from the out-of-touch "old" people around the table. "Your fantasies. You think that once the National Front gets into power, you'll finally be able to go off and fight, like your parents in '68 and your grandparents in World War Two. Part of you even *wants* the extreme right to take over, just so you can feel alive. And that goes for the left-wing political leaders, too. You're all just waiting for the worst to come, so something will finally *happen* in your lives."

"You'll have to excuse my son," said William. "He's clearly lost his mind."

"No! No, on the contrary. What he's saying is very interesting," François said.

"The worst . . . well, now wait," said Lola, clearly trying to lower the temperature in the room. "Even if the National Front does win the elections, which I don't think they will—even if something so extreme does happen, I don't see why we, as Jews, would suffer any more than anyone else from the situation. Let's be

228 · ANNE BEREST

realistic. I agree with your son, William. Even though I'm Jewish, I think it'll be undocumented workers, Africans, immigrants who will be the ones in danger. Sorry to disappoint you, gentlemen, but you're not the ones they'll be arresting in the streets."

"And why not?" William argued.

"Come on, you know Lola is right! Nothing will happen to you or me," said Nicole, William's wife. "It's not like they're going to make us wear a yellow star."

"Maybe not, but there will be another kind of violence against the Jews."

"You're way off base. It's the Africans and the Arabs who will be at risk, even the ones who have citizenship, if the National Front comes to power. Far more than us."

"Yeah, but here's the problem: are you prepared to fight for people other than yourselves?" It was William's son again. "Are you suddenly going to turn into one of the Righteous? Look at all the families living in the street, children dying of hunger on filthy mattresses. Doesn't that remind you of anything? What if *you* had to be the generous ones? Would you take someone into your house and let them sleep on your sofa? How much would you risk? What if you weren't the victims, for once, but the people who could actually help?"

"The Jews had enemies in France, before the war. Immigrants today don't have those kinds of enemies here."

"Oh, so your indifference isn't a kind of collaboration?"

"Hey, calm down. Don't speak to your father like that."

"That kind of self-righteous talk is too simplistic," William retorted. "And it makes Jews feel guilty. We live in a country where there is still a huge amount of anti-Semitism; just watch the news on any given day. Now imagine the National Front coming to power and trying to challenge the system when the people at the highest levels of the government aren't on your side. For me, that changes the perception of being Jewish in this country. No doubt about it."

"The only thing that kind of doomsday talk does is soothe your conscience about not doing anything for anyone else."

"You can't possibly understand!" William shouted. "Georges and I—our generation dealt with a lot of anti-Semitism, and that leaves permanent scars. Doesn't it, Georges?"

Georges had started chuckling at William's sudden theatricality.

"Listen, William," he said after a moment. "It's not that I don't agree with you about all of this. But to be honest, I've never had anything anti-Semitic happen to me personally. Not at school, and not at work."

William crossed his arms. His expression was one of frank disbelief that his cousin would say something so idiotic. Then he smiled, and asked, "Are you sure? Really positive?"

"Yes," said Georges. "I'm sure."

"So you've never wondered about what happened the year of your bar mitzvah?"

Georges understood the allusion immediately.

"Okay, okay," he said, conceding defeat. "I was inside the synagogue the evening of the attack on the rue Copernic."

"If that wasn't an anti-Semitic act, nothing is!" William bellowed. He got up so fast that his chair tipped over backwards. It was as if the two cousins were acting out a scene in a play.

"Yes. It was October 3, 1980, a few months after my bar mitzvah," Georges explained to the rest of us. "I was still deep into Judaism at that point. One of the few periods in my life when I went to synagogue regularly."

"I don't mean to interrupt," put in William, "but I want to clarify something for my son. The date of October 3 had been chosen to commemorate the night of October 3, 1941, when six synagogues were attacked in Paris, including the one on the rue Copernic."

"It was the Friday evening service, and the synagogue was packed," Georges continued. "I was praying with my sister. Ten minutes before the service ended, during the *Adon olam asher*, the bomb went off. We heard an explosion, and the windows shattered; some people were hit by flying glass. The rabbi hustled us all out a back door. My sister and I saw cars on fire. We turned left, toward the avenue Kléber, where we caught our bus. When we got home, our nanny, Irène, was watching the news on FR3; they'd just announced the attack. She understood right away what a lucky escape we'd had."

"Did *you* understand it?"

"Me? No, not at first. But that night, in bed, my legs started shaking uncontrollably."

"And then—remember? Raymond Barre's anti-Semitic statements," William prodded.

". . . yeah. He was Prime Minister at the time. He said the attack was all the more shocking because 'innocent French people' who'd happened to be in the street in front of the synagogue had gotten hurt."

"He actually said 'innocent French people'?"

"Yes! As if in his mind, Jews weren't quite French, or truly innocent, either."

"But you don't think that attack scarred you at all?"

"No, I don't believe so."

"You're just in denial."

"You think?"

"Yeah. It's denial. You've just buried the trauma. And also, you feel like you're assimilated enough to be protected."

"What is that supposed to mean?"

"Look at all of us around this table," François said. "We're all the children or grandchildren of immigrants. Every single one of us. But do we think of ourselves that way? Absolutely not. We think of ourselves as middle-class French men and women, the children of parents who made a success of themselves. We all consider ourselves totally assimilated. All our names sound foreign, and yet we know the best domestic wines, we've read all the classic

French literature, we all know how to cook *blanquette de veau*. But take a good, hard look at yourselves and ask the question: isn't this feeling of being deeply anchored in France the same way French Jews felt in 1942? A lot of them had fought for this country in the first World War. And yet they were put on those trains."

"Exactly. It's the same kind of denial. Thinking nothing bad could ever happen to you."

"But no one's asking to see ID when you take the metro. This is just crazy talk," argued William's son.

"It's not crazy. France is going through a period of incredible economic and social violence. If you look at the history of Russia in the late nineteenth century, or Germany in the '30s—those situations have always led to anti-Jewish sentiment. Since the dawn of time. Why should it be any different now?"

"Actually, Anne's daughter just had a problem at school," put in Georges. "Didn't she, Anne? Tell them what happened."

Every eye turned to me. I had contributed nothing to the debate so far, and Georges's friends were curious to hear what I had to say. He'd told them so much about me.

"Well . . . it isn't totally clear what happened yet," I began. "But something upset her . . . and she asked my mother if she was Jewish . . ."

"Wait, you mean your daughter doesn't know she's Jewish?" Déborah asked, cutting me off.

"I mean—yes, she does, but not really. I'm not observant. So, no, I've never woken up one day and said to her, 'By the way, we're Jewish.'"

"You don't celebrate the holidays?"

"Sure, we celebrate all of them! Christmas, and Twelfth Night, and Halloween, and she gets an Easter basket . . . it all probably blends together in her head."

"So tell them what happened," Georges prompted again.

"My daughter said, 'I don't think they like Jews very much at school.'"

"*What?!*"

"How awful!"

"What on earth happened to make her think something like that?"

"I . . . I'm not sure, actually . . ."

"What do you mean?"

". . . I haven't asked her . . . not yet."

My heart sank. I looked like the worst mother in the world, just some featherbrained bimbo, in front of all Georges's friends whom I was meeting for the first time.

"I haven't really had time to talk to her about it since . . ." I added lamely. "It only happened a few days ago."

Georges hadn't joined in the horrified exclamations, but I knew he couldn't think of any way to come to my defense.

The tension in the room had become palpable. Georges's friends, his cousins—their faces had changed. Everyone was looking at me with suspicion now.

"I didn't want to make a big deal out of it," I said, still trying weakly to defend myself. "I don't want to reinforce the clique mentality. And besides, if we start taking schoolyard insults seriously . . ."

I could tell my arguments had had all the effect they were going to. All Georges's friends wanted now was to change the subject; they were just going along with whatever was said. And it was time for everyone to move into the living room, anyway. But Déborah wasn't ready to let it go. She shot at me, "If you were truly Jewish, you wouldn't take it so lightly."

Every face registered surprise at the ferocity of her words.

"What is that supposed to mean?" Georges snapped. "She's told you her mother is Jewish. Her grandmother was Jewish. Her family members were killed at Auschwitz. What more do you want? A medical certification?"

But Déborah refused to back down.

"Do you ever mention Judaism in your books?"

I didn't know what to say. My wits deserted me. I started to babble something meaningless. And then Déborah looked me straight in the eye and said, "The truth, as far as I can tell, is that you're only Jewish when it suits you."

CHAPTER 4

G eorges,

Déborah's remarks hurt me, but if I'm being honest, I have to admit that there was truth in them.

I wasn't comfortable coming to your house for Pesach.

Because of a misunderstanding that happened between us on our very first date.

I told you about my family, about what happened to them. You thought, naturally, that I'd grown up in the same culture as you did, and you said it was something that connected us. And I didn't correct you, because I wanted it to "connect us."

But it wasn't the truth.

I *am* Jewish, but I know nothing about Jewish culture.

You have to understand that after the war, my grandmother Myriam joined the Communist Party, embracing the same revolutionary ideals her parents had when they lived in Russia. She believed that her children and grandchildren should be born into a new world, with no links to the old one. My grandmother, the sole survivor of her family by war's end, never set foot in a synagogue again. For her, God had died in the death camps.

My parents didn't raise us, my sisters and me, in the Jewish faith, either. The fundamental mythos of my childhood, my culture, my family models, sprang mostly from secular, republican socialism, as dreamed of by a generation who were young adults in the late twentieth century. In that, my parents were a lot like the great-grandparents I told you about, Ephraïm and Emma Rabinovitch.

My parents were both twenty years old in 1968, and it made them who they were. *That* was my religion, so to speak.

That's why I've never been in a synagogue. My parents saw religion as the opiate of the masses. There was no Shabbat for us on Friday nights. No Pesach. No Yom Kippur. Our family's big occasions were the Fête de l'Humanité for its concerts, Barbara Hendricks singing "Le Temps des cerises" in the Place de la Bastille, and "Parents' Day," a holiday we made up ourselves, a non-Pétainist, anti-capitalist version of Mother's Day. I don't know any Biblical texts. I don't know any religious rites. I never went to Hebrew school. Instead, my father sometimes read me extracts from *The Communist Manifesto* as bedtime stories. I can't read Hebrew, but I've read all of Barthes, whose works I borrowed from my parents' shelves.

I don't know the chants for Yom Kippur, but I know all the words to "Le Chant des partisans." We didn't go to synagogue to listen to the hazzan on high holidays, but my parents played The Doors for us, and I knew every one of their songs by heart by the time I was ten. No one taught me about a chosen people fleeing Egypt, but my parents always taught me that I had to work hard because I was a woman and because no one was going to leave me a big inheritance.

I wasn't familiar with the prophet Elijah, but I read about the exploits of Che Guevara and Subcomandante Marcos. I'd never heard of Maimonides, but my father advised me to read François Furet when I studied the Revolution. My mother never had a bat mitzvah. But she had May 1968.

My education didn't arm with me weapons to fight through life with, it's true. But I wouldn't trade the romantic culture I was raised in, the mother's milk that nourished me, for anything in the world. My parents taught me the values of equality among humans; they really believed that a utopian future was possible. They gave my sisters and me the tools to become women who were intellectually free, in a society where the bright light of Culture would banish all forms of religious darkness with its brilliance and clarity. They may not have succeeded—may not even have come close—but they tried. They *really* tried. And I admire them for that.

And yet.

And yet, there was a disruptive element that showed up regularly to contradict their teachings.

That disruptive element was a single word. *Jew.* That strange word that popped up from time to time, usually uttered by my mother, and defied my understanding. That word, or that concept, or rather that secret, unexplained history that my mother brought up at the most random moments, and that never failed to startle me.

I found myself confronted with a latent contradiction. On one side, there was the utopia my parents described as a model society to be built, instilling in us, day after day, the idea that religion was an evil to be fought against. And on the other side, hidden away in some dark crevice of our family life, was the existence of a hidden identity, a mysterious heritage, a strange lineage that drew its *raison d'être* from the very heart of religion. We were all one big family, no matter the color of our skin or our country of origin; we were all connected to one another through our *humanity*. But, in the midst of this enlightened discourse, there was that word that kept returning, circling back like a dark star, like some bizarre constellation, surrounded by a halo of mystery. *Jew.*

And ideas began to fight with each other in my mind. Heads: my distaste for any kind of male-transmitted legacy. Tails: the revelation of a Jewish heritage transmitted through the mother. Heads: the equality of all citizens under the law. Tails: the feeling of belonging to a chosen people. Heads: the rejection of any so-called "inherent" characteristic. Tails: an affiliation existing from the moment of birth. Heads: we were universal beings, citizens of the world. Tails: our roots lay in a world as unique as it was closed in on itself. How could I make sense of it all? From a distance, my parents' teachings seemed clear, but close-up, everything turned blurry.

I've forgotten months, even whole years of my life. I've forgotten cities I visited, things that happened to me. I've forgotten things that people don't usually forget: my high-school grades, the names of my teachers, and a lot of other things, too. But despite my shoddy memory, I can pinpoint every single one of the exact moments when I heard the word "Jew" in my childhood, starting with the first time. I was six years old.

September 1985.
Someone spray-paints a swastika on our house during the night. I have no idea what it means, of course.
"It's nothing," my mother says.
But I can tell she's disturbed.
Lélia tries to scrub the swastika away with bleach and a sponge, but the black paint won't come off. It stays there on the wall, dense and dark.
The next week, our house is graffitied again. This time it's a circle with a cross through it, which I think looks sort of like a target. My parents say some words I've never heard before. One of them is the word "Jew," which shocks me like a slap this first time it invades my life. And I also learn another word, "GUD," which they spell out: gee–you–dee. The funny, sing-song sound of it sticks in my little-girl mind.
"Don't worry," my mother says to me. "It doesn't matter. Don't think about it anymore. These drawings have nothing to do with us."
But I know, despite these reassuring words, that Lélia feels threatened by "something" and that that "something,"

anti-Semitism, exists in a world near my own, a zone of space and time orbiting the tiny planet of my young life.

January 1986.

When my mother talks, the words hover in the air over my head like night-flying insects, buzzing in my ears. One of these words is never pronounced quite like the others; it has a particular sound to it, a particular tone. A word that scares and excites me at the same time. My natural repulsion at hearing it is contradicted by the shivery thrill it gives me—because I know that this word has something to do with me; I feel . . . *designated* by it.

On the playground with the other children, I don't like playing hide-and-seek anymore, because I feel terror at the thought of being hunted. The fear of being someone else's prey. When one of the monitors asks me why I'm crying, I say: "My family is Jewish." I still remember her shocked expression.

Autumn 1986.

I'm seven years old and in the second grade. Most of my classmates attend Bible class and meet on Wednesday afternoons for church activities.

"Maman, I want to join the church group."

"You can't," answers my mother, upset.

"Why not?"

"Because we're Jewish."

I don't know what that means, but I can tell it's better not to argue. Suddenly I feel guilty for having wanted to join the church group. It was only because little girls get to wear pretty white dresses to church on Sundays.

March 1987.

For a little while, Malabars come with a prize in their

sweet-smelling wrappers: temporary tattoos. You have to peel the protective paper off carefully, dampen it with water, and then press it to your skin and wait for the image to stick. I put one on the inside of my wrist.

"Wash that off right now," Lélia orders me.

"But I like it, Maman."

"Mamie will be very angry if she sees it on you."

"Why?"

"Because Jews don't get tattoos."

Another mystery. Unexplained.

Early summer 1987.

Claude Lanzmann's *Shoah* airs on television for the first time, over four nights. I can tell, despite being only eight, that it is about a very important event. My parents decide to record the episodes on the VCR bought last summer for the World Cup.

The videotapes containing *Shoah* are stored by themselves, separately from the other tapes. My big sister has drawn a star of David on each label, with an exclamation point in red ink and the words DO NOT ERASE in capital letters. Those tapes scare me. I'm glad they're kept separate.

My mother spends long hours watching them. We mustn't disturb her while she does.

December 1987.

I finally ask my mother, "What does it mean to be Jewish, Maman?"

Lélia doesn't really know how to answer my question. She thinks for a few moments, then goes to get a book from her office. She puts it down on the floor, where it nestles in the thick white wool pile of the carpet.

Faced with these black-and-white photographs, these images of ravaged bodies in striped pajamas, of barbed wire in the snow, of corpses stacked atop one another, of mountains of clothes and shoes and eyeglasses . . . my eight years of life aren't enough to have given me any kind of mental resistance. I feel physically attacked by them, wounded.

"If we'd been born back then, we'd have been turned into buttons," Lélia said abruptly.

The thought of being "turned into buttons" was so bizarre, so unfathomable, that I found it utterly devastating. Those words were burned permanently into my brain, leaving a scorched place that remains, even today, a black hole where no thoughts can exist, where nothing will grow.

Did my mother misspeak that day, when she used the word "button"? Or was it me? Did I somehow confuse the French word *bouton* with *savon*, the word for soap? Experiments *were* carried out on the remains of Jews, but with the aim of using human fat to make soap, not buttons.

Nevertheless, it's the latter word that has stayed with me forever. I loathe sewing buttons back onto clothing even now, because of the horrifying idea that I might be piercing one of my ancestors with the needle.

June 1989.

It's the bicentenary of the French Revolution. My school puts on a show about the year 1789. The roles are cast, and I'm chosen to play Marie-Antoinette. The boy chosen to play Louis XVI is named Samuel Lévy.

On the day of the show, my mother and Samuel's father are talking. Lélia comments ironically on the choice of actors to portray the crowned heads destined for decapitation. Again the word *Jew* hits my ear with the shocking coldness of the guillotine. I experience a strange, uncomfortable mixture of emotions: pride at being different, tinged with the threat of death.

Still 1989.

My parents buy the graphic novels *Maus I: My Father Bleeds History* and *Maus II: And Here My Troubles Began*. I stare at the covers of these books as if they're nightmarish mirrors, portals to be entered. I'm reluctant to read them. I'm ten years old, and I can sense that if I plunge into these two graphic novels, I'll be embarking on a journey that might change me forever. In the end, I open the covers. The pages of *Maus* stick to my fingers, particles of the paper becoming embedded in the flesh of my hands until they won't come off. The black-and-white characters settle in my body, lining my lungs. My ears become very hot. At night I have trouble falling asleep. I watch on the walls of my skull the macabre dance of cats and pigs pursuing mice like some terrifying magic lantern. Pale presences sit around me on my bed, forms wearing striped pajamas. This is when the nightmares start.

October 1989.

I'm still ten years old. My mother and I watch *Sex, Lies, and Videotape*, the Steven Soderbergh film that has just won the Palme d'Or at Cannes, at our little neighborhood movie theater. The cashier, who is also the usher and projectionist, lets me in to see the movie despite my tender age.

In the film, someone says a word I don't understand. Back at home, alone in my room, I consult the dictionary. *Masturbation.* I decide to put the definition into practice, stretched out on the floor with the dictionary open beside me. A new world opens up, an undiscovered and powerful world.

In the days that follow, I am made to understand by adults' reactions that I should never have been allowed to see the movie, despite the fact that I loved it. The lunchroom monitor, with whom I get along very well, doesn't want to believe me. She calls me a liar and tells me to stop claiming that my mother took me to see the film in a theater. This is when I realize that adults are preoccupied by two things, both of which they hide from kids: sexuality and concentration camps.

Images from *Sex, Lies, and Videotape* superimpose themselves on images from *Maus* in my head. Gradually I begin to deny myself pleasure because of the suffering endured by the mice, because of the Jewish race to which I feel I belong without fully understanding why.

November 1990.

I'm in sixth grade. I'm at the top of my class in reading, grammar, and especially writing. I'm the best student, the teacher's pet. Our French teacher is a tall, thin, gray woman who always wears wool skirts. She asks us to draw up our family tree over the autumn school holidays. The project won't be graded, but our trees will be displayed in class when we get back from vacation.

The family names on my mother's side are difficult to write; there are too many consonants in relation to vowels, and the French teacher is made uncomfortable by the frequent recurrence of the word "Auschwitz" on my family tree.

From that day onward, I sense that something has changed. I'm no longer the teacher's pet. I work even harder, get even higher grades, but it doesn't help. Kindness and affection have been replaced by a kind of wariness.

And I feel even more as if I'm swimming in troubled waters, ever more linked to dark times.

April 1993.

This spring, I win fourth prize in the *Concours national de la Résistance et de la Déportation*, a national essay and multimedia competition established in 1961 that's open to all middle- and high-school students in France. I've spent several months reading everything I can find in the history books about the war. My father comes with me to the awards ceremony, which is held in an ornately appointed room in the Hôtel de Lassay. I'm happy to have him with me. During the speeches, the word "Jews" comes up often, and once again I feel that sense of pride mixed with fear of belonging to a group whose history is studied in books. I want to tell the assembled crowd that I'm Jewish, to add value to the award I've just received. But something holds me back. I'm uncomfortable.

Spring 1994.
Every Saturday, I take the RER to the Clignancourt flea market with my friends. We buy Bob Marley t-shirts and leather bags that smell like cow. One afternoon, I come home with a star of David pendant around my neck. My mother doesn't say anything. Neither does my father. But I can read their expressions; they don't like it that I'm wearing this piece of jewelry. We never do talk about it. I put it away in a box.

Autumn 1995.
There's a tenth-grade handball tournament in the gym at school. Four or five girls explain to the phys ed teacher that they won't be participating "because it's Yom Kippur." I envy them and feel excluded from a world that should be mine. I'm vexed at having to play with the "non-Jews" on the handball court.
Back at home that day, I feel sad. I feel like the only thing I truly belong to is my mother's pain. That's my community. A community made up of two living people and several million dead ones.

Summer 1998.
At the end of my *hypokhâgne* year, I join my parents, who are spending a semester in the United States. My father's been offered a visiting professorship at the University of Minneapolis. The atmosphere when I arrive isn't great; since

setting foot on American soil, Lélia has been plagued by intrusive dark thoughts, strange "attacks."

"It's because I keep thinking about my family members who weren't able to escape to the United States. I feel guilty for surviving. That's why I feel so bad."

I'm struck by the fact that my mother talks to us about her "family" as if we, her own daughters, have suddenly become strangers.

I'm also struck by what seems like an intrusion of the past into the present. There's something very unsettling about it. Suddenly my mother seems to be confused about genealogical links, about the identities of each person. Fortunately, the crisis passes once we're back in France, and everything goes back to normal.

At the end of the summer, I move out of my parents' house and start living my "own" life.

I studied at the same school my grandmother Myriam and her sister Noémie attended seventy years before me—without knowing it. I failed my exams, then endured a difficult decade during which I only felt better when I was writing, when I fell in love, and when I had a child.

All of it took a lot of energy. I poured my entire self into it.

And after all that, I met you. Georges.

You can't imagine how beautiful I found that Pesach celebration. How could I have missed something so deeply that I'd never done before? I could feel the gentle caress of my ancestors, you know.

Georges, the sun is rising. I've stayed up all night writing this e-mail; you'll read it when you wake up. I don't regret the lost sleep because I feel like I spent the night with you.

In a few minutes, I'll go into Clara's room to wake her up. And I'll say, "Your breakfast is ready. Hurry up, sweetheart. I want to talk to you about something important."

C lara, honey, your grandmother said you told her about a problem you were having."

"No, I don't have a problem, Maman."

"But you told her . . . you said you thought they didn't like . . ."

"Didn't like what, Maman?"

Clara knew very well what I was talking about, but she made me coax it out of her.

"Clara! You told your grandmother they didn't like Jews very much at school."

"Oh, yeah. Right. It's no big deal, Maman."

"I want you to tell me what happened."

"It's okay, don't get mad. My football friends and I were talking in the playground about heaven and life after death, and so everyone said their religion. And I said I was Jewish—because I've heard you say it—and then my friend Assan said, 'That's too bad. I'm not going to pick you for my team anymore.' And I asked him why, and he said that his family didn't like Jews very much. And then I asked him why again, and he said it was because they didn't like Jews very much in his country."

"I see."

"I was disappointed," Clara went on, "because Assan's the best football player, and you always win if you're on his team during recess. So I thought about it for a minute, and then I asked him what his country was. And he said his parents were from Morocco.

"I was hoping he'd say that, because I had the perfect solution. So I said, 'Don't worry, Assan, there's no problem. You know what? Your parents are wrong. They really like Jews in Morocco.' He asked me how I knew that, and I told him that my mother and I had stayed in a hotel there on vacation, and they were really nice to us. So that proves that they like Jews.

"And then Assan said, 'Oh, okay, that's fine, then. You can play on my team.'"

"And did you talk about it any more after that?" I asked.

"No. Then we just kept playing like before."

I was proud of my daughter. And proud of the other child's reaction, so simple, so logical. I kissed Clara's broad, intelligent forehead, blotting out the absurdity of the world for a moment. Everything was all right. Reassured, I took her to school.

"I'm sorry," Georges said on the phone, "but for the sake of everything you wrote to me last night, and everything you've told me, you've got to tell the principal what happened. You can't just let anti-Semitic talk slide in a public school."

"It wasn't anti-Semitic talk. Just a stupid remark by a little boy who didn't even understand what he was saying!"

"But that's just it. Someone needs to explain it to him. And that someone needs to be the secular, state-funded school he attends."

"His mother's a cleaning woman. I'm not going to complain to the principal about a cleaning woman's kid."

"Why not?"

"You don't think it would be a bit . . . socially irresponsible . . . for me to complain about him?"

"So if it had been the son of a middle-class French person who told Clara his family didn't like Jews, *then* you would speak to the principal?"

"Yes, probably. But that isn't what happened."

"Don't you realize—I don't want to hurt your feelings, but—don't you see how condescending your reaction is?"

"Yes, I do realize it. And I'll own up to it. I'd rather that than feel guilty about making trouble for a woman from an immigrant family."

"And just what kind of family are *you* from?"

"Okay, Georges, fine. You win. I'll e-mail Clara's principal and request a meeting."

Before we hung up, Georges told me to keep my birthday weekend free.

"That's two whole months away," I said.

"Exactly. I figure you're not booked up yet. I'd like to have a little getaway together, just the two of us."

All that day, I thought about how I would frame the situation to the principal. I wanted to rehearse the meeting thoroughly in my head, so I wouldn't get carried away by emotion in the moment, and I wanted to be prepared for any questions he might ask so they wouldn't rattle me.

I wanted to tell you about an exchange that happened in the schoolyard between my daughter and another pupil. Please understand, I'm not trying to make it more serious than it actually was . . .

I'm listening.

. . . and I'd also like this to remain between you and me. I'm not planning to tell the teacher about it.

Certainly.

Here it is. A little boy told my daughter that his family doesn't like Jews.

Excuse me?

Yes. The kids were talking about religion . . . and that ridiculous phrase came out. And let's say my daughter was mildly aggravated by it. No more than that, really. I think we adults are more upset about it, to be honest.

Which little boy said this?

Sorry, but I'd rather not disclose the student's identity.

Look, I need to know what's happening in my school.

I know, that's why I wanted to meet with you. But I still won't point the finger at anyone.

I'd like Clara's teacher to speak to the students about the secular values of state-run public schools.

Look, Monsieur, I respect your reaction, but—

Everything blew up after that, and I lost control of the conversation. The consequences I imagined for my daughter were even more serious; she had to transfer schools, and I could already see the reporters and journalists with their microphones: *Do you think anti-Semitism is a problem in this school?* And the news vans at the front door . . .

I continued to picture a series of worst-case scenarios right up to the moment of the actual meeting.

I waited in the school entrance hall, looking at the children's drawings on display, the foam balls abandoned in corners, the little petrol-blue mats, the brightly painted walls, until a woman appeared and showed me to the principal's office. Passing the windows of the cafeteria, where stacks of clear Duralex drinking glasses stood ready for lunchtime, I remembered how my friends and I used to pretend to tell our ages from the numbers on the bottom of the glass.

The principal opened his door, and I shook his hand, the whole scene feeling slightly unreal. His office was exactly how I'd imagined it: a battered cork bulletin-board with class schedules, a calendar, and a few postcards from far-flung destinations tacked to it. Shelves full of binders. On his desk, a mug of paper clips.

Settling himself behind the desk, the principal smiled at me, showing square, gappy teeth that reminded me of a hippopotamus.

Gathering my courage, I took a deep breath and explained why I was there. The principal listened to me, his head bent slightly forward, his face calm and impassive. He blinked from time to time.

"I don't want to turn this into a big brouhaha, you

understand," I said. "I just want you to know what took place in your schoolyard."

"Okay," he said. "Duly noted."

". . . I don't need you to speak to the teacher, or the student's parents about it . . ."

"That's fine. I won't mention it. Anything else?"

"Er—no . . ."

"Well, thank you for coming in."

I was so startled that I didn't move, just sat there, staring at him.

"Was there something else you wanted to tell me?" he asked uneasily, wondering why I didn't get up.

"No," I said, still not budging. "Do you have anything else to say to *me*?"

"No."

We sat in silence for what felt like an eternity, just looking at each other.

"Well . . . have a good day, then," the principal said at last, rising and moving toward the door, a clear signal that our interview was over.

I left his office in a state of shock. Looking at my phone, I saw that the meeting had lasted a grand total of six minutes.

I hadn't had to convince him to keep the story under wraps.

I hadn't had to persuade him not to talk to the children about it.

"You did him a favor by telling him you wanted the incident kept quiet, plain and simple," my mother said.

"Yes . . . I figured that out, a little late and a little painfully," I said.

"What were you expecting, exactly?"

"I don't know. I thought he would be . . . concerned."

CHAPTER 6

You thought the principal would be '*concerned*'?"
Gérard Rambert's laugh echoed off the walls of the
Chinese restaurant, a great booming belly-laugh that
made the other diners look around.

Gérard splits his time between Paris and Moscow. We have
lunch together every ten days or so, depending on his travel
schedule, always in the same Chinese restaurant halfway between his apartment and mine, always at the same table, and we
always get the daily special. When the weather gets warmer, we
each add an extra; me a dessert, and him a glass of beer, which
he never does more than sip.

Gérard is tall and broad-shouldered, always clean-shaven,
with gorgeous skin. He speaks loudly and smells good, and he's
always cheerful, even when he doesn't actually feel that way. He
makes me think of a Roman who ended up in Paris somehow; he
could definitely be Italian, with his custom-tailored suits, violet
sweaters, and socks from Gammarelli, where the Vatican cardi-
nals also shop.

"You're never bored with Gérard" is the universal verdict of
the few people lucky enough to spend time with him. And he
agrees.

"You know, I'm not such bad company, even for myself."

That day, I'd told him all about what happened. The meeting
at Clara's school, the principal's reaction.

"You're actually surprised that he isn't bothered? I'm sorry
for laughing; it's just so I don't cry. You wouldn't want me to cry,

would you? Just let me make fun of you a *little* bit, then. *Feygele*. That's you. A little bird. I'll tell you why you're a little bird, but first, let me taste your egg rolls, and listen closely. Are you listening? They're scrumptious! I'm going to order myself some. Excuse me, Mademoiselle? Give me the same thing the little lady here is having! Okay. Now, are you listening?"

"Gérard, that's the only thing I'm doing, I promise."

"All right. So: I'm eight years old, and my gym teacher says to me, 'Gérard Rosenberg, you're a worthy representative of a mercenary race.'

"This was in the early '60s. Dalida was singing 'Itsi bitsi petit bikini'—and France was still anti-Semitic. You see what I'm saying? This teacher, like all the French back then, knew about the gas chambers. The ashes were still warm. But he says to me, 'You're a worthy representative of a mercenary race.' I didn't understand what he meant at the time. Now, you might say to me, well, that's normal; I was eight, and I didn't understand what every word meant, you know? But that phrase stayed in my mind, like it was saved on my hard drive. And I've thought about it often ever since. You want to hear the rest?"

"Of course I do!"

"Two years later, it's 1963, and I'm ten, and my father decides to go to the Conseil d'Etat and have our name changed . . . Our last name. Why? Because my father wanted my older brother, who was only fifteen at the time, to be a doctor one day. And he'd heard there was a lot of anti-Semitism in medical schools. And my father was afraid they'd bring back the *numerus clausus*, which would have hurt my brother's chances of getting into med school. You know what a *numerus clausus* is?"

"Yes . . . yes, in Russia, the May Laws—but also the Vichy laws in France. Only a small number of Jews were allowed to attend university."

"That's right! So you know what I'm talking about. People didn't want to be 'invaded' by us. Always the same old story, which in reality is also a very new story. You'll see. Anyway, my father decides overnight that our whole family will change from Rosenberg to Rambert. You can't *imagine* how angry I was!"

"Why?"

"Because I didn't want to change my name! And my parents had decided to transfer me to another school, too! Changing names, changing schools—it's a lot for a little boy of ten, you know. I wasn't happy. Not happy at all. I made a scene. Swore to my parents that I'd take back my real name the day I turned eighteen. Anyway, on the first day of school that fall, the homeroom teacher calls the roll.

"'Rambert!' he says.

"I don't answer, because I'm not used to the name yet.

"'Rambert!'

"Silence. I think to myself, this Rambert had better answer quick, because the teacher doesn't seem too happy.

"'RAM-BERT!'

"Shit! Suddenly I remember: wait, *I'm* Rambert! So I yell out, 'Here!'

"Of course, all the kids laugh. That's normal. But the teacher thinks I did it on purpose, that I'm clowning around, that I want to draw attention to myself, you know, that kind of bullshit. Long story short, I was pissed off. *Pissed. Off.* But, little by little, I started to realize that at school, being called Gérard 'Rambert' was totally different than being called Gérard 'Rosenberg.' And you know what the difference was? I stopped hearing 'dirty Jew' every day in the schoolyard. I stopped hearing the other kids say things like, 'It's too bad Hitler missed your parents.' And in my new school, with my new name, I realized that I really liked being left the hell alone."

"So what did you do, when you turned eighteen?"

"What do you mean, what did I do?"

"You said that you swore to your parents you'd take your real name back on your eighteenth birthday."

"If someone had asked me on that day, 'Gérard, do you want to go back to being Gérard Rosenberg?,' you know what I would have said? 'Not on your life.' Now, darling, be a good girl and finish your egg rolls. You've hardly eaten a thing."

"I have a French name, too. The most French name anyone could have. Your story makes me think—"

"What?"

"Deep down, I'm glad that with me, it 'doesn't show.'"

"It certainly doesn't! You might as well be singing the mass in Latin! I'll admit something: when you told me—after we'd already been friends for ten years—that you were Jewish, I just about fell out of my chair!"

"Really? It was that much of a surprise?"

"Oh, yes! Before you told me, if someone had said to me, 'Did you know that Anne's mother is Ashkenazi?' I'd have told them to get the hell out of town with that bullshit. You look like the epitome of a 'Frenchwoman.' A real *goy*. An *echte goy!*"

"You know . . . all my life, I've had trouble actually saying the words 'I'm Jewish.' I never felt like I had the right to say it. And . . . it's weird, but it's almost like I'd taken on my grand-mother's fears. In a way, the secret Jewish part of me was glad to be hidden by the *goy* part. Made invisible. No one would ever suspect me. I'm my great-grandfather Ephraïm's dream come true. I've got a perfectly French face."

"And you're an anti-Semite's worst nightmare," Gérard said.

"Why?"

"Because even *you* are Jewish!" he said, with his booming laugh.

M aman, I've spoken to Clara, I've met with the principal; I've done everything you asked me to. Now you have to keep your promise."

"Fair enough. Ask me some questions, and I'll try to answer them."

"Why didn't you try to find out?"

"Hang on, let me get my cigarettes, and I'll explain," Lélia said.

She disappeared into her office and returned to the kitchen a few minutes later, lighting a cigarette.

"Have you heard of the Matteoli Commission?" she asked. "In January 2003, I was right in the thick of it. It was . . . so strange to get that postcard at that exact time. It felt like a threat."

I didn't see the connection between the commission and my mother's feeling threatened. I frowned, and Lélia realized that I needed more information.

"It might make things clearer if we rewind a bit, if you have time."

"I've got all the time in the world, Maman."

"After the war, Myriam wanted to file an official record for each member of her family."

"What kind of record?"

"Death certificates."

"Oh. Yes . . . of course."

"It was extremely complicated. It took almost two years of dealing with endless bureaucratic red tape for Myriam to file a record. And bear in mind: at that time, the French government still wouldn't officially use the terms 'killed in concentration camp' or 'deported.' The term they used was 'not returned.' Do you understand what that meant? The symbolism?"

"Yes. The French government was saying to the Jews, your families weren't murdered because of our actions. They just . . . haven't come back."

"Can you believe the hypocrisy?"

"And the pain, for all those families who weren't really able to grieve properly. They hadn't had a chance to say goodbye; there were no graves to visit. And to top it all off, the government was using such asinine terminology."

"The first record Myriam was able to file concerning her family is dated December 15, 1947. It was signed by her and countersigned by the mayor of Les Forges on December 16, 1947."

"The same mayor who signed the letters ordering her parents' deportation? Brians?"

"The very same. She dealt with him directly."

"That was De Gaulle's doing. He wanted the French to forgive one another. He kept people on in their political roles who had 'only done their duty.' He wanted to rebuild the nation, not divide it further. But that must have been a bitter pill for Myriam to swallow."

"It took another year, until October 26, 1948, for Ephraïm, Emma, Noémie, and Jacques to be officially declared 'missing.' Myriam accepted delivery of those certificates on November 15, 1948. Now the next phase began for her: the fight for official death certificates. Only a judgment by a civil court could compensate for the absence of their bodies."

"Like for sailors who go missing at sea?"

"Yes, exactly. The judgments were handed down on July 15, 1949, seven years after their death. But—get this—on the death certificates issued by the French government, the official places of death were Drancy for Ephraïm and Emma and Pithiviers for Jacques and Noémie."

"The French government didn't recognize the fact that they died at Auschwitz?"

"No. They went from 'not returned' to 'missing' to 'deceased on French soil.' The official death dates were the days the deportation convoys left France."

"I can't believe it."

"A letter from the National Office for Veterans and Victims of War to the trial court prosecutor even requested that the place of death be specified as Auschwitz. The court decided otherwise. But that's not all. They also refused to say that the Jews had been deported because of race. They said it was for political reasons. It was only in 1996, after a lot of lobbying, that official recognition of 'death by deportation' was granted and the death certificates were corrected."

"So what did people have to say about all those images from the liberations of the camps? And the survivors' testimonies? Primo Levi's books?"

"There was that crisis of conscience just after the war, when the camps were liberated and the surviving deportees came home. But then, little by little, French society shoved it all under the rug. No one wanted to hear about it anymore. No one. Not the victims, not the collaborators. There were a few people who spoke up every now and then, but it took Beata and Serge Klarsfeld in the '80s, and Claude Lanzmann around the same time, to say 'We must not forget.' They were willing to do the work. An unthinkably enormous task. The work of a lifetime. But other than them, it was just silence, you know?"

"It's hard for me to imagine it, because when I was growing up there was a lot of talk about it all—yes, thanks to Lanzmann and the Klarsfelds. I didn't realize how many years—decades— of silence there had been before that."

"Which brings me to the Matteoli Commission. You know what that was?"

"Oh, yes. The Study Mission on the Spoliation of Jews in France."

Alain Juppé, then Prime Minister of France, had defined the parameters of this mission in a March 1997 speech:

> In order to fully inform the authorities and our fellow citizens about this painful part of our history, I wish to entrust you with the task of studying the conditions under which personal property and real estate belonging to Jews in France was confiscated or, generally speaking, acquired by fraud, violence, or theft, both by the Occupier and by the Vichy authorities, between 1940 and 1944. In particular, I request that you seek to assess the extent of spoliation perpetrated thusly and that you indicate which categories of persons, natural or legal, profited from it. I also request that you specify what happened to these assets from the end of the war until the present day.

"A commission was then appointed to examine individual applications filed by victims of anti-Semitic legislation propagated during the Occupation, or by their heirs. If it could be proven that assets belonging to our family had been confiscated in or after 1940, the French government would be obligated to pay reparations with no statute of limitations."

"It had to do mostly with paintings and works of art, if I remember correctly."

"No! It applied to any assets! Apartments, businesses, cars, furniture, and even cash stripped from detainees in the various transit camps. The Commission for the Compensation of Victims of Spoliation Resulting from the Anti-Semitic Legislation in force during the Occupation was theoretically set up to monitor the processing of applications and to make reparations."

"And in practice?"

"I managed to file a successful application in the end, but . . . it wasn't simple. How could I prove that my family members had died in the camp at Auschwitz when the French government had officially stated that they died in France? It was right there on their death certificates, issued by the 14th arrondissement prefecture. And how could I prove that their assets had been confiscated? The government had made sure that no trace of spoliation operations remained! I wasn't the only one who struggled, of course. There were many other descendants who were encountering the same obstacles."

"What did you do?"

"I launched an investigation. It all started because of an article that appeared in *Le Monde* in 2000. A journalist gave the addresses of all the places to write for information, if you wanted to file a case with the commission. You know, 'If you're looking for documentation, write here, here, and here; say it's for the Matteoli Commission.' That was why the government's archives became accessible."

"You couldn't access the archives before then?"

"Let's just say they might not have been 'officially' closed to the public, but they weren't exactly easy to get into, either, and they sure as hell didn't advertise themselves. It wasn't like today, with the internet. You didn't know who to contact, or even how. That article changed everything for me."

"You wrote to them?"

"I wrote to the addresses listed in *Le Monde*, and I got responses pretty quickly. I lined up two appointments: one at the National Archives and one at the central police archives. And I received photocopies of documents from the archives in Loiret and Eure. That was how I got my hands on the entry and exit records from the camps, which meant I could show that they'd been deported."

"Still had to prove the stolen assets, though."

"Yes. That wasn't easy. But I found the records of SIRE, Ephraïm's company, which proved that the business had been commandeered by the Compagnie Générale des Eaux during the Aryanization of commerce. I also had family photos I'd found in Les Forges, which allowed me to show that they'd had a car, a piano, et cetera. And that all of those things had vanished."

"So you filed the case?"

"Yes, in 2000. It was case number 3816. I'd been summoned to give oral testimony, which was supposed to take place—get this—in early January 2003."

"When the postcard arrived."

"Yes. That was why it made me so uncomfortable, with everything that was going on."

"I understand. Like someone was threatening you, maybe to make you abandon your case. How did it go with the commission after that?"

"I was in front of a sort of jury, a bit like when I defended my PhD thesis. The president of the commission was there, and also some government representatives, plus the rapporteur. Quite a few people. I introduced myself briefly, and they asked if I wanted to say anything or had any questions. I said no. And then the rapporteur told me he'd never seen such a well-put-together case."

"That doesn't surprise me at all, given it was you, Maman."

"A few weeks later, I got a letter indicating the amount of money the government was going to pay me. A . . . well, we'll call it a 'symbolic' amount."

"How did you feel about that?"

"You know, for me it wasn't about the money. What I wanted most was for France to recognize that my grandparents had been deported from French soil. That was all I cared about. Some part of me . . . just wanted to exist in France . . . through that official recognition . . ." Her voice trailed off.

"But do you think the postcard had any connection to the commission?"

"That was what I thought at the time. But I've come to believe it really was a complete coincidence."

"You seem very sure."

"I am. I thought about it a *lot*. For weeks and weeks. Who on that committee would have been in a position to send me such a thing? And why? To intimidate me? So I wouldn't appear for my testimony? And because I'd spent so much time racking my brain and rereading all the documentation I'd gathered, I had a revelation. It wasn't until a few months later."

Lélia got up to fetch an ashtray. I watched silently as she left the room and then returned.

"You remember when I told you that Russians could have more than one first name?" she asked me.

"Yes, like in the novels. 'You end up getting lost in it.'"

"Well, they also had more than one spelling. 'Ephraïm' could also be spelled 'Efraïm.' In his administrative letters he wrote his first name with an 'f,' but in personal ones, he used 'ph.'"

"And?"

"One day I realized that, in the case I'd filed with the commission, I'd written 'Efraïm' with an 'f.' Everywhere. Never a 'ph,' like on the postcard."

"And that made you conclude that the card had nothing to do with the commission—"

"—but had to have come from someone close to the family."

CHAPTER 8

1. Statistically speaking, anonymous letters are almost always sent from within a person's intimate circle. Family members most often and, after that, friends, then neighbors, and finally work colleagues. (= Someone close to the Rabinovitches)
2. Also statistically speaking, neighbors are often involved in various criminal acts. In the Paris metropolitan area, for example, more than one in three murders is due to conflicts between neighbors. (= Neighbors of the Rabinovitches)
3. The prominent handwriting analyst Suzanne Schmitt confirms that, "With experience, it becomes apparent that people who write anonymous letters are very often quiet, self-effacing individuals. Writing an anonymous letter is a way to express what they cannot say verbally." (= Self-effacing personality)
4. Anonymous letters are usually written in capital letters, in order to disguise the handwriting. The author will use his or her left hand if they are right-handed, and vice versa, to further change their writing. "But even with the left hand, specific individual characteristics emerge," Suzanne Schmitt has observed. (= The author of the postcard didn't use capitals. Did they alter their handwriting? Or, on the other hand, did they *want* it to be recognized?)

I read Lélia the notes I'd taken. She listened, her gaze focused on something in the distance, the way it always is when she's concentrating deeply. I drew three columns on a page of my notebook and labeled them: *Neighbors, Friends, Family.* Those three words, so small and lost-looking on the white blankness of the page, suddenly looked pathetic to me. Paltry. Meaningless. And yet they were our only landmarks, our only way of navigating this unknown land: a boulder, a belfry, a tower. We would cling to them.

"Okay, I'm listening," Lélia said, lighting a cigarette she'd cut in half with a pair of scissors, a method she'd devised of smoking less.

"Let's start with Myriam and Noémie's friends. Who do you know of?"

"I can only think of one. Colette Grés."

"Yes—I remember. You've mentioned her. Do you know if she was still alive in 2003?"

"She was indeed. She died in 2005. I went to her funeral. After the war, Colette became a surgical nurse at the Pitié-Salpêtrière Hospital. She was a very good person, and she and my mother remained close. Colette looked after me a lot when I was little, when Myriam was rebuilding her life. She lived at 21 rue Hautefeuille. I used to sleep in the little tower room on the third floor."

"Do you think she could have been the author of the postcard?"

"No. Not a chance. I can't imagine her sending me an anonymous postcard."

"Was she shy?"

"Shy, no. I wouldn't say shy. Quiet, though. Rather reserved."

"Did she have dementia when she got old?"

"No. She even wrote me a very thoughtful, clear letter just a year or two before she died. The problem is—where is that letter? You know, I find things, I archive them . . . but I don't really *file* them. It's a bit chaotic . . . I couldn't tell you where exactly everything is."

We both looked up at the shelves filled with archive boxes. Where might the letter be, in those hundreds of laminated pages, in those dozens of binders? It would take us hours to find it.

We'd have to open every single box and look at everything in it, go through binders stuffed with copies of administrative papers and old photographs. But it had to be done. As the two of us began to search, rather like two children digging in the sand on a vast beach, I shared my latest thoughts with Lélia.

"I contacted the company that published the postcard, Éditions La Cigogne—Sodalfa. Their address is right there in the middle of the card in tiny print, along with the photographer's name. Zone industrielle BP 28, 95380 Louvres. I thought they might be able to tell me when the photo was taken, but no luck."

"Too bad," Lélia commented.

"The postmark is the one from the Louvre central post office. I looked into that, too."

"But it's closed since 2003, hasn't it?"

"Yes, I did some online research. In 2003, it was the only post office open every day of the year, even on Sundays and holidays. All night, too. The card was stamped on January 4, 2003. I checked—that was a Saturday."

"So?" Lélia began rummaging through another box.

"Well, it means we can say with certainty that the author of the postcard went to the Louvre post office sometime between Saturday morning at 12:01, and Saturday night at 11:59, 'except for the slot between 6:00 and 7:30 A.M., during which the post office closes for computer maintenance and backup,' to quote the website."

"And what can you conclude from that?"

"I looked at the weather report for that day. Here's what it said: '8 cm of snow in the 12th arrondissement, which hasn't happened in Paris since January 13, 1999. Rain turning to snow at 11:30 A.M., first lightly and then in pellets. Visibility practically zero.'"

"Oh, yes—I remember that! There was a lot of snow that weekend."

"You've got to be unusually determined to go out and mail

an anonymous postcard in the middle of a blizzard, don't you think?"

We sat there for a few moments, each of us wondering why the postcard's author had decided that day to brave snow heavy enough to reduce visibility to nothing.

"Here it is!" my mother crowed, brandishing a sheet of paper. "The letter from Colette Grés!"

She handed me an envelope. It was addressed to my grandmother Myriam, but at my mother's address—exactly like the postcard had been. The handwriting, though, bore no resemblance to what was on the card. The letter was written on sky-blue stationery, the paper thick and coarse-grained. Lélia scanned the letter quickly, then held it out to me silently. I could tell she was troubled.

> July 31, 2002
> My dear Lélia,
>
> What a wonderful surprise to hear from you! So happy you haven't forgotten me. You've done so well to recreate your Rabinovitch family history; your mother was so deeply traumatized by the loss of No and Jacques, and of her parents. It was so hard for her. I always loved Noémie—she used to send me letters, beautiful ones. She would have been a very good writer.
>
> I've always felt such remorse, because I had a little house there, near La Picotière, but there were always soldiers going back and forth—who knows. It was right on the road, and they were always going to the neighboring farm for rabbits and eggs.
>
> I've held on to your letter for a long time. I'll phone you in September . . . if I go. I'm sorry.
>
> With all my love,
>
> Colette

"Why did she say 'you haven't forgotten me'?" I asked.

"Oh, that's simple. 2002 was when I was doing my research,

and it occurred to me to write to her and ask about the war and her memories."

"Do you remember which month it was that you wrote to her?"

"February, I think, or March, 2002."

"So, you wrote to her in March, and she didn't write back until July. Four months," I mused. "And she's an old lady; it's not like she wouldn't have time to write. You know, it makes me think how the month of July was significant for the Rabinovitches. She's talking about the children's arrest here. As if she were remembering."

"But none of that explains why Colette would have sent me an anonymous postcard six months later."

"I think it does! In the letter, she says 'I've always felt such remorse, because I had a little house there, near La Picotière.' That a pretty strong word, 'remorse.' Not one to be used lightly. There's something there, something that's been eating away at her since the arrest. July 2002 . . . July 1942 . . . what's unsettling is that she talks about it as if it were yesterday. The soldiers, the rabbits. She thinks she should have hidden the children in that little house. She feels like she owes you an explanation. It's like she's saying, *I could have hidden Jacques and Noémie in my house, maybe, but they would have been found anyway, so please don't be angry with me.*"

"Yes. It does seem like she feels obligated to explain herself to me. Like she's trying to justify her actions."

All of a sudden, everything became clear in my mind, pieces of the puzzle falling into place.

"Maman? Give me a cigarette."

"You're not smoking again, are you?"

"Oh, whatever—it's only a half. Look, this is how I see things. After the war, Colette feels guilty. She never dares to bring up the subject with Myriam. But she never forgets Jacques and Noémie's arrest. Sixty years later, she receives your letter, and

266 · ANNE BEREST

she thinks you want her to take responsibility for what she did during the war. She's surprised and upset, and she writes back, telling you in so many words that she feels guilty—that she feels 'remorse,' as she puts it. She's eighty-five years old; she knows she's going to die soon, and she doesn't want to take that guilt into the afterlife with her. So she sends the postcard as a way of getting it off her shoulders."

"That does make sense . . . but I still have a hard time believing it."

"It all fits, Maman. She was still alive in 2003; she knew the Rabinovitches intimately. And she had your address handy, because you'd sent her a letter a few months earlier. What more do you need?"

"So you're saying the card was a kind of confession?" Lélia asked, still clearly unconvinced by my argument.

"Exactly. With a Freudian slip! Because she sent it to you— but with Myriam's name on it. Subconsciously it was *Myriam* she'd always wanted to confess everything to. You say Colette took care of you a lot; couldn't that have been because she felt she owed something to her friend? The postcard is, in a way, what Jodorowsky would have called an act of 'psychomagic.'"

"I'm not familiar with . . ."

"Jodorowsky says, and I'm paraphrasing here, 'There are, in the genealogical tree, traumatized, unprocessed places that are eternally seeking relief. From these places, arrows are launched toward future generations. Anything that has not been resolved must be repeated and will affect someone else, a target located one or more generations in the future.' You're the target in a future generation. Maman, did Colette live near the Louvre post office?"

"No, nowhere near it. I told you—she lived in the 6th, on the rue Hautefeuille. I just can't imagine Colette, at the age of eighty-five, venturing out in a blizzard, when one wrong step could mean a broken arm or leg or hip, just to go to the Louvre post office on a Saturday. It just doesn't hold water."

"She could have asked someone to mail it for her. Someone who worked for her, who came to her house, for example. That person might have lived near the Louvre."

"The handwriting on the postcard and the letter don't match at all."

"So what? She could have disguised it!"

I was silent for a few seconds. It all fit. The logic was faultless. And yet. I trusted my mother's gut feelings, and *she* didn't think Colette had done it.

"Okay, Maman. I hear you. But I'd like to have someone compare the handwriting. Just to be absolutely sure."

Dear Monsieur Falque, I think my mother and I might have found the author of the postcard. Her name was Colette Grés. She was a friend of my grandmother's, and she knew all the Rabinovitch children very well. She died in 2005. Can you help me find out any more?

As usual, Franck Falque replied to my e-mail within a couple of minutes:

You should write to Jésus, the criminologist whose card I gave you.

I knew I should have done that ages ago.

Dear Monsieur,

On the recommendation of Franck Falque, I am sending you a photograph of the anonymous postcard my mother received in 2003. Could you tell me what you think of it? Would it be possible for you to create a psychological profile of the author? Their age or gender? Or any information that could help us identify them? I'm attaching a scan of both sides of the postcard.

Many thanks in advance for your help,

Anne

Dear Madame,
Unfortunately, the writing on the postcard isn't sufficient for me to generate a psychological profile through handwriting analysis. I can tell you that the writing does not look natural to my eye. Nothing further, however.
Regards,

Jésus

Dear Monsieur,
I can fully understand how you'd be reluctant to analyze such a small quantity of words, given that it might affect the accuracy of your work. But could you give me just a few impressions anyway? I promise to consider them with a grain of salt.
Many thanks,

Anne

Dear Madame,
Here are a few impressions, then, to be taken with a grain of salt, as you put it.
The 'a' in Emma is not common. I'd go so far as to say that it's quite rare. This way of forming the letter is a hallmark of handwriting that has been deliberately disguised or belongs to someone who is not accustomed to writing.
One confusing characteristic is that the writing of the first names, on the left-hand side of the card, appears to be disguised, while the writing used in the address on the right-hand side seems 'natural' (the term we graphologists use to describe spontaneous, unaltered handwriting). There is some question of whether it's the same writer on the left and right sides of the card. I think it is, but I can't be certain.
The numbers in the address don't provide any conclusive

information; numbers are never very conclusive for graphologists because we only have 10 numbers to work with, from 0 to 9, whereas we have 26 letters. Numbers are never truly individualized: we all learn to write them the same way in school, and the style changes very little throughout our lives. So they're never of much interest in our field. On your postcard, apart from the '3's, which are unusually angular, the numbers are written in quite a common way (capital letters pose exactly the same problem as numbers).

That's about all I can tell you.
Cordially,

Jésus

Dear Monsieur,
There is something else I wanted to ask you about. There's someone I think might have written the postcard, and I'm also in possession of a letter written by that person.

Would it be possible for you to compare the writing on the postcard with a two-page letter?

Kind regards,

Anne

Dear Madame,
Yes, that is certainly possible, on one condition: the handwritten letter must date from the same period as the postcard. A person's handwriting changes every five years on average.

Cordially,

Jésus

Dear Monsieur,
The letter was sent in July 2002 and the postcard in January 2003, so just six months apart.

Kind regards,

Anne

Dear Madame,
Send it to me, and I'll see what I can do, if it's possible to determine any handwriting matches with the letter.
Cordially,

Jésus

Dear Monsieur,
Please find attached the handwritten letter, received in July 2002. Do you think it could have the same author as the postcard?
Many thanks,

Anne

J ésus had told me he would get back to me, but not for at least two weeks. In the meantime, I had to find something else to occupy myself: getting my work done, running errands, picking my daughter up from school and judo, making crêpes and after-school snacks, lunching with Georges, and keeping in touch with Gérard, who was back in Moscow. But mostly, I had to be patient.

And yet, everything seemed to lead back to the postcard. I remembered meeting Nathalie Zajde at Georges's house, the woman whose book he'd given me. She'd mentioned Yizkor books, or memorial books: "books compiled after World War Two, filled with the memories of people who had escaped before the war and the accounts and testimonies of those who had remained and survived, in order to preserve some record of Jewish communities." I thought of Noémie, of the novels she'd had in her that would never be written. And then I thought of all the books that had died along with their future authors in the gas chambers.

After the war, women in orthodox Jewish families had made it their mission to have as many children as possible to replenish the population—and it seemed to me that the same was true for books. That subconscious drive to write as many books as possible, to fill those places left empty on the library shelves, not just by the books burned during the war, but by the ones whose authors had died before they could write them.

I thought of Irène Némirovsky's two daughters who, as grown women, had unearthed the manuscript of *Suite Française* from beneath some clothes in an old suitcase. How many more forgotten books were there, hidden away in trunks and armoires?

I went for a walk in the Luxembourg Gardens and sat on a wrought-iron chair, soaking in the wistful charm of the park where the Rabinovitches had strolled so many times.

Suddenly there was a scent in the air of honeysuckle after rain, and I headed toward the Théâtre de l'Odéon, just like Myriam had on the day she put on five pairs of underwear and left to be smuggled across France in the trunk of a car. The posters in front of the theater today weren't for a Courteline play but one by Ibsen, *An Enemy of the People*, directed by Jean-François Sivadier. I walked down the rue de l'Odéon and the stairs of the narrow rue Dupuytren, which opens out onto the rue de l'École-de-Médecine. This took me past 21 rue Hautefeuille with its octagonal corner turret, where Myriam and Noémie Rabinovitch had spent hours dreaming of their future lives with Colette Grés. I strained my ears, trying to hear the long-ago voices of those little Jewish girls. A few meters further along the street, an information board explained: "The area of land delineated by the rue Hautefeuille between numbers 15 and 21, the rue de l'École-de-Médecine, the rue Pierre-Sarrazin, and the rue de la Harpe, was a Jewish cemetery during the Middle Ages, until 1310."

The past was calling out to me more and more urgently all the time.

I made my way through the streets of Paris, feeling as if I were wandering, tormented, through the corridors of a house too large for me. The next stop on my itinerary was the Lycée Fénelon, where I had spent two years doing my *hypokhâgne*.

Just as I used to do twenty years ago, I stepped from the bright sunlight of the rue Suger into the dim coolness of the school's entrance hall. Those two decades had gone by so fast. I hadn't known back then that Myriam and Noémie had been students here, and yet something in me had felt I *had* to study at Fénelon and nowhere else. "It speaks to me in a way others can't understand," the artist Louise Bourgeois had written of her years at the school. She'd written another phrase, too, one that had stayed with me always: "If your need is to refuse to abandon the past, you must recreate it."

Passing beneath the high wooden portico, I had never felt Myriam and Noémie so close to me. We'd felt the same emotions, the same young girl's desires, in this same schoolyard. The dark wooden clock with its hands wrought in the shape of a pair of scissors; the ancient chestnut trees in the courtyard with their dappled trunks; the wrought-iron banisters on the staircases—all these things had been the same for them as they were for me. I went upstairs to look out over the courtyard, and it seemed to me that the war was still here, everywhere, in the minds of the people who had lived through it and the ones who hadn't, the children of those who had fought, the grandchildren of those who had stood by and done nothing, who could have done more. The war continued to influence our actions, our destinies, our friendships, our loves. All roads led us back to the war. Its deflagrations still resonated within us.

It was here at Fénelon that I'd discovered my love of history, learned to study the factors that led to crisis, the triggering events. Causes and consequences. Like a game of dominoes, in which each piece causes the next one to topple. That was how I'd been taught about the logical sequencing of events, as if there were no random phenomena. And yet our lives were composed of nothing but clashes and fractures. And, to borrow Némirovsky's words, "we understand none of it."

I jumped as I felt a hand on my shoulder. "What are you looking for?" It was the school monitor.

"That's just it; I'm not sure," I answered. "I used to be a student here. I just wanted to see . . . if things had changed. I'll go now. Sorry."

I met Gérard Rambert at our usual Chinese restaurant, and we ordered the daily special as always.

"You know," Gérard remarked, "in 1956, the Cannes Film Festival announced that one of the films selected to represent France in competition for the Palme d'Or would be the Alain Resnais documentary *Night and Fog*. What do you think happened next?"

"I don't know . . ."

"Well, open those ears wide—though of course your ears are tiny; I've rarely seen such dainty ears, but anyway—listen to this. The West German Ministry of Foreign Affairs asked the French government to withdraw the film from competition. Can you believe that?"

"But for what reason?"

"Franco-German reconciliation! They claimed it was being jeopardized!"

"And did France withdraw the film?"

"Yes. Yes. I'll say it again: *yes*. Censorship, plain and simple."

"But I thought the film was shown at Cannes."

"Oh, it was! There were protests, naturally. They still showed the film, but it was no longer in the running for the Palme d'Or. And that's not all. The French Censorship Board demanded that a clip be deleted from the footage—a photograph where you can see a French policeman guarding the camp at Pithiviers. They didn't want to put too much emphasis on the fact that it was the French who helped to organize all of that.

"The thing is," Gérard continued, "after the war, people were sick of hearing about us. It was even the same at home. No one ever talked to me about what had happened during the war. Not ever. I remember one Sunday in the spring—my parents had invited a dozen or so people to the house. It was hot, and the women were in light dresses, the men in short sleeves. And I noticed something: all my parents' guests had a number tattooed on their left arm. Every single one of them. Michel, my mother's father's brother. Arlette, his wife. Both of them had those numbers. My mother's cousin and his wife, too. And Joseph Sterner, my mother's uncle. There I was, in the middle of all these old people, buzzing around like a mosquito. I'm sure I was annoying, running all over the place and staring at them. So Uncle Joseph decides to tease me a little, and he says to me, 'Hey! Your name's not Gérard.'

"'It's not? What is it, then?' I ask.

"'Your name is Supermalin,' he says. You know, like Superman, except he used the French *malin*, not 'man.' *Wiseass*, basically. And he had a Yiddish accent so thick you could cut it with a knife, so he put all the emphasis on that first syllable: *'SI-PER-ma-lin.'*

"Of course, I didn't take that very well, because I was a kid, and all kids take themselves too seriously. I didn't like Uncle Joseph's little joke at all. And suddenly I'd just had it with all these old people. So I decide to get my mother's attention, to have her all to myself for a minute, and I pull her aside, and I ask, 'Maman, why does Joseph have a number tattooed on his left arm?'

"She makes this face, sort of a frown, and tries to deflect the question. 'Can't you see I'm busy? Go away and play somewhere else, Gérard.'

"But I insist. 'Maman, it's not only Joseph. Why does EVERYONE here have a number tattooed on their left arm?'

"So my mother looks me right in the eye and says, without batting an eyelash: 'Those are their telephone numbers, Gérard.'

"'Their telephone numbers?'

"And then she starts nodding, to make it more convincing, and she says, 'Yes, their phone numbers. You see, they're quite elderly, so it's to help them remember.'

"'What a good idea!' I say.

"'There you go,' my mother says. 'Now, don't ever ask me that question again, Gérard. Do you understand?'

"And I believed my mother for *years*. For *years* I thought how nice it was that these elderly people wouldn't get lost in the street, thanks to their telephone number tattoos. Let's order an appetizer, shall we? They look delectable. Now, I'll tell you something—my whole life I was haunted by it. Every time I met someone, I'd wonder: victim, or perpetrator? Until I was around fifty-five. After that, I stopped thinking about it so much. And now I rarely ask myself the question—except when I meet a German of eighty-five or thereabouts, which doesn't happen too often, fortunately. Because they were all Nazis! All of them! *All* of them! And they *still* are! And they will be until they die! If I'd been twenty years old in 1945, I would have joined the Nazi hunters and dedicated my whole life to their cause. I tell you, it's better not to be Jewish in this world. It doesn't make you a lesser being, but it doesn't make you a greater one, either. Now, let's share a dessert. You pick."

My mother phoned me after I'd left Gérard. She wanted to show me something important, some papers she'd come across in her archives. She asked me to come over.

When I got to her office, she handed me two typewritten letters.

"We won't be able to have these analyzed," I said.

"Read," she replied simply. "You'll find them interesting."

The first letter was dated May 16, 1942. Two months before Jacques and Noémie were arrested.

Mamushka darling,

Just a quick note to tell you I've arrived safely. I can't write much just now, because I've been given an important task: filling in for someone who's absent!

(...)

Didn't you think No seemed very different? Far less sunny and cheerful than before. But I think she was glad to spend those 24 hours together, when I abandoned you so shamefully. It won't stop raining today—my poor bean patch! (...) You aren't angry with me for having spent so little time in dear old Pic Pic, are you? Anyway, big hugs, my darling, and I'll write a longer letter tonight.

Love,

Colette

The second letter was dated July 26, thirteen days after the Rabinovitch children's arrest.

Paris, July 23, 1942

Dear Maman,

Found your letter of the 21st when I got home. I'm typing this because it's twice as fast as writing, not that I want to rush my letter, but I've got a lot to do, really a whole lot. (...) Some bits of news:

Office: all sorts of arguments between Toscan and the rest of us; Etienne still going to Vincennes. (...)

Got a letter at noon from Monsieur and Madame Rabinovitch that made me very sad: No and her brother have been picked up like so many other Jews. Parents have heard nothing from them since. That was the same week I was supposed to go to Les Forges—you know, I think my lack of enthusiasm was a bad omen. I'm going to try and get in touch with Myriam. Poor little No is nineteen and her brother not yet seventeen. It was awful in Paris, people say; they were separating children,

278 · ANNE BEREST

married couples, mothers, etc. The only children they let stay with their mothers were those younger than three!

Wrote to Raymonde. Glad she's coming, because I've been a mess since the news from Les Forges.

Love,

Colette

The letter seemed so odd to me. "No and her brother have been picked up like so many other Jews. Parents have heard nothing from them since." Picked up? The term was baffling. As was the trivial, everyday nature of these letters. The carefully planned extermination of the Jews was casually tossed in amid mentions of rationing, rainstorms, and the family cat. I shared my impressions with my mother.

"You can't really judge people in the past from a modern perspective, you know. Our daily lives might seem glib and irresponsible to our descendants, too."

"I know you don't want me to judge Colette, but these letters only confirm my suspicions. Colette was deeply impacted by what happened to the Rabinovitches during the war. She felt guilty about it for the rest of her life."

Lélia raised her eyebrows. "Maybe," she murmured.

"Why won't you admit that it all fits? She wrote to you on the very same subject only six months before you received the postcard! Don't you think that's absolutely crazy?"

"It's a disturbing coincidence, I'll admit."

"But?"

"But it wasn't Colette who sent the postcard."

"Why do you keep saying that? How can you be so sure?"

"Because it just doesn't feel right. I don't know how to explain it. It's like you're telling me 2 plus 3 equals 4. You can tell me how well it fits until you're blue in the face, but it doesn't feel right. That's all. I just don't believe it."

CHAPTER 11

D ear Madame,
As we discussed on the telephone, the small number of words examined are not sufficient to reach
a definitive conclusion; however, we can confirm that these
few words do not seem to have come from the same writer as
the handwritten letter. We remain at your disposal should you
require any further information.
Cordially,

Jésus F.
Criminologist, Expert in Handwriting and Documents

Jésus and my mother were in agreement on this point. Colette
was not the author of the anonymous postcard.

I felt not only deep disappointment but also a kind of profound weariness.

I went back to my normal, everyday life, putting the whole
thing behind me. I would tuck Clara into her little bed and read
her the story of *Momo the Bad-Tempered Crocodile*, then lie in
my own bed, close my eyes, and listen to the upstairs neighbors
playing the piano, letting the music surround me. One night I
felt as if the notes were falling into my bedroom like a gentle rain.

As the days following Jésus's e-mail passed, I became more
and more depressed. Nothing interested me. I was cold all the
time, and only scalding-hot showers seemed to revive me. I didn't
meet Georges for lunch. I was exhausted. All I wanted to do was
go to the Cinémathèque Française and buy Jean Renoir films so
I could see Uncle Emmanuel in them. I was able to find *The Sad*

Sack and *Night at the Crossroads*, but not *The Little Match Girl*. Seeing his pseudonym, Manuel Raaby, in the credits was both surreal and deeply sad. After that I was seized with the overwhelming desire to sleep, as if I'd taken a sedative. I balled my sweater up beneath my head and thought about Emmanuel. I wanted to call Lélia and ask her the exact date and circumstances of his death. But I couldn't summon up the courage to do it.

The doorbell woke me.

Georges stood there in the shadowy doorway, holding a bouquet of flowers and a bottle of wine.

"Since you don't feel like going out. I had to do something, otherwise you'll end up missing me too much," he said, laughing.

I let him into my apartment, motioning for him to be quiet so as not to wake Clara, who was sleeping. We went into the kitchen to open the wine.

"Did you ever hear from Jésus?" he asked.

"Yes, and it wasn't Colette. Discouraged me a bit. I started thinking, what's the point of all this?"

"Don't give up. You need to see this through to the end."

"I thought you'd tell me to drop the whole thing."

"No. You've got to keep going. Keep believing in it."

"I'll never find the answers. I'll just waste hours and hours for no reason."

"I'm certain there's more to learn."

"What do you mean?"

"I don't even know. Just . . . pick it up where you left off. See where it leads you."

I opened my notebook and showed it to Georges.

"This is where I left off."

The page contained three columns. *Family. Friends. Neighbors.*

"Family . . . there was no one left. Friends . . . Colette was the only one. All I've got left are the neighbors."

CHAPTER 12

Y ou want to go and ask the people in the village what happened in the 1940s?"

"Yes. We'll go to Les Forges and question the neighbors. Ask them what they saw, what they remember."

"You honestly think we're going to find anyone who knew the Rabinovitches?"

"Of course! People who were kids in 1942 will be in their eighties now. They might remember some things. We'll go tomorrow morning, early, right after I drop Clara off at school."

The next morning, Lélia was waiting for me at the Porte d'Orléans in her little red Twingo, the radio playing the news at full blast. The car smelled of stale tobacco and perfume, a scent I'd known my whole life. To make room for myself in the front seat, I had to shove aside a pencil case, an old detective novel, a single glove, an empty paper coffee cup, and her handbag. *It's like Lieutenant Columbo's car*, I thought.

"Do you have the exact address of the house?"

"No," Lélia said. "I've got all kinds of documents about Les Forges in my archive, but none of them have the house number and street, believe it or not."

"It's okay; I'm sure we'll find it once we're there. It's a small village."

The drive would take an hour and twenty-seven minutes, the GPS informed us. The news on the radio was full of the European elections and the big national debate. Suddenly, the sky darkened. We focused on our mission. I turned down the volume on

282 · ANNE BEREST

the radio and began to speculate out loud about what might have become of the house in Les Forges once the Rabinovitch parents left it on an October day in 1942.

"They knew they were going to be arrested," I said. "They wanted to find their children in Germany. So before they left, they put the house in order and gave instructions to the neighbors. You always give a copy of your house key to someone you trust, don't you? If there was a spare key, it's got to be around somewhere."

Lélia nodded. "They gave one to the mayor."

She took advantage of my surprise to light a cigarette.

"To the *mayor*?" I repeated, coughing. "How do you know?"

"Look in the folder on the back seat, and you'll see."

I reached back and retrieved a green cardboard folder.

"Maman, at least roll down your window, or I'm going to throw up."

"I thought you'd started smoking again."

"No, I only do that so I can bear *your* smoking. Open the window!"

The folder held photocopied papers that my mother had obtained when she was putting together her case for the Matteoli Commission. I took out a sheet of paper on the Les Forges town hall letterhead, handwritten by Monsieur le Maire himself. It was a letter dated October 21, 1942, twelve days after Ephraïm and Emma's arrest.

The Mayor's Office
To the Director of Agricultural Services of Eure

Dear Monsieur,
It's my privilege to inform you that after the arrest of the Rabinovitch family, I have proceeded to close up the residence and have retained the keys. I have subsequently drawn up, in the presence of a representative of the recently appointed

municipal property management company, a basic inventory of the household goods. The two remaining pigs are currently in the custody of Monsieur Jean Fauchère, along with the grain located on the premises. However, this situation will not remain tenable for long, as Fauchère, a farm laborer, is asking for a daily allowance of 70 francs (he is currently threshing barley by hand). Moreover, in the garden there are some fruits and vegetables which should be made use of. In order to liquidate the property, an official administrator must be appointed.

I would be grateful for some guidance on your part, as the prefecture has informed me that it is not currently able to resolve the present abnormal situation.

With thanks in advance and my sincere best wishes,

The Mayor

The mayor's handwriting was ostentatiously ornate, the capital Ds embellished with slightly ridiculous curlicues and the Es finished with complicated scrollwork.

"Such a pretty way to write such horrors."

"He must have been a real jackass."

"Maman, we've got to find the descendants of this Jean Fauchère."

"Read the next letter. It's the reply from the Director of Agricultural Services of Eure, who reacted immediately—the next day, in fact. He wrote to the prefecture."

REPUBLIC OF FRANCE
Director of Agricultural Services of Eure
To the distinguished Prefect of Eure (3rd division)
ÉVREUX

Monsieur,
I am attaching a letter in which His Honor the Mayor of Les Forges informs me that he desires to liquidate the property

of the Jewish RABINOVITCH household, which previously resided in his municipality, through the appointment of an official administrator responsible for upkeep of the home belonging to the aforementioned household.

Being wholly incapable of assuming responsibility for this situation, which my office is not equipped to handle, I can only ask that you give His Honor the Mayor of Les Forges the instructions he is requesting.

The Director

"The authorities just kept passing the situation around like a hot potato."

"Yes. No one seems to have wanted to reply to the mayor of Les Forges. Not the prefecture, not the director of agricultural services."

"Why was that, do you think?"

"They were overloaded with work. They didn't have time to worry about a couple of pigs and some apple trees belonging to the 'Jewish Rabinovitch household.'"

"Don't you find it strange that they were raising pigs even though they were Jewish?"

"Oh, they didn't care about that! This thing about not eating pork, *honestly*." Lélia rolled her eyes. "Fresh meat didn't keep well in hot climates during Biblical times; it could be deadly—but that was two thousand years ago! And Ephraïm wasn't religious."

"You know, I wonder if the agricultural director refused to deal with the Rabinovitch farm as a kind of resistance. It would have been one way to keep anything from getting done."

"You're such an optimist. God knows where you got that from."

"Quit saying that! I'm not an optimist at all! I just think you have to look at both sides of the coin. You know, one of the most fascinating things about this whole story, to me, is thinking that in a single government, the French government, good people and totally evil ones could be operating side by side. Take Jean Moulin and Maurice Sabatier. They were members of the same generation; they had similar educations; they both became civil servants and had similar career paths. But one of them became head of the Resistance and the other a prefect under the Vichy government and supervisor of Maurice Papon. One's buried in the Panthéon, and the other was convicted of crimes against humanity. What determines that? Maman, I swear—put out that cigarette or we're both going to suffocate!"

My mother threw the still-burning stub of her cigarette out the window. I bit back an irritated remark.

"Look at the third letter in the folder," she told me. "As you'll see, the mayor of Les Forges didn't sit around twiddling his thumbs. He took the matter in hand and went to the prefecture of Évreux himself. And in return he received this letter, dated November 24, 1942—an entire month later."

> General Administration and Police Services Office
> Control of Foreigners Division
> Reference: Rabinovitch 2239/EJ
> Évreux, November 24, 1942
> His Honor the Mayor of Les Forges
>
> Monsieur,
> Following your visit of last November 17 to the General Foreigners Office, it is my pleasure to inform you that I hereby authorize you to sell as general supply the two pigs belonging to the Jew Rabinovitch interned last October 8. Please contact the quartermaster-general for general supply, Amey Barracks, Évreux, to make these arrangements. Please direct the profits of this sale to the provisional administrator to be named in the near future.

"There was a provisional administrator for Emma and Ephraïm's property?"

"Named in December to handle the matter of the Rabino-vitches' gardens and land."

"Did he live in the house?"

"No, no. It was the land that was recouped—spoliated, if you prefer—for Germany by the French government, like all businesses belonging to Jews, and then given to French entre-preneurs. In the case of the Rabinovitches, the role of the provi-sional administrator was to hire workers to manage the land, but they didn't go into the house."

"Then what happened to the house?"

"After the war, Myriam decided to sell it. Quickly. Without setting foot there herself. It was too painful for her. Everything was handled by attorneys and agents. This was in 1955. After that, she never mentioned Les Forges again. But I knew the house existed. I was eleven when she sold it. I must have over-heard some snippets of conversation, I suppose . . . at any rate, I certainly knew that my unknown relatives, this family of ghosts, had lived in a village called 'Les Forges.' It was always there in the back of my mind, and it must have troubled me—kind of like it's bothering you now—because in 1974, when I was thirty, fate led me to that village.

"We were a family of three back then: your father, your big sister, and me. Our group of friends practically lived together; we always traveled as a pack. Anyway, one weekend we ended up at the family home of one of our buddies, near Évreux. I bought a Michelin map, and, suddenly, following the road with a pencil, I saw the name Les Forges—only about eight kilometers from where we were. It was a shock, as you can probably imagine. The village wasn't just a name; it wasn't a myth. It really existed. That Saturday night, there was a big party at our friends' house. It was a great time, lots of people, but I was distracted. All of a sudden I couldn't stop thinking about the fact that I could actually go to

Les Forges, just like that. Just to see it. I lay awake all that night, and in the morning I got in my car and just started driving. It was like some force was guiding me—I didn't get lost; I turned at the right place and stopped in front of a house at random. I rang the bell on the garden gate, and a woman came out after just a few seconds—an older woman, with a nice, friendly face and white hair. She made a good impression on me right away.

"'Excuse me, I'm looking for the house that belonged to the Rabinovitches, who lived in Les Forges during the war. Does that name mean anything to you? Would you by any chance know where I might be able to find the house?'

"She looked at me with the strangest expression on her face. She actually turned white. And she said, 'Are you Myriam Picabia's daughter?'

"I couldn't even move. I just stood there, staring at this woman. She knew exactly what I was talking about, and for good reason. She was the person who bought the house in 1955."

"Wait, Maman. Are you actually telling me that the first house you stopped at, totally at random, turned out to be your grandparents' house? Just like that? Are you kidding me?"

"I know it seems impossible, but that's what happened. I told her that yes, I was Myriam's daughter, that I was spending the weekend not far from there with my husband and daughter, and that I'd wanted to see the village where my grandparents had lived.

"'But I don't want to disturb you,' I said.

"'Not at all! Please, come in. I'm so happy to meet you.'

"She said it very sweetly, very politely. I stepped into the front garden, and I remember that when I saw the front of the house everything got sort of foggy, and my knees turned weak, and I felt really ill. The lady sat me down in the living room with a cold glass of orangeade. I think she understood why I was so emotional. I felt better pretty quickly, and we talked, and eventually I asked her the same question you're asking me this morning: what condition was the house in when you took possession of it? And this is what she said:

"'I bought the house in 1955. The first time I looked at it, I noticed that some furniture and things were missing; you could sense that it had been emptied of anything of value. And then, when I came back on the actual moving day, I saw that people had come, in the meantime, and taken more things. They must have done it quickly because chairs were overturned, that sort of thing. You know—like thieves, acting in a hurry. I remember vividly that a very beautiful framed photograph of the house, which had caught my eye on my previous visit, had disappeared. You could still see the rectangular outline on the wall where it had been, and the empty hook it had hung from.'

"Everything the woman said was like a knife in my heart. Those were our memories they had stolen. My mother's memories. Our family's memories.

"'The few things I was able to keep,' the woman told me, 'are in a trunk in the attic. If you would like it, it's yours.'

"I followed her up to the attic like a robot. I couldn't believe what was happening. All these years, these things had been waiting here, patiently, for someone to come looking for them. When she opened the trunk, I broke down in tears. It was just too much.

"'I'll come back for the trunk another day,' I said.

"'Are you sure?' she asked.

"'Yes, I want to come back with my husband.'

"The woman walked me to the door, but just as I was leaving, she said, 'Wait, there is something I'd like you to take now.'

"She went into another room and came back with a little painting in her hands, no bigger than an average sheet of paper. It was a gouache of a glass carafe, a little still life in a rustic wooden frame. It was signed 'Rabinovitch.' And I recognized Myriam's pointed, elegant handwriting. My mother had painted it, back when she lived here, happy, surrounded by her parents and her brother and her sister Noémie. I've kept it with me ever since."

"Did you go back for the trunk?"

"Of course! A few weeks later, with your father. I didn't say anything to my mother right then. I wanted it to be a surprise."

"Oh, dear. What a *terrible* idea."

"The *worst* idea," Lélia agreed. "I went down to Céreste that summer to spend a month with Myriam, and I brought the trunk with me. I was so proud and emotional about being able to give her such a treasure. Her whole face changed, and she opened the trunk without saying a word. Then she closed it immediately and put it in the basement. All in total silence. At the end of that month, before going back to Paris, I took a few things from the trunk with me. A tablecloth, a drawing of her sister, and the few photographs that are in my archive. Some administrative documents. Nothing much. When Myriam died in 1995, I looked for the trunk in Céreste. It was empty."

"You think she threw it all out?"

"Burned it. Gave it away. Who knows."

A few fat, heavy drops of rain plunked against the windshield of the car with a loud noise, like marbles. We arrived in Les Forges in torrential rain.

"Do you remember where the house was?"

"Not very well. I think it was on the way out of the village, toward the forest. We'll see if I can find it as easily now as I did the first time."

The sky was black with rain clouds, dark as twilight. We tried to clear the fogged-up windshield with the sleeves of our sweaters. The windshield wipers had become useless. We drove in circles, Lélia not recognizing anything in the village, always ending up back where we'd started, like in a nightmare where you never find the exit from the roundabout. And the rain lashed down all the while.

We reached a street made up of a single row of no more than five or six houses across from a field.

"I think this might be the street," Lélia said suddenly. "I remember that there were no houses opposite."

"Hang on, I see a sign: 'rue du Petit Chemin.' Does that sound familiar?"

"Yes—I think that was the name of the street! And I think this is the house," my mother said, pulling up in front of number 9. "I remember it was almost at the end of the row, not the house on the corner, but the one before it."

"I'll see if there's a name on the front gate."

I got out of the car in the rain and ran to look at the name next to the bell. We hadn't brought any umbrellas with us, and I came back utterly soaked.

"'Mansois.' Was that the name?"

"No. There was an *x* in it, I'm sure."

"Maybe this isn't the right place."

"I have an old photo of the front of the house among those papers in the folder. Have a look; we'll compare them."

"How are we going to do that? The fence is too tall. You can't see anything."

"Climb up on the roof," Lélia suggested.

"The roof of the house?"

"No! Climb onto the roof of the car! That way you'll be able to see over the fence."

"No way, Maman, I'm not doing that! What if someone sees us?"

"Come on," Lélia coaxed, the same way she used to do when I was little and didn't want to pee on the side of the road during long car journeys.

I opened the car door and, using the passenger seat as a step, hoisted myself onto the roof. Standing up was difficult; the rain had made the metal slippery as ice.

"Well?" my mother called.

"It's definitely the right house, Maman!"

"Go ring the bell!" shouted Lélia, who had never given me an order in my whole life.

Completely drenched, I clambered down and rang the bell on the gate of number 9 several times. I found myself deeply moved to be standing in front of the Rabinovitch home. It seemed to me that, behind the gate, the house knew I was there, and it was waiting for me, smiling.

I stood there for long moments. Nothing happened.

"I don't think anyone's home," I called to Lélia, disappointed.

But suddenly there came the sound of barking, and the gate of number 9 opened a crack. A woman of about fifty appeared. Her shoulder-length hair was dyed blonde, her face plump and slightly flushed. She spoke angrily to the barking, gamboling dogs, and despite the wide smile I gave her to assure her of my good intentions, her expression remained wary. The dogs, German shepherds, swarmed around her legs, and she snapped at them again to be quiet, clearly fed up with her own pets. I wondered why some dog owners spent all their time complaining, when nobody was forcing them to have dogs in the first place. I also wondered whether I was more afraid of the woman or her German shepherds.

"Was it you who rang the bell?" she asked sharply, darting a glance at my mother's car.

"Yes," I said, trying to keep smiling despite the rain pouring onto my head and down the back of my neck. "Our family lived in this house during the war. They sold the house in the '50s, and we were wondering if we could—without bothering you, of course—maybe just have a look around the garden? To see what it was like?"

The woman stepped into the open gateway, blocking my path. She was large, and I couldn't see around her to get a glimpse of the house. She frowned. Now I was the one she was fed up with.

"This house belonged to my great-grandparents," I tried

again. "They lived here during the war. The Rabinovitches. Does that name mean anything to you?"

She recoiled slightly, staring at me, her mouth twisting as if I'd just waved something foul-smelling under her nose.

"Wait here," she said, closing the gate.

The German shepherds started barking loudly again, and the other dogs in the neighborhood took up the call, as if they were warning the residents of our presence in the village. I stood there in the rain for a long time. It was like taking an endless ice-cold shower. But I was willing to do anything to see the garden Nachman had planted. The well he and Jacques had dug. Every stone of the house where the Rabinovitches had been so happy before their disappearance.

After a while I heard footsteps on the gravel again, and the woman opened the gate. It was Marine Le Pen she reminded me of, I realized. She carried a large, incongruous flowery umbrella that again blocked my view of the house. There was someone else behind her, a man, wearing green plastic Wellington boots.

"What is it that you want, exactly?" she asked me.

"Just . . . to see . . . our family used to live here . . ."

I didn't have time to finish my sentence before the man spoke to me. He looked older than the woman, and I wondered whether he was her father or her husband.

"Look here, you don't just show up at people's houses like this! We bought this place twenty years ago. It's our home now," he spat at me, rudely. "Next time, call first. Sabine, close the gate. Goodbye, Madame."

Sabine slammed the gate in my face. I stood there without moving, and sadness swept through me so overpoweringly that I dissolved into tears that didn't show, thanks to the rain already streaking my cheeks.

My mother settled herself more comfortably in her seat and stared straight ahead with grim determination.

"We'll question the other neighbors," she said. "We're going to find the people who stole from us."

"Stole?"

"Yes. Whoever took the furniture, and the artwork, and all the rest! It has to be around here somewhere!"

She rolled down the window to light a cigarette as she spoke, but the driving rain kept putting out her lighter.

"Where to next?"

"Those two houses look like someone's at home."

"Yes," she murmured thoughtfully.

"Which one should we start with?"

"Let's take number 1," Lélia said. I knew she'd picked that one because it was the house farthest from the car, which meant she'd have time to finish her cigarette on the way.

We sat there for a few more moments, summoning our courage and shaking off the unpleasantness of our first encounter, and then we both got out of the car.

At number 1, a woman came out to the gate. She was friendly and seemed around seventy, but she probably looked younger than she was. Her hair was dyed red, and she wore a leather motorcycle jacket and a red bandana around her neck.

"Hello, Madame—we're sorry to bother you, but we're looking for people who might remember our family. They lived on this street, at number 9, during the war. Do you, by any chance know—"

"During the war, you say?"

"Yes, they lived in Les Forges until 1942."

"The Rabinovitches?" she asked. Her voice was deep and gravelly, a smoker's voice.

It was so strange to hear this woman say the Rabinovitch name, as if she'd just bumped into them that morning.

"That's right," my mother said. "Do you remember them?"

"Very well," the woman replied, with unnerving simplicity.

"Would you mind if we came in?" Lélia asked. "Just for five minutes, just to talk?"

Suddenly the woman seemed hesitant. It was obvious that she didn't want to let us into her home. But, equally clearly, she didn't feel she could refuse us, as descendants of the Rabinovitches. She asked us to wait in the living room—but told us not to sit on her sofa in our soaking-wet coats.

"I'm just going to tell my husband," she said.

I took advantage of her absence to have a quick glance around the room—but she returned startlingly quickly, making us jump, with a couple of towels.

"It's to protect the sofa. I hope you don't mind. I'll make some tea," she said, disappearing into the kitchen.

When she came back, she was carrying a tray laden with steaming cups, English-style china with pink and blue flowers.

"I have these same cups at home," Lélia said, which made the woman smile. My mother has always known instinctively how to win people over.

"I knew the Rabinovitches. I remember them very well," the woman said, offering us the sugar bowl. "Once, the maman—I'm sorry, I don't remember her first name—"

"Emma."

"That was it. Emma. She gave me some strawberries from her garden. I thought she was very nice. Was she *your* maman, then?" she asked Lélia.

"My grandmother. Do you have any more . . . precise memories? I would be so interested to hear them."

"I remember the strawberries," the woman mused. "I loved strawberries. The ones from her garden were lovely. And they had a vegetable garden, and these magnificent espaliered apple trees. And I remember sometimes we'd hear music out in our garden. Your maman was a pianist, wasn't she?"

"My grandmother. Yes." Lélia corrected her again. "Did she give piano lessons in the village, maybe? Does that ring a bell?"

"No . . . I was very little. Those memories are quite hazy."

The woman looked at us.

"I was four or five when they were arrested."

She was quiet again for a moment.

"But my mother told me something."

She looked into her teacup, remembering.

"When the police came to arrest them, my mother saw the children come out of the house. When they got into the car, they were singing 'La Marseillaise.' She never forgot that. She used to mention it often: 'Those little ones were taken away singing "La Marseillaise."'"

Who would have told them to stop? Not the Germans, and not the French. No one would dare demean the national anthem that way. The young Rabinovitches had found a way to defy their killers. Suddenly it was as if we could hear them singing, faintly, outside in the street.

"There were some things that vanished from the house. A piano. Do you remember anything about that?" I asked.

The woman was silent for a few more moments.

"I remember the apple trees," she said again. "They were espaliered all along the wall."

She looked down at her teacup again, still pensive.

"We were occupied by the Germans during the war, you know. They were at the Château de la Trigall. There was also a teacher who disappeared."

She seemed to be rambling now, as if her brain had become fatigued.

"Yes," I prompted her.

"The current owners—they're very nice," she said, looking at us as if someone were listening, someone we couldn't see.

Her voice had changed, becoming higher, almost childlike, and I could see in her face the little girl she had been, seventy years earlier, eating strawberries from Emma's garden. Was this a deliberate act?

"Let us explain why we're here. A few years ago, we received a strange postcard in the mail, a postcard that said things about our family. We're wondering if someone from the village might have sent it."

I saw something spark in the woman's eyes. She was no fool. I could almost hear the wheels turning in her mind as she made a series of mental decisions. She seemed caught between two urges. She didn't want to take this conversation any further, or be backed into a corner. But a kind of moral uprightness compelled her to answer our questions.

"I'll just go and get my husband," she said abruptly.

The gentleman himself entered the room at that exact moment, like an actor who'd been waiting in the wings for his cue. Had he been listening to our conversation from behind the door? I was sure he had.

"My husband," the woman said by way of introduction. He was significantly shorter than her, his hair and mustache snow-white, his eyes a piercing blue.

He sat down on the loveseat silently, his eyes on us. He was waiting for something to happen, but we didn't know what.

"My husband's from Béarn," the woman said. "He didn't grow up here. But he's always been interested in history in general, so he's done some research on the village of Les Forges during the war. He might be able to answer any questions better than I could."

The husband immediately took over.

"The village of Les Forges, like most villages in France, particularly northern France, was profoundly affected by the war. Families were divided; many suffered bereavements. It's hard to imagine how difficult it must have been for people to recover from all that, almost impossible to put ourselves in their shoes, in the context of the time. We can't judge their actions. Do you know what I mean?"

The man spoke thoughtfully, deliberately, with a certain wisdom.

"Les Forges was also deeply shaken by the Roberte affair. You know of it, I'm sure."

"No. We've never heard of it."

"Roberte Lambal? No? There's a street named after her. You should go and see it; it's very interesting."

"Would you tell us the story?"

"If you like," he said, hitching up his trouser legs and settling himself more comfortably on the loveseat. "In August 1944, if I remember correctly, a group of Resistance fighters from Évreux killed two Nazi soldiers. This was a very serious matter to the Germans, of course. The Resistance fighters fled Évreux and came here to Les Forges, where they were taken in and hidden by an elderly lady named Roberte, a widow aged seventy—which was very old in those days—who lived alone on a little farm with her goats and chickens. After a few days, someone in the village informed on her to the Germans. Another resident learned of this and came running to the farm to warn the Resistance fighters to clear out immediately. They wanted to take Roberte with them, because they knew the Germans would interrogate her, but she refused. She wouldn't say anything, she promised; all she wanted was to stay on her farm and look after her animals. And besides, she said, she was much too old to flee into the forest. So the Resistance fighters left without her. And hardly had they gone when the Germans came storming onto the farm, with cars and motorcycles and machine guns. There were probably fifteen of them surrounding poor Roberte. They asked her where she was hiding the Resistance fighters. She said she didn't know what they were talking about. So they turned the farm upside down, and eventually they found the radio transmitter the Resistance fighters had hidden among some bales of hay in the barn. They beat old Roberte to make her confess, but she wouldn't say a word. Then another car arrived. A patrol had managed to capture one of the Resistance fighters, with his armband and his rifle. Gaston. They tried to pit him and Roberte

298 · ANNE BEREST

against one another, but neither one would talk; neither would admit anything; neither would say where the other Resistance fighter had gone; neither would give names. The Germans tied Gaston to a tree and tortured him. They took turns beating him, but he would not talk. They tore out his fingernails. Still nothing. In the meantime, they ordered Roberte to cook a meal for them, with her chickens and goats, and the wine from her cellar, and all the food in the house. She was forced to set up a banquet table in front of the tree where Gaston was tied, bloody and mutilated from the torture. Then the Germans spent the evening eating and drinking, being waited on by Roberte. Every so often one of them would hit her, and she'd fall down, which the Nazis thought was very funny. The next morning, Gaston, who had spent the night tied to the tree, still wouldn't talk, so they untied him at dawn and took him into the woods, where they made him dig a grave, and then they buried him alive. After that they went back to Roberte's house and told her what they'd done to Gaston, and threatened to hang her if she didn't talk. But she stayed strong. She refused to say what she knew about the Resistance fighters. The German sergeant went mad with rage that this obstinate old lady wouldn't talk and ordered that she be hung from the tree. The men put a rope around her neck and strung her up, and before she was completely dead, while her legs were still kicking, the sergeant finished her off with a machine gun, to get his revenge. And that's the story."

"Do you know who it was from the village that informed on Roberte?"

Stressing this point, I knew, was like stirring up a sludge-filled pond. It might dislodge things buried deep in the muck.

"No. No one knows who betrayed her," the man answered, before his wife could speak.

"Has your wife told you why we're here, exactly?"

"Explain it to me."

"We received an anonymous postcard about our family, and

we're trying to find out if it could have been written by someone from the village."

"May I see it?"

The old man examined the photo on my phone silently, carefully.

"And this postcard is a kind of betrayal; is that how you see it?"

He'd asked the right question.

"The fact that it's anonymous does make us feel a bit strange about it."

"I understand completely," the man said, nodding.

"That's why we're wondering if there was anyone in Les Forges who might have been particularly close to the Germans."

This remark visibly disturbed him. He grimaced.

"Does it bother you to talk about it?"

Now it was his wife's turn to step in. They were protective of one another, these two.

"As my husband has said, no one wants to revisit the past. But there were some very good people in the village."

"Yes—some very good people," the man repeated. "There was the schoolteacher."

"No—he wasn't the teacher; he was *married* to the teacher," his wife corrected him. "He worked for the prefecture."

"Can you tell us anything else about him?" my mother asked.

"He lived here in the village, but he worked in Évreux. At the prefecture. I don't know which department—it wasn't a high-ranking position, I don't think, but he had access to information. And when he had the opportunity to help people, to warn them, he did it. He was a very good guy."

"Is he still alive?"

"Oh, no. Someone informed on him," the woman said, tears filling her eyes. "He died before the war ended."

"He fell into a trap," her husband clarified. "Two vigilantes went to see him and said, 'We hear you know how to get people

300 · ANNE BEREST

to England. The police are looking for us. Help us.' So he arranged a rendezvous with them, to save them, but when he got there, the Germans were waiting to arrest him."

"What year was this, do you know?"

"1944, I believe. He was taken to Compiègne, and then to the concentration camp at Mauthausen, in Germany, where he died."

"How did the teacher cope after the war?"

The woman looked down. When she spoke again, her voice was soft.

"She was our village teacher, and we loved her very much, you understand. Right after the war, that was all anyone could talk about. The informers. Everything that had happened. But then, after a while, everyone decided it was better to move on. Our teacher, too. But she never remarried."

Her voice quivered, and she was close to tears again.

"I just want to ask you one last thing," I said. "Do you think there's anyone left in the village who would have known the Rabinovitches? People who remember them and could tell us about them?"

The husband and wife looked at each other, as if an unspoken question were passing between them. They knew much more than they were saying. I had no doubt of that.

"Yes," the woman said, dabbing at her eyes. "I can think of someone."

"Who's that?" her husband asked nervously.

"Monsieur and Madame François."

"Oh—of course, yes. Them."

"Madame François's mother was the Rabinovitches' housekeeper," the woman explained.

"Really? Can you tell us where she lives?"

The husband reached for a block of Post-It notes and wrote down the address. Handing us the slip of paper, he said, "Tell her you found her in the phone book. And now we'll walk you out, as we both have a lot to do."

The Post-It had given me an idea.

Maybe I could ask Jésus to analyze the handwriting.

When we emerged from the house, the sky was blue again. Bright sunlight reflected off the puddles in the street, blinding us. We walked to the car in silence.

"Give me the Françoises' address," I said to my mother.

We keyed the address into the GPS on my phone and followed the arrows. We both felt as if something was unfolding almost in spite of us, something that simmered beneath the phony calm of the village.

We parked the car and rang the bell at the address the man had given us. A short-haired woman in a geometrically patterned blue apron came out to the gate.

"Hello, are you Madame François?" I asked.

She looked surprised. "Yes, that's me."

"I'm sorry to bother you, but we're trying to find people who might remember our family. They lived in this village during the war. You might have known them. Rabinovitch was the name."

The woman's face froze. Her eyes darted back and forth.

"What do you want, exactly?" she asked. It wasn't suspicion I saw in her eyes; it was more like fear. Fear of something that had nothing to do with us.

"Just to know if you remember them, if you can tell us anything about them."

"For what reason?"

"We're their descendants. And since we didn't know them, we'd really like to have a few stories about them, that's all."

The woman had backed away from the gate. I got the sense that we weren't taking the right tack with her.

"I'm sorry—we've probably come at a bad time," I said. "Could you just give us your contact information? Maybe we could meet up again another day."

Madame François seemed relieved by my suggestion.

"Of course," she said. "That will give me a little more time to think."

"Here," I said, "you can use this." I rummaged in my bag and then held out my notebook, open to a blank page. "Would you mind just writing down your name and telephone number? That way, whenever you're ready . . ."

She didn't seem thrilled by the idea, but she clearly wanted to get rid of us as quickly as possible. She scribbled her last name, address, and telephone number in the notebook.

An old gentleman, probably her husband, had come into the garden. He was obviously disturbed by the sight of his wife talking to two strangers at the front gate. He had a cloth napkin tied around his neck.

"Hey ho, what's going on, Myriam?" he asked the woman.

Lélia's gaze flew to meet mine. My face went slack with shock. I knew the woman could see our thunderstruck expressions.

"Your . . . your first name is Myriam?" my mother asked, haltingly.

But instead of replying, the woman spoke to her husband.

"They're descendants of the Rabinovitch family. They have a few questions."

"We're eating. It's not a good time."

"We can speak later, on the phone," the woman said. She seemed terrified of her husband, who clearly wanted to get back to his lunch.

But my mother persisted. "We know it's terribly impolite to bother you at lunchtime, but I'm sure you can imagine—it's quite emotional for us to meet a Myriam in the village of Les Forges . . ."

"I'm coming," the woman said to her husband. "Take the potatoes out of the oven before they burn, and I'll be right there."

The husband turned immediately back into the house. The woman spoke to us very quickly, all in one breath. All we could see of her through the crack in the barely opened gate was her mouth and one eye.

"My mother worked for them. They were a wonderful family, you know; I can tell you that for sure. Believe me, they treated my mother like no other employer ever treated her; she told me that all her life. They were people who made music—the lady, especially, and my mother decided to name me Myriam because of them—I mean, not *because* of them, but you know what I mean. She called me Myriam because I was her oldest daughter, and their oldest daughter was named Myriam. So that's the story. Now I have to go; my husband will be angry."

Her recitation finished, she closed the gate without saying goodbye. My mother and I stood there silently, unmoving.

"Let's grab something to eat. I saw a bakery just past the town hall," I said to Lélia. "My head is spinning."

"Okay."

We sat in the car and ate our sandwiches, still dazed by what had just happened. Both of us chewed silently, staring into space.

"Let's go over everything," I proposed finally, taking out my notebook. "So, the new owners of number 9 have nothing to do with our family. No one was home at number 7."

"We'll have to try them again after lunch."

"Nobody home at number 3, either."

"And then there was the strawberry lady at number 1."

"Do you think it could have been her who sent the postcard?"

"Anything's possible. We can compare her writing to the postcard."

"It might also have been the husband."

"You think they did it together? Jésus did say it might not have been the same person who wrote on the right and left sides of the postcard. It would make sense . . ."

I retrieved the Post-It on which the man had written down the François' address.

"I'll send these to Jésus; we'll see what he thinks. I've got Myriam's handwriting, too."

"*That* whole thing was so strange," my mother mused.

Just then we heard Lélia's phone ringing in the bottom of her handbag.

"Blocked number," she said nervously.

I took the phone from her and answered it.

"Hello? Hello?"

All I could hear was the faint sound of someone breathing. Then the call was cut off. I looked at Lélia, surprised. The phone rang again. I put it on loudspeaker.

"Hello? I'm listening. Hello?"

"Go to Monsieur Fauchère's home. You'll find the piano there," said a voice, before hanging up.

My mother and I stared at each other, wide-eyed.

"Does that name sound familiar to you? Fauchère?" I asked.

"Of course it does! Read the letter from the mayor of Les Forges again."

I seized the folder and pulled out the letter.

> Dear Monsieur,
>
> It's my privilege to inform you that after the arrest of the Rabinovitch family, (. . .) The two remaining pigs are currently in the custody of Monsieur Jean Fauchère, along with the grain located on the premises.

"We should have thought of this. We were just talking about it in the car."

"Look in the White Pages. Maybe we can find this Fauchère's address. We definitely have to go see him."

I glanced in the rearview mirror. I couldn't shake the vague feeling that someone was watching us. I got out of the car to walk a bit, breathe some fresh air. A car started up behind me. I searched the White Pages on my phone. There was no trace of a Jean Fauchère, but when I searched again without the first name, an address appeared on my screen.

"What have you got?" my mother asked, seeing my face.

"Monsieur Fauchère, 11 rue du Petit Chemin. That's where we just came from."

Lélia started the car, and we retraced our journey, our hearts hammering as if we were deliberately heading toward something very dangerous.

"If we say we're members of the Rabinovitch family, they'll never let us in."

"We'll have to make something up. But what? Any ideas?"

"No."

"Okay . . . we'll have to think of . . . a reason for him to take us into his living room and show us his piano . . ."

"We could say we're piano collectors," my mother suggested.

"No, that'll make him suspicious. What if we said we were antiquarians? That's it—that we provide expert assessments of antique objects, and that he might be interested . . ."

"What if he says no?"

I rang the bell at a gate with a nameplate that said "Fauchère." A man came out of the house. He was elderly but still handsome, his clothes crisply ironed. Suddenly the street seemed too quiet, too empty.

"Hello," he said affably.

He was impeccably groomed and clean-shaven, his hair neatly combed and his cheeks shining with some undoubtedly expensive moisturizing cream. I spotted a strange, extremely ugly sculpture in his garden. That gave me an idea.

"Hello, Monsieur," I said. "We're sorry to bother you, but we work for the Centre Pompidou in Paris. Perhaps you know it?"

"It's a museum, I believe," he said.

"Yes. We're planning a major exhibition of a modern artist. You have some interest in art, it looks like."

"Yes," he said, running a hand through his hair. "Well, I'm just a fan . . ."

"Then you might like to know what we're looking for. Our

artist works from old photographs. Photographs taken in the 1930s, to be precise."

My mother was nodding along with everything I said, looking the man right in the eye.

"And our job at the moment is to find photographs from that period for him, in flea markets, antique shops, private homes . . ."

The man listened attentively. His knitted brows and crossed arms indicated, however, that he wasn't the type to swallow just any old nonsense.

"For his installation, our artist needs a lot of photos from the era—"

"—we're paying anywhere from two to three thousand euros for the right photos," put in my mother. I stared at her, astonished.

"Really?" asked the man, surprised. "What kind of photos, exactly?"

"Oh, they can be landscapes, pictures of monuments, or just family photographs," I said. "But only from the 1930s."

"We pay cash," added my mother.

"Well," the man said, smiling, "I know I have some photos in the house that date from those years. I can show them to you, if you like."

He smoothed back his hair again. His teeth were extraordinarily white.

"Wait here, please," he said, ushering us into the living room. "I'll just go and have a look; everything's in my office."

We saw it right away. The piano. A magnificent rosewood grand piano. It had been made into a piece of decorative furniture, an assortment of porcelain knick-knacks on a lace table runner sitting on top of its closed lid. We couldn't tell if it was a baby grand piano, a parlor grand, or some other size—but it was definitely far too substantial to belong to a casual player. A person would have to be a dedicated pianist to own and play a piano like that. It was majestic, its teardrop-shaped pedals gilded, the letters PLEYEL delicately sculpted into the wood. The white ivory and black ebony keys seemed to be in original—and splendid—condition. It seemed to me that I saw Emma's ghost, seated on the piano bench with her back to us, turn around and whisper, "At last, you've come."

Monsieur Fauchère came into the room. He was visibly surprised—and displeased—to see us examining his piano.

"This is a beautiful piano you've got. It looks quite old," I said, struggling to hide my emotion.

"Nice, isn't it?" he agreed. "Here, I've found several photos you might be interested in."

"Is it a family piano?" my mother asked.

"Er, yes," he said awkwardly. "Look—these photos date from the 1930s, and they were taken in the village. I think you'll find them interesting."

He seemed very pleased with his find, grinning widely, those bright white teeth on full display. He handed us a box containing about twenty photographs. They were photos of the Rabinovitches' house, photos of the Rabinovitches' garden, the Rabinovitches' flowers, the Rabinovitches' animals. My mother, I saw, was reeling. I felt sick. The presence of the piano behind us was almost unbearable.

"I have a framed one, as well. I'll get it."

At the bottom of the box, my mother saw a photo of Jacques, taken in front of the well during the summer when Nachman had come to help plant the garden. Jacques was gripping the handles of his wheelbarrow proudly, standing there in his too-short trousers, smiling at his father behind the camera.

Lélia took the photo in her hands, bowing her head over it. Tears began to run down her cheeks.

Obviously, the man whose house we were in wasn't responsible for the war, or the fate of her relatives, or the thefts. But even so, we both felt anger rising hotly within us. He came back into the room just then, holding a photo of the Rabinovitch house, a beautiful photo in a lovely frame—the same one, undoubtedly, that had been on the wall before the owner my mother met in 1974 had moved in.

"Who is the boy in this photo? Your father, maybe?" Lélia asked the man, indicating Jacques.

Monsieur Fauchère looked utterly bewildered, completely at a loss as to why my mother had spoken so sharply, or why she was crying.

"No . . . they were friends of my parents . . ."

"Close friends?"

"I believe so, yes. I think the boy there, in the photo, was a neighbor."

I stepped in to explain, trying to keep the situation from getting out of hand.

"We're asking you all these questions because the matter of rights could be an issue. The descendants of the people in these photos would need to give permission for them to be used. Do you know them?"

"There aren't any."

"Any what?"

"Descendants."

"Ah," I said, trying to keep my face impassive. "At least that solves the problem."

"Are you really sure there are no descendants?"

Lélia asked the question so aggressively that the man immediately became suspicious.

"What's the name of your gallery again?" he asked.

"It's not a gallery—it's a museum of modern art," I said quickly.

"But which artist are you working for?"

I had to think of an answer quickly. Lélia had stopped listening at all. Suddenly, I had a flash of inspiration.

"Christian Boltanski," I said. "Are you familiar with him?"

"No. How is it spelled? I'll look on the internet." He pulled his phone from his pocket, still suspicious.

"Just like it's pronounced. Bol-tan-ski."

He typed the name into his phone and began reading the Wikipedia page aloud.

"Hmm," he said when he'd finished. "I don't know him, but he seems very interesting."

The landline rang in the next room. The man stood up.

"I'll leave you to look at the photos while I take this call," he said, and stepped out of the room.

Lélia took the opportunity to slip several photos from the shoebox into her purse. Seeing it took me back to my childhood. I'd watched her do it countless times in cafés and bistros; she'd stuff a handful of sugar cubes into her bag. Packets of salt, pepper, mustard. It wasn't really stealing; it was there for the customers, she said. Back at the house, she'd stash them in an old Traou Mad cookie tin we kept in the kitchen. It was only years later, when I saw the Marceline Loridan-Ivens film *The Birch-Tree Meadow*, that I realized where the habit came from; in one scene, Anouk Aimée steals a teaspoon from a hotel.

"Don't take all those photos," I hissed. "It'll show."

"Not as much as if I took the piano," she retorted, slipping more pictures into her bag.

The quip made me snort with laughter like a Jewish joke.

All of a sudden, we realized that Monsieur Fauchère was standing in the doorway, watching us.

"Who are you?" he asked.

We didn't know how to answer.

"Leave or I'm calling the police."

Ten seconds later, we were in the car. Lélia started the engine, and we drove off. But she stopped the car as soon as we reached a small parking lot just across from the town hall.

"I can't drive," she said. "I'm shaking too much."

"We'll wait a little while."

"What if Fauchère calls the police?"

"May I remind you that those photos are our property? Come on, let's have a coffee while we get our heads on straight again."

We went back to the bakery where we'd bought tuna sandwiches for lunch an hour earlier. The coffee they served was excellent.

"Do you know what we're going to do now?" Lélia asked me.

"Go back home."

"No. We're going to the town hall. I've always wanted to see my parents' marriage certificate."

The town hall was scheduled to reopen at 2:30, and it was 2:30 on the dot. A young man was in the process of unlocking the front door of the building, a large red-brick structure surmounted by a slate roof with three chimneys.

"Excuse us—sorry to bother you, we don't have an appointment—but if it's possible, we'd like to see a copy of a marriage certificate."

"Well," he said amiably, "I'm not usually the one who does those things, but I can find it for you."

The man ushered us into the building.

"My parents got married here," my mother said.

"Ah, I see. I'll look for the certificate. What year was it?"

"1941."

"Give me the names, and I'll see if I can dig it out. It's Josyane who normally does this, but I think she's running a bit late."

"My father's name was Picabia, like the painter. And my mother's was Rabinovitch. R-A-B-I"—

The man stood stock still at this, staring at us as if we might be figments of his imagination.

"You're just the person I've been hoping to see, Madame!"

Entering his office, we saw an official photograph on the wall. It showed our host, wearing a tricolor sash. The young man who'd let us into the building was the mayor of Les Forges.

"I've been wanting to contact you because I received this letter from a history teacher at the high school in Évreux," he explained, leafing through the papers on his desk. "He's teaching his students about World War Two."

The mayor handed us a file.

"Take a look at this while I hunt down your parents' marriage certificate."

For that year's *Concours national de la Résistance et de la Déportation*, some students at the Lycée Aristide Briand in Évreux had looked into whether any Jewish pupils from their own school had been deported during the war. They'd begun with class lists and then taken their research further, to the Eure departmental archives, the Shoah Memorial archive in Paris, and the *Conseil national pour la mémoire des enfants juifs déportés*. That was how they'd come across Jacques and Noémie, and, along with their history teacher, they'd sent a letter to the mayor of Les Forges.

> Dear Monsieur le Maire,
>
> We are trying to get in touch with the descendants of these families in order to gather more information, particularly about their time as students at the high school in Évreux. We also want to correct the omission of their names from the school's commemorative plaque as soon as possible in remembrance.
>
> Sincerely,
>
> The students of tenth grade class A

"I'd love to meet them," my mother said to the mayor, touched to learn that these young students were trying, like we were, to learn more about the all too brief lives of the Rabinovitch children.

"I think they'd be thrilled," he replied. "Here—your parents' marriage certificate."

On the fourteenth of November, nineteen hundred and forty-one, at six o'clock P.M., appeared before us Lorenzo

Vicente Picabia, designer, born in the seventh arrondissement of Paris on the fifteenth of September nineteen hundred and nineteen, aged twenty-two years, residing in Paris
at 7 rue Casimir Delavigne, the son of Francis Picabia, artist
and painter residing in Cannes, Alpes Maritimes, no specific
address given, and of Gabriële Buffet, his wife, of no profession, residing in Paris at 11 rue Chateaubriand, and Myriam
Rabinovitch, of no profession, born in Moscow, Russia, on
the seventh of August, nineteen hundred and nineteen, aged
twenty-two years, residing in this municipality, the daughter of Efraïm Rabinovitch, farmer, and of Emma Wolf, his
wife, farmer, both residing in this municipality. Both future
spouses hereby declare that their marriage license was issued on the fourteenth of November nineteen hundred and
forty-one by Robert Jacob, Esquire, notary in Deauville,
Eure. Lorenzo Vicente Picabia and Myriam Rabinovitch
having both declared that they wish to be united in marriage, I have pronounced in the name of the law that they
are husband and wife. So done in the presence of witnesses
having attained the age of majority Pierre Joseph Debord,
drafter for the prefecture, and Joseph Angeletti, day laborer,
both residing in Les Forges, both of whom have read the
above and appended their signatures along with the spouses
and myself, Arthur Brians, mayor of Les Forges.

Signed:
L.M. Picabia
M. Rabinovitch
P. Debord
Angeletti
A. Brians

"Do you know who these two witnesses were? Pierre Joseph
Debord and Joseph Angeletti?"
"No idea! I wasn't born yet," replied the mayor, who looked

314 · ANNE BEREST

no older than forty, smiling. "But I can ask Josyane, our secretary. She knows everything. I'll get her."

Josyane turned out to be an ample, rosy-cheeked blonde of about sixty.

"Josyane, I'd like you to meet the Rabinovitch family," the mayor said, introducing us.

It was strange to be called that, for the first time in our lives. "The Rabinovitch family."

"The kids will be so happy to have found you," Josyane said, beaming with almost maternal pleasure.

She meant the students from the Lycée d'Évreux, of course, but my immediate thoughts were of Jacques and Noémie.

"Josyane," the mayor continued, "do the names Pierre Joseph Debord and Joseph Angeletti mean anything to you?"

"Joseph Angeletti doesn't. But Pierre Joseph Debord—of course." She said this with a shrug, as if it were only too obvious.

"What do you mean 'of course'?" asked the mayor.

"Pierre Joseph Debord. The teacher's husband. You know. The one who worked at the prefecture."

It touched me deeply to think of this man agreeing to stand witness to the marriage of a member of the "Jewish RABINOVITCH household." He had died not long after that, of too much willingness to help his fellow man. And whoever it was that had led him into a trap might still be alive today, doddering old residents of a nursing home somewhere.

"Do you have any other records on file concerning the Rabinovitches?" Lélia asked.

"Actually," Josyane said, "when I read the students' letter, I looked for other documents, but I didn't find any here. I spoke to my mother about it. Rose Madeleine is her name; she's ninety-two, but she's still sharp as a tack. And she told me that, back when she was the mayor's secretary, she got a letter requesting that the names of all four Rabinovitches be added on the Les Forges monument to the war dead."

Lélia and I had the same reaction.

"Did your mother remember who'd sent that letter?"

"No, all she remembered was that it came from somewhere in the south of France."

"Do you know when it was sent?"

"Sometime in the '50s, I believe."

"Can we see it?" I asked.

"I looked for it here in the town hall archives, but I didn't find it anywhere. I think it must have been in one of the boxes of records belonging to the prefecture, and those were moved at some point."

"That would mean that even back in the '50s, someone wanted their four names to be back together again," murmured my mother, thinking aloud.

The mayor seemed as touched as we were by what we'd just discovered.

"I would very much like for the town council to organize a ceremony in remembrance of your family," he said. "And I want to make sure their names are engraved on the memorial, because that was never done."

"That would be wonderful," Lélia said warmly. We were both overwhelmed by the mayor's kindness.

Leaving the town hall, we sat down on the edge of a low wall so Lélia could smoke a cigarette before getting behind the wheel again.

She crushed the butt with the heel of her boot, and we walked back toward the car. We were still some distance away when we both spotted it: a manila envelope the size of a half-sheet of paper, stuck beneath the windshield wipers the way a parking ticket might be.

"What is *that*?" I wondered aloud.

"How should I know?" my mother retorted, as taken aback as I was.

"It has to be someone who knows that's our car."

316 · ANNE BEREST

"And who's been watching us."

"I'm sure it's someone whose house we've been in today."

The envelope held five postcards. Nothing else. They were bound together with a tattered ribbon. Each postcard showed a monument in a large city: La Madeleine in Paris; a bird's eye view of Boston in the United States; Notre Dame in Paris; a bridge in Philadelphia. Just like the Opéra Garnier.

All the cards dated from the war years. And all bore the same address:

Efraïm Rabinovitch
78 rue de l'Amiral-Mouchez
75014 Paris

All the writing on them was in Russian, dated 1939. As I examined the Cyrillic sentences, none of which I could read, I was hit with a sudden realization about the writer of our postcard—something as obvious as it was crucial.

"I know why the writing is so strange!" I said to my mother. "The person who wrote it doesn't know our alphabet!"

"Of *course* . . ."

"The author has 'drawn' the Roman letters rather than writing them. But their native alphabet is Cyrillic."

"Very possibly."

"Where were these postcards sent from?"

"Prague. Uncle Boris wrote them," Lélia said.

"Who was Uncle Boris again? I can't quite remember."

"The naturalist. Ephraïm's older brother. The one who patented the method for determining the sex of baby chickens."

"Can you translate the Russian?"

Lélia read each postcard carefully, handing them to me one by one as she did so.

"It's fairly standard stuff," she said. "He wants to know how the family is. He sends his love to everyone. Birthday greetings here and there. He talks about his garden and the butterflies. He says he's working a lot. Sometimes he's worried because he hasn't had an answer from his brother. That's it, really. Nothing special."

"Do you think Uncle Boris could have sent *our* postcard?"

"No, sweetheart. Boris went the same way as all the others. He was arrested in Czechoslovakia on July 30, 1942. His comrades from the Socialist Revolutionary party tried to keep him from being deported, but according to an account I found, he refused to be saved: 'He decided to share the fate of his people.' He was sent to the concentration camp at Theresienstadt, the Nazis' famous 'model camp,' and then on August 4, 1942, he was transferred to the extermination camp at Maly Trostenets, near Minsk, in Byelorussia. He was killed as soon as he got there, shot in the back of the head, kneeling at the edge of a pit. He was fifty-six years old."

"Then . . . if it wasn't Boris, who wrote it?"

"I don't know. Someone who didn't want to be found."

"Even so," I mused. "I feel like we're getting closer."

BOOK III
FIRST NAMES

C laire,
I called this morning to tell you I wanted to talk to you about something, but that I needed to put my thoughts down in writing. Organize them. So here they are.

You know I'm trying to find out who sent the anonymous postcard to Lélia, and obviously, this whole investigation has stirred up a lot of things inside me. I've been reading a lot, and I stumbled across this quote from Daniel Mendelsohn in *The Elusive Embrace*: "Like a lot of atheists, I compensate by being superstitious, and I believe in the power of first names."

The power of first names. That little phrase did something to me. Made me think.

I've realized that, when we were born, our parents gave us both Hebrew first names as middle names. Hidden first names. I'm Myriam, and you're Noémie. We're the Berest sisters, but on the inside, we're also the Rabinovitch sisters. I'm the one who survives, and you're the one who doesn't. I'm the one who escapes. You're the one who is killed. I don't know which is the heavier burden to bear, and I wouldn't dare to guess. It's a lose-lose situation, this inheritance of ours. Did our parents even think about that? It was a different time, as they say.

Anyway, Mendelsohn's words shook me up. And I'm wondering what I—you—we should do with these names. I mean . . . I'm wondering what we've done with them so far, and I'm wondering how they've affected us, silently, invisibly. Affected our personalities and how we look at the world. Basically, to go back to Mendelsohn again, what power have those first names had in our lives? And in our relationship as sisters? I'm wondering what conclusions we can draw, and what we can make of this whole first-name business. First names that showed up out of the blue on the postcard, as if they were being thrown in our faces. First names hidden in our family names.

The effects, for better or worse, on our temperaments.

Those Hebraic-sounding names are like a skin beneath the skin. The skin of a story bigger than us, that came before us and goes far beyond us. I can see, now, how they instilled something disturbing in us. The idea of fate.

Maybe our parents shouldn't have given us such heavy names to carry. Maybe. Maybe things would have been easier, lighter inside us, lighter between us, if we weren't Myriam and Noémie. But maybe they would have been less interesting, too. Maybe we wouldn't have become writers. Who knows.

Recently I've been asking myself: how am I Myriam? In what ways?

Here are the answers I've come up with.

I am Myriam in that I'm the one who's always escaping. Who never stays at the table after dinner. Who's always leaving, going somewhere else, feeling like I have to save myself.

I am Myriam in that I can adapt to all kinds of situations. I know how to blend in, to lie low. I know how to contort myself to fit into a trunk; I know how to become invisible; I know how to change my environment, change my social milieu, change my *self*.

I am Myriam in that I know how to seem more French than any Frenchwoman. I anticipate situations, I adapt, I can blend into the wallpaper so that no one wonders where I'm from. I'm discreet, I'm polite, I'm well brought up. I'm a bit distant, and a bit cold, too. I've been criticized for that a lot. But it's what has allowed me to survive.

I am Myriam in that I am tough. I don't show tenderness even to the people I love. I'm not always comfortable with shows of affection. Family, for me, is a complicated subject.

I am Myriam in that I always know where the exit is. I run away from danger. I don't like dodgy situations, and I see problems coming long before they actually happen. I take the side streets; I pay attention to how people act. I prefer still waters, and I always slip through the net. Because I was chosen to be that way.

I am Myriam. I'm the one who survives.

You are Noémie.

You are Noémie even more than I am Myriam.

Because in your case, the name wasn't even hidden.

We used to call you Claire-Noémie sometimes, like a hyphenated first name.

I remember, when we were little—you must have been five or six, and I was eight or nine at most—one night you called to me from the other side of the bedroom. I came over to you in your little bed, and you said, "I'm the reincarnation of Noémie."

How very strange that was, when you think about it. Wasn't it? Where on earth did that idea come from? You were so tiny! Lélia never talked to us about her past or her family history back then.

We never spoke about that night again, and I don't even know if you remember it. Do you?

Anyway, those are my thoughts.

I don't know what I'm going to find out from my investigation, or who wrote the postcard. And I don't know what the consequences of all this will be. We'll see.

Don't worry about writing me back right away; there's no hurry. I'd imagine you're almost finished correcting your trial proofs. "Trial"—that is *definitely* the right word for them. Good luck with it. I can't wait to read your book on Frida Kahlo; I just know it's going to be beautiful and powerful and huge for your career.

Big hugs to you, and Frida, too,

A

Anne,

I've read your e-mail half a dozen times since you sent it. I'll admit it—the first two times both made me cry. The way you cry when you're a kid and you've hurt yourself. Uncontrollably, and loudly, hiccupping and shaking. Probably because you think your pain is unfair somehow.

But then, the third time I read it, I didn't cry. And then I read it again and again, and I was able to sort of . . . neutralize my initial reaction, which was denial, and a kind of dread.

And that allowed me to focus on your questions. So now I'm going to try to answer them.

Yes, I remember.

I remember calling out to you one night when I was really little, to tell you I was the reincarnation of Noémie. It's one of my few early-childhood memories, and I remember it as clearly and vividly as if it were a movie scene playing in my head.

Yes, it's true that Lélia didn't actually *talk* about all that stuff back then, but she communicated it in other ways. It was everywhere. In all the books in the study, in her pain, in the things she said and did that didn't quite make sense, and in the "secret" photos that weren't very well hidden at all. The Holocaust was like a treasure hunt in our house. You just followed the clues.

Isabel didn't have a middle name. Neither did Lélia.

Yours was Myriam. And mine was Noémie.

Maman told me once that she originally wanted Noémie to be my first name, but Papa suggested that it would be better as my middle name. "But Noémie is so pretty as a first name too," she said to me. And it is.

Then she said, "But 'Claire' was a good choice. It means 'light.' And I think that's really lovely too."

This, coming from Maman, whose name in Hebrew means "night."

When I was little, I used to look at the photo of Noémie Rabinovitch I'd swiped from Maman's desk, to envisage a truth. En-visage, in the literal sense. I wanted to look into this dead girl's face—her *visage*—to see if there was anything of myself in it. I remember realizing that we had the same cheeks (I'd say cheekbones now, of course, but I didn't understand the concept at that age). We had the same blue eyes.

Whereas yours are green. Like Myriam's.

I had the same long braids.

But did I braid my hair that way for ten years because I was imitating Noémie? That's the question. Though I'm not really looking for an answer.

In Maman's photo, Noémie looked almost Mongolian, with her slightly slanted eyes and those famous high cheekbones. My eyes almost disappeared when I smiled in pictures, narrowing to slits, and people would have seen our Mongolian ancestry in my face, too. And let's not forget the Mongolian birthmarks. They show up on a baby's buttocks at birth and then disappear, apparently. Remember how Maman used to talk about how we'd all had them? Of course, as I'm writing this e-mail, my thirty-eight-year-old self is blurring together with my six-year-old self, and I'm writing to you from that perspective. All mixed up and confused.

For reasons I didn't really understand, I became a passionate volunteer for the Red Cross at the exact age Noémie was when she found herself working in the infirmary at her transit camp before being sent to Auschwitz. I was spending every single weekend at the Red Cross—and then all of a sudden, overnight, I just stopped going.

I used to wonder about all kinds of strange things at night when I couldn't sleep.

I remember with cruel clarity the day when someone said to me—I was still very little—"Your family died in an oven." For a long time after that, I used to look at the oven in our kitchen and try to figure out how that was possible. How had they managed to cram everyone in there? It's the kind of mental gymnastics that leave you exhausted. When I was a teenager, during a party I threw impulsively when our parents were away, I broke that fucking oven, and I remember how it made me feel strangely better. Relieved.

When I ditched everything and ran off to New York on a whim at the age of twenty, I went to the Holocaust Museum. So many rooms. And in one of those rooms, on a wall, a photograph. Tiny. It was Myriam. I recognized her. I started to feel sick. I went closer and looked, and there was a caption: Myriam and Jacques Rabinovitch, from the Klarsfeld Collection.

I fainted. They took me out of the museum through an emergency exit. I remember that.

But yes. When I was six, I did call you over to tell you that thing. Monstrous, in a way. That I was the reincarnation of that dead girl I didn't know, whom no one knew, because she died too soon, and the people who knew her died with her. All of them, all at once. And because she didn't survive. And I don't know anything about her. And it's horrible.

But I know—we know—that she wanted to be a writer.

And so, when I was little, I said I would be a writer. And I stuck to it, with persistence and endurance, until I became one for real.

For real, as little kids say.

And yes, during my wild days, sometimes I felt like I was living the life that another girl didn't have the chance to live, because it was my duty. I don't feel that way anymore, though. But I would say it in my mind when I felt bad about myself, like an exorcism. And here we are.

I'm the one who played leapfrog with her fears, jumping over them to see how far I could get. And the one who got tattoos all over her arms, to cover up the shadows.

But I'm willing to admit that in an e-mail now, because I have nothing to be ashamed of. I'm not ashamed anymore. Not ashamed of my arms, I mean.

So yes, in that way, you are Myriam. You're discreet, you're polite, you're well brought up. You're the one who always knows where the exit is, and you run away from danger and dodgy situations. The opposite of me. I've gotten myself into all kinds of dodgy and dangerous situations—to say the least.

Myriam saves herself, and everyone in the story dies.

She didn't save any of them.

But how *could* she have?

I've asked you to save me. So many times. What a burden I've been on you.

When I was six and told you I was Noémie reincarnate. When I told you I loved you and said I didn't understand why you never said it to me, or hugged me (another incredibly vivid early-childhood memory). Because, as you say, you or Myriam, you seem tough and cold. You have trouble expressing your feelings. It makes you uncomfortable.

And I've called you on some of those nights when the shadows were too deep, too strong.

All that is far behind me now, you know. That was somebody else. I've made my peace, and I'm not dead.

What do these first names say about us? You're asking me the question, so:

Anne-Myriam, required to save Claire-Noémie again and again so that she doesn't die. Just like you're saving the Rabinovitches now, by following the trail of that postcard.

What effects have these names had on our personalities and on the bond between us, on our sometimes fraught relationship? You're asking that, too. Damn it.

Now, and for a good few years now, your drive to save me has disappeared. It wasn't your role. And I've stopped trying to kill myself. I don't resent you for being cold anymore, either, and I hope you've stopped thinking I'm infuriating, too. I'm sure you would have used words far stronger than "infuriating" at one point, but you were too polite to do it, even though I deserved it. I gave you such a hard time.

But I know how to be discreet and polite now, too, and you're not a woman who blends into the wallpaper or leaves the table early. Quite the opposite, in fact.

I think that, as we both approach forty, we're only just beginning to get to know each other. Even though we lived together for so many years.

I think Myriam and Noémie never got the chance to begin to get to know each other.

I think we've survived our arguments, our betrayals, and our inability to understand one another.

I think I would never have been able to write all this to you if you hadn't sent me that e-mail, with its questions from beyond the grave.

This is what I think. But I really don't know.

We survived.

And Myriam couldn't have saved her family.

It wasn't her fault.

Noémie didn't have the chance to write.

You and I became writers.

We've written books together, the pair of us. And it wasn't easy. But it was beautiful and intense.

I hope so much, Anne, that one day I can be your strength. *Your* shelter.

A kind of strength drawn from the light. From Claire.

Godspeed with the postcard.

A hug and a squeeze to you and Clara.

Love,

C

PS:

A dokh leben oune liebkheit. Dous ken gournicht gournicht zein. To live without affection is not living at all.

BOOK IV
MYRIAM

M aman, I've been thinking. What if the postcard
was meant for Yves?"
"What?"
"Yeah—look. You could read 'M. Bouveris' as 'Monsieur
Bouveris,' not 'Myriam Bouveris.'"

"I really don't think so. Yves has nothing to do with any of
this."

"Why not?"

"It doesn't make any sense. You're not thinking straight. Yves
had been dead for years by 2003. It's impossible."

"But remember—the postcard is from the early '90s."

"Okay, stop. Yves . . . that was Myriam's other life. One that
had nothing to do with her life before the war."

Lélia got up, stubbing out her cigarette. "It's always the same
with you. You were like this even when you were little. So stubborn," she said, and stalked out of the room.

I knew she'd be back. Her pack of cigarettes was empty. She'd
just gone to get a new one from the carton upstairs.

"Fine," she said, sighing, when she came back into the room.
"Tell me your theory about 'M. Bouveris.'"

"Here it is. The author of the postcard *could* have chosen
to write to Myriam under another name. They could have addressed it to Myriam Rabinovitch, or Myriam Picabia. But they
chose 'Myriam Bouveris.' The name of her second husband. So I
think I need to find out more about him. Yves."

"What do you want to know?"

"What your relationship with him was like, for one thing."

"There was no relationship, really. He was rather distant. I'd even say . . . indifferent."

"Was he nice to you?"

"Yves was a very nice man. Refined and intelligent. He was nice to everyone, especially his own children. Except me. As for why . . . I don't know."

"Maybe he saw you as a reminder of Vicente."

"It's possible. He and Myriam both took so many secrets to the grave."

"I remember you told me once that Yves used to have anxiety attacks. How did those manifest themselves? What happened?"

"He would just sort of lose it, very suddenly. Panic. Like he was disoriented. And then, in June 1962, something very bizarre happened. He was on the phone, a work call, and he just started stammering, like he couldn't speak properly. And he wasn't able to work for a full ten years after that."

"Did anyone ever figure out why he broke down like that?"

"Not really. Shortly before he died, he wrote a strange letter: 'More than once I have imagined that certain evil things were absolute, final. And until now, I had completely forgotten all of that.'"

"What things did he mean? What had he forgotten that came back? What was he talking about?"

"I have no idea. But my hunch is that it had to do with things that happened among the three of them at the end of the war. I don't know much about that time, though. I can't really shed any light on it for you."

"You don't know anything at all?"

"No. I lose Myriam's trail as soon as she crosses the demarcation line with Jean Arp in the trunk of Gabriële Buffet's car and wakes up in that château in Villeneuve-sur-Lot."

"When do you pick it up again?"

"At my birth in 1944. But the period between the two . . . it's a blank."

"You don't even know how Yves came into your father and Myriam's lives?"

"No."

"Didn't you ever wonder?"

"Darling, it would have meant going into my parents' bedroom, if you know what I mean."

"And that bothers you."

"Let's just say things happened that I'm in no position to judge. They lived their life the way they wanted to. And it *was* the war, after all."

"I'll do the research myself, then, Maman. I'll figure out what happened during that part of Myriam's life."

"Then I'll leave you to it."

"If I find out who sent the postcard, do you want me to tell you?"

"That will be up to you, when the time comes."

"How will I know?"

"There's a Yiddish proverb that might give you your answer: *A khave iz nit dafke der vos visht dir op di trern ni der vos brengt dikh bekhlal nit tsi trern.*"

"What does it mean?"

"A true friend isn't the one who dries your tears. It's the one who never causes them to be shed."

August 1942. Myriam has been in hiding at the château in Villeneuve-sur-Lot for almost two weeks. One night, she is awakened by her husband. Vicente has come from Paris. He lies, says he's talked to her parents on the telephone. He tells her everything's fine. Myriam closes her eyes. These days of uncertainty and suspense will soon be a thing of the past, she thinks. They leave Villeneuve before sunrise in a car Myriam has never seen before, heading for Marseille.

Don't ask questions, she reminds herself.

Every city has its own smell. Migdal was full of the bright perfume of oranges, mixed with the odor of stone, deep and lingering. Lodz smelled like linen and garden flowers, their rich scent mingling with the hot metallic smell of tram wheels against asphalt. Marseille, Myriam discovers, smells like scented baths and salt water, mixed with the warm odor of the wooden crates unloaded on the docks. Unlike Paris, here the market stalls are overflowing, giving rise to a miraculous feeling of abundance. Vicente and Myriam have almost forgotten what it's like for the sidewalks to be full of pedestrians. The bustle and rush of street crossings. They drink cool beer at one of the waterside bistros. It's the cocktail hour, the social hour, the air tinged with the scents of eau de Cologne and shaving cream. They sit at a table outside on the terrace like young lovers, smiling and sipping from foamy glasses, slightly giddy. They order the *plat du jour*, lamb chops flavored with fresh thyme, and eat them with their fingers. Around them they can hear people speaking countless languages; since the armistice, Marseille has become one of the main cities of refuge in the unoccupied zone, foreigners and French fugitives alike resting here before putting out to sea. The daily newspaper *Le Matin* has published a venomous article disdainfully dubbing Marseille "the new Jerusalem of the Mediterranean."

Vicente makes himself a pair of shoes from pieces of a car tire, held together by strips of leather. He takes mysterious trips with his sister Jeanine. Two days here, four days there. He never talks about where they go, or why.

Myriam spends three months in Marseille, most of that time on her own. Sitting alone on café terraces, tipsy on beer, she imagines scenarios in which she receives news of Noémie and Jacques.

"But of *course*, I know your sister! I've met her! And your brother! Your parents came to find them! Oh, yes—they're together as we speak!"

Sometimes, in a crowd, she spots them. For a moment she can't move. Then she runs and seizes a young woman by the arm. But when she turns, the young woman is never Noémie. Myriam apologizes, dejected. The night that follows is invariably a bad one, but hope always returns by morning.

In November, she hears German being spoken on La Canebière. The "free zone" has been invaded. Marseille is no longer a *bonne mère*, a city of refuge. Signs begin to appear in shop windows: "Entry strictly reserved for Aryans." ID checks become more and more frequent, even outside the movie theaters where American films are now prohibited.

Marseille is like Paris now, with its curfew and its patrolling German soldiers, its streetlamps that are no longer lit at night.

Myriam envies the rats that can disappear into a crack in the walls. She doesn't have the taste for risk that she used to, back in the days of the Rhumerie Martiniquaise on the boulevard

Saint-Germain. She no longer feels like there is an invisible force protecting her. Since Jacques and Noémie's arrest, something inside her has changed. Now she knows what fear is.

Vicente insists that they walk toward the port to get some fresh air, despite the presence of uniformed Germans. He lingers on the cours Saint-Louis. Myriam grasps his arm; a young woman is walking toward them, wearing sunglasses and a summer dress like a holidaymaker.

"Look," Myriam says. "She looks like Jeanine."

"That is Jeanine," says Vicente. "We're meeting her here."

Jeanine, in her slightly ridiculous outfit, leads her brother down a narrow side street. Myriam waits for them in front of the newspaper kiosk. She chats with the vendor, who is removing the Mickey Mouse and Donald Duck comic books from his shelves.

"Have to replace them with coloring books. Vichy regime's orders," the man says, shaking his head.

Meanwhile, Jeanine is informing her brother that the young woman who produced their false *Ausweis* has been arrested. A pretty little thing with blonde curls and pearly teeth, whose family in Lille possessed a very good set of "kitchen utensils"— phony administrative stamps. Her job was to travel back and forth between Lille and Paris, transporting papers. Every time she took the train, she would head straight for the German officers' compartment, smiling and dimpling, asking if there might be room for her to sit down. The officers were always charmed, of course, clicking their boot-heels together with a courteous "*Fräulein!*" and gallantly helping with her luggage. The young woman would spend the rest of the journey seated smack dab in the middle of the group of Nazis, the false papers sewn snugly into the lining of her coat.

When the train reached its destination, she would ask a German to help carry her suitcase and, thus escorted, she would pass through the station without having her luggage inspected. A pretty, porcelain-skinned china doll.

But eventually, by sheer chance, a Nazi officer found himself in the same train car as the young woman three times in a row. In the end, he figured out what she was up to.

"A dozen men took turns raping her while she was being interrogated," Jeanine tells Vicente, her anguish palpable.

Brother and sister inform Myriam that they're returning to Paris, where they have "things to do."

"We'll take you to a youth hostel out in the countryside. You'll need to wait for us there."

They cut Myriam off before she can protest: "It's too dangerous for you to stay here."

Getting into the car, Jeanine at the wheel, Myriam feels as if she's moving just that much farther away from Jacques and Noémie. She asks Jeanine for one last favor. She'd like to send her parents a postcard, to reassure them.

Jeanine refuses.

"It would put us all in danger."

"How the hell could it hurt *you*?" Vicente snaps at his sister. "We're getting the fuck out of Marseille anyway. It's fine," he says to Myriam.

So Myriam buys an "interzone card" for 80 centimes at a post-office service counter. This is the only type of mail permitted to circulate between the two zones, the "nono," which stands for non-authorized, and the "ja-ja," the German translation of "*oui-oui*." All postcards are read by the postal control office, and if the message appears suspicious in any way, the card is destroyed then and there.

After completing this card, which is strictly reserved for family correspondence, strike out any of the following indications which do not apply. You must write legibly to facilitate German government inspection.

The cards are pre-filled out. On the first blank line, Myriam writes "Madame Picabia."

Next, she has to choose between:

in good health
exhausted
killed
prisoner
deceased
whereabouts unknown

She circles "in good health."
After that, she has to choose between:

needs money
needs belongings
needs provisions
is back in
is working in
is going to start school in
has been admitted to

Myriam circles "is working in" and writes "Marseille" in the blank.

At the bottom of the card, the closing has been pre-written by the authorities: "Fondly. Sending kisses."

"Unbelievable," Jeanine snaps, reading over Myriam's shoulder. "*I'm* Madame Picabia. And yes, I'm wanted in Marseille."

Sighing, Jeanine tears the card in half and buys another, which she fills out herself.

"Marie is in good health. She has been admitted to take her exam. Don't send any parcels; she has everything she needs."

"*God*, you're tiresome, both of you," she says, as they get back into the car. "You don't understand *anything*."

Jeanine and Vicente don't say a word to each other for the entire drive. They stop the car near Apt, in the department of

Vaucluse, in front of an ancient, ruined priory that has been converted into a youth hostel.

"We're leaving you here," Jeanine tells Myriam. "You can trust the man who runs the place. His name is François. He's on our side."

It's the first time Myriam has ever been in a youth hostel. She used to hear about them, before the war. Songs around the fire, long walks in nature, nights giggling in the dormitory. She'd promised herself back then that she'd stay in one sometime, to see what it was like, with Colette and Noémie.

I n the early 1930s, the writer Jean Giono, who was born in Manosque and would later be famous for writing *The Horseman on the Roof*, published a novella that became an enormous success and launched a "back to nature" movement. Young urbanites were seized with a sudden desire to live in the unspoiled countryside as the book's hero had done, moving to rural villages and renovating abandoned old farms, rejecting the cramped big-city apartments their grandparents had moved to during the industrial revolution.

The young men and women who frequented youth hostels were dreamily idealistic, anarchists, pacifists, and communists debating vigorously around the fire while someone strummed a guitar. Later in the night, mouths found each other hungrily, disagreements forgotten, desire igniting in the dark between reconciled bodies.

And then the war came.

Some refused to join the army and were thrown in prison. Others were sent to the front and killed. There were no more fireside guitars. All the hostels were obliged to close their doors.

Marshal Pétain appropriated the back-to-nature movement, coining the slogan "The land does not lie." In 1940, following the armistice, he authorized the reopening of the youth hostels. But now the themes of evening entertainment had to be approved by the government, as did the lists of songs to be sung around the fire. And co-ed hostels became a thing of the past.

François Morenas, one of the founders of the youth hostel movement, refused to comply with the Vichy regime's rules.

Forced to close his hostel, which he had named Le Regain in homage to Giono, he retreated into the obscurity of a ruined twelfth-century priory, Clermont d'Apt. This hostel was no longer official, but it was common knowledge in the area that you could always find a hot meal there, and a bed for the night. These dissident underground hostels continued to operate clandestinely, becoming places of refuge for young people on the margins of society: pacifists, members of the Resistance, communists, Jews, and, soon, those fleeing the STO, or Service du travail obligatoire, the forced enlistment of French workers to serve as laborers in Germany for the Nazi war effort.

Myriam keeps to her room. François Morenas leaves a tray outside her room each morning with a piece of Melba toast soaking in a cup of ersatz coffee, which she never touches until lunchtime. She doesn't wash, doesn't change her clothes. She's still wearing the same five pairs of underwear. Not taking care of herself is her way of stopping time. She thinks constantly of Jacques and Noémie.

Where are they? What are they doing?

One week, the wind blows from the east. One evening, Myriam looks out the window of her room and sees Vicente and Jeanine, emerging from the olive trees as if spat out by a frothing green sea. She knows, as soon as she sees her husband's face, that he isn't bringing news of her parents, or of her brother and sister.

"Come on," Vicente says, "let's take a walk. I have something to tell you. It's about Jeanine."

Jeanine Picabia has always kept a deliberate distance from her parents' world. Great artists, she has found, usually have egos to match. She's like the child of a magician who, having grown up backstage, doesn't believe in the illusion of the performance.

Jeanine's mind has always been set on freedom, on not being dependent on a husband. She passed her nursing exams at a young age and immediately began earning her own living.

From the earliest days of the war, she has worked for what isn't yet called "the Resistance," but will be one day.

A Red Cross nurse and ambulance driver, she transports confidential documents between Paris and the British consulate, now relocated to Marseille. The papers are hidden among bandages, beneath syringes of morphine.

Later, she joins a group in Cherbourg that helps English aviators and parachutists get out of the country. A sort of early escape network.

Her name gets around. Jeanine is scouted by the SIS, or Secret Intelligence Service, the British foreign intelligence service also known as MI6. In November 1940, she meets Boris Guimpel-Levitzky, who puts her in contact with the English. Two months later, she receives the order to set up a new network specializing in maritime intelligence. She accepts the mission, knowing she'll be risking her life.

She's assigned to work with another French operative, Jacques Legrand. The network Jeanine and Jacques create is christened Gloria SMH. "Gloria" is Jeanine's code name, and "SMH" is Jacques Legrand's—three letters that, when read backwards, stand for "Her Majesty's Service."

In February 1941, Gloria SMH scores a major coup. Agents of the network spot German ships in the Brest harbor: the *Scharnhorst*, a Kriegsmarine battlecruiser; her sister ship the *Gneisenau*; and the *Prinz Eugen*, a heavy cruiser. Thanks to the information provided by the French agents, the English are able to stage an aerial raid that puts all three ships out of action. It's a significant victory. Gloria SMH receives 100,000 francs from London to expand the network.

Jacques Legrand recruits new operatives from among university students and high-school teachers. Most of them are "*boîtes aux lettres*"—that is, people who simply agree to have secret documents left in their mailboxes.. They don't know the contents of these papers—they merely accept them—but all the same, they are willingly putting their lives at risk, and they all deserve to be named and commended for their courage: Suzanne Roussel, teacher at the Lycée Henri IV; Gilbert Thomazon; Alfred Perron, teacher at the Lycée Buffon. And others. Legrand also recruits a clergyman, the Reverend Alesch, vicar of La Varenne Saint-Hilaire near Paris. Young people wishing to join a Resistance network make a "confession" to Alesch, and he refers them to his various contacts.

Jeanine, for her part, recruits from among her parents' entourage artists accustomed to traveling all over Europe, many of whom speak several languages. In the Resistance, any profession that can facilitate the international transport of documents is important. Employees of the SNCF, the French national railroad service, are highly sought-after agents.

Marcel Duchamp's companion Mary Reynolds, an American from Minnesota, becomes a network agent under the name "Gentle Mary." So does an Irish writer who has already worked for the SOE, or Special Operations Executive, a secret British espionage and reconnaissance organization also known as the "Baker Street Irregulars." An eminently trustworthy man and skilled translator, the Irishman goes by the code name "Samson," but his real name is Samuel Beckett. Initially promoted to staff sergeant within the Gloria SMH network, he rises rapidly through the ranks to become a second lieutenant.

Samuel Beckett works out of his apartment on the rue des Favorites, analyzing documents, compiling and comparing them, determining their degree of importance, putting them in order of urgency, and then translating them all into English before typing up clean copies. Then he hides these secret documents among the pages of his manuscript novel *Murphy*. Alfred Peron, a Gloria SMH agent, ferries the manuscript to the network's photographer to have the documents put on microfilms, which are then sent to England.

It is during this period that Jeanine recruits both her younger brother Vicente and her mother Gabriële, the latter joining the network at age sixty and taking the code name of "Madame Pic."

"There, now you know everything," Vicente says to Myriam.

"You're one of us now," adds Jeanine. "If we go down, you go down with us. Is that understood?"

Yes. Myriam had realized all of this a long time ago.

J eanine departs the hostel for Lyon. A few days ago, two members of the Gloria SMH network, the Reverend Alesch—alias "Bishop"—and Germaine Tillion, were tasked with traveling there to deliver a microfilm containing twenty-five photographic plates: the coastal defense plans for Dieppe. But the mission hadn't gone as planned.

Germaine Tillion was detained by German police at the Gare de Lyon, questioned, and arrested. Reverend Alesch, though, was able to slip through the net—and, fortunately, he was the one who had the microfilm, hidden in a large box of matches.

And so Bishop had to continue the mission alone. He was supposed to give the microfilms to his contact in Lyon, a Miss Hall. But they failed to make contact at the rendezvous point in front of the Hôtel Terminus. Miss Hall came back the next day, but Bishop wasn't there. It was only the following day that Bishop was able to deliver the microfilms—before vanishing into thin air. Since then, the network has been unable to find any trace of him.

Worried, Jeanine tries to find out what happened. In Lyon, she meets with an SOE special agent, Philippe de Vomécourt, alias "Gauthier," who is in contact with Miss Hall. They open the matchbox, and Jeanine discovers that the microfilm doesn't contain the coastal defense plans for Dieppe, but documents of no interest instead. Jeanine and Philippe de Vomécourt realize immediately what has happened: the Reverend Alesch, alias Bishop, has sold out the network.

Arrests occur simultaneously in Paris, confirming the betrayal.

Jacques Legrand, alias SMH, is arrested by the Gestapo, as is Philippe de Vomécourt, along with the photographer who produced the microfilms. Samuel Beckett tells his lover, Suzanne Déchevaux-Dumesnil, to warn the other members. But Suzanne is watched in the street and forced to turn around. The couple goes into hiding at the home of their friend, the writer Nathalie Sarraute. Twelve network agents are imprisoned at Fresnes and Romainville before being shot. Eighty others are deported to Ravensbrück, Mauthausen, and Buchenwald. In the span of just a few days, Gloria SMH's numbers are reduced by almost half.

Jeanine follows the standard procedure to be applied in the event of a betrayal, ordering the immediate cessation of the group's activities throughout France and then cutting all ties with its members.

Jeanine has now become one of the most wanted female fugitives in France. She has no choice but to leave the country. Now it's her turn to travel in the trunk of a car, a Renault 6CV modified by Samuel Beckett with the help of a friend. Beckett and Suzanne drive to Roussillon, in the south of France, dropping Jeanine at the youth hostel in the ruined priory along the way.

She tells Vicente and Myriam that she is going to try to get to England by way of Spain—which means crossing the Pyrenees on foot.

"I'd rather die up there than be arrested," she says.

Jeanine knows the fate that awaits female Resistance fighters. Rape. The perfect, silent crime.

Myriam and Vicente bid Jeanine farewell under cover of darkness, with no hugs, no reassurances. No *coupo santo* or promises to see one another again. No words of encouragement. No words at all, in fact. Just a handshake to ward off bad luck.

And so they are left alone together. Myriam and Vicente. Both of them have now lost their sisters to the endless black night that is the war.

The next day, François Morenas, the director of the youth hostel, informs them that the place is under surveillance.

"It's too dangerous for you to stay here. The police are coming to go through my registers."

François drives them to Buoux, the next village, up in the hills, where there is a café-inn that accommodates travelers. Unfortunately, the place has no vacant rooms.

"That's all right," François says. "We'll go and see Madame Chabaud."

Everyone in the area knows and respects this lady, who was widowed in the Great War.

"Yes, I have a place free," she tells Myriam and Vicente. "It's not big, but there's enough room for two. It's up on the Plateau des Claparèdes. The Hanged Man's House."

"Perfect," murmurs François. "The police hate ghosts. And it's very high up. You'll see."

Sure enough, it takes them a full thirty minutes of hiking up a relentlessly steep slope covered in almond trees to reach the plateau from the village.

"There are parachutists around here, so the Germans are always patrolling," François warns them. "If you want to avoid trouble, close the shutters tight before you turn on the lights in the evening. Don't smoke cigarettes outside, or near the window. And if I were you I'd plug any gaps or cracks around the window frames that might let the light through. Stop up the keyholes, too, while you're at it. You can't be too careful."

CHAPTER 6

Maman,

This morning I remembered something. I must have been about ten. Myriam had suggested that we go for a walk in the hills. It was a hot summer day, I remember, and she picked up a bee pupa from the side of the road. She handed it to me, telling me to be very careful with it because it was fragile. And then she started talking to me about the war. I felt very uncomfortable.

When we got back home, I wanted to tell you. But everything was a blur in my head, and I couldn't find the right words for any of it. I remember your reaction. It's seared into my memory like a burn-mark. You asked me questions and I just kept saying "I don't know." It was perhaps one of the most character-defining moments of my life.

Ever since then, whenever I don't know how to answer a question, or when I've forgotten something I should have remembered, I fall into a kind of black hole because of that old, old feeling of guilt about Myriam, and about you. So I'm asking you not to be angry with me for trying to awaken the spirits of the dead, to make them live again. I think I'm looking for what Myriam was trying to tell me that day.

On that note, I've made a discovery.

In one of the snippets of writing she left behind, Myriam talks about a Madame Chabaud, in whose house she lived for a year, in Buoux, during the war. I looked in the phone book, and the name was there. Still in the village.

I called the phone number right away and ended up

speaking to a very nice woman who's married to a grandson of the Madame Chabaud Myriam mentioned. She said, "Oh yes, the Hanged Man's House still exists. And I know my husband's grandmother hid Resistance fighters there. If you call back tomorrow, my husband will tell you about it better than I could." Her husband's name is Claude. He was born during the war. I'm going to call him, and I'll let you know what he says.

Maman, I know this is interesting and painful for you all at the same time. I'm sorry. And I'm sorry for forgetting what Myriam tried to tell me on that summer day.

A

There's nothing in the Hanged Man's House. No linens, no cutlery or utensils. Nothing but a bed frame without a mattress, an old wooden bench, and the milking stool the former occupant stood on to hang himself. And the rope, which no one has ever dared to take down.

"Well, this is still usable," Myriam remarks, untying the rope from the rafter and winding it around her hand.

"Until I can find the two of you a mattress, you can make a bed out of Spanish broom. You know—the yellow flowers. Everyone does it around here," the landlady tells them.

And so the two city-dwellers set off to gather heaping armfuls of the vividly colored plants from the thickets behind the house, their yellow blossoms resembling small irises. Back in the house, they pile them on the bed to make something like a straw mattress, then stretch out on it gingerly.

Myriam, feeling uneasily as if she and Vicente are lying in a flower-bedecked coffin, gazes out the window at the moon, which has risen round and bright as a new penny.

The situation suddenly feels completely unreal. This bedroom in the middle of nowhere, this husband she hardly knows. She finds some comfort in thinking that somewhere, far from here, Noémie is looking at the moon, too. The thought gives her strength.

The next morning, Vicente decides to visit the market in Apt to buy some things for the house. The town is only seven kilometers away. He sets out on foot at dawn, following the crowd of farmers, artisans, and country folk, with their sheep and produce and merchandise to sell at the market.

But once there, Vicente is quickly disappointed. There are no mattresses or bed linens for sale. And even the smallest saucepan costs as much as hiring a cook. He returns home empty-handed—except for a bottle of laudanum, to soothe his nerves, and a bar of nougat for his wife.

Vicente and Myriam begin to become better acquainted with their landlady, the widow Chabaud. A courageous woman with a big heart and a spine of steel, she does the work of three men while raising her only son. Everyone in the region respects her. She's rich, certainly, but she is invariably generous to those in need. She never says "no" to anyone. Except the Germans.

Once a week, the German soldiers requisition Madame Chabaud's car—the only one in the area. She acquiesces because she has no choice. But never—not ever—does she invite them in for a drink.

Myriam and Vicente portray themselves to Madame Chabaud as a young married couple in search of a life in the open countryside. The kind of life depicted in Giono's novels. Vicente says he's a painter and Myriam a musician. She doesn't let on that she's Jewish, obviously. Madame Chabaud has dealt with all sorts of people in her time. All she asks of her tenants is that they respect the villagers and their way of life and behave correctly. And that they *not* have the police after them, of course.

Since the dismantling of the Gloria SMH network, Vicente has had nothing to do. And for the first time, he and Myriam are living under the same roof in a typical, everyday, married existence. Eating, washing, getting dressed, keeping warm, and going to bed. For the whole history of their relationship before now, they were living in a constant state of urgency and fear. Their entire love story had played out against a backdrop of danger. And Vicente liked it that way. *Needed* it, apparently. Myriam, on the other hand, is quite happy with their new, simple, peaceful way of life, just the two of them, in the middle of nowhere.

Several days into their sojourn, Myriam notices that Vicente has gone very quiet, withdrawing into himself. She watches him, observing him as if he were a *tableau vivant*.

He seems never to become attached to anything, or anyone—and this is actually what has always made him so irresistible. He lives entirely in the present. He can pour one hundred percent of his energy into a game of chess, or the cooking of a meal, or building a fire. But the past and the future don't really exist for him. He has no memory and no sense of keeping his promises. He can strike up a friendship with a farmer at the market in Apt, spend the whole morning talking to him, ask him a thousand questions about his work, drink an entire bottle of wine with him, and buy him another—but the next day, he'll hardly recognize him. And he's the same way with Myriam. After a night of joy and laughter with his wife, he can wake up in the morning and look at her as if some stranger has turned up in his bed. The days they spend together don't add up to anything; their marriage has no foundation. Every morning, it's like they're starting all over again.

Gradually, it dawns on Myriam that her husband is deliberately distancing himself from her, physically. As soon as she enters a room, he finds a reason to leave.

"I'll go to the market while you're visiting Madame Chabaud."

He takes every possible opportunity to be away from her.

One evening, Myriam goes to Madame Chabaud's house to pay the rent and ends up lingering for quite a while, drinking the cordial "the Germans will *never* taste," as the widow declares emphatically while refilling their glasses. Myriam asks about the former tenant of the house she and Vicente are living in—the famous Hanged Man.

"Camille. He was stiff as a board when they found him, poor soul. His donkey next to him, licking his feet."

"Do you know why he killed himself?"

"They say it was the solitude that drove him half-mad. And the wild boars, too; they kept tearing up his garden. The odd thing was that he often talked about death. He always said he was afraid of dying painfully. He was obsessed with the thought."

They talk for a long time. On the way home, Myriam quickens her steps; it's late, and she doesn't want Vicente to worry. It's almost midnight by the time she reaches the house, but she finds Vicente in bed. He almost always lies awake until dawn, but tonight he's been so completely *un*worried about her that he's sound asleep.

In the days that follow, Myriam notices that her husband's gaze has become unfocused. There's a sort of dull pain in his eyes. He breaks out in itchy hives, and his forehead often shines with a thin film of sweat. After a week of this, he tells her he's going back to Paris.

"It's for my hives," he says. "I need to see a doctor. And I'll try to find out how everyone's doing. I'll go to Les Forges and see your parents and then to Étival—the attic in my mother's family home is crammed with old sheets and blankets no one's using. I'll bring them back. I don't think it'll take me more than about two weeks; I'll be home before Christmas."

Myriam isn't surprised. She's been sensing that restless quality that Vicente always has just before he announces he's going off somewhere.

He leaves on November 15. It's their one-year wedding anniversary. *A sign if ever there was one*, Myriam thinks. She accompanies him to the end of the path even though she knows she shouldn't be trotting along after him this way, like a dog following its master. Vicente is irritated. He wants to be alone and far away from here.

So she stops and watches him disappear among the almond trees in the cold November light. She stands still, rigid. She doesn't want to cry. But there has been so little affection between them since they came here. One night—just one—Vicente rubbed up against her, curling into her arms like a little boy. There were a few awkward kisses, a few shuddering movements in the dark—but then everything stopped as suddenly as it began, and Vicente, his eyelids swollen, sank into a sweaty, sluggish sleep.

That night, Myriam saw her husband as a burden. A useless encumbrance.

But in spite of everything, despite his enigmatic nature and his lack of desire for her, Myriam wouldn't trade Vicente for anyone else. He is hers, this sad, beautiful man. A husband who is childish at times, but always with that irresistible glint in his eye. And the fragile, tenuous intimacy that binds them, a cord no wider than a wedding band . . . it's enough for her. Yes, he sometimes goes entire days without speaking to her, but so what? He's made her a promise. *'Til death do us part.* Nothing matters more than that. There's a dignity between them, a solitude, that she finds beautiful. He may not share his thoughts with her, or the tiny details of his existence, but all he has to do is introduce her to someone as "my wife," and all the rest falls away, her heart swelling with pride because this man in all his male beauty belongs to her. Vicente may not say much, but he is exquisite to look at, and that's enough for her to build a life on.

Over the next few weeks, Myriam goes down to the village periodically to buy eggs and cheese. Buoux, with its tiny population of sixty at most, boasts all of two businesses: a café-inn and a grocery-tobacconist.

"Well now, Madame Picabia, where is your husband these days? We never see him anymore," someone invariably says to her in the village.

"He's gone to Paris; his mother is ill."

"Ah, of course," the villager always says, nodding. "He's a good son, your husband."

"A very good son," she agrees, smiling.

She tries to keep her spirits up. Vicente has gone away often since they first met. But he has always come back.

Chapter 8

To reach Paris, Vicente has to cross the demarcation line without an *Ausweis*. He makes his way to Chalon-sur-Saône, where he seeks out a bar called ATT, which is run by the wife of a railroad engineer who smuggles clandestine mail. He goes to the counter and places an order, "A Picon-grenadine, with lots of syrup."

While continuing to wipe glasses, the engineer's wife nods at a doorway in the back of the bar hung with a curtain of wooden beads. Casually, as if heading to the men's room, Vicente goes through the curtain, which clacks like a hailstorm. *Not very discreet*, he thinks, entering a kitchen where a man is busy cooking a luscious-looking omelet.

"Madame Pic says hello," Vicente says to the man. He pulls a 500-franc note from his pocket, but the man makes no move to take the money.

"You're her son, aren't you?"

Vicente nods.

"No charge for Madame Pic," the man says.

Vicente puts the money back in his pocket, accepting the favor as his due. He and the man agree to meet at eleven o'clock that night. The rendezvous takes place in front of a footbridge some way outside town. At the other end of the bridge, barbed wire marks the demarcation line. Vicente and the man crawl alongside this barbed wire for nearly five hundred meters until they reach a hole in the ground concealed by shrubbery. Following the smuggler's instructions, Vicente slithers into the hole, which is actually a narrow tunnel, and then walks for several kilometers along a main road, careful not to be spotted, until he arrives at a train station. There, he waits for the first morning train, which will take him to Paris.

A few hours later, he disembarks at the Gare de Lyon. Paris is as bustling as ever, as if the rest of the world doesn't exist. Vicente goes directly to the apartment on the rue de Vaugirard. He feels dirty after his journey, his clothes dusty from station benches and train seats, and he's eager to change. There are no letters from his in-laws in the mailbox. That isn't like them. He remembers his promise to Myriam to go to Les Forges and find out what's going on.

Reaching the top floor, he finds a note that has been slipped beneath the door of the flat. It's from his mother, who says she needs to see him "urgently."

Vicente arrives at Gabriële's apartment to find her very busy, a porcelain doll in her hands.

"What are you doing?" Vicente asks.

"I still have work to do."

"For whom?"

"The Belgians," Gabriële replies, smiling.

Since the demise of the Gloria SMH network, Gabriële has been operating not as Madame Pic but as "La Dame de Pique," smuggling correspondence for a Franco-Belgian resistance group. This new network is called Ali-France. It has links to the Zéro network, formed in Roubaix in 1940.

Vicente looks at his mother. She's sixty-one years old, her back still perfectly straight, flitting around the room like a young girl.

"How are you managing this, with your painful arms?" he asks. He has had to administer morphine injections to her more than once.

Gabriële leaves the room and comes back pushing a large, dark blue baby carriage with enormous wheels. She puts the doll into the carriage, thickly swaddled in blankets within which the secret correspondence is hidden. She smiles impishly. *My god, this mother of mine*, thinks Vicente.

"Are you with us?" Gabriële asks. "We need a contact in the southern zone."

"All right, Maman," Vicente says. He sighs. "Is this why you wanted me to come?"

"Of course it is," she replies. "I'll have someone contact you with orders."

"Have you had any word about Jeanine?"

"She's supposed to cross the Spanish border soon, I think. So, I can count on you?"

"Yes, yes," Vicente says impatiently. "But in the meantime, I need money. I've got to go to Les Forges and see my parents-in-law. And then I want to go to Étival and get the sheets and blankets that are in the attic, for—"

"Fine, yes, certainly," Gabriële cuts him off. She has no interest in listening to dull accounts of newlyweds setting up house.

She opens a drawer and takes out a wad of banknotes. She counts them and gives four to Vicente.

"Where did that come from? Did Francis give you all this money?"

"No," Gabriële shrugs. "It was Marcel."

"Isn't he in New York?"

"Oh, yes. But we find ways to stay in touch."

Walking down the stairs, Vicente can feel the money burning a hole in his pocket. When he reaches the street, instead of turning right toward home, he goes left, toward Montmartre and Chez Léa.

He'd first visited the opium den when he was fifteen years old. It was with Francis, father and son discovering a mutual pleasure at last. On the rare occasions when they were alone together, it had always gone badly. Vicente was desperate to please his father, but Francis didn't trust him—he thought he was too handsome. The truth was that, for reasons of his own, he would have loved the wistful, fine-featured boy more if Vicente had been the product of a good fuck enjoyed by Gabriële and Marcel Duchamp—but unfortunately the child, with his dark coloring and his hips slim as a matador's, was indisputably Spanish.

After four children with Gabriële, Francis had concluded that, sometimes, great minds cancel each other out. Their relationship might have produced transcendent paintings, but their offspring had turned out disappointingly mediocre.

At a loss as to what to do with his melancholy teenage son, Francis had decided on that particular day to buy him his first session with an opium pipe.

"It enlightens the mind. You'll see," he promised.

Léa's opium den wasn't one of the fashionable ones frequented by actors and denizens of the demi-monde, reserved for the happy few. No, at Chez Léa you rubbed shoulders not with esthetes, but with shadows.

When they first arrived at the place, Francis and Vicente had lingered for a while in the bar overlooking the street. Francis had asked Léa herself, who was still around and pouring the drinks back then, to give his son a little something to put hair on his chest. She'd handed the teenager a tiny glass of transparent rice liquor that burned a fiery trail from his throat to his gut. Vicente had been shocked by the sensation, and that had made his father laugh. Not mockingly, but with genuine pleasure. That sound had filled Vicente with profound happiness—helped along by the alcohol, of course. It was the first time his father had ever laughed with him, rather than at him.

"Shall we go in?" Francis had asked, downing his own glass of rice liquor in one swallow. "Not a word of this to your mother, my boy," he'd added, thumping his son on the shoulder.

Vicente had been overwhelmed by an extraordinary emotion. To be here, in this forbidden place, sharing a secret with Francis! To be called "*his* boy"! And that affectionate gesture! He'd seen his father clap his friends on the shoulder that way so many times. Sometimes even the waiters in a café. Always followed by a hearty laugh. But Vicente had never been one of the privileged ones. Until now.

Eight years later, pushing open the door of Chez Léa, Vicente remembers that first time with his father. He's visited every opium den in Paris since then, from the most luxurious to the most sordid. But this place still makes him feel like a virgin to the pipe. Old Léa is dead now, of course. And his father has become his worst enemy.

Vicente makes his way to the back of the establishment, toward the stairs that lead to the basement. The damp odor of sewers and mold grows thicker in his throat with every step down into the vaulted underground space.

Lifting a curtain as thick as a Persian rug, he finds himself in a labyrinth of stone caves opening into one another, stretching away into infinity like fun-house mirrors. The first time he came here, he was surprised—and nauseated—by the smell: the hot, bitter scent of opium mixed with human feces and the sweet perfume of flowers. Now, though, the sharp, moist odors of excrement and patchouli are soothing. They make him feel calmer immediately.

As a teenager, the red oriental hangings and silky embroidered fabrics covering the walls here had transported him to the Far East. Shabby and tawdry as the décor may be, he loves it for what it is: theatrical and phony, dirty, deceptive. Here, everything is fake: the rhinestone jewelry worn by the old Chinese woman at the counter; the large statue of Buddha; the felt headgear worn by the boys. But, Vicente knows, what people come here for does not lie. He puts the money Gabriële has just given him on the counter. The old Chinese woman signals for one of the boys to take care of him.

Vicente follows the boy through the tiny, smoky rooms, where people lie in semi-darkness, hardly moving, like invalids on the verge of seeing their souls leave their bodies. They cough softly, their eyes shining with otherworldly pleasure. Vicente feels excitement mounting within him. His sex twitches.

Men and women lie boneless and bloodless on low couches. The slim bamboo-stem pipes held between their fingertips give them the look of flute players intertwined in a sensual symphony, lips caressing the stiff lengths. Vicente envies them, eager to be one of them. His whole body relaxes in anticipation of the delicious poison.

Reaching the divan assigned to him, he unbuttons his shirt-sleeves, then takes off his leather belt, getting comfortable. He lies down. A tiny, hairless individual with bulging eyes and waxy, yellowish skin brings him a blood-red lacquer tray that shines like a mirror, laden with the accoutrements of the opium user. Vicente remembers his father saying to him, the first time he smoked, "It's impossible to be sad here. All your worries get left behind at the door."

But the fifteen-year-old Vicente had gotten violently ill, vomiting until there was nothing left to purge but a watery liquid.

He'd sweated, felt awful. The promised happiness had come, finally, with the third pipe. The divine snakebite.

Lying on the divan, comfortably disheveled, Vicente listens for his neighbors' groans of pleasure, for the low gasps and muffled cries of the eternal, secret, obscene night that reigns in this place, bodies finding each other in the dark. But the youth with the waxy skin brings him a pipe that is poorly made and far too light, which annoys Vicente. The youth drops his gaze in shame and goes to exchange the bad pipe for one that is already burning. Vicente fidgets impatiently. He wants to feel the smoke burning his lungs, to hold it in as long as possible. When the youth finally returns and hands him the lit pipe, Vicente closes his eyes, holding the length of bamboo carefully in both hands, happy as a child grasping its mother's hand.

Finally, he breathes in the yellow smell of the opium. The little oil lamps placed around the room emit tendrils of smoke into the air, giving it the solemn feel of a church. Lying on his side, Vicente's eyes are half-closed, the pipe dangling from between his lips. He lets his head loll back on a wooden rest, and the brown fairy does her sublimely whorish work, sucking him off like the queen courtesan of Siam, his skin first tautening at the nape of his neck, the hairs rising all over from scalp to shin. In a frenzy of exaltation, the heavy smoke drifting around him, he slides a hand into his trousers and finds, at last, without moving, what he came here for: pure, golden ecstasy, fantastical dreams, sensual pleasure flooding every fiber of his motionless being.

Francis had watched that first time, smiling, as his son's sex became swollen and engorged with blood. The teenage boy had felt a kind of supple, yielding desire, endless and free from any feeling of shame. A peaceful, peaceable pleasure utterly lacking in bitterness.

Vicente doesn't even need to stroke himself; the simple touch of his hand on his erect sex transports him to a place where he is no longer even aware of his physical body, but simply of an infinite goodness binding him to everything he loves: a harmony of bodies; the beauty of a young girl's skin; the ripe, heavy breasts of mature women; the perfection of men, their ivory buttocks like those of Greek statues. Without moving, his whole body melds with everything around him in unrestrained, all-encompassing sexuality. He is no longer a little boy, but a stallion like his father, whose enormous manhood could satisfy any woman or man who sought it out. Tiny swan-feathers drift around him like snow, and beautiful girls drape themselves over his body in rose-and-cream voluptuousness, their armpits smelling like sugar and lilacs. He doesn't even need to lave them with his tongue in order to drink them in, his erection floating in the fragrant air like a downy-feathered bird. He satisfies them that way for hours, levitating, adrift in endless pleasure.

That first time, when he was fifteen, a man came and rubbed himself against Vicente's crotch. He had looked around for his father, seeking his protection or maybe his approval—but Francis had lain motionless, his spirit elsewhere, his son forgotten. And so Vicente had given himself up to the tender caresses of the opium, gentle and almost chaste, like an aimless stroll, like a day spent doing nothing, a night pressed against a warm, sleeping body . . .

It's a feeling that can last for whole hours together, the opium daze, somewhere between sleep and wakefulness—until his mother makes her appearance in his fantasies.

Gabriële always has to come and tarnish the golden beauty of his dream-world. And his sister Jeanine, too. Seeing them appear through the smoky haze, Vicente feels as if he is suddenly trapped between two towering granite mountains, two enormous breasts, smothering him. His father, too, the greatest genius of the century—he comes to crush his son as if Vicente were nothing but a maggot, a piece of filth beneath his shoe, compared to the glorious paintings he created. Vicente is their puppet. A rag doll. A plaything. And they all mock him for it.

Vicente begins to laugh, all alone, like a madman. He pinches the heroic little figures of his mother and sister between his fingers until they crumble to nothingness. Then he is seized by the desire to weep for his brother. The false twin. The bastard Francis sired with another woman at the very same time he was conceiving Vicente. Where is he, the detested brother? Gone, sailed away, across the sea. *I should have gone with him, instead of hating him*, Vicente thinks. His eyes glittering with delirium in his chalk-white face, he returns to his own body for a moment— only because it's time for a new pipe. He signals to the waxy-skinned youth. He wants a blanket to cover his legs. One of the goatskin ones that smell rank but keep you warm. And then he'll lie without moving, for a decade maybe, the pipe always within easy reach of his lips.

When he wakes again, he has no idea what day it is. He has no more money. And no more will to act. The opium has stripped him of any motivation to do anything at all. Instead of traveling to Les Forges, Vicente spends days shut up in his apartment, incapable of lifting a finger.

He wonders why he's in Paris.

Why did he leave? His wife is waiting for him somewhere, he remembers. But his brain refuses to supply the name of the village they've been living in.

How will he get back to her?

The only thing he can recall is that he was supposed to go to his mother's family home in the Jura, to get a saucepan and some bedsheets.

M yriam still hasn't heard anything from her husband. Alone in the Hanged Man's House without running water or electricity, she waits. The wind, which has begun to blow every day, is growing colder and colder.

Madame Chabaud comes up to visit her from time to time. The widow is like a crab, soft-hearted beneath the steely carapace. On the *jours de raïsse*, days when the weather is particularly nasty, she invites Myriam down to her house in the village, where it's less damp. There Myriam can luxuriate in hot water heated over the fire, kneeling to bathe naked in the low sink carved from a single block of stone. Madame Chabaud shows her how to burn logs "economically," laying them in the fireplace not horizontally but with their ends poking out onto the hearth.

"Even though the fire doesn't always draw very well that way," she says.

Myriam always returns home with a basket of vegetables and cheese.

On December 23, Madame Chabaud invites her over to celebrate Christmas Eve with her son and daughter-in-law and their newborn baby Claude.

"Neither one of us is very religious, I think, *non*?" she says to Myriam. "We have other things to do. But I think it would be good for both of us to go to the midnight mass. Dress warmly; these December nights are so cold."

Myriam has no choice but to accept. No one must suspect that she's Jewish, not even Madame Chabaud. Her absence from the mass would be noticed and talked about in the village. Will she have to perform the rituals? Read a Bible? Recite prayers? She has no idea how a Christmas celebration is supposed to work. She appeals to François Morenas to help her prepare.

So the atheist François shows the Jew Myriam how to make the sign of the cross. *In the name of the Father, the Son, and the Holy Ghost.* Two fingers to the forehead, then the heart, then the left and right shoulders. Myriam practices the gesture until it looks natural.

On Christmas morning she goes to gather holly in the Aiguebrun valley, so as not to arrive at Madame Chabaud's empty-handed. The Alpilles are snow-capped and shining white, and she takes it as a sign that her husband will be home soon.

Before leaving for the village, she writes a note for Vicente. *It would be just like him to show up unannounced on Christmas Eve*, she thinks. She imagines him arriving, arms loaded with gifts, like one of the Three Wise Men.

"The key is in the usual spot," the note reads. "I'm at Madame Chabaud's. Join me there or wait for me here."

Fingers stiff with cold, she props the note against the front door and sets off, murmuring "Amen" to herself the way François taught her to, as "ah-menn," and not "oh-mayne," as Ashkenazi Jews say it.

The church is packed, and no one pays attention to Myriam during the mass—she was clearly worried for nothing. Afterward, Madame Chabaud is waiting for her at the door. The parish priest greets the widow warmly.

"Madame Chabaud! You should come and visit me more often! Just look," he says, indicating Myriam. "Tonight you set a good example, and it was followed."

"May I remind you, Father, that work *is* prayer?" Madame Chabaud replies smoothly. She takes Myriam by the arm and leads her away.

The priest lets them go without saying anything more. He knows that the widow harvests her own grain, gathers her own fruit and almonds to sell, tends her own flock of sheep for meat, milk, and wool, and cares for her own four horses, which she gladly loans to anyone who needs them. She doesn't have time to come to church every Sunday, but more than one family in the village owes its life to her.

Madame Chabaud takes Myriam to her house, where the table is already set with three snowy white linen tablecloths laid one on top of another like fresh sheets on a grand antique bed, to be stripped off as the festivities progress. The middle cloth will be used for the next day's lunch, a meal solely composed of various meats. The bottom cloth will be used on the evening of the 25th, when leftovers are eaten. But right now, the uppermost cloth is covered with what the people of Provence call "the Thirteen Desserts of Christmas Eve."

The table is heaped with olive and holly branches, representing happiness. The three candles of the Holy Trinity are burning next to *le blé de Sainte-Barbe*—a saucer of lentils that Madame Chabaud has been germinating since December 4. The pulses have sprouted a thatch of thick green shoots, like the beard they're named for. A loaf of bread has been torn into three pieces—one for Jesus, one for the assembled guests, and one for the beggar—and stored in a cupboard, wrapped in cloth. Myriam remembers her grandfather breaking a loaf of bread at the beginning of the kiddush. Remembers, too, that at Pesach dinner, a cup of wine was always set aside for the prophet Elijah.

All along the length of the table, platters hold the traditional thirteen desserts.

"Take a good look! You won't see this anywhere but in Provence," Madame Chabaud says. "This is *la pompa a l'òli*, sweet bread made with wheat flour. We call it that because it soaks up the olive oil like a thirsty donkey."

Myriam breathes in the aroma of the yeasted bread perfumed with orange blossom water, its insides yellow as butter, its top sprinkled with crystals of cane sugar.

"You must never cut this bread with a knife," Madame Chabaud explains. "It brings bad luck."

"You can find yourself ruined in the year to come," adds her son.

"And these, Myriam," the widow says, with obvious pride in her ancestral Provençal traditions, "are *li quatre pachichòis*—the four beggars."

The four beggars are arranged on four plates, symbolizing the four religious orders having taken a vow of poverty. There are dates, each with an "O" carved in its pit to represent the exclamation of the Holy Family when they tasted the fruit for the first time.

"If you can't get dates, you use dried figs with a nut stuffed inside," Madame Chabaud tells Myriam.

"It's the nougat of the poor," says her son.

The ninth platter contains seasonal fresh fruits: arbutus berries and grapes, Brignoles plums and pears poached in wine—and *le verdaù*, a green melon, the last melon of autumn, never picked until its skin is slightly wrinkled. And there are pastries: deep-fried *bugnes*; flat waffles called *oreillettes*; boat-shaped *navettes* perfumed with cumin and anise; almond biscotti; *galettes de lait*; and crunchy biscuits made with pine nuts.

The sight of the lavish table reminds Myriam of Yom Kippur dinners in Palestine, when the Ten Days of Repentance were capped off by the sound of the shofar. When they came back from the synagogue, there would be poppy-seed cakes waiting on the table, and little buns spread with soft white cheese, which her grandfather Nachman loved to eat with herring, accompanied by a cup of coffee with cream.

"So! Is this how they celebrate Christmas in Paris?" Madame Chabaud asks, seeing Myriam lost in thought.

Myriam smiles. "No—nothing like this!"

"I have a gift for you," Madame Chabaud says after dinner.

She leaves the table and comes back with an orange. Myriam's heart clenches at the sight of the delicate paper the fruit is wrapped in, the same paper used by the citrus-farm workers in Migdal. She remembers the bitter taste of the peel, which lingered beneath one's fingernails. She thinks back to the day her mother announced that the whole family would be moving to Paris. The words rang in her small ear like promises then. *Paris. La tour Eiffel. France.*

Ephraïm, Emma, Jacques, Noémie. Where are you? she wonders on the way home, as if an answer might rise up in the silent stillness of the night.

CHAPTER 11

It takes between four and five days of walking to cross the Spanish border by way of the Pyrenees. The journey costs 1,000 francs at the very least—and can cost as much as 60,000. Some *passeurs* demand part of their fee in advance and then fail to show up for the rendezvous. Sometimes their customers get killed on the way to their destination. But there are also brave and generous *passeurs*, to whom you can say, "I don't have any money on me, but I'll pay you one day."

And who reply, "Come on, then. We can't just leave you to the Germans."

Jeanine has heard all the stories. The *passeur* who's been recommended to her is a mountain guide, accustomed to the terrain. He's done at least thirty of these trips.

The man's first sight of his young female customer makes him nervous. Not only is she no taller than a child, but her clothes and shoes are totally inappropriate for a mountain crossing.

"They're the best I could find," she says.

"Well, don't complain when it gets bad," the man says.

"I'd originally planned to go by way of the Basque country," she explains.

"That would have been better for you. The crossing is less dangerous."

"But it's not safe anymore, not since the southern zone was invaded."

"I've heard that, yes."

"That's why I was told to take the Mont Valier route. The German soldiers won't go that way, apparently, because it's too dangerous."

The *passeur* eyes Jeanine, then says, dryly, "Better save your energy for walking."

Jeanine isn't typically chatty, but she needed to talk to calm her fear. She knows that others before her have found death, rather than freedom, at the end of the journey. But she fixes her gaze on the horizon, puts one foot in front of the other, and tries to forget that she suffers from vertigo.

Their feet sink into the powdery snow. It's more solid than it looks, the *passeur* reassures her. They walk across stream-beds filled with solid ice.

"What if someone breaks a leg?" Jeanine asks.

"I won't lie," the *passeur* answers, "it ends with a bullet in the head. It's either that or freeze to death."

When Jeanine looks up, Spain seems very close, as if she could reach out and touch its mountaintops, where lights can be seen burning in the night. But the more she walks, the farther away the lights get. She knows she must not despair. She thinks of the philosopher Walter Benjamin, who killed himself just after crossing the border because he thought the Spanish were about to turn him away. "My situation is hopeless," he'd written in his suicide note, "and I have no choice but to end it." And yet, if he'd stayed hopeful, he would have been all right.

After three days of walking, the *passeur* lifts a gloved hand, points into the distance, and says to Jeanine, "Go that way. This is where I leave you."

"What? You're not coming with me?"

"*Passeurs* never cross the border. You go the rest of the way alone. Just keep going straight until you reach a small chapel. They look after fugitives there. Good luck," he adds, turning around.

Jeanine remembers something her mother said once, when she was little, something she's never forgotten. A list of the ways a person could die.

Fire.
Poison.
Stabbing.
Drowning.
Suffocation.
"If you ever have to choose how you're going to die," Gabriële had said, "pick freezing to death. It's the easiest way. You don't feel anything. It's like you're just falling asleep."

CHAPTER 12

M yriam is woken up in the middle of the night by someone knocking on the kitchen window. It's Vicente,
she's sure of it. She slips her bare feet into an over-
sized, icy-cold pair of boots and pulls a cardigan on over her
nightgown. But the silhouette she sees outside in the darkness
isn't her husband's. This man is very tall, with broad shoulders.
He's resting one hand on a bicycle.

"Monsieur Picabia sent me," he says, in a thick local accent.

Myriam opens the door and lets him in. She looks around for
some matches to light a candle, but Jean Sidoine gestures that
they should keep the house dark. He takes off his hat and says,
"Your husband is in prison. He's been incarcerated in Dijon. He
sent me to get you. We'll take the next train. Hurry."

Myriam has inherited her mother's ability to think quickly
and calmly. She rapidly makes a mental list of the things that
must be done before leaving. *Check to make sure the coals in the
stove are extinguished. Don't leave any food out. Tidy the house.
Write a note to Madame Chabaud.*

"We've got two trains and a bus to catch," Jean says. "We'll
reach Dijon just before midnight."

At dawn, they make their way silently to the station in Saignon,
which serves the Cavaillon-Apt line. On the deserted platform,
Jean hands her an identity card.

"You're my wife," he says.

She's prettier than me, thinks Myriam, looking at the false ID.

The journey is long, a succession of buses and regional trains, every minute dangerous. It's cold, and Myriam isn't dressed warmly enough. At Montélimar, Jean drapes his large, heavy woolen cardigan over her shoulders.

At Valence, "husband and wife" hold their breath as uniformed Germans conduct identification checks. They hand over their false papers, and Jean admires the composure of this young woman, so cool-headed when faced with the enemy.

Aboard the train to Dijon on the last leg of the journey, the two of them alone in the car, Myriam allows herself to relax a little. She loves trains at night, when all is quiet and her fellow passengers are sleeping. It's when the mind can rest, no more decisions to make.

They both know they shouldn't tell each other anything about themselves. That, in these times, silence is key. But in the muffled quiet of this empty train car passing through the dark countryside, Jean and Myriam both feel the urge to confide in one another.

"The first time I ever took a train," Myriam says, breaking the silence, "I was crossing through Poland into Romania. There was this enormous lady who was in charge of the samovar. I remember her face vividly."

"Why were you going to Romania?"

"To board a ship. To Palestine. We lived there for a few years, my family and I."

"But you're Polish?"

"No. My mother's family is Polish, but I was born in Moscow," Myriam says, looking out the window at the ink-black outlines of the trees. "What about you?"

"I was born in Céreste. It's not far from Buoux. Two hours by bicycle, if you take the Manosque road. My father's a wheelwright and plays the cornet in the village band. And my mother is a trouser-maker." He beams proudly, slapping a hand on his thigh to show off his trousers.

"Lovely work," Myriam says, smiling. "And what do you do for a living?"

"I'm a teacher. Been a while since I set foot in a school, though, unfortunately. I've done some time in prison myself. One day, in the bistro in my village, I said I didn't like the war. The military court at Fort Saint Nicolas in Marseille immediately slapped me with a summons for making 'defeatist comments.' I got a year in prison for it. So I know what it's like, and I can tell you that what your husband needs most right now is fortitude. Inmates fight one another over toilet privileges or tobacco. You get thrown in the hole. The guards treat you like dirt. They shave your head. Your husband will have to learn to walk in wooden clogs and trade in cigarette butts and bear the humiliation of strip-searches. He'll drink rot-gut alcohol and get bullied by the screws. But the only thing that matters is that, one day, he'll get out."

"When did you get out?"

"January 21, 1941. I'd changed so much in a year, gotten so thin, that my own parents didn't recognize me. And I'd changed on the inside, too. No more pacifism for me. I made up my mind to help the Resistance."

"You're very brave."

"It isn't bravery. I do whatever I can, in my own way. In Céreste, there's a man. René. You go and see him, and he tells you what to do. Gives you small missions. Look, I even provide snacks," he says with a grin, taking two neatly-wrapped pieces of bread from his satchel.

Myriam smiles and shares Jean's bread with pleasure.

"We should be there soon," he says. "That's where we'll part ways. I'm going to drop you off at the house of the woman who's married to your husband's cellmate. Tomorrow, she'll take you to see him."

In Dijon, Myriam thanks Jean Sidoine. She grasps his arm just as he's walking away and says, "I want to be sent on missions, too."

"Very well. I'll speak to René."

René Char had been placed under surveillance in his hometown of L'Isle-sur-la-Sorgue. So, in 1941, he and his wife packed their bags and sought refuge with friends at their home in Céreste, fifty kilometers away.

Here he discovered the little village square with its chestnut trees and its houses rising up immediately in front of the church, like choir boys standing to attention before the vicar. It was beside the well in the middle of the square that he fell in love at first sight with a beautiful village girl, Marcelle Sidoine.

René went to the fountain every day, just to see her. The old ladies of the village watched from their benches, from behind their windows, and from the doorstep of the church, anticipating the moment when René would arrive to watch Marcelle drawing water from the well.

"You've dropped your handkerchief," he said to her one day.

Marcelle didn't say anything, just tucked the handkerchief into her pocket and walked away. She could feel the eyes of the old ladies boring into her back, and she knew they hadn't missed a single nuance of the scene.

She slipped a hand into her pocket. Her fingers found the scrap of paper tucked into the folds of the handkerchief. She knew it suggested a rendezvous. The old ladies of Céreste were quite familiar with the old handkerchief trick themselves. The sight of it had set their weary hearts fluttering again. They'd been slim and supple young women, too, once, drawing water from the well. They knew the words hidden in the handkerchief, the handkerchief hidden in the hand, the hand hidden in the pocket.

Marcelle would be immortalized as the vixen in *Feuillets d'Hypnos*, René Char's poetic journal of the war, published in 1946.

But in 1941, she was already married to a boy from the village, Louis Sidoine—whom no one could blame for not keeping a closer eye on his wife, as he was being held as a prisoner of war in Germany.

In a village, nothing is ever secret for long. The whispers spread quickly. An outsider had stolen the wife of a *Cérestain*. But the settling of accounts would have to wait. In the meantime, René left his wife and set up headquarters in the home of Marcelle's mother. It was here that he became the commander of a secret army, organizing in the shadows.

Throughout the region, there were men and women ready to fight. Sometimes whole families; sometimes isolated individuals who didn't even know they were on the same side as their neighbors. Little by little, these scattered fragments of the fledgling Resistance united around a number of leaders. One of those was René Char. He knew how to bring men together, to galvanize them into action, and—most importantly—to organize them, and to spot the most promising among their numbers. It was René who drew up the list of those he felt could be relied on, and René who assigned the missions. Using the name "Alexandre," in 1942, he was made a regional commander in the military collective grouping together the three most important Resistance movements in France's southern zone—the famous *armée secrete*, formed by Jean Moulin on the orders of General Charles de Gaulle. His code name was chosen in reference to Alexander the Great, the legendary warrior-poet, king of Macedonia and pupil of Aristotle.

René criss-crossed the region, traveling by bicycle and train and bus, finding friends where they had gone into hiding, inviting them to join the fight, working to connect anyone in and around Céreste who might be able to aid the Resistance. He drew up an underground Resistance map that showed hiding places in stables, houses with hidden entrances, streets to avoid so as not to be arrested. In a field where parachutists were scheduled to land, he had a tree cut down that had been a source of irritation for local farmers—he knew how to quiet the concerns of those who found him too enterprising.

René Char's men weren't yet armed, but they trained like soldiers awaiting the call to the front. In the meantime, they busied themselves carrying out intelligence missions, drawing Crosses of Lorraine on walls, and rigging the house of Jean Giono with explosives during the night of January 11–12, 1943, blowing up the front door and inflicting heavy structural damage. Why attack such a great writer and committed pacifist? Not everyone understood it.

"Anyone who's not with us is against us."

I n Dijon, Myriam spends the night at the home of a woman whose hair has been bleached so aggressively it's almost burned, in a damp apartment on the route de Plombières.

"I was a trapeze artist when I met my husband," the woman says, making up a bed for Myriam.

Myriam finds it hard to see any trace of the former athlete in the woman's fleshy body.

"Better get some rest. We're getting up early for the visit," the woman says, tossing her a blanket.

Myriam doesn't sleep. It's been a long time since she last heard the sound of planes strafing the city. She watches the sunrise out the window. Her legs feel as if they're still vibrating from the train, the same way the ground seems to shift and heave after a boat trip.

It takes an hour of walking through fields to reach the Fort d'Hauteville, overlooking Dijon. The building is a gray edifice with thick stone walls. Myriam is allowed to visit her husband. She hasn't seen him in two months. His face is pale and bleary, his eyes half-lidded.

"I've been getting these awful headaches," he says. "Pains in my kidneys, too."

That's all Vicente talks about—that and the terrible cold he has. His nose runs incessantly.

"Aren't you going to tell me what *happened?*" Myriam asks.

"I went to Étival, in the Jura. Like I said I would. I got some sheets and blankets. Silverware, too. The next day—it was December 26—I was on my way home with the suitcases. I had to cross the *déma*. The first time, I had a *passeur*, but I figured I could get back by myself. No such luck. At around midnight, I reached the bridge, and I ran into some Germans on patrol—and there I was with a suitcase stuffed to the gills. They accused me of being a black marketeer, and well, sweetheart, here I am."

Myriam says nothing. Her husband has never called her "sweetheart" before. And he won't meet her gaze. His skin is waxy, and his eyes have a glassy quality.

"Why are you scratching yourself like that?" she asks.

"Lice," he says bitterly. "Lice! Nits! The judge is supposed to hand down my sentence today or tomorrow. Then we'll see."

Myriam hardly notices her husband's sour mood. Something else is foremost in her mind.

"Have you heard anything from my parents?"

"No. No news," Vicente says. His tone is cold.

It's as if he's punched her in the gut. Myriam can't breathe. Visiting hour is over. Vicente leans forward to whisper something in her ear.

"Did Maurice's wife give you anything for me?"

Myriam shakes her head. Vicente straightens up, frowning.

"Okay, then I'll see you tomorrow. Tomorrow, don't forget," he says, with a token attempt at a smile.

On the way back, the trapeze artist apologizes. She'd forgotten; she did have something for Vicente, actually. In the apartment, she shows Myriam a little wad of some black substance.

"Tomorrow, keep this between your fingers. That way, the guards don't see anything when you show them the palms of your hands at the prison entrance. And then slip it to your husband under the table. Make sure no one sees."

"What is it?" Myriam asks.

The trapeze artist realizes that Myriam has no idea what her husband is expecting her to do for him.

"It's one of my grandmother's old folk remedies," she says. "Relieves painful joints."

The next day, everything goes to plan. Vicente puts the shiny black wad under his tongue. Myriam watches her husband's face relax and brighten as if under the effect of some magical camera filter. For the first time, Vicente lays a hand on his wife's cheek. He stays that way for a long time without moving, gazing at something far away, behind her eyes.

The day after that, January 4, 1943, they learn that Vicente has been sentenced to four months in prison and a fine of 1,000 francs. Myriam was afraid it would be far worse, afraid he would be deported to Germany. As long as her handsome husband remains in France, she can bear anything.

B ack at the Hanged Man's House, Myriam finds the Plateau des Claparèdes the same as it has always been. Everything still in exactly the same place as before. Indifferent. The month of January 1943 is a frozen wasteland that chills her to the bone.

One night, as she's getting ready for bed, a knock at the window makes her jump.

"I have something for you," Jean Sidoine calls, tapping on the glass.

Balanced on the luggage rack of his bicycle is a large toolbox, from which he takes a carefully wrapped object. Myriam immediately recognizes a brown Bakelite wireless.

"You told me your father was an engineer, and he taught you a bit about radios," he says.

She nods. "I can even fix it for you, if it's broken."

"Mostly I just want you to listen to it. Have you been to Fourcadure?"

"The farm? I know where it is."

"The owners have electricity, and they've agreed to help us. We're going to put this radio in a little shed on their property, and you'll go there and listen to it. We need you to listen to the late BBC news bulletin. The one that airs after nine o'clock at night. Write down everything you hear on a piece of paper and then take it to François's hostel. There's a cookie tin in the kitchen pantry, hidden behind bags of dried herbs. Leave all messages in that tin."

"Every night?"

"Every night."

"Does François know about it?"

"No. Just say you're stopping by for a cup of tea and a chat because you're feeling a bit lonely. Don't worry him, whatever you do. He mustn't suspect anything."

"When do I start?"

"Tonight. The news bulletin comes on at 9:30 sharp."

Myriam plunges into the night toward Fourcadure. When she reaches the farm, she goes straight to the shed, sets up the anti-jamming antenna, and turns on the radio. The transmission crackles with static, and she has to press her ear against the wireless to hear what's being said, especially when the wind gusts. In the darkness of her hiding place, she writes down the bulletin, unable to see the sheet of paper or her own hand. It's not easy.

Once the broadcast has finished, she emerges from the shed, careful not to be seen, and makes her way to the hostel run by François Morenas. It's a thirty-minute walk in inky darkness, the cold burning her skin. But she feels useful, so it's all right.

Myriam enters François's hostel without knocking and invites herself to have a cup of herbal tea with him. She's shivering, and François drapes one of the hostel's blankets over her—so rustic that dried herbs are embedded in the wool. Woolen and absorbent cotton clothing has been rationed for some time, and a blanket like this one, scratchy as it is, is a rare commodity.

Myriam offers to prepare the herbal tea herself. As she is putting the bags away in the pantry afterward, she slips the folded paper into the cookie tin. Her hands shake on the first few nights that she does this, from cold, from fear.

During the day, she teaches herself to write with her eyes closed. The messages become more legible as time passes. Soon, the nightly news bulletin is all she lives for.

After two weeks, François says to Myriam, "I know you're listening to the radio."

Myriam tries to keep her face impassive. François shouldn't know this.

Jean has told him everything. Why? To protect Myriam's honor. Because one evening, François said to him, "Madame Picabia keeps coming to see me. She wants to chat. Talk. Every night."

"She's quite alone in the world at the moment, poor girl, without her husband."

"You don't think . . ."

"Think what?"

"You know . . ."

"I don't know what you're talking about."

"You think she's waiting for me to . . . you know, make the first move?"

François had asked the question simply, not lewdly or lasciviously, but because the matter was on his mind. Jean had felt guilty, and so he'd explained why Myriam was coming to the hostel every night. He'd broken the rules of silence to safeguard the respect that was a married woman's due.

CHAPTER 16

Maman,
I'm making a lot of progress with my investigation.

I read Jean Sidoine's memoirs. So much information in them. He talks about Yves, and Myriam, and Vicente.

He even includes a photo of your parents. They're milking a sheep. Myriam is holding a baby lamb in her arms, and Vicente's squatting down by the mother's udder. They look happy.

I've ordered the memoirs of Marcelle Sidoine's daughter, too, who talks about her childhood in Céreste with René Char during the war. I think she's still alive.

Do you remember her? Mireille is her name. She was about ten years old during the war.

I also need to talk to you about something else I found out. In one of her notes, Myriam refers to a man named François Morenas. He ran a youth hostel. He also wrote several books, talking about his memories. He mentions Myriam quite a few times, too.

One day, when you're ready, I'll photocopy those passages for you—if you want. One of them made me particularly emotional. It's on page 126 of *Clermont des lapins: chronique d'une auberge de jeunesse en pays d'Apt, 1940–1945*. François Morenas writes, "Myriam came to live on the Plateau des Bories. In a solitary little house where a man had recently hung himself, this young woman lived all by herself. She often came to visit me for company. She worked for a Resistance group and paid rent to Fourcadure because it had electricity. She went there at night, in secret, to listen to the radio broadcast from London."

It overwhelmed me completely to stumble across Myriam in that book, Maman.

And I thought of you. Doing your research and finding Noémie, purely by chance, in Adélaïde Hautval's book. I know it's hard for you to watch me going so deep into all that history. Your parents' history. You never tried to find out exactly what happened on the Plateau des Claparèdes that year, the year before you were born.

And I can guess why. Of course.

I'm your daughter, Maman. You're the one who taught me how to do research, to gather information, to make even the smallest scrap of paper speak. Really, I'm just doing what you showed me how to do. I'm carrying on your work, that's all.

The strength I'm drawing on, to put together the pieces of the past . . . I got that from you.

Anne,
My mother never spoke about that part of her past.

Except once. She said to me, "Those were probably the happiest times of my life. Know that."

Something came in the mail from the mayor's office in Les Forges just this morning, believe it or not.

You remember the secretary? I think she's found some documents for us. I haven't opened the envelope yet. But remind me about it next time you come to the house with Clara.

S hortly before the beginning of Lent, a band of traditional Provençal *bouffet* dancers wends its way from village to village, a crowd of children at its heels. The lead dancer holds aloft a fishing pole with a paper crescent moon at its tip; this is the celebrants' *dame blanche*, their pale goddess. In front of the church in Buoux, Myriam lets herself be swept along by the snaking line of dancers, to the sound of horns and bells. The young people hop and stamp their feet on the ground, strings of tiny bells on their ankles tinkling, entreating Mother Earth to awaken and bring forth her life-giving bounty. The *bouffets* also carry bellows, and they blow spurts of air into the villagers' faces like insults and then hobble away, limping theatrically—*à pèd couquet*, in the local dialect—in a grotesque dance. They grin horribly, their faces covered with a mask made from flour and egg-whites: clowns, but with old-man wrinkles. Children run from house to house like a swarm of field mice, faces blackened with burnt cork, seeking the traditional gifts of an egg or a bit of flour from the homeowners.

In the midst of this clamor, a voice murmurs in Myriam's ear, "You're going to have a visit tonight."

They arrive shortly before sunrise. Jean Sidoine and a pale, exhausted young man.

"You've got to hide him," Jean says. "In the little shed out back. Just for a few days. I'll let you know. No more news bulletins for now. We'll just keep an eye on the boy. He's young. Seventeen, if that. His name is Guy."

"I have a brother your age," Myriam says to the teenager. "Come into the kitchen; I'll find you something to eat."

She takes care of him the way she hopes that someone, somewhere, is taking care of Jacques. She gives him some bread and cheese and drapes François's heavy woolen blanket over his shoulders.

"Eat and get yourself nice and warm."

"Are you Jewish?" the boy asks, abruptly.

"Yes," Myriam answers, unprepared for the question.

"Me, too," he says, wolfing down the bread. "Can I have some more?"

His tired eyes are fixed on the remainder of the loaf.

"Of course," Myriam says.

"I was born in France. Where were you born?"

"Moscow."

"It's because of you, all of you, what's happened . . ." he says, now staring at a bottle of wine on the table.

The wine was a gift from Madame Chabaud. Myriam has been saving it for Vicente's return. But seeing the hopeful gleam in the boy's eyes, she seizes the bottle without hesitation.

"I was born in Paris. My parents were born in Paris," he says. "Everyone here liked us. Before you came. Before all you *foreigners* invaded us."

"Really? Is that how you see it?" Myriam asks calmly, busy with the corkscrew.

"My papa fought in the Great War. He wanted to enlist again in '39, too—put his uniform back on and defend his country."

"The army wouldn't take him?"

"Too old," Guy mumbles, draining the glass of wine Myriam hands him in one long swallow. "My big brother fought, though. He didn't come back."

"I'm sorry," Myriam says gently, refilling the boy's glass. "So, what's happened to you?"

"My papa's a doctor. One day, a patient warned him that we

had to leave. The whole family moved to Bordeaux. My sister, my parents, and me. From there, we went to Marseille. My parents managed to rent an apartment, and we stayed there a few months. When the Germans came, my parents decided we should go to the United States. But at the last minute, we were betrayed. The neighbors. The Germans took us to the camp at Les Milles."

"Where is Les Milles?"

"Near Aix-en-Provence. There were regular convoys."

"Convoys? What's a convoy?"

"They put everyone on trains. To a place a lot of you call 'Pitchipoi,' or so I've heard . . ."

"Who is this 'you' you keep talking about? Foreigners? You seem to hate Jews even more than the Germans do."

"Your language is so ugly."

"So, your parents left in a convoy to Germany, is that right?" Myriam asks, remaining calm in the face of the boy's anger.

"Yes, with my sister. On September 10. But I escaped the night before."

"How?"

"There was a kind of panic in the camp, and I took advantage of it and ran. I ended up in Venelles; I don't know how. A farmer and his wife hid me there for three months, but they argued about it a lot. He wanted to let me stay; she didn't. I was afraid she'd turn me over to the Germans. So I left on Christmas night. I spent several days in a forest. A hunter found me sleeping and took me to Meyrargues with him. He lived alone. He was nice. Except when he drank; then he went crazy. One night he started firing his rifle in the air. I got scared, and I ran away again. An old couple in Pertuis took me in. They'd lost their son in the Great War. I slept in his bedroom, with all his things. It was fine there, but . . . I don't know, one night I just ran away again, for no reason. Then the forest again. I fainted, I think. And when I woke up, I was in a barn. Your friend was there, and he brought me here."

"In the camp where you were, do you remember meeting a boy your own age? Jacques? And a girl called Noémie?"

"No. Doesn't sound familiar. Who are they?"

"My brother and sister. They were arrested in July."

"July? You'll never see them again. Gotta face facts. That 'work' in Germany . . . it doesn't exist."

"All right," Myriam says, taking the bottle of wine from him. "Time to rest."

She avoids the teenager over the days that follow. One evening, leaning out the window, she hears the sound of Jean's bike.

"You have to take the boy up to Morenas's. A fellow's going to pick him up and take him to Spain. The hostel is the rendezvous point. François doesn't know. Tell him Guy's a friend of yours from Paris. You bumped into each other by chance on the train, but he can't stay with you because you've got to visit your husband."

"Myriam," François writes in his memoirs, "the mysterious girl from the plateau, brought a friend to stay with me. He had nothing of the hostel spirit in him. He wanted to live in Clermont, claimed he was Jewish. She'd run into him on the train and took him home to give him a good meal."

The next day, Jean comes to see Myriam again, to make sure everything went according to plan.

"What do I do now?" she asks. "The news bulletins again?"

"No. Hold off for now. It's dangerous. We need to lie low for a while. Let everyone forget about us."

Weeks creep by in the Hanged Man's House. Myriam feels her world shrinking, freezing. The wind blows night and day, whistling through the closed shutters and beneath the doors, as if warning of a distant enemy. It's enough to drive one insane. The still, icy veil of winter settles over the endless bare trees of the plateau.

The landscape of Haute-Provence is nothing like the plains of Latvia or the deserts of Palestine; rather, it's like something Myriam has known for a long time. Since her birth, since her first journey by wagon through the forests of Russia.

Exile.

She's angry with herself for obeying Ephraïm when he ordered her to hide in the orchard that night. Why do girls always do what their fathers tell them? She should have stayed with her parents.

She goes over those last months spent with her family, but it's as if she's viewing them through a dark filter. The coolness that had sprung up between her and her sister. Noémie often reproached her for it; she wanted to spend more time together. Myriam had blamed everything on her marriage—but the truth was that she'd felt the need to distance herself from Noémie, to fling open the windows of a room grown too small. They weren't little girls anymore. Their bodies had grown; they were two women now. Myriam had needed her space.

The older sister had begun frequently treating the younger with disdain. She was tired of Noémie's moodiness, her embarrassing outbursts in front of everyone, even at the dinner table.

Myriam felt as if Noémie lived her whole life as an open book, even the most private moments, and sometimes it drove her crazy.

How she regrets that now.

She'll make it all up to Noémie, she promises herself. They'll take the metro from the Sorbonne together again, and giggle together on a bench as they watch people pass in the Luxembourg Gardens. And she'll take Jacques to see the tropical forests in the enormous, humid greenhouses of the Jardin des Plantes.

She stays curled up in bed, newspapers and clothing piled on top of the blankets to keep in the warmth. She lets herself drift into a kind of half-sleep, a state of indifference, where nothing matters anymore.

She opens her eyes from time to time, as slowly as possible. She moves as little as she can, only getting out of bed to fetch a new oven-warmed brick to shove beneath the covers or eat a slice of the bread left by Madame Chabaud, then returning to her room. She doesn't know what day it is anymore, or even what time. Sometimes she doesn't even know if she's asleep or awake, if the whole world is after her, or if it's forgotten her altogether.

How can you tell you're alive, when there's no one to witness your existence?

Sleep. As much sleep as possible. One morning she opens her eyes, and there's a small fox sitting there in front of her, looking at her.

It's Uncle Boris, Myriam says to herself. *He's come from Czechoslovakia to watch over me.*

The thought gives her courage. She allows her spirit to roam free. She sees the sunlight filtering through the boulders and aspen trees of a forest a long way away, the bright sun of Czech holidays warm on her skin.

"Man can't live without nature," Boris whispers to her, through the fox. "He needs air to breathe, water to drink, fruit to eat. But nature is quite able to live without man. Which proves just how superior it is to us."

Myriam remembers how enthusiastically Boris used to speak about Aristotle's writings on the natural sciences and about the Greek physician who treated several Roman emperors.

"Galen says that nature is always giving us signals. For example, peonies are red because they heal the blood. Celandine sap is yellow because it can treat biliary illnesses. *Stachys byzantina*, called hare's ear because of its shape, can be used for problems with the auditory canal."

Uncle Boris skipped through nature as lightly as a sprite. Aged fifty, he looked at least fifteen years younger. He attributed this to his habit of taking cold baths, following the example of Sebastian Kneipp, a German priest who had cured himself of tuberculosis through the science of hydrotherapy. A copy in the original German of Kneipp's 1894 book, *Thus Shalt Thou Live: Hints and Advice for the Healthy and the Sick on a Simple and Rational Mode of Life and a Natural Method of Cure*, could always be found on Boris's nightstand.

Uncle Boris used to scribble notes on his shirtsleeves because there wasn't room for any more paper in his already bulging pockets. Pausing next to a white willow, he would say, "This tree is aspirin, you know. The laboratories want to convince us that only the chemicals they manufacture can cure human disease. Eventually people will end up believing it."

He showed his nieces how to pick flowers, which part of the stems to pinch so they wouldn't lose their medicinal properties. Sometimes he would stop walking and, taking Myriam and Noémie by the shoulders, turn their young bodies to face the horizon.

"Nature isn't just scenery," he would say. "It's not around you, but within you. It is *inside* you, just as you are inside it."

One morning, the fox is gone. Myriam senses that it will not be back. For the first time in a long time, she opens her bedroom window. The almond trees on the Plateau des Claparèdes are covered in tiny white buds. Winter has been driven away by the weak rays of the sun. Light glints on the Alpilles, heralding the arrival of spring.

Vicente is released from the prison in Hauteville-lès-Dijon on April 25, 1943. But he doesn't go directly home to his wife. First, he has to see Jean Sidoine.

CHAPTER 19

Every French male between the ages of twenty and twenty-two is summoned to the town hall to show their ID papers and undergo a medical exam. Once registered, they must wait to receive their notice to report. The Service du travail obligatoire (STO), or compulsory work service, is, as the name suggests, compulsory. Draftees are required to serve two years.

> By working in Germany, you will be an ambassador of French excellence.
> By working for Europe, you are protecting your home and family.
> The hard times are over; Papa is earning money in Germany.

The Vichy government promises the French that the young men sent to Germany will be given the opportunity to acquire new skills, and that each one's professional qualifications will be taken into account. In the end, nearly six hundred thousand young Frenchmen will go. But not all of them. Many refuse to obey the summons.

Raids and police checks are carried out all over the country, and "insubordinates" and "draft dodgers" are arrested. Families are threatened with punishment. Anyone who helps a young man evade STO is slapped with a fine of up to 100,000 francs.

These men who refuse to be sent to Germany have no choice but to go into hiding. They seek refuge in rural areas, hiding on farms. And many of them join the Resistance. The ranks of France's shadow army swell by approximately forty thousand.

René Char, from his headquarters in Céreste, takes command of the effort to recruit draft dodgers from the Durance zone. He organizes lodging for them, tests their abilities, and gauges the strength of their convictions. Then he coordinates their missions. Jean Sidoine comes to speak to him about a cousin. He's a gentle boy, bookish but reliable, Jean assures René. They agree to hide the young man in the home of the young Jewish woman on the Plateau des Claparèdes.

That young man is Yves Bouveris. He's the one I'm looking for.

Myriam stands in the doorway of the Hanged Man's House. Shading her eyes from the sun with one hand, she squints into the distance. She knows the man coming toward her is her husband, but she hardly recognizes him. His cheeks are hollow like an old man's, but his body has lost all its muscle, and he looks like a child from the neck down. He's smaller than the Vicente in her memory. There is a faded green-and-yellow bruise at the corner of one eye.

Vicente is being escorted by the two Sidoine cousins, Yves and Jean, each grasping one of his arms as if they were hospital orderlies, or police officers. The three men approach the house like exhausted soldiers returning from war, their trouser pockets bulging, their mouths dry with dust from the roads.

"I thought you could put up my cousin here," Jean says to Myriam. "He's an STO."

Myriam agrees without really paying attention, overwhelmed by her husband's presence.

Before he leaves, Jean Sidoine warns her, "When I got out of prison, it took me weeks to adjust. Be patient with him. Don't get discouraged."

And indeed, Vicente doesn't want to sleep in the bedroom that night. He wants to spend his first night as a free man outside, under the stars. Myriam is almost relieved. Contrary to what she imagined during her weeks of hibernation, seeing Vicente again isn't a relief. She would even say it's the opposite. At least he was *safe* in prison. Safe from the Germans, and the French police, and most importantly, safe from the obscure dangers Myriam senses but is unable to name.

Over the next few days, Myriam jumps every time Yves comes into her field of vision. She can't get used to his presence. Completely preoccupied by her husband's health, nothing else matters. Twice a day she brings him a tray, with soup she makes herself and bread she fetches from the village. When she sits down next to him, Myriam feels that she is too fleshy somehow, her round hips curving out from her waist like a cello. Sometimes she feels as if she's become her husband's mother.

After several days, Vicente has regained strength—but now it's Myriam's turn to fall ill. She develops a high fever, her body giving off an acrid odor as her temperature rises. Vicente takes charge of the tray, bringing it up to the bedroom twice a day. Yves tells him about an infusion his grandmother used to make for fever. He takes Vicente to gather calamint in the fields.

Thanks to Yves's tisane, Myriam gets better. Vicente decides that this is cause for celebration. He goes to the market in Apt to buy the ingredients for a special dinner, and for the first time Myriam and Yves are alone in the house together.

Yves's presence bothers Myriam. She knows he's doing the best he can, but somehow this annoys her even more.

Vicente comes back from the market with two bottles of wine, turnips, cheese, a jar of jam, and a loaf of bread. A feast.

"Look," he says to Myriam. "Look how they wrap goat cheese in dried chestnut leaves here."

Neither Myriam nor Vicente has ever seen anything like it. They peel the leaves apart carefully, as if unwrapping a fragile gift. This method keeps the cheese soft for a long time, even in the winter, Yves tells them. Vicente is delighted by the explanation.

"A Roman emperor, Antoninus Pius, died from eating too much cheese, you know," Yves adds.

He bought a book from a traveling bookseller recently, just

because he was tickled by the title. It's a novel by Pierre Loti, published in 1883, called *My Brother Yves*.

"Why don't we read it aloud?" he suggests to Myriam and Vicente now. "We can take turns."

Vicente opens a bottle of wine. While Myriam peels the vegetables and Yves sets the table, Vicente reads to them, smoking contraband cigarettes that stain his fingers.

The book opens with a description of the titular character, a sailor Pierre Loti once knew aboard a ship and seems to have really loved.

"'Kermadec (Yves-Marie), son of Yves-Marie and Jeanne Danveoch. Born August 28, 1851, in Saint-Pol-de-Léon, Finistère. Height: 5 foot 9. Chestnut hair, chestnut eyebrows, brown eyes. Unremarkable nose, ordinary chin, ordinary forehead, oval face.' Now you!" he says to Yves, who has to describe himself in the style of the book on the spot: "Bouveris (Yves-Henri-Vincent), son of Fernand and Julie Sautel. Born May 20, 1920, in Sisteron, Provence. Height: 5 foot 9. Brown hair, brown eyebrows, brown eyes. Unremarkable nose, ordinary chin, ordinary forehead, oval face."

"Perfect!" Vicente exclaims, pleased by how fast Yves has grasped the rules of the game.

He continues reading, "'Distinctive features: tattoo of an anchor on the left pectoral; tattoo of a bracelet with a fish on the right wrist.'"

"I don't have any tattoos," Yves says.

"We can fix that," says Vicente, leaving the room.

The remark makes Myriam uneasy. She knows her husband is capable of strange things sometimes.

Vicente comes back with a piece of charcoal. He takes Yves's wrist and ceremoniously draws a thin black line around it, like the bracelet described in Loti's novel. It tickles, and Yves laughs. The laugh irritates Myriam. Then Vicente says he wants to draw an anchor on Yves's left pectoral. *He's taking the game too far,*

Myriam thinks uncomfortably. But Yves unbuttons his shirt will-ingly. His body is lean and well-formed. His skin gives off a strong odor of sweat that surprises Myriam—and arouses Vicente.

In that kitchen that evening, Vicente realizes just how naïve and innocent both Myriam and Yves are. The country boy and the young foreigner. Vicente, accustomed to the jaded children of his parents' circle, finds this both vexing and provocative.

When Myriam and Vicente first met two years prior, he'd made suggestive remarks about the nights he'd spent in the home of André Gide. Myriam, who had read Gide, hadn't understood the allusions.

She wasn't like the free-thinking, sophisticated girls he nor-mally ran with, Vicente had realized. And then it was too late to explain things to her. And too complicated. They were already married.

The very little Myriam had heard about relationships be-tween men—always writers: Oscar Wilde, Arthur Rimbaud, Verlaine, and Marcel Proust—had been abstract notions. Their books hadn't helped her to understand her husband any more than they'd taught her about life. It was only through *living* that, much later, she gained a true understanding of the books she'd read in her youth.

Vicente wants to know everything about Yves. He asks him endless questions, gazing intently at him, the same way he used to look at Myriam when she was the one who interested him.

Yves tells them that he was born in Sisteron, a village one hundred kilometers to the north of Apt, on the road to Gap. His mother, Julie, was from Céreste, the home of Jean Sidoine and most of Yves's own family. As a child, Yves lived in the schools where his mother was a teacher. He used to envy his classmates, who went home when the day's lessons were done. He never got to go anywhere.

Eventually he was sent away to boarding school in Digne. These were bleak years, years of unheated classrooms and damp beds in dormitories and cold-water baths. Food was strictly rationed and sweaters rarely mended. Yves had hated the place and failed to make any friends, taking refuge in his books instead. He loved travel adventure stories: Joseph Peyré, Roger Frison-Roche, and the great mountain-climbers. He was a shy, gentle boy who knew how to fight—but preferred fishing and outdoor sports.

"I'll say goodnight," Yves announces after dinner. He apologizes for talking too much as he leaves the room.

Vicente asks Myriam what she thinks of their lodger.

"Very . . . open," Myriam says.

"Sometimes that's a good thing," Vicente replies.

Vicente and Yves become inseparable. On one clear night when the moon is full, Yves shows Vicente how to catch crayfish in the Aiguebrun river. They laugh so much that they don't catch anything, the crayfish wriggling through their fingers. They come back to the house at dawn with a single large trout, which practically launched itself into their hands. They eat the trout for breakfast, and the boys nickname it *la goulue*, "the glutton," because of how fat it is.

Myriam has never seen Vicente so enthusiastic about fishing; he usually shows no interest in "manly" pursuits. She remarks on it to him.

"Things change," he says, enigmatically.

The boys spend whole days together, coming and going from the house, sometimes vanishing for hours, shaking the rafters with their boisterous laughter and thumping footsteps when they're at home. One day, Myriam reproaches Vicente for the noise. It's dangerous, she says.

He shrugs disdainfully. "Who's going to hear us?"

Yves and Vicente begin to grate on Myriam's nerves, especially when they try to act older, sometimes even all of *thirty*. They smoke pipes to make themselves seem sophisticated and converse loftily about Life. Sometimes they even try to talk philosophy, which makes Myriam want to scream.

Yves asks Vicente a lot of questions about Paris and the artistic scene. He can't believe he knows someone his own age who's on a first-name basis with André Gide.

"Have you read his books?" he asks Vicente.

"No, but I told him they were rubbish anyway."

Yves is dazzled by having a friend who speaks of Picasso like an old uncle. Myriam, listening to them talk in the living room, bites back her exasperation.

"And so Marcel gave the Mona Lisa a mustache," Vicente recounts. Grabbing a sheet of paper, he sketches the painting, complete with facial hair.

"I can't believe it," Yves says.

"It's true. And then he wrote underneath it . . ."

Vicente writes five capital letters in pencil.

"L.H.O.O.Q.," Yves reads aloud. It takes him a moment to grasp the meaning of what he's just said. *El . . . ah-sh . . . oh . . . oh . . . kou. Elle a chaud au cul.* She has a hot ass.

They laugh uproariously. Myriam goes into the bedroom and shuts the door.

Yves proposes a day trip to the Fort de Buoux, a medieval fortress on the heights.

"It's beautiful," he says to Vicente. "Like an island. You'll love it."

Myriam hurriedly slips on a pair of her husband's trousers and goes with the boys. She's sick of being home alone.

The three of them take the road through the Serre valley that leads to the fort. They're silent at the sight of the enormous sheer cliffs at the mountaintop. Rock-cut stairs lead up to the round tower, their treads cut long and flat so mules can climb them. Ravens perch, proprietary and unchallenged, among the ruins.

Myriam deciphers the Latin dedication etched into the stone pediment of the ancient church with its barrel-vaulted ceiling: "*In nonis Januarii dedication istius ecclesiae. Vos qui transitis . . . qui flere velitis . . . per me transite. Sum janua vitae.*" She translates it for the boys.

"I dedicate this church on the 9th of January. You who pass by here . . . who wish to weep . . . pass through me. I am the gateway to life."

Yves shows Myriam and Vicente how to tell sparrowhawks from mountain eagles. Pointing with his finger, he shows them Mont Ventoux in the distance. He knows the names of plants and animals and rocks by heart. He is fond of definitions and loves to identify things in nature. He reminds Myriam of Uncle Boris, who loved to categorize and define, too. This unexpected bond between the country boy and her uncle, purely imaginary as it is, affects Myriam. She begins to look at Yves differently.

As they explore the ramparts and rock-cut buildings, Myriam watches the boys up ahead of her. Yves and Vicente are exactly the same height; they could trade clothes and shoes. But they are so different. Vicente is a surface being. An exquisite surface, but impossible to penetrate. All the mysterious things going on beneath his skin, in his veins and his bodily fluids and his mind, remain a permanent enigma to Myriam and the rest of the world. Yves, on the other hand, is cut from a single, homogeneous block of stone. What he shows you on the outside is the same as what's going on inside him. Two men, like the two faces of one coin.

After the Fort de Buoux, Yves takes them to see the *bories*. These are round dry-stone shelters, mysterious huts built solely of ingeniously stacked flat stones.

When Myriam and Vicente go inside one of the *bories*, the contrast between the bright sunlight outside and the complete darkness within renders them temporarily blind. Gradually their eyes adjust, and their bodies become aware of the space around them. The air is cool. The ceiling, made of overlapping stones, resembles a huge overturned bird's nest.

"It's like we're inside a giant tit," Vicente quips, caressing one of Myriam's breasts in the darkness.

Then he kisses her, right in front of Yves. Myriam lets him do it. She senses that something is happening, but what? She doesn't know how to put a name to it. She and Yves are both startled and uncomfortable.

"The origins of the *bories*," Yves says, to cover his embarrassment, "lie in the earth itself. The soil here is very rocky and has to be cleared. As people were removing the stones, they put them aside in piles. Eventually they made shelters out of the piles. Shepherds rest in them when the weather gets too hot."

On the way back, they hear laughter coming from the Seguins tavern near Buoux. Life out here in the countryside seems so *normal*, in the gentle warmth of the late afternoon.

The humid air dampens the senses. Yves thinks women are

impenetrable mysteries. Vicente tries to manufacture secrets where
they don't exist, merely to keep boredom at bay. He was thrown
into so many strange situations at such a young age. He got used
to the smut and obscenity of adults the same way he got used to
opium. Eventually there was no more mystique to be found in
the bedroom of a woman or a man. His brain has come to
require ever-greater doses of excitement, ever more exotic plea-
sures, spiced with the tang of heat and blood.

And yet, sometimes, his jaded cynicism gives way to a sudden
purity. His thoughts turn artless and clear, and he wants nothing
in the world but simple love, childlike joy.

Myriam has never seen her husband so happy or healthy as he
is now, every day of this life an adventure. Eating escargots one
day, beet greens and sprouted wheat the next. Gathering dead
wood and building a fire to cook their chops. Making rope from
nettle-stems after tearing them in half lengthwise and stripping
out the insides. Washing the sheets and spreading them in the
sun to dry. And reading Loti aloud in the evenings, each of them
taking their turn.

"'Yves, my brother,'" Vicente picks up, with emphasis, "'we
are but grown-up children, often very merry when there is no
reason, and now rambling off into sadness because of a chance
moment of peace and happiness.'"

Vicente *is* happy, but the reasons for this happiness are mysterious, obscure, incomprehensible to Myriam. The truth is that
Vicente is living his own version of the period before he was
born. When the Picabias were invited to dinner back then, the
host had to set three places. One for Francis, one for Gabriële,
and one for Marcel Duchamp.

Vicente has inherited his father's taste for illicit substances,
and also for the number three. A number that, in its inherent
disequilibrium, allows for infinite motion, unexpected combina-
tions, and accidental friction . . .

One day, Vicente comes back from the market and announces that they're out of money. He has spent the last of what his mother gave him. From now on, they'll have to work.

Vicente, who is the only one of the three not wanted by the Germans, tries to get a job at the small candied-fruit factory on the Apt road. But the foreman doesn't like the look of him, and he returns home empty-handed.

The next day, Yves goes to Céreste, to borrow a ferret from one of his cousins.

"We're not going to *eat* that, are we?" Myriam asks apprehensively.

"No! Of course not! It's for the rabbits."

Since the Vichy government made it illegal to own a gun, it has become impossible to hunt for rabbits or any other forest game. But Yves knows a technique involving a ferret and a large canvas sack.

"You have to find a rabbit hole. You stuff the ferret in one end of the hole, and put the sack over the other end to catch the rabbits when they run out."

That evening they dine hungrily on one rabbit and take a second to Madame Chabaud as rent. Myriam explains their financial situation—and Yves's presence.

The widow, whose son only narrowly avoided the Service du travail obligatoire himself, offers them work on her various properties.

Madame Chabaud, Myriam realizes, is one of those people who is never disappointing, where others always are.

"Once is never a surprise, but twice always is," she says, thanking their landlady. "Even though it should be the reverse."

The trio gets up at dawn to help gather cherries and almonds, cut hay, and pick borage and great mullein. Their hair is powdered with wheat-dust, their skin flushed red by heat and hard work. They find that they don't mind the fatigue, the sunburn, the insect bites and thistle scratches. Sometimes they're even joyfully content, especially in the hottest part of the afternoon, when everyone naps on piles of hay in the shade, the men on one side and the women on the other.

One morning, Vicente wakes up with one eyelid swollen to the size of a quail's egg. A spider bite, says Yves, showing Myriam two little red fang-marks. Yves and Myriam leave for the day, while Vicente stays home alone. When they come back in the evening, he's in a good mood. The swelling has gone down and the pain subsided, and he's even made dinner. In bed that night, Vicente says to Myriam, "When I saw the two of you coming home tonight, I thought you looked like a pair of lovers."

Myriam doesn't know what to say. She finds the remark very strange. It should be a reproach. But Vicente said it with such ease and good humor. She remembers Jean Sidoine's warning. He was right. Vicente isn't the same man anymore.

The month of July is meltingly hot. In Paris, people swarm to the spas, men and women in bathing suits packing the Seine's riverside terraces. Myriam, Vicente, and Yves decide to go in search of fresh air and cool water among the clifftops between Buoux and Sivergues, where one of the sources of the Durance river flows down from the heights into a man-made lake, lush green vegetation contrasting with pale, dry stone. It's a magical spot, tucked away amid the towering rocks like something out of a fairy tale. When they find it, they're almost delirious with joy. It's Vicente who strips off his clothes first.

"Come on!" he shouts to the other two, plunging into the cold water.

Yves shucks off his shirt and trousers in his turn and jumps naked into the water, splashing Vicente mischievously. Myriam stays on the bank, overcome by bashfulness.

"Come on in!" Vicente calls to her.

"Yes, come in!" Yves urges.

Their voices echo off the rocks. Myriam asks them to close their eyes. She's never swum nude. The water feels soft and thick as liquid silk, sliding over her skin like a caress.

On the way back, Myriam walks between Yves and Vicente, linking arms with both of them. Yves is flustered, but he doesn't show it. Vicente presses his wife's arm strongly to his side, pleased at her initiative. He has never touched her this way, not even on their wedding day. Myriam feels like she's floating.

They're walking like that, arm in arm, when the sky abruptly goes dark.

"*La raïsse*," Yves says.

Seconds later, fat, warm, heavy drops of rain begin falling. Vicente and Myriam dash under a tree for protection. Yves laughs at them.

"You want to get struck by lightning?" he asks.

Rainwater streams down their faces and necks, plastering their wet hair to their cheeks and turning their clothes into a second skin.

Myriam slips on a stone and Vicente, pretending to do the same, falls on top of her. She can feel his erection against her thigh. She laughs as he kisses her face. He presses his body hard against the length of hers. Closing her eyes, Myriam allows herself to be swept up in her husband's passion, the hot rain soaking her thighs. Turning her head, she sees Yves, some distance away, watching. She can almost feel the tumult of his emotions. All three of them are caught up in this moment, bound together by it, under its spell.

The next morning, in the Hanged Man's House, they're woken by the police knocking at the door. Myriam starts to tremble from head to toe. She is seized by a fierce desire to run.

"Everything'll be all right," Vicente says, taking her hand firmly. "Just stay calm. No one here's got anything against us."

He's right. The police have just come to meet these Parisians everyone's been talking about. A simple courtesy call, to see for themselves if what people are saying is true: "Those Parisians are very nice, actually . . . for Parisians."

While Vicente chats with the police, Myriam helps Yves hide. She quickly tidies the shed, but the cops don't even ask to have a look around. They leave as cheerfully as they came.

Even after they've gone, Myriam is horribly anxious, unable to relax, seeing danger everywhere. She pelts Madame Chabaud with questions about current events in the region.

"There's been another arrest in Apt."

"Violence in Bonnieux."

"The news from Marseille isn't good; things are even worse than before."

Myriam insists on going back to Paris. Vicente arranges for their departure.

Sitting on the train with her false ID card, Myriam feels relieved to be getting away from Yves and their strange, unsettling relationship. Emerging from the Gare de Lyon, the hot smell of asphalt and dust makes her feel sick. The buses have stopped running in Paris, and the metro runs only twice an hour.

It's been a year since she last saw Paris.

She feels dizzy and demands that Vicente take her to Les Forges then and there. She wants to see her father and her mother.

Myriam and Vicente catch a train from the Gare Saint-Lazare. She doesn't speak for the entire journey. She feels that something is wrong, that something terrible is waiting in Les Forges.

Reaching her parents' house, the first thing she sees are all the postcards she has sent them over the past year, telling them she's all right.

No one has picked them up. No one has read them.

Myriam feels as if she might faint.

"Should we go inside?" Vicente asks.

Myriam can't speak. Can't move. Vicente peers into the house through one of the windows.

"Looks deserted. Your parents have draped sheets over all the furniture. I'll knock on the neighbors' door and ask if they know anything about it."

Myriam stands stock-still. Anguish has begun coursing through her body.

"The neighbors say your parents went away not long after Jacques and Noémie were arrested."

"Where did they go?"

"Germany."

Rumors are swirling that Allied forces will be landing in France sometime in the weeks to come. Pétain has travelled up to Paris to address the people from a balcony of the Hôtel de Ville.

"I have come here to relieve all of the suffering that is afflicting Paris. You are never far from my mind. I find Paris somewhat changed, as it has been nearly four years since I was last here. But rest assured that, as soon as I can, I will come again—and it will be an official visit. And so I say with hope, *à bientôt.*"

After his speech, he pays a visit to some Parisians who have been wounded in air raids. The cameras follow his car to the hospital and film everything for the newsreels. Reporters crowd the Place de l'Opéra Garnier, and the crowd cheers for the marshal as his motorcade passes.

Yves moves to Paris without telling anyone he's coming. He rents a tiny room on the top floor of an ancient building near the Porte de Clignancourt. His landlady warns him to keep away from the window in the event of an aerial bombardment.

It's a direct metro journey from there to Vicente and Myriam's place, but Yves manages to get lost anyway.

Things don't go the way Yves expected them to. The trio can't recapture the spirit of those carefree summer days in Provence. It all seems very far away now. Vicente and Myriam keep Yves at arm's length, sometimes going entire days without contacting him. He doesn't understand what's happening and grows depressed. Vicente seems to have lost all interest in him, and Myriam visits him only every now and then, and never stays very long.

This isn't what Yves had pictured for the three of them. He stops leaving his tiny apartment and has what Myriam will later call a nervous breakdown. His first one.

Myriam comes to the Porte de Clignancourt and tries to reason with Yves. Times are hard. Paris is under constant attack from the air as part of the Allied efforts to liberate it. Then she tells Yves she thinks she's pregnant with Vicente's child.

Yves spends one more night in his attic room. It's the loneliest he's ever felt. He goes back to Céreste the next day.

But Vicente and Myriam haven't told Yves the whole truth.

Since returning to Paris, they have been among the 2,800 agents working for the Franco-Polish intelligence network F2.

Vicente has gotten his hands on some of the amphetamines used by the military to keep soldiers awake for as long as possible. The drug strips him of any sense of danger, but miraculously his recklessness hasn't gotten him killed yet. Myriam, for her part, feels protected by her pregnancy, and takes extreme risks on a regular basis.

Lélia is still just a fetus, but she can taste on her lips the bitterness of the bile a body produces when it experiences fear. The same bitterness Myriam tasted in her own mother's womb, when she heard the terrified thumping of Emma's heart as she faced down the Moscow police.

CHAPTER 24

The months pass. April, May, June. The Allied forces land in Normandy, and Paris is liberated soon afterward. Vicente watches Myriam's belly grow into a grotesque protuberance and wonders what will emerge from it. A girl? Yes. He hopes it's a girl. The parents-to-be listen at the window to the distant noise of battles taking place across Paris. They sound oddly like fireworks.

By August 25, 1944, the storms have passed. Paris stands free beneath a mackerel sky. Vicente makes his way toward the Place de l'Hôtel de Ville to hear General de Gaulle's speech. But at the sight of the people mobbing the square, he changes his mind. Crowds frighten him, even when they're on the right side. He goes to Chez Léa instead.

For the first time, the French have an actual glimpse of the general they've only known as a voice on the BBC. He's like a marble statue, towering a head taller than anyone else in the throng pressing around him.

Myriam is still without news of her parents, her brother, her sister. But she continues to believe, to hope, insisting over and over to Jeanine in the last exhausting weeks of the summer, "The baby will be such a wonderful surprise when they come back from Germany."

Four months later, on December 21, 1944, the winter solstice, my mother Lélia, the daughter of Myriam Rabinovitch and Vicente Picabia, is born at number 6 rue de Vaugirard. Jeanine holds Myriam's hand throughout her labor. She knows what it's like to bring a baby into the world far from your loved ones, in a country in chaos. She has a son of her own now: Patrick, who was born in England.

A year earlier, when Jeanine finally came within sight of the distant Spanish border on Christmas night 1943, she'd promised herself that, if she survived, she would have a child. She'd walked in the direction indicated by the *passeur*, and then everything had become a blur.

She'd woken up in Spain, in a women's prison. She was bathed, registered, and interrogated by the Spanish authorities, refugee and prisoner at the same time. From there, thanks to her Red Cross connections, she'd been transferred to Barcelona, and from Barcelona she'd made her way to England, to join the women's corps of the Free French Forces.

Upon arriving in London, Jeanine had learned that the Reverend Alesch, the white-haired, kind-faced clergyman, was in reality working for German military intelligence, paid 12,000 francs per month to be a double agent. A priest and member of the Resistance by day, by night he lived on the rue Spontini, in the 16th arrondissement, with his two mistresses—whom he supported with the money he earned as a collaborator. His specialty was encouraging young people to join the Resistance—then betraying them and pocketing the reward.

It was also in London that Jeanine learned of the deaths of most of her comrades in the Gloria SMH network, including Jacques Legrand, her male counterpart, deported to Mauthausen after Alesch's betrayal.

She soon made the acquaintance of a young Breton woman from Morlaix, Lucienne Cloarec, whose brother had been shot before her eyes by the Germans. Lucienne had decided to join General de Gaulle's forces and had shipped out—the only woman among seventeen men—aboard a small *goémonier,* or kelp-gathering sailboat, called the *Jean.* The crossing had taken twenty hours. Maurice Schumann, impressed by the young woman, had featured her on his BBC radio broadcast as soon as she reached London.

Lucienne Cloarec and Jeanine Picabia were the first two women to be awarded medals by General de Gaulle for their work in the Resistance, by a decree dated May 12, 1943.

Soon afterward, as she had vowed to do, Jeanine became pregnant.

Now back in Paris, Jeanine and her son Patrick are staying at the Lutetia. The hotel, recaptured from the Germans by the Free French Forces, is initially reserved for important Resistance figures, and Jeanine rests there for several weeks with her newborn. Her room is in one of the round turrets topped by a pointed roof with an *oeil-de-boeuf* window on whose sill her cat loves to lounge. So luxurious are these accommodations that Jeanine asks her brother Vicente if he and Myriam would like her to look after little Lélia for a while.

She can tell that the couple's marriage has become strained since the birth of their baby.

CHAPTER 25

Maman,

I'm sitting in the back seat of your little white Renault 5. I'm around six or seven years old, maybe, and we're crossing the Boulevard Raspail. You point out an enormous hotel—a palace—and tell me you spent the first few months of your life there. I press my face against the car window and stare at the building, which looks big enough to take up the whole 6th arrondissement. I wonder how it's possible that my mother could ever have lived in a place like that. It's one more mystery, one more riddle to add to all the other riddles in my childhood.

I used to imagine you running down hallways with thick cream-colored carpets and stealing cakes from waiters' carts to eat in some secret hiding-place, just like in a storybook you read to me when I was little.

But with you, Maman, those strange episodes from the past were never children's stories; they were real. They actually happened. And even though I understand now why you spent the first months of your life at the Lutetia, and even though I know your childhood after that was marked by a lack of creature comforts, an image remains in my mind, one that's simultaneously false and real. The fantastical image of having a mother who learned to walk in the hallways of a palace.

A

I n early April 1945, the government Ministry of Prisoners, Deportees, and Refugees, or MPDR, begins organizing the return of several hundred thousand men and women to French soil. Paris's largest buildings are requisitioned for the purpose: the Gare d'Orsay, the Reuilly barracks, the Molitor swimming baths, the Rex and Gaumont Palace movie theaters. And the Vélodrome d'Hiver. (The Vél d'Hiv no longer exists. It was torn down in 1959, a year after it had been used as a detention center for Algerian French Muslims on the orders of then-Prefect of Police Maurice Papon.)

The Lutetia is not among the buildings pressed into service by the ministry. Not at first, anyway. But the government's existing provisions quickly prove inadequate, and General de Gaulle orders the hotel to make its 350 rooms available to returning deportees. The Lutetia is then revamped under the advice of doctors, its interior spaces restructured to create fully stocked infirmaries.

De Gaulle also arranges for taxis to bring nurses to the Lutetia after their shifts at the city's hospitals. Medical students lend their skills to the repatriation effort, as well, as do social workers. The Red Cross is present, along with other organizations, including the Boy Scouts, who are assigned to carry messages through the hotel's maze of high-ceilinged corridors, supervised by members of the Women's Auxiliary Army Corps.

The Lutetia must also provide meals at all hours of the day and night, not just for newly arrived guests, but for medical and managing staff as well—there are fully six hundred personnel seeing to the needs of returned deportees. The hotel kitchen produces up to five thousand dishes a day, which means that supplies must be constantly inventoried and reordered. Provisions seized from the black market fill the Lutetia's storerooms, the police distributing new hauls of contraband food every day. Shoes and clothing are delivered, as well, trucks and vans making frequent round trips between the hotel and the city's warehouses full of confiscated goods.

It's also necessary to make arrangements for the families who will soon be showing up *en masse* at the Lutetia's revolving doors, hoping to be reunited with sons, husbands, wives, fathers, grandparents. A system is devised under which families will be instructed to submit a form that includes a photograph and any identifying characteristics of their missing loved one, as well as the family's contact information. These forms will then be posted in the lobby of the hotel.

All along the boulevard Raspail, two dozen large wooden signboards have been put up advertising the municipal elections scheduled to begin April 29, 1945. These signboards are collected and installed in the Lutetia's lobby, stretching all the way to the grand staircase. Little by little, they will be covered with hundreds of thousands of sheets of paper, each filled out by hand and containing photos and information provided by desperate families in the hope of reunion.

The arriving deportees will have to be registered and vetted, as well, of course. The MPDR estimates that these formalities will take between one and two hours, long enough for each person to be added to the necessary administrative lists, receive any minor medical treatment needed, and be given ration coupons, as well as metro and train tickets for those returning from Germany to Paris and elsewhere in France. Surviving prisoners will also be issued with official cards declaring their "returned deportee" status and a small amount of money.

By April 26, everything is ready. Jeanine arrives at the Hotel Lutetia to lend a hand to the already-overstretched staff.

But things don't go the way the MPDR expected them to. The condition of the returning prisoners is indescribable. The arrangements that have been made are totally unsuited to the reality of the situation. No one imagined anything like this.

"How was it?" Myriam asks, when Jeanine returns to the rue de Vaugirard after the first day.

Jeanine doesn't know what to say.

"Well . . ." she begins. "We weren't expecting . . ."

"Expecting what? I want to come with you."

"Give it a little time," Jeanine says. "Wait for things to settle down a bit."

Over the days that follow, Myriam becomes more insistent.

"It's not the right time yet," Jeanine tells her. "We had two people die of typhus on the first day. A maid and the Boy Scout who was manning the coatroom."

"I won't get too close to anyone."

"They're spraying everyone who sets foot in the hotel with DDT. I don't think that would be very good for your milk, with the baby."

"I won't go inside. I'll wait out in front."

"You know they're reading out the lists of everyone who returns every day on the radio. It's better for you to stay here and listen, instead of dealing with all the crowds."

"I want to put up a form in the lobby."

"Just give me the photos and information. I'll fill one out for you."

But Myriam fixes Jeanine with a look of steely determination. "No. It's time for you to listen to me, for once. I'm going to the Lutetia myself tomorrow, and no one's going to stop me."

CHAPTER 27

U nder the Parisian sun, an open-platform bus crosses the gleaming Seine. At the point where the river goddess spreads her legs near the Place Dauphine, the bus takes the Pont des Arts, which is crowded with beautiful, manicured, scarlet-lipsticked women and automobiles coming and going in both directions. The drivers of these cars rest lazy forearms on the edge of their rolled-down windows, cigarettes held loosely between their fingertips, and passing American soldiers stare at the French girls in their stiletto heels, delicate rings on every slim finger, the swell of their breasts made more prominent by their tiny, cinched waists in flowered dresses. The air of the capital is growing warmer and sweeter every day, linden trees shading the sidewalks, children walking home from school with backpacks full of books.

The bus follows its route from the Right Bank to the Left Bank, from the Gare de l'Est to the Hotel Lutetia, and everyone—the automobile drivers hurrying home, the shopkeepers on their doorsteps, the pedestrians with their thousand mundane preoccupations—everyone stops as they catch their first sight of the strange passengers on board, with their jutting brow-bones, hollow-eyed gazes, and bumpy, shaven heads.

"Have they let all the inmates out of the asylum?"

"No, it's just some old men coming back from Germany."

But they aren't old. Most of them are between the ages of sixteen and thirty.

"Is it only men they're bringing back?"

There are women on the bus, too. But their ravaged bodies

and bald heads make it impossible to recognize them as such. Some of them will never again be able to bear children.

Trains from the East arrive every hour, streaming into Paris's various stations. Planes land at Le Bourget and Villacoublay sometimes, too. On the first day, a uniformed brass band welcomed the returning deportees with a rousing rendition of "La Marseillaise." Passengers returning from extermination camps were helped off the train first, and then prisoners of war, and finally those who had been drafted into the Service du travail obligatoire.

That was on the first day.

Outside the stations, the returning survivors are told to board buses—the very same buses that, months earlier, transported rounded-up men and women to the transit camps that were their last stop before the stock cars and trains to the East.

"There really weren't any suitable alternatives," they are told.

The deportees remain standing on the bus, crowded closely together, watching the streets of the capital slide past beyond the windows. Some of them are seeing Paris for the first time.

They can see the eyes of the Parisians widen as they pass, the pedestrians and drivers pausing for a few seconds, wondering where these hairless beings in striped pajamas flooding into their city have come from. Like creatures from another world.

"Did you see that bus full of deportees?"

"They could have given them a bath."

"Why are they dressed like convicts?"

"They're being given money, apparently . . ."

"Oh. Well, they'll be just fine, then."

And then life resumes its normal course.

At a red light, an old gentleman thunderstruck by this vision of horror offers the passengers a bag of juicy red cherries. He lifts the bag up toward the bus window, and dozens of arms thin as matchsticks reach out for it, their spidery fingers grasping for the fruit.

"Don't feed the deportees!" cries the Red Cross nurse aboard the bus. "Their stomachs can't handle it!"

The returning prisoners know very well that the cherries are poison for their systems, but the temptation is too great.

The bus starts moving again, toward the Left Bank and the Place Saint-Michel, the boulevard Saint-Germain. And the cherries don't stay down and are vomited up again.

"They should mind their manners," a watching pedestrian comments.

They should eat more politely, thinks another.

"They smell so bad. They should shower."

O ne man recognizes the bus waiting outside the Gare de l'Est. It's the very same bus that took him from Paris to Drancy. He slips away from the rest of the passengers waiting to board and out a side exit on the rue d'Alsace. Now, though, he is lost.

"Are you all right, Monsieur? Do you need help?" a passing man asks.

He shakes his head. The last thing he wants is for someone to help him board that bus.

People—kind, well-meaning people—surround him.

"You don't look very well, Monsieur."

"Careful—don't jostle him."

"I'll get a policeman."

"Monsieur, do you speak French?"

"He needs something to eat."

"I'll go and buy him something, just a moment."

"Do you have your identification papers?" asks the policeman who has been called over.

The sight of his uniform terrifies the man. But the officer is kind and thinks he should be taken to the hospital, this poor gentleman. He's never seen anyone in such bad condition.

"Follow me, please, Monsieur. I'll take you someplace where they can give you some medical attention. You don't have a returnee ID card?"

The man thinks to himself that it's been a long time since he had any kind of ID. Or any money. Or a wife, or a child, or hair, or teeth. He's afraid of all these people, crowding around, staring at him. He feels guilty for being here, guilty for being alive when his wife, and his parents, and his two-year-old son are not. When so many others are not. Millions of others. He feels as if he's done something wrong, and he's afraid that all these people are going to start throwing rocks at him, and that the police officer will take him to prison and haul him up before a tribunal, with the SS on one side and his dead wife and dead parents and dead son on the other. And the millions of other dead. He wishes he had the strength to run, because the policeman's truncheon hurts just to look at. But he has no strength. He remembers coming to this part of the city, a long time ago. He knows that he used to dress just like these people crowding around him, that he had hair on his head and teeth in his mouth just like them, but he also knows he will never be like them again.

One of the bystanders has very kindly gone into a nearby shop and asked for something "for one of the returnees who's dying of hunger; he doesn't have any teeth left," and the shopkeeper thinks of yogurt and lets the bystander have it for free, saying, "No charge, of course we have to help them," and the bystander gives the yogurt to the man, and it perforates his stomach because it's too heavy for someone hanging on to life by a single thread after being evacuated from Auschwitz by the SS in January, three whole months ago, after having somehow survived the final massacres and death-marches and forced walks through the snow beneath the blows of the soldiers' truncheons, the constant humiliations, the chaos of the fall of the Reich, and the journeys in the same stock cars, on the same trains, and hunger, and thirst, and the fight to stay alive long enough to get home, a fight that has been almost impossible for his exhausted body, and so his heart finally stops beating there and then, on the day of his arrival home, on the gray pavement of Paris, at the bottom of the stairs on the rue d'Alsace, after weeks and weeks of fighting. His body is so thin that it folds in on itself as it crumples to the ground softly, like a dead leaf, and settles there slowly, without making any sound at all.

The bus from the Gare de l'Est pulls up in front of the Hotel Lutetia. The waiting crowd surges forward, and Myriam, without really knowing what's going on, moves along with it. A bicycle runs over her foot, but no one apologizes. She hears the names of towns being read out. Words she's never heard before. Auschwitz. Monowitz. Birkenau. Bergen-Belsen.

The doors of the bus open. The deportees inside can't climb down unaided, so Boy Scouts come to help them into the hotel. Stretchers are brought for some of them.

The crowd of waiting family members rushes toward them. Myriam is appalled by the rudeness of some of these people, who hurl themselves at the new arrivals in desperation, waving photographs in their faces.

"Do you recognize this boy? He's my son."

"This is my husband. He's tall, with blue eyes. Do you think you might have met him?"

"My daughter's twelve in this picture, but she was fourteen when they took her away."

"Where are you coming from? Have you heard of a place called Treblinka?"

But, Myriam sees, the people getting off the buses don't speak. They can't answer. They hardly have the strength to think their own silent thoughts. How can they possibly tell the story? No one would believe them.

Your child was put in an oven, Madame.

Your father was stripped naked and put on a leash, like a dog. For entertainment. He died from the cold, insane.

Your daughter was made a camp prostitute, and when she became pregnant they cut open her belly to do medical experiments.

When they knew the war was lost, the SS stripped all the women naked and threw them out a window. Then they made us stack the bodies like firewood.

No chance they've survived. You'll never see any of them again.

Who would take the risk of talking and not being believed? And who could bear to say things like this to the waiting families? The survivors know these naïve people are to be pitied. Some of them even go so far as to give some hope:

"That picture of your husband looks familiar to me. Yes, he's alive."

Myriam hears phrases like this more than once as the crowd pushes its way toward the revolving doors of the Lutetia.

"There are still ten thousand people over there, waiting to be brought home. Don't worry; they'll come back."

The deportees know the chances of this are laughably small. But hope is the only thing that kept them alive in the camps. One of the returning men is jostled by a woman who doesn't seem to realize how exhausted he is, just asks him if he's seen her husband. A Red Cross nurse steps in.

"Let the returnees get by, please. Mesdames, messieurs—*please*, you'll kill them by shoving them like this. You can come back later. Let them through!"

The deportees are ushered toward a requisitioned hydrotherapy clinic overlooking the Récamier public garden. To get there they must pass the Lutetia's patisserie on the corner of the boulevard Raspail and the rue de Sèvres, its window displays empty of cakes. At the clinic, the deportees' striped pajamas are removed, and they are disinfected, with any personal belongings placed in plastic bags they wear around their necks. It's here that they are usually sprayed with DDT powder, which kills any typhus-carrying lice. The deportees must stand nude in front of men wearing rubber suits and protective gloves with canisters of DDT strapped to their backs. These men spray the deportees with this powder using long hoses. It's hard for the survivors to endure. But, the men explain, there is really no other way.

Once they have been disinfected and bathed, they are given clean clothes. After that they are directed to offices on the second floor for questioning, in order to spot any "false" deportees among them.

It happens sometimes that those who were complicit with the Vichy regime, in an attempt to avoid the consequences of their actions, hide among the returning deportees, hoping to take on a new identity. They're trying to escape the retaliatory assassinations taking place all over France as the country purges itself of collaborators, to slip through the net, to avoid being put on trial by one of the many special courts being formed. Some French militia members even tattoo their left forearms with a false registration number to make it look like they've come back from Auschwitz. They slip in among the deportees just as they leave the train stations and board the buses to the Lutetia.

In order to catch these impostors, the Ministry of Prisoners, Deportees, and Refugees requests that the registration offices in the hotel set up a monitoring system. This means that each returning person must be questioned to make sure that he or she is a "real" deportee. Some of them see this new ordeal as a humiliation.

Questioning the deportees is no easy task. Those who have survived the camps are so disoriented that they have trouble talking. Their brains are muddled; they dwell on insignificant details and are incapable of giving precise information. The impostors, however, tend to tell highly structured stories, built of memories they've stolen from others.

The sessions often go badly, with the deportees unable to bear being confronted by the French police, whom they see as cold and abrupt.

"Who are you to question me?"

"Why is this happening again, this interrogation?"

"Leave me alone!"

Some of the reactions in the registration offices even turn violent. Men upend tables; women rise to their feet and point at the officers, screaming, "I remember you! You're the one who tortured me!"

When an impostor is discovered, they're locked into one of the Lutetia's rooms under armed guard. A police wagon comes each day at six o'clock in the evening to collect them for imprisonment and trial.

Once the questioning is finished, the "real" deportees receive ID papers, a sum of money, and transport vouchers for buses and the metro. Then they are checked into the hotel, where they can rest for a few days. Here they're attended to by *"petites bleues,"* female volunteers who manage the reception desk and those floors of the Lutetia set aside for deportees. The floor of the hotel just upstairs from the lobby is used for administration; above that is the infirmary; and then there are bedrooms up to the seventh floor. The fourth floor is reserved for women only.

"Don't worry, the rooms are very well heated."

The radiators are turned to their highest setting even though it's the middle of summer, because the deportees' malnourished, stick-thin bodies are always cold.

"They'd rather sleep on the floor even though the rooms have comfortable beds. It's so strange."

The deportees lie on the floor because they can't sleep on the softness of a mattress anymore. Often, three or four of them need to lie together, pressed against one another, in order to fall asleep. They're all ashamed of their shaved heads and the sores and abscesses covering their bodies. They know just how horrific the sight of them is.

In the Lutetia's opulent dining room, graceful potted palms

emphasize the straight, clean lines of the stone walls, massive stained-glass windows, and ornamental columns. The space is a luxurious, geometrical Art Deco wonder.

The deportees are served their meals at tables in this dining room. They haven't eaten from plates in so long. Not since they lived in a world which now feels like it never existed. Their shining goblets contain clean water. They've forgotten what that's like, too.

A vase sits on each table, each holding a pretty bouquet of blue, white, and red carnations. Canada's ambassador to France and his wife have had milk and jam sent from their country for the deportees.

A man whose age is impossible to tell, his head bent so far forward it doesn't seem securely attached to his neck, scrutinizes the plates of meat being set down in front of him. He's accustomed to stealing his food—"organizing" it, as they said in the camp—and now he's not sure he's allowed to sit down and keeps asking the permission of a *petite bleue*. These young women aren't always equipped to deal with every situation that arises at the Lutetia. Some deportees no longer speak anything but German, while others repeat their registration number over and over.

"You can't take that knife with you, Monsieur."

"I need it. To kill the person who betrayed me to the Germans."

M yriam manages to get through the Lutetia's revolving doors, jostled along by others in the stampede. She looks around for the "Family Information" signboard and sees a number of them at the foot of the grand staircase, covered with hundreds of forms, hundreds of beseeching letters, hundreds of photographs of weddings and happy vacations, family dinners and soldiers in uniform. They plaster the hotel lobby from floor to ceiling, sheets of paper peeling away from the walls like blistered skin.

Myriam approaches one of the panels just as the deportees who have just arrived do the same, drawn by all these photographs of the world from before, now buried beneath ash. Their eyes examine the images but no longer seem to understand what they mean. They aren't even sure they'd be able to recognize themselves in the many portraits displayed.

"How do I know if I used to be the man in that picture?"

Myriam backs away from the signboard to make room for others. She's looking for the information office when a distraught man grasps her arm. He's obviously mistaken her for one of the female volunteers there to aid the families.

"Excuse me—I found my wife—she fell asleep in my arms, and I can't wake her up . . ."

Myriam explains that she doesn't work here, that she's looking for people, too, but the man is insistent.

"Please, please," he insists, tugging at her arm.

Seeing the woman in the armchair, Myriam realizes that she isn't asleep. She isn't the only one who will die here. There are dozens every day, their fragile, exhausted bodies unable to withstand the emotion of returning, of reuniting.

Myriam joins the line waiting in front of the information office. Next to her, a French couple is holding a Polish child in their arms, whom they hid for the whole war. She was two years old when they took her for safekeeping; now she's five and speaks perfect French with a Parisian accent. They've come to the Lutetia because they heard her mother's name read out on the daily radio broadcast.

But the little girl doesn't recognize her *maman* in the thin, bald figure reaching out for her. Seized with sudden panic, she begins to cry, and then scream at the nightmarish sight of this woman she wants nothing to do with, clinging tightly to the legs of the lady who is not her mother.

Myriam learns nothing at all in the information office. They hand her a form to fill out and tell her to wait for the radio to broadcast the returned survivors list each day. They discourage her from coming to the Lutetia often.

"It's pointless," they tell her.

Myriam approaches a group of people standing in the corner of the lobby who look like they're regulars here. As it turns out, they come every day to exchange information and the latest rumors.

"The Russians have taken some of the French deportees."

"They took doctors and engineers."

"Furriers and gardeners, too."

Myriam thinks of her engineer father, of her Russian-speaking parents. If they've been taken East, it might explain why they aren't on the lists of returnees.

"My husband's a physician. I'm sure they've kept him."

"They say at least five thousand people have gone to Russia."

"But how can we find out who they are?"

"Have you asked in the office?"

"No, they don't want to see me anymore."

"One of you try, then! They're friendlier to unfamiliar faces."

"All those people have to be *somewhere*."

"We have to be patient. They'll bring them back."

"Did you hear what happened to Madame Jacob?"

"Her husband was on the list of people killed at Mauthausen."

"When they read out his name, she fainted."

"And then three days later, there was a knock at the door. She opened it, and—"

"—her husband was standing there. There had been a mistake."

"It's happened more than once. There's always hope."

"They say there's a camp in Austria where they're sending everyone who's lost their memory."

"In Austria?"

"No—I heard it was in Germany . . ."

"Have they taken photos of the people with no memory?"

"I don't think so."

"Then how is anyone supposed to identify them?"

Myriam posts her form in the lobby. She doesn't have any photos of her family—all the albums are in Les Forges—so she writes their first names in large capital letters, so they'll be able to spot them easily amid the dozens, hundreds, thousands of forms papering the lobby. *EPHRAÏM EMMA NOÉMIE JACQUES.* Then she signs her name and writes her and Vicente's address on the rue de Vaugirard so that her parents will know where to find her.

Standing on tiptoe to post her form good and high for better visibility, arms outstretched, Myriam wobbles, almost losing her balance. A man stands next to her, watching, the faint trace of a smile on his lips.

"I read on a list that I was dead," he says.

Myriam doesn't know how to respond. Her form safely tacked up, she is heading toward the exit when a woman grabs her by the shoulder.

"Look, this is my daughter."

Myriam turns around. Before she can say anything, the woman thrusts a photo in her face, so close that she can't really even see it.

"She was a little older than she is in this picture when they arrested her."

"I'm sorry," Myriam says. "I don't know—"

"Please, help me find her," begs the woman, whose cheeks are red and blotchy.

She takes Myriam's arm and squeezes it hard, leaning forward to whisper, "I can pay you a lot of money."

"Let me go!" Myriam cries.

Leaving the hotel, she sees the group of Lutetia regulars rushing off somewhere; they've grabbed their things and are heading toward the nearest metro stop. She follows them to see what's going on. There's been a routing error, someone tells her, and a group of about forty women who were supposed to be brought to the Lutetia were taken to the Gare d'Orsay instead. *Forty women—that's a lot*, thinks Myriam. And Noémie is among them. She can *feel* it. She takes the metro with the group from the hotel and enters the station with her heart pounding. She's filled with a kind of light, an anticipatory joy.

But none of the women at the Gare d'Orsay is Noémie.

"Jacques? Noémie? Do those names sound familiar to you?"

"Do you know which camp they were sent to?"

"I thought all the women were sent to Ravensbrück."

"We don't really know anything for certain, Madame. They're only suppositions."

"Can't the people who were there tell us?"

"I'm sorry, Madame. We haven't had any convoys from Ravensbrück. And we don't think there will be any."

"But why haven't you sent someone to look for them? I can go myself if you want!"

"Madame, we did send people to arrange repatriations from Ravensbrück. But there was no one left to repatriate."

The words are clear, but Myriam doesn't understand them. Her brain simply refuses to register the meaning of the phrase. *There was no one left to repatriate.*

She goes home. Jeanine opens the door, holding Lélia in her arms. There is no need to speak. Both women know what the outcome of the day has been.

"I'll go back tomorrow," is all Myriam says.

And every day, she returns to the Lutetia to wait for her family. She has no capacity for shame left, either. She fires questions unrestrainedly at the deportees as they emerge from the hotel, trying to catch their attention for even a few seconds.

"Jacques—Noémie—do those names sound familiar?"

She envies those who have heard a name on the radio or received a telegram. You can tell which ones they are the moment they enter the hotel lobby, their steps confident and sure.

Day after day, Myriam tries to make herself useful to the people running the repatriation efforts. She tries to find out what's happening in Poland, Germany, Austria. She loiters on one floor, then another, until someone tells her, "There won't be any more convoys today, Madame. Go home."

"Come back tomorrow. There's no point in staying any longer."

"Please. You need to leave the premises now."

"We've told you there won't be anyone else arriving tonight."

"The first buses are scheduled for eight o'clock tomorrow. Come on, now. Don't give up hope."

Lélia, now nine months old, has terrible stomach pains. She starts refusing to nurse, and Jeanine urges Myriam to spend more time with her daughter.

"She needs you. You have to help her eat."

For a week Myriam stays at home, feeding and watching over her baby. When she goes back to the hotel, she sees the same women, still brandishing their photographs. But something has changed. There are far fewer people than before.

"They say there won't be any more convoys after tomorrow."

On September 13, 1945, the newspaper *Ce soir* publishes an article by M. Lecourtois:

> ## THE LUTETIA NO LONGER A HOTEL FOR THE LIVING DEAD
>
> In just a few days, the requisitioned Hotel Lutetia on the boulevard Raspail will be returned to its owners. It will take three months to return the hotel to its former condition. (. . .) For now, the Lutetia stands empty, having closed its doors on the most abject human suffering, secure in the promise of welcoming happy guests once again.

Myriam is furious. Everywhere in the press, she reads the same thing: the repatriation of deportees is now considered to be finished.

"It *isn't* finished, though. My family isn't on any of the lists, but they haven't come home, either."

Caught between waning hope and the absence of proof, Myriam is in agony. She remembers the rumors she heard in the hotel lobby:

"There are still ten thousand people out there somewhere. Don't worry. They'll be back."

"They say there's a camp in Germany where they're putting people who have lost their memory."

Myriam has seen pictures of the extermination camps in the papers and in newsreels. But she's utterly incapable of connecting those images to the disappearance of her parents and Jacques and Noémie.

They have to be somewhere, she tells herself. *It's just a matter of finding them.*

At the end of September 1945, Myriam joins the troops occupying Germany, in Lindau.

She works as a translator for the air force. She speaks Russian, German, Spanish, Hebrew, a little bit of English, and, of course, French.

In Germany, she keeps searching.

Maybe Jacques or Noémie managed to escape.

Maybe they're somewhere in a camp for people with amnesia.

Maybe they don't have enough money to get back to France.

Anything is possible. She has to keep believing.

CHAPTER 31

D id you ever visit your mother in Germany when you were little?"

"In Lindau? Yes, my father took me there at least once. I have a picture of myself in a washtub in the back garden of a house, where my mother would bathe me. Somewhere in the military camp, I suppose."

"But if I understand correctly, your parents weren't really living together anymore by then, is that right?"

"I don't know. They were living in two different countries, certainly. And I think my mother had an affair with an air force pilot in Lindau."

"Really? You never told us that!"

"I think he even asked her to marry him. But he didn't want to raise me. Wanted me sent away to boarding school. So she broke it off."

"So then, when did the trio get back together?"

"What trio?"

"Yves, Myriam, and Vicente. They saw each other again, right? After you were born?"

". . . I don't really want to talk about that."

"Okay. Don't get upset. That isn't really what I came to talk to you about, anyway. I wanted to ask you about the letter you got from the mayor's office."

"What letter?"

"You said the town hall secretary in Les Forges had sent you a letter, and you hadn't opened it yet."

"Look, I'm tired, and I don't know where I put that letter. We'll have a look at it some other time if you want."

"I'm pretty sure it'll be something that can help my investigation. I could really use it."

"Do you really want me to say it? I don't think you're going to find the person who sent that postcard."

"I know I *am* going to find them."

"Why are you doing all this? What are you getting out of it?"

"I don't know, Maman. There's just some invisible force pushing me to do it. Like a voice urging me to see it through."

"Well, I'm sick to death of answering your questions. It's my past! My childhood! My parents! None of it has anything to do with you! Just move on, all right?"

CHAPTER 32

D ear Anne,
    I'm so sorry for just now. Let's put it all behind us.

I never reconciled with my mother. I don't think it was possible. But we could have come to a better understanding, at least, if she'd just told me why she abandoned me for so many years. If she'd just come right out and said that there was no other way.

I think she kept silent out of guilt for being alive. And guilt over all those long absences when I was bounced around from friend to relative.

If she'd explained to me why, I would have understood. But I had to figure it out for myself, and by then it was too late. She was already gone.

All of this is bringing up some deep questions, and honestly I'm struggling with it, because it makes me feel like I'm betraying my mother somehow.

Maman,
Myriam thought the war was hers, and hers alone.

She didn't see why she should talk to you about it. So of course you feel like you're going against her wishes by helping with my research.

Even in death, Myriam is imposing her own silence on you.

But Maman, don't forget that you *suffered* because of those silences of hers. And not just her silences—the feeling that she was shutting you out of a story that didn't involve you.

I understand that what I'm finding out is overwhelming for you. Especially the parts having to do with your father, life on the plateau, and Yves showing up in your parents' lives.

But Maman, this is my story, too. And sometimes, almost like Myriam, you treat me like I'm a foreigner in the land of your past. You were born into a world of silences. It's only natural that your children would be thirsty for words.

Anne,

Call me when you've read this email, and I'll answer the question you asked me yesterday. The one that made me angry.

I'll tell you exactly—not when the trio saw each other again after being separated, because I'm not sure of that, but about the very last time Myriam, Yves, and my father were all together.

CHAPTER 33

It was during the autumn school holidays, in November 1947. In Authon, a tiny village in the south of France. How do I know? Simple. I only have one picture of myself with my father. I've looked at that photo so often I know it by heart. But there was never anything written on the back. So for a long time I didn't know where or when it had been taken, and there was no point in asking my mother, of course. But then, one day in the late '90s, I was visiting one of my Sidoine cousins in Céreste, and we were just talking about nothing and everything . . . you know, as you do . . . and my cousin said, 'Actually, I just came across a very nice picture of you and Yves. You're sitting on his lap. Here, I'll show you.' She opened a drawer and took out a photograph, and what a surprise. I was in the same place as in the photo with my father. I'm in the same clothes, same hair. Both pictures had to have been taken on the same day—probably even the same roll of film. I turned the photo over—I remember trying not to show how confused I was—and written on the back it said: 'Yves and Lélia, Authon, November 1947.'"

"That date . . . it must have been upsetting for you."

"Of course. My father committed suicide on December 14, 1947."

"Do you think there's any link?"

"We'll never know."

"I don't remember how Vicente died, exactly. I'm just realizing how fuzzy that whole thing is in my head."

"I'll let you read the coroner's report from the Paris police archives. You can draw your own conclusions."

CHAPTER 34

Vicente had discovered an amphetamine newer than Benzedrine, and more suited to recreational use, called Maxiton. It was the perfect treat. An excellent stimulant for the nervous system, but without the dizziness or shaking, or that heavy, fatigued feeling behind the eyes. Maxiton made life feel simple and easy for Vicente. It brought him peace.

Amphetamines are known to diminish potency, but on that particular night the opposite had been true, and Lélia had been conceived during a night of seemingly endless passion. That was precisely what Vicente loved about drugs: the surprise. The body's unexpected reactions. The chemical interactions between a living body and a substance that was also alive in a way, the infinite number of physical experiences that could result, depending on the day, time, situation, dose, ambient temperature, and what he had eaten before ingesting the drug. He could talk about it for hours, with the expertise of a trained pharmacist. In this domain Vicente was a true scholar, with significant knowledge of chemistry, botany, anatomy, and psychology; he would have been among the highest scorers if there had been a competitive exam in toxicology.

Vicente had always sensed that he would die young, that life was an ordeal he wouldn't have to endure for long. His parents had given him a birth name he disliked, Lorenzo, so he had rechristened himself Vicente, after an uncle who had himself died prematurely, in an accident on the factory floor. The uncle had breathed in the fumes of a corrosive product, and they had eaten away at his lungs, resulting in an agonizing death from internal bleeding. He'd been the father of a three-year-old daughter.

Vicente died just a few days before Lélia's birthday. She, too, was about to turn three years old.

"Vicente overdosed on the sidewalk in front of his mother's apartment building. It was the concierge who found him."

"And the concierge called the police?"

"Yes. The police file included a description of the scene, which I found in the archive. It's in an old college-ruled notebook with yellowed pages. Each page is divided into five columns: Number, Date, Division, Civil Status, and Summary of Case. The page that includes my father mainly lists robbery cases. His death is right in the middle. All the cases are written up in the same black ink, except Vicente's. Why? The police officer used sky-blue ink, very light. So faded that it had almost disappeared. He wrote: 'Investigation of the death of *Sieur* Picabia, Laurent Vincent.' Isn't that a strange way to put it? He's Frenchified the names. 'Laurent' for 'Lorenzo,' 'Vincent' for 'Vicente.'"

"The policeman must have liked old-fashioned phrasing. That 'sieur' is a bit anachronistic."

"'Occurred on 14 December at around 1:00 A.M. in his bed,' he wrote. That information is incorrect. I know it. Vicente died outside, on the pavement, and the police subsequently investigated the reason for that. It's also confirmed by the records of the Institute of Forensic Medicine, which I was able to consult."

"But why would the police officer lie?"

"What happened is that the concierge called the police when she saw a body outside. Then, recognizing Vicente, she woke up Gabriële and told her that her son was dead. Gabriële refused to let her son lie out in the street like that, and she insisted that he be brought upstairs and put in his bed. So the confusion stems from that. In the notebook, the police officer jotted down a series of questions: 'Drugs? Alcohol abuse? Bootleg liquor? IFM

1 rep. Med. Ex. Dr. Frizac.' That's how I found out a medical examiner's report had been done.

"That report told me three things about my father. One, that the presumed cause of his death was suicide. Two, that his body was found lying on the ground outside Gabriële's building. And three, that in December, in the middle of the night, he had nothing on his feet but a pair of sandals."

CHAPTER 35

D idn't you ever wonder about your origins?"

"No. I know it's crazy, but I didn't. I looked so much like Vicente; there was never any doubt. I'm the spitting image of him. But I did ask Myriam and Yves the question once, just to annoy them."

"Which question?"

"Ha! I asked them whose daughter I was!"

"Why?"

"Why do you think? To get my mother to talk! Myriam never said anything. She never told me *anything*. I was so sick of it, you know? So sick. I wanted her to tell me about Vicente. So I went after her. I knew I'd have to hit her where it hurt, to get her to talk. Your father and I were in Céreste with them for the long summer vacation, and I asked her and Yves that question in the early evening. Yves in particular took it very badly, and the whole night after that was terrible. A lot of shouting."

"Did Yves feel responsible for your father's death?"

"Looking back now, I hope not. Poor man. But maybe he felt that way at the time. In any case, the next morning your father and I packed our bags and came back to Paris."

"We hadn't been born yet?"

"Oh yes, you were. We all came back to Paris. And three days later, I received a letter from your grandmother."

"Was it everything you'd been hoping for?"

"I'd say so, yes. Back then, I knew absolutely nothing about my father, or about Myriam's life during the war. She never, ever talked about it. I was so desperate for dates, places, words, names. And by asking her whose daughter I was, I'd forced her to give them to me."

"Will you show me the letter?"

"Yes. It's in one of my archive boxes. I'll get it."

CHAPTER 36

Thursday, four o'clock P.M.
Dear Pierre, and my darling Lélia,
Lélia's question about her origins, asked at such an inopportune moment, took Yves and I completely by surprise. We would probably have reacted much more calmly at a different time. Yves is far too sensitive of a man (and he has paid dearly for that sensitivity) to be asked something like that so abruptly. That said, I am happy to address your question.

In June 1943, Jean Sidoine, a friend of the hostel owner François Morenas, asked us to hide one of his cousins in the little shed behind our house. That was how Yves came to live with us.

It was '43, as I said, and we were staying out of sight on the plateau, near Buoux. Stalingrad had awakened a faint spark of hope, but the Nazis were becoming more and more aggressive. The plateau was idyllic, but the danger of being informed on was constant. So, that December, Vicente and I decided to leave and go back to the place on the rue de Vaugirard (rented under a false name, thanks to some forged ID papers Jean Sidoine gave us). You were conceived shortly after that, Lélia. In Paris, in March 1944, and not during our time on the Plateau des Claparèdes in 1943.

In Paris during that same period, from the first of April 1944 onward, Vicente and I worked for an intelligence network. I was assigned to ciphers—that is, the coding and decoding of messages. My rank was P2, serial number 5943, permanent network operative, with military combatant status. I used the code name "Monique," and I belonged to the *"Filles du Calvaire."*[2] Vicente was a second lieutenant, serial number 6427, P2 as well, and he was head of the encryption center. His code name was "Richelieu," and he was a *"pianiste."*[3] Both of us were demobilized on September 30, 1944, two months before you were born.

I need to tell you that, if things during that first trimester of my pregnancy in 1944 hadn't gone well for the Allies, neither Vicente nor I would ever have brought a child into the world. With the constant shooting in the streets, police raids on the metro, and the strong probability that those of us in networks would be arrested by the Gestapo, it would have been too dangerous. Really, you owe your life to the June '44 landings at Normandy and the liberation of Paris. It was because things went our way that Vicente was able to go to the 6th-arrondissement registry office on Thursday, December 21, 1944, with his true identity papers and declare the birth of his daughter.

"What happened after you were born?"

"After my father left the registry office, he disappeared for three days. Instead of going back to the rue de Vaugirard, he vanished into thin air."

"No one knew where he'd gone?"

"Not a soul. He must have been in a hell of a state, because his statement at the registry office was nonsense. Everything on my birth certificate is wrong. Dates, places. He made it all up."

"Was he on drugs at the time, do you think?"

"Maybe. Or maybe it was a reflex left over from the Resistance. I don't know. But I can tell you that it caused me a lot of problems later on, when I became a civil servant. I even had to appear

---

[2] *Filles du Calvaire*: a French Resistance cell named after a Paris Metro station. [Translator's note]

[3] *Pianiste*: Resistance jargon for a radio operator. [Translator's note]

before a lower court judge in the 6th arrondissement. You see, when Charles Pasqua was Interior Minister, civil servants had to be '*French* French,' and I wasn't. Then I had to redo my ID documentation years later, under Sarkozy this time, because everything had been stolen—my passport, driver's license, ID card. That was a whole ordeal, too. Some government bureaucrat told me that I had to prove I was French. 'How am I supposed to do that, when all my documents have been stolen?' I asked. 'Prove that your parents were French,' was the answer. Because my mother was born in a different country and my father had a Spanish name *and* the information on my birth certificate was incorrect, I was seen as a highly suspicious character, apparently. I remember thinking, *shit, here we go again.*"

"Maman, what happened to you after your father's death?"

"That was when they sent me to stay with Yves's family in Céreste."

CHAPTER 37

After two years in Germany, Myriam finally returns to France. Yves takes Vicente's place in her bed and encourages her to become a teacher. To allow her to concentrate on studying for her exams, he arranges for Lélia to stay near the Sidoines in Céreste, in the home of a lady named Henriette Avon, who was widowed in the First World War. Yves himself remains in Paris to soothe and support Myriam. It's them against the world.

Henriette is reluctant to take on her tiny new boarder at first. Children usually end up costing more money than they bring in; there's laundry that has to be done more often than usual, and broken dishes, and bread pilfered from the pantry. But she feels sorry for this little brown-haired girl, clinging to her mother's legs like a dog who senses that his master wants to get rid of him.

Henriette is poor—*very* poor, even—and her boarders are even poorer. In addition to Lélia, there is Jeanne. People in the village say that Jeanne is a hundred years old because no one can remember when she was born. Her tightly corseted little body resembles a lobster. She's blind, but her hands can still work wonders. All one has to do is plunk her in a corner and put a cloth full of peas or lentils in her lap, and Jeanne will shell, sort, hull, and peel as nimbly as if the pupils of her blank eyes have been magically transported to her fingertips. But Jeanne scares Lélia. She always smells so strongly of urine that the little girl stays as far away from her as possible.

Jeanne never bathes. Henriette is as strict as a drill sergeant when it comes to Lélia's cleanliness, though. When it's time to wash her hair, she sets Lélia on a little stool at the sink, a washcloth over her eyes and a dishtowel around her neck. Then Henriette empties a whole packet of creamy white Dop shampoo over the girl's hair. Shampoo is expensive, but Henriette doesn't skimp. After that she pours tepid water slowly from a pitcher to rinse away the suds. It runs in trickles along Lélia's ears and down her neck, making her shiver.

At the village school in Céreste, Lélia learns to read, write, and count. The head teacher remarks on her abilities, which are far beyond those of other children her age. She tells Henriette that Lélia's parents should plan on their daughter pursuing higher education. For Henriette, it's like telling her the little girl will walk on the moon someday.

Céreste becomes Lélia's village, just as Riga was the unexpected landscape of Myriam's childhood. Lélia knows everyone who lives there, their habits and personalities, just as she's intimately familiar with every stone, every nook and cranny of the chemin de la Croix, beyond which children aren't allowed to venture, the paths heading off toward La Gardette, and the hill topped by Céreste's water tower—a capricious giant that often refuses to provide the village with water for days at a time.

Henriette's house stands almost on the corner of the rue de Bourgade and the little path that winds down to the village square. The slope is so steep that Lélia always ends up hurtling down it in a near-uncontrollable dash. The adjoining house, the one actually on the corner, is inhabited by two brats called Louis and Robert, who like to amuse themselves by trapping little Lélia against a wall before scurrying off.

Lélia, tanned nut-brown by the southern sun, becomes a true daughter of the region. Her favorite day is Mardi Gras, when all the children dress up as *caraques*—a Provençal term designating gypsies or Bohemians. They assemble in the village square like a swarm of field rats, dressed in rags, their faces blackened by burnt cork, and make their way through the streets from house to house with a large basket, asking everyone who opens their door for an egg or a cup of flour. In the evening, they parade behind a wagon bearing the *Caramantran* effigy, a brightly painted monstrosity that is then tried, condemned, and burned in the square. The smallest children shriek at the top of their lungs and throw stones at the figure, ferociously gleeful at the sight of the sacrifice.

"The young people used to do the *danse des Bouffets* just before Lent began," the older villagers recall. "Of course, that was years ago . . ."

On religious procession days, the priest is followed by two townspeople carrying a banner, and then the boys of the choir, and finally a group of little girls dressed all in white, carrying baskets of flowers trailing long pink, white, and pale blue ribbons.

The first time Lélia participates in this ritual, Henriette hears the other women murmuring, "That little Jewish girl shouldn't be in the procession."

Henriette is furious. She speaks up on Lélia's behalf as if she were her own daughter, and the women watch their tongues from then on.

But the incident preys on Henriette's mind, and she begins to wonder what God thinks of Lélia's presence among the baptized girls.

In church, Lélia is fascinated by the statue of the Virgin Mary, with her lovely, sorrowful gaze, her hands joined in eternal prayer, her white-belted robes draping in azure folds. Lélia has seen people reverently crossing themselves in front of Mary, and one Sunday she imitates the gesture. But Henriette stops her, saying, "No, not you."

Lélia doesn't ask why.

One day in the schoolyard, someone throws a stone at her, which narrowly misses hitting her in the eye.

"Dirty Jew," she hears.

Lélia understands immediately that the word is referring to her, but she doesn't really know what it means. Back at Henriette's, she doesn't mention the incident. She wants to confide in some-one, but who? Who can explain to her the meaning of this new word that has just entered her life?

No one.

CHAPTER 38

T hat was how my mother learned that she was Jewish. That incident in the schoolyard in 1950. *Thunk*. Suddenly, and without explanation. The stone that hit her was much like the stone that had hit Myriam at the same age, that one thrown by Polish children in Lodz when she went to meet her cousins for the first time.

1925 and 1950 weren't so very far apart.

For the children of Céreste, like the children of Lodz—and the children of Paris in 2019, for that matter—it was nothing more than a joke, a schoolyard taunt like any other. But for Myriam, and Lélia, and Clara, it was an interrogation.

When my mother became *our* mother, my sisters and I never once heard her say the word "Jew." She just never mentioned religion. It wasn't a conscious or deliberate omission; I just think she honestly didn't know how to address it, or even where to begin. How could she explain it all?

My sisters and I were confronted with the same viciousness on the day the wall of our house was tagged with a swastika.

1950 and 1985 weren't so very far apart.

And, I realized now, I was the same age as my mother and grandmother were when they were hit with the insults, the stones. The same age as my daughter when she was told by a classmate, in a schoolyard, that his family didn't like Jews.

The pattern was undeniable.

But what was I supposed to do about it? The answer eluded me. How could I avoid drawing conclusions that weren't just overly hasty, but also clumsy and simplistic?

Something had to be learned from all these lives. But what?

Reflection. Examination. A deeper questioning of that word whose definition remained ever elusive.

What does it mean to be Jewish?

Maybe the answer was contained within another question:

What does it mean to wonder what it means to be Jewish?

The book Georges gave me, Nathalie Zajde's *Children of Survivors*, told me everything I should have said to Déborah during that Pesach dinner, just a few weeks too late.

Déborah, I don't know what it means to be "truly Jewish" or "not truly Jewish." All I can tell you is that I'm the child of a survivor. That is, someone who may not be familiar with the Seder rituals, but whose family died in the gas chambers. Someone who has the same nightmares as her mother, and is trying to find her place among the living. Someone whose body is the grave of those who never had a proper burial. You said I'm only Jewish when it suits me. But, Déborah, when my daughter was born, when I held her for the first time, do you know what I thought of? The first image that went through my mind? It was the mothers who were breastfeeding when they were sent to the gas chambers. So yes, it would *suit* me not to think about Auschwitz every day. It would suit me for things to be different. It would suit me not to be afraid of the government, afraid of gas, afraid of losing my identity papers, afraid of enclosed spaces, afraid of dog bites, afraid of crossing borders, afraid of traveling by airplane, afraid of crowds and the glorification of virility, afraid of men in groups, afraid of my children being taken from me, afraid of people who obey orders, afraid of uniforms, afraid of being late, afraid of being stopped by the police, afraid whenever I have to renew my passport. Afraid of saying that I'm Jewish. I'm afraid of all those things, all the time. Not "when it suits me." I carry within me, inscribed in the very cells of my body, the memory of an experience of danger so violent that sometimes I think I really lived it myself, or that I'll be forced to relive it one day. To me, death always feels near. I have a sense of being hunted. I often feel subjected to a kind of self-obliteration. I search in the history books for the things I was never told. I can't read enough; I *always* want to read. My hunger for knowledge is never sated. Sometimes I feel like a stranger here. A foreigner. I see obstacles where others do not. I struggle endlessly to make a connection between the thought of my family and the mythologized occurrence that is genocide. And that struggle is what constitutes me. It is the thing that defines me. For almost forty years, I have tried to draw a shape that resembles me, but without success. Today, though, I can connect those disparate dots. I can see, in the constellation of fragments scattered over the page, a silhouette in which I recognize myself at last: I am the daughter, and the granddaughter, of survivors.

CHAPTER 39

L élia handed me the large envelope she had received from the town hall in Les Forges. Inside was a note, addressed to her.

"May I . . . ?"

"Yes," she said, immediately. "Yes, read it."

I scanned the note eagerly. It was a page of thick white cardstock, the handwriting neat and graceful.

Dear Madame,

Following your visit to the town hall of Les Forges, I searched the archives for the letter I mentioned to you: the request for the names of the four Rabinovitches deported to Auschwitz to be inscribed on the Les Forges memorial to the dead.

I didn't find anything in the town hall archives.

However, I did find the enclosed envelope, which may be of interest to you. It was stored in a manila folder. I have not opened it and am sending it to you just as I found it.

Kind regards,

Josyane

Lélia indicated a sealed envelope on her desk. Handwritten on the back of it were the words "NOTEBOOKS—NOÉMIE."

I knew what it was immediately. No one had touched this envelope since 1942.

"Anne," my mother murmured. "It's too emotional. I can't open it."

"Do you want me to do it?"

Lélia nodded wordlessly. I took a deep breath. With trembling hands, I unsealed the envelope. Something went through the room then, a kind of silent, electric exhalation. A letting-out of breath. Both of us felt it. I gently extracted two notebooks, completely blackened with Noémie's handwriting. Every page was full; not a single line was left empty. I opened the first notebook, which began with an underlined date.

I began to read aloud to my mother.

September 4, 1939

It's Maman's birthday today. Twenty-five years ago, during the other war, it was Uncle Vitek's. We're living in Les Forges now, turning our little country escape into our real, everyday home. It took me two days to understand what war is like. How to recognize it when the sky outside is so blue. Trees, greenery, flowers. And yet beautiful human lives are already being stolen away. Still, we remain in good spirits. We must hold on, and we will hold on. For us, there is even something attractive about so much change. Cynical, maybe, but it's true. Our physical bodies haven't changed yet; our actions are still the same. But everything around us is different. Our life itself has come off its axis, and adjusting to that, changing ourselves to fit, will take some time. The most important thing is to emerge from this metamorphosis strong and brave. London was bombed for two hours today. A passenger ship was sunk. These are dark times for civilization. Ominous flashes and lights in the sky near Paris. We go outside to watch them. We're getting used to the fact that it's wartime now. Nightmares when I sleep. My first thought when I wake is to remember that we're fighting. That men are dying in the fields, and women and children are being killed by bombs falling on city streets.

September 5

We expect Lemain at five o'clock. No news of any kind. "It

appears that," "they say that." No letter from the countess. Hitler is crazy. Has he actually suggested to Sir Nevile Henderson that Germany and England split Europe "fairly"? And yet from the way he put it, he obviously thinks he's being selfless. The English are bombarding Germany (?) They're dropping leaflets. Les Musiciens do re mi fa so Myriam's trombone. I'm reading Pierre Legrand. Maybe we can go to Russia soon and finally meet all our relatives. We sure do make things easier for our descendants, don't we? 150 years after the revolution, a war to liberate the people is taking place. Let's just hope it doesn't last too long. Something I'm beginning to realize is that, as long as the battle isn't over, we don't have the right to think about the consequences of the war on our own lives and those of others (Myriam and pessimism).

September 6
Beautiful weather. Knitting. Letter. Wardrobe, maybe. Lemain 5:00.

September 9
Sometimes there's no point in even bothering to write. Bad day today. Polish discussion today. Everyone knows that certain arguments are meaningless, but they make them anyway, to convince themselves. The Dans are in Paris; they'll arrive sometime next week. And, would you believe, we're still coolly discussing the usefulness of a philosophy degree and our life in Les Forges while people are dying. Are all our loved ones in Lodz still alive? Hideous nightmare. Yes, very bad day.

At the mention of the relatives in Lodz, Lélia asked me to stop. It was too much for her. I could feel how deeply shaken she was.

"How far does it go? What date?" she asked.

I opened the second notebook, also full of writing. But I saw immediately that this wasn't the next part of Noémie's diary.

"Maman . . ." I murmured. "It's . . ."

Even as I spoke, I was scanning the pages of handwritten text.
". . . the beginning of a novel . . ."

"Read it to me," Lélia said.

I leafed through the notebook. There were notes, chapter outlines, whole passages, all mixed together. In that chaos, I immediately recognized the creative process of a novelist groping, seeking, needing to get ideas out on paper and to write out certain passages that spring to mind fully formed.

And then.

I read something that stopped me in my tracks. I couldn't believe it. I closed the notebook, unable to speak.

"What's wrong?" Lélia asked sharply.

I couldn't answer.

"Maman . . ." I whispered finally, ". . . are you sure you never opened this envelope?"

"Never. Why?"

I couldn't manage an explanation. My head was spinning. All I could do was read the first page of the novel aloud to Lélia.

Évreux was cloaked in mist that late September morning. A cold mist that signaled the coming of winter. But the day would be bright; the air was pure, the sky cloudless.

Anne passed the time wandering the streets of town, waiting for the girls to get out of school so they could gossip. Of course, to get to the school you had to pass the barracks and the Hôtel de Normandie, where the English officers lodged.

Anne put down her music book and gazed at the tomatoes, the cabbages and pears. Across the street was a row of cottages and five pairs of black socks drying on a line.

"It appears," said Anne, listening to the town, "that the first English convoys will arrive tomorrow. There's already a small staff at the Grand Cerf. They're very chic, you know."

The heroine of Noémie's book was named Anne.

CHAPTER 40

G eorges and I had arranged to meet at the Gare de Lyon, which always holds the promise of sunshine and summer holidays. I'd stopped at a pharmacy on the way to buy a pregnancy test, but I didn't tell Georges that. On the train, he told me the plan for the weekend, which was packed. We'd pick up our rental car at the station in Avignon and drop off our things in a hotel in Bonnieux, before going back down to a chapel where an art-history student would give us a private presentation on the Louise Bourgeois sculptures exhibited there.

It was because of Louise Bourgeois that Georges had chosen Bonnieux for my fortieth birthday celebration. After the guided visit, we would eat lunch in a hilltop restaurant with spectacular panoramic views. And for dessert, we'd have a stroll in the vineyards, plus a wine tasting.

"And then I have a surprise or two in store."

"But I don't like surprises. They make me anxious."

"Oh, okay. Well then, the birthday cake will be brought out as a surprise right before the wine tasting."

The birthday weekend started out beautifully. I was happy to be with Georges, happy to be taking a train to the south of France. I was certain I was pregnant; I knew my body, and I knew the signs. But I decided to wait until the return journey to Paris to take the test in the train bathroom. If it was positive, the news would make for a joyful Sunday evening for us both, and if it wasn't, our weekend getaway wouldn't be ruined by disappointment.

The rental car was waiting for us at the station, and we set off for Bonnieux, Georges behind the wheel. I took my sunglasses out of my bag so I could look out at the scenery. For the first time in a long while, I wasn't thinking about anything except being there, with a man, imagining a life with him and the kind of parents we might be. But something I saw wiped everything else from my mind. I asked Georges to stop the car and go back a little way. I wanted to get another look at the candied-fruit factory on the Apt road, which we had just passed. That ochre façade with its Roman-style arches looked very familiar.

"Georges, I've been this way before. Dozens of times."

Suddenly, *everything* was familiar. Apt, Cavaillon, L'Isle-sur-la-Sorgue, Roussillon. The villages rose up out of my past, all the names recalling childhood trips to visit my grandmother. Bonnieux, where Georges had reserved the hotel room, was a place I remembered. I'd been there with Myriam.

"I know Bonnieux really well!" I exclaimed. "My grandmother had a friend who lived there, and she had a grandson my age."

The memories were flooding back. The grandson had been called Mathieu, and he had a pool, and knew how to swim, but I didn't.

"I was embarrassed because I had to wear water-wings. After that I told my parents I wanted to learn how to swim."

I stared out the window, scrutinizing each house, each shop-front, the way you gaze at an old man's face, trying to see the features of the young man he used to be. It was all so strange. I took out my phone and pulled up a map of the area.

"What are you looking at?" Georges asked.

"We're only thirty kilometers from Céreste. My grandmother's village."

The village where Myriam had sent Lélia to stay as a toddler, and where she'd moved after the war, to marry Yves Bouveris. Céreste, the village of my childhood vacations.

"I haven't been back there since my grandmother died. Twenty-five years ago now."

As we were checking into the hotel, I looked at Georges and smiled.

"You know what I'd really like? For us to go and take a walk around Céreste. I'd love to see my grandmother's little house again."

Georges chuckled. He'd spent a lot of time arranging to-day's private activities. But he gave in with good grace, and I rummaged in my bag for my notebook, which I took with me everywhere.

"What's that?" Georges asked.

"The notebook where I write down everything that might be useful for my investigation. There are people in the village that knew Myriam. I might run into some of them . . ."

"Well, let's go, then!" Georges said with enthusiasm.

We immediately got back in the car. On the way to Céreste, Georges asked me to tell him about Myriam, and her life, and my memories of her.

CHAPTER 41

F or a long time—until I was about eleven—I thought my ancestors had come from Provence."

"You're kidding!" Georges said, laughing.

"It's true! I thought Myriam had been born in France, in this little village straddling the Via Domitia, because it was where we always went for the summer holidays. I also thought Yves was my grandfather."

"You didn't know about Vicente?"

"No. How can I explain it . . . everything was sort of . . . blurred. My mother never said, 'Yves is your grandfather.' But she never said he wasn't, either. Do you see what I mean? I remember so clearly, when I was little, when someone asked me where my parents were from, I'd say 'Brittany on my father's side, and Provence on my mother's.' I was half Breton, half Provençal. That was just how it was. And Myriam never brought up any memories that would have made me question it. She never said 'once in Russia,' or 'when I used to spend my vacations in Poland,' or 'when I was a little girl in Latvia,' or 'at my grandparents' house in Palestine.' We had no idea that she'd lived in all those places."

When Myriam showed us how to shell peas for *soupe au pistou*, to make a *quenouille de lavande* out of a few springs of lavender and a hair ribbon, to dry linden flowers on a clean bedsheet for our evening herbal teas, to macerate cherry pits for ratafia, to fry zucchini-blossom fritters, I thought we were learning our family's old Provençal recipes. It was the same when she taught us to leave the shutters half-closed to keep the coolness inside, or to take a *sieste* in the afternoon—I just assumed they were local traditions handed down by our ancestors. And even though I know now that I don't have any blood ties to Provence, I still have a special love for its rocky peaks, its ferocious summer heat that you have to learn how to cope with.

Myriam was like a seed, blown by the wind across entire continents, that had finally come to rest here, in this little, sparsely populated patch of land. And here she had stayed for the rest of her life, as if time had stopped moving.

She had been able to put down roots at last, on this vaguely inhospitable hillside that might have reminded her of the heat and rocky soil of Migdal, of that brief period in her childhood when, on her grandparents' property in Palestine, for once she hadn't been hunted.

All the time I spent with my grandmother Myriam happened here, in the south of France. It was always here that I saw her, between Apt and Avignon, in the hills of the Luberon, this woman whose hidden name I bore.

Myriam was one of those people who needed to keep a certain distance between herself and others. She didn't want anyone to get too close. I remember her watching us sometimes with a kind of haunted look in her eyes. I'm certain, now, that it was because of our faces. Some sudden resemblance to the ones who were gone, a way of laughing, a reaction. That must have been so painful.

Sometimes I felt like she saw us as a kind of adoptive family. She was happy to share a moment of warmth or a meal in our company, but deep down, all she really wanted was to be back with her *real* family.

For me, it was difficult to bridge the gap between Mirotchka, the daughter of Ephraïm and Emma Rabinovitch, and Myriam Bouveris, the grandmother I spent summers with between the peaks of the Vaucluse and the mountains of the Luberon.

It was no simple matter to put everything together. I had trouble keeping track of all the different periods of history. This family was like an overlarge bouquet of flowers that I couldn't quite keep a grip on.

"I'd like to go and see the cottage where I spent summers as a little girl. We'll have to walk up into the hills a bit, behind the village."

"Let's go," Georges said.

Reaching the end of the path, I had a vivid mental image of Myriam, her skin tanned and leathery from the sun, walking among the rocks and succulents despite the hot, dry weather.

"There it is," I said to Georges. "You see that little house? That's where Myriam lived after the war, with Yves."

"It must have reminded them of the Hanged Man's House!"

"I'm sure it did. I spent all my summers there with her."

It was a small cabin built of bricks and concrete and tile, with no indoor bathroom and a summer kitchen outside. We all lived there together from early July onward, the days moving in slow motion because of the heat, which made it impossible for people and animals to move, turning us all into statues of salt. Myriam had recreated a life which, I had no doubt, was much like the one she'd known at her father's dacha in Latvia, and on her grandparents' farm. My mother and father both let their hair grow long, and we bathed in a yellow plastic tub. For the bathroom, you had to go into the forest; I remember squatting behind a huge moss-covered rock and watching, fascinated, as my warm pee made a river that flowed among the leaves, terrorizing insects as it went, sweeping gnats and ants along like lava from a volcano.

For a long time, I thought that all children spent their summer vacations in a country cabin, taking *siestes* on mattresses under the trees and doing their business in the forest.

Myriam taught us to make jam and honey and to preserve fruits in syrup, as well as how to maintain the vegetable garden and the orchard of quince, apricot, and cherry trees. Once a month, the distiller came to make *eaux-de-vie* from our leftover fruit. We collected dried flowers, put on shows for the grown-ups, and played cards. We whistled on blades of grass held between our fingers the way Myriam showed us—you had to choose wide, solid blades to get a good sound. We made candles out of hollowed-out oranges, too, using the stem for a wick and putting olive oil in the bottom of the peel. Occasionally we went into the village to buy sausages to barbecue, or chops, or stuffing for the tomatoes, or the tightly rolled beef-and-prosciutto dish called *alouettes sans têtes* that is a Provence specialty. You had to go through the forest to get into the village, and it was a long walk in the burning sun beneath the silvery leaves of the cork oaks. As kids, we could walk on the paths in our bare feet without hurting ourselves. We knew which stones would be the smoothest, and we could also recognize the fossils: seashells and shark's teeth. We knew how to handle the heat, to conquer it the way you win a battle against a fearful enemy, so terrifying that it paralyzes everyone and everything in its path. We always felt we'd won a magnificent victory when the coolness arrived to save us at twilight, a breeze caressing our foreheads like a cool washcloth soothing a fever. Then Myriam would take us to feed the fox that lived on the hillside.

"Foxes are gentle," she told us.

She always said the fox was her friend, and the bees were, too. And we really believed that she had secret conversations with them all.

The summer holidays always went quickly, like a child's dream, with my uncle and aunt and all the cousins there, too. Myriam had given the children she'd had with Yves the names of Jacques and Nicole.

Nicole became an agricultural engineer. Jacques became a mountain guide and poet, and for a long time he was a history teacher, too.

They'd each had something tragic happen to them when they were teenagers, Jacques at age seventeen, Nicole at nineteen. No one had connected the dots. Because of the silence. And because, in this family, we didn't believe in psychoanalysis.

My uncle Jacques, who I adored, nicknamed me Nono. I loved it. It sounded like a little robot in a cartoon.

Little by little, Myriam lost her memory. She began to do strange things. One morning, very early, she came to wake me up in bed. She seemed anxious, upset.

"Get your suitcase. We have to leave," she said.

Then she snapped at me about my shoelaces. I don't remember if it was because they were tied or untied, but she seemed really angry. I followed her out of the room automatically, but all she did was go back to bed.

After a while, she started hearing voices talking to her on the hillside. Objects, faces, forgotten memories came back to her. But at the same time as these distant memories returned, her speech and even her writing became clumsier, harder to decipher. Despite this, she continued to write. She was always writing. But she threw away, or burned, almost everything. All we have left are a few pages we found in her desk.

Things have become difficult I feel so strange and ill, can't shake it.

Very attached to nature, plants, I find certain characters around me very disagreeable.

I cut the words off short; I think there's a misunderstanding.

Sitting near the plane tree and the linden, which are becoming nicer and nicer. I find myself not asleep, but dreaming, and I hope that little by little my mind will grow tired of all these stupid things. And I don't doubt the beauty of our woods, our happiness in this place, but I also have to admit that I still go back to Nice for a few months in the winter.

It's there, as one apart, that I find happiness and friendship again.

Jacques will be back on Wednesday.

In the last few years of Myriam's life, her children had to have someone come to Céreste to help take care of her because she could no longer live on her own. Something very strange had happened: Myriam had forgotten how to speak French. She'd learned the language late, at age ten, and it was simply gone from her memory. She only spoke Russian now. As her mental capacity waned, she fell back into the language of her childhood, and I vividly remember writing letters to her in Cyrillic so we could still have contact with her. Lélia asked some Russian friends for an alphabetical key, and we copied it. The whole family did it; we would sit around the dining room table writing out sentences in Cyrillic, and it ended up being a happy, special thing, to write in the language of our ancestors. But it was very complicated for Myriam who, in a way, had once again become a foreigner in her own country.

After we'd had a look at the cabin, Georges and I went back to the car. That was when I told him I'd bought a pregnancy test at the pharmacy.

"I'm sure you're pregnant," he said. "If it's a girl, we'll call her Noémie. And Jacques if it's a boy. What do you think?"

"No," I said. "We'll pick a name that belongs only to them, and no one else."

CHAPTER 42

I leafed slowly through the pages of my notebook, waiting for something to leap out at me. If I racked my brain hard enough, I knew I could come up with a good idea.

"Mireille!" I exclaimed. "I've read her book! I think she still lives here!"

"Mireille?"

"Yes! Yes! Little Mireille Sidoine—Marcelle's daughter! She was raised by René Char. She must be ninety years old by now. I know because I read her memoirs not long ago. And . . . and she mentioned that she still lived in Céreste! She knew Myriam, and she knew my mother. No doubt about it. She was a cousin of Yves's."

As I spoke, Georges was scrolling through the White Pages on his phone.

"Yes—here's her address. We can go and see her now, if you want."

I recognized the narrow streets of the village I had roamed as a child, the houses crowded closely together, the hairpin turns. Nothing seemed to have changed in the past thirty years. And there it was, just across from Henriette's old place: the home of Mireille, the daughter of Marcelle, the vixen from *Feuillets d'Hypnos.*

We rang the bell on the front gate. I was reluctant at first, because we hadn't phoned ahead. But Georges insisted.

"What do you have to lose?" he asked.

An old gentleman opened a front window of the house: Mireille's husband. I explained that I was Myriam's granddaughter, and

I was looking for people with memories of her. He asked us to wait, and then he opened the door and very kindly asked us in for a cordial.

Mireille was there, sitting at a table in the garden behind the house, dressed all in black. Neatly dressed and impeccably groomed. Ninety years old, maybe more. Waiting for us, as if we'd had an appointment.

"Come closer," she said to me. "I'm nearly blind. You must come closer so I can see your face."

"You knew my grandmother Myriam?"

"Of course. I remember her very well. And I remember your mother, too, who was only a little girl back then. What was her name again?"

"Lélia."

"That's it! Such a pretty name. So original. Lélia. I've never met anyone else with that name. Now, what is it you want to know?"

"What was she like? My grandmother? What kind of woman was she?"

"Oh, she was very reserved. She didn't talk much. No one in the village ever gossiped about her. She wasn't at all flirtatious, I remember that."

We stayed for a long time, talking about Yves and Vicente, about the love triangle they and Myriam had formed and its consequences. We talked about René Char, too, and how he'd spent the war in Céreste. Mireille spoke frankly, without going off on tangents. I wondered how I would tell my mother about all of this: Mireille, her secluded garden, her memories of Myriam. I wished she were there with me.

Eventually I sensed that it was time for us to go, that Mireille was beginning to get tired. Before we left, I asked her one last question: whether it would be possible to meet others in the village who could tell me about my grandmother.

"Someone who would have known her intimately."

J uliette offered us glasses of the lemonade she'd made for her grandchildren. She was a cheerful, chatty woman, and we talked for a long time about everything: Myriam, her Alzheimer's disease, her funeral. Back when Juliette was a nurse, she had moved in with Myriam to take care of her in her final illness. She'd been thirty years old at the time, and she remembered it all vividly.

"She used to tell me about all of you! Her grandchildren, and especially Lélia, your mother. She always said she was going to go and live with you."

"Why? She didn't like it in Céreste anymore?"

"Oh, she loved Céreste and the countryside, but she always used to say, 'I must go to my daughter, because she knew them.'"

"Oh . . . yes . . . it's coming back to me now."

I turned to Georges and explained, "Myriam got very confused at the end of her life. She thought Lélia had known Ephraïm, Emma, Jacques, and Noémie. She even said to my mother once: 'You know what your grandparents were like,' as if Lélia had grown up with them."

That was when Georges suddenly had the idea of showing the postcard to Juliette. I had a photo of it on my phone.

"Oh yes, of course I recognize it," Juliette said.

"*What?*"

"I'm the one who sent it."

"What do you mean? You wrote this postcard?"

"Oh, no! I only put it in the mailbox."

"But who *wrote* it?"

"Myriam. Very shortly before she died. A few days, maybe. I had to help her a bit, guide her hand. She had trouble forming letters at the end."

"Can you tell me exactly what happened?"

"Your grandmother often wanted to write her memories down. But with her illness, it was difficult. She wrote things I had a hard time reading. There was French, Russian, Hebrew—all the languages she'd learned in her life, all mixed up in her head, you know? And then one day she chose a postcard from her collection—you remember, her collection of postcards with historic monuments on them."

"Just like Uncle Boris."

"Yes—that name sounds familiar; she must have told me about him. Anyway, she asked me to help her write those four names. I remember that she absolutely insisted on using a ballpoint pen. She wanted to be sure the ink wouldn't fade or run. And then she said to me, 'When I go to live with my daughter, I want you to send me this postcard. Promise?' And I said, 'Yes, I promise.' I took the postcard home with me and put it away with my personal papers."

"And then?"

"She never went to live with your mother as she'd hoped to. She passed away here in Céreste. I'd forgotten all about the postcard, to be honest. It just stayed there, filed away with my papers. And then, a few years later, I was spending Christmas in Paris with my husband. This was in the winter of 2002."

"Yes. January 2003."

"That's right. I'd brought a manila envelope with me, with all the documents for the trip: our ID cards, the hotel reservations, etc. And while we were in Paris, I found the postcard in that envelope. It was on the last day of our holiday, just before we went back to Céreste."

"A Saturday morning."

"Must've been. I said to my husband, 'I absolutely have to

mail this postcard. It was so important to Myriam. I promised her.' And also, I don't know . . . I just didn't want to go back to Céreste with that card. There was a big post office right near our hotel."

"The Louvre post office."

"Exactly. That's where I mailed it."

"Do you remember putting the stamp on upside-down?"

"I don't, no. It was dreadfully cold, and my husband was waiting for me in the car. I must not have been paying attention. Then we rushed to the airport—and after all that, our plane wasn't even able to take off!"

"You could have put the postcard in an envelope, with a note, just to explain! It would have spared us all this wondering."

"I know. But as I said, we were running late, and there was a blizzard, and my husband was grumbling in the car, and I didn't have an envelope handy . . ."

"But why did Myriam want to send this postcard to herself?"

"Because she knew her memory was failing, and she said to me, 'I can't forget them. If I do, there will be no one left to remember that they ever existed.'"

This book could not have been written without my mother's research. Nor without her own writing. It's hers, just as much as it is mine.

This book is dedicated to Grégoire,
and to all the descendants of the Rabinovitch family.

ACKNOWLEDGEMENTS

Thank you to my editor, Martine Saada.

Thank you to Gérard Rambert, Mireille Sidoine, Karine and Claude Chabaud, Hélène Hautval, Nathalie Zajde and Tobie Nathan, Haïm Korsia, Duluc Détective, Stéphane Simon, Jesus Bartolome, Viviane Bloch, and Marc Betton.

Thank you to Pierre Bérest and Laurent Joly, for their insights and advice.

Thank you to all the readers who accompanied this book on its journey: Agnès, Alexandra, Anny, Armelle, Bénédicte, Cécile, Claire, Gillian-Joy, Grégoire, Julia, Lélia, Marion, Olivier, Priscille, Sophie, Xavier. Thank you to Émilie, Isabel, Rebecca, Rhizlaine, and Roxana.

And Julien Boivent.